A VERY PE

The BBC TV series of
A VERY PECULIAR PRACTICE

Stephen Daker	PETER DAVISON
Jock McCannon	GRAHAM CROWDEN
Bob Buzzard	DAVID TROUGHTON
Lyn Turtle	AMANDA HILLWOOD
Rose Marie	BARBARA FLYNN
Ernest Hemmingway	JOHN BIRD
John Furie	TIMOTHY WEST
Mrs Kramer	GILLIAN RAINE
Chen	TAKASHI KAWAHARA
Maureen Gahagan	LINDY WHITEFORD
Chinese Girl	SARAH LAM
Helen Furie	PHILIPPA URQUHART
Lilian Hubbard	JEAN HEYWOOD
Angie Fry	FRANCESCA BRILL
Megan Phillips	KATE EATON
P. R. Prettiman	PAUL JESSON
Jimmy Partington	DAVID GWILLIM
Rust	JOE MELIA

Produced by KEN RIDDINGTON
Dramatized by ANDREW DAVIES
Script Editor DEVORA POPE
Directed by DAVID TUCKER

Andrew Davies divides his time between writing and teaching in a university. His play ROSE, starring Glenda Jackson, played to full houses at the Duke of York's and was subsequently produced on Broadway and in many other countries. Awards: Guardian Children's Fiction Award (for CONRAD'S WAR): Boston Globe Horn Award (for CONRAD'S WAR): Broadcasting Press Guild Award for Best Series or Serial (for TO SERVE THEM ALL MY DAYS): Pye Colour Television Award for Best Children's Television Writer (for MARMALADE ATKINS IN SPACE). His most recent work, the screenplay for TIME AFTER TIME, was selected for the London Film Festival 1985 and will be seen on BBC 2 in 1986. A VERY PECULIAR PRACTICE is his first novel for adults.

A VERY PECULIAR PRACTICE

Andrew Davies

CORONET BOOKS
Hodder and Stoughton

Copyright © 1986 by Andrew Davies

First published in Great Britain in 1986
by Coronet Books

British Library C.I.P.

Davies, Andrew
   A very peculiar practice.
   I. Title
   823′.914[F]   PR6054.A875/

   ISBN 0 340 39114 6

Printed and bound in Great Britain for
Hodder and Stoughton Paperbacks, a
division of Hodder and Stoughton Ltd.,
Mill Road, Dunton Green, Sevenoaks,
Kent (Editorial Office: 47 Bedford
Square, London, WC1B 3DP) by
Cox and Wyman Ltd.,
Cardiff Road, Reading.

The University of Lowlands, thank God, does not yet exist. The doctors in this novel are not real doctors. They are figments of the imagination. If one of them happens to resemble your doctor, that is your misfortune. Real lecturers and students never carry on as lecturers and students do in this book. Rust does not exist, though he thinks he does. And "Jonathan Powell" and "Ken Riddington" are fictional characters, nothing to do with the real people who bear those names. It's just a *story*. All right?

A VERY PECULIAR PRACTICE

The Arts Council Fellow in Creative Writing is picking his nose in his room. It is a very small room. There is just space enough for a single bed (quite adequate for present needs), a few books (more than adequate), uneasy chair, second chair, grim work table, cupboard for clothes, cupboard with washbasin, and the Arts Council Fellow in Creative Writing himself.

The window affords a view of a narrow strip of grass, a narrow strip of lake, and a generous dollop of the room opposite, ten feet away, where a large, sad-looking African stands staring out of the window. The Arts Council Fellow yearns briefly for his spacious flat in Muswell Hill, then remembers sodding Carol and her sodding pal and stops yearning. Sodding dog's breakfast that was. (He reserves the mot juste for his creative work. Sodding and the like will serve perfectly well for ordinary thinking.)

This place will do to bounce back from. Just partake, they told him. Just mingle; be a presence. But term hasn't started. There's no one to mingle with but the African. Above all, feel free to get on with your own work. Ah, well. He has captured the bogey, a sturdy greeny-grey job, well worth the effort. Nothing else for it now. He reaches for the least threatening-looking of his notebooks, picks up his Pentel, and begins to write.

1

A VERY LONG WAY
FROM ANYWHERE

The University of Lowlands is a dump – no, wait, hold on, we can do better than that.

In a certain light, from a certain angle, viewed in late afternoon from the far side of the lake, it looks like a modern version of a medieval fortified town, with its subtly interlocked towers and flat roofs and buttresses casting patterns of light and shadow, its elegantly brutal concrete walkways and bridges crisscrossing the façades, creating unexpected teasing links between tower and piazza, refectory and boiler room, Arts and Cybernetics, in an endless labyrinth of multi-level interfacing.

Going every bloody way except the way you need to go, thought Jock McCannon, not for the first time. And what was more, when it rained, which was usually, these walkways, their gratings clogged with empty cigarette packets, crisp bags, leaflets, lecture notes, condoms and the like, filled up to a depth of seven or eight inches, and refused to drain away. Other universities are famous for gonorrhea and drug-induced hallucinations. Lowlands, though no stranger to either of these inflictions, was noted for trench foot as well.

Jock McCannon knew all about that. It was his job. He was the head of the Medical Centre at the University. He had held that post from the beginning, when it was a new New University, and Jock was little, as he liked to say.

Now, although it was twenty years old and falling to bits, it still looked unfinished. Unlike Jock. He was falling to bits and he looked finished. Henderson in Social Administration argued that Jock had actually been dead for several years, but Jock knew better than that. Usually.

Nobody knew exactly how old Jock was, but his age could be confidently estimated at somewhere between fifty-five and eighty. This morning was one of his better days: he looked well on the right side of seventy. Indeed he cut a fine and rather frightening figure as he stood at the window gazing moodily down at a couple of nuns picking over an overflowing rubbish skip. He stood six feet three inches tall in his handmade brogues, odd socks, a tweed suit so hairy it seemed to have a life of its own, and a strikingly horrible bright yellow tie. His eyes were his most remarkable feature. From the folds and furrows and creases and blotches of his ruined face, they stared down at the world with startling liveliness and candour. Their expression changed from moment to moment – glee, malice, compassion, amnesia, you name it – but their colour was always the same: a pure, clear, translucent, alcoholic blue.

It was seven a.m. A bit early for a doctor to be in his consulting room, it might be thought, but in fact all the medical team were in their consulting rooms, even though term had not started and nobody had had time to get ill yet. The reason was as follows: Jock McCannon was by way of being an insomniac (as well as one or two other things with the same suffix); Bob Buzzard liked to get in early because seven to nine were the hours when you got ahead of the opposition; and Rose Marie needed to be there to keep an eye on the other two. It was, in this as in other ways, a very peculiar medical practice.

Jock turned from the window, sighed loudly, and pressed a button on his intercom.

"Bob," he said, or rather groaned. "Bob. I am experiencing a sense of boredom so acute that it borders on rage. Can you tell me anything interesting today, Bob?"

Bob was reading the *Sunday Times*, gloomily pricing low mileage BMW 635s. How was he to know what could possibly interest the old fart at seven in the morning? Ronnie Laing just dropped in with a case of Jack Daniels Green Label, perhaps?

"Um . . . I've got the printout back for my new rationalisation scheme. Results are fascinating."

"Try again," said Jock bleakly.

Bob put his razor-keen brain onto fast picture search. Ten grand of Gulbenkian money up for grabs, finally decided to enter the twins for Winchester, Daphne's going to sue her ex-cleaning lady in the Small Claims Court, no, none of that would do. Then he remembered.

"New man's coming."

"Ah, yes," said Jock. "The new man."

Stephen Daker would have liked being thought of as the new man. A new man was what he aspired to be, without very much confidence. He had not very much enjoyed being the man he had been for the last six years, the Walsall years. There had been a lot of pain in Walsall. It is a statistical fact that there are more ill people in Walsall than anywhere else in the country. That means that it is absolutely marvellous to be a doctor there, and also absolutely terrible, both at the same time. Stephen had felt needed, been stretched, and pulled down a high income. At the same time he had been desperately overworked, tormented by guilt, and had spent such long hours at the job that the only healthy person he had talked to for years, or so it felt, had been his wife.

And that hadn't been so good either. Quite recently his wife, a rather beautiful girl called Angela, had told Stephen that she didn't want to be his wife any more. At the same time she had taken the trouble to tell him one or two other things: that she had never really enjoyed having oats with him, as she put it, that he had never managed to touch her in the right way, and that she was sorry but she didn't think she could bear to look at his ears any more. Stephen, who loved his wife very much, was very distressed, though he felt unable to blame her. He spent a considerable time at the bathroom mirror turning his head this way and that, but his ears seemed to him well within the normal distribution

7

curve. (In fact he had a sweet and potentially rather sexy face, including his ears, but he didn't know this; nor would he have cared if he had known, the point being that Angela didn't like it any more.) Quite soon after the crucial conversation he found himself incapable of having oats at all.

He had applied for the Lowlands job, as he had for seventy-six others, in a spirit of quiet desperation, and had been astonished to hear, rather a long time after the interview, that his application had been successful. A new man. A new life. Anything seemed possible. Anything seemed possible except, at the moment, finding his way into the place. For some minutes he had been driving around the outer edges of the campus, obeying a series of increasingly enigmatic and minatory road signs, and wishing that he was something to do with Library Deliveries or Site Levelling. One sign particularly pleased him; it said: CAUTION: ALTERED PRIORITIES AHEAD. When he had passed it for the third time, he hung a bold left into RESERVED PARKING AREA: PERMITS ONLY, narrowly missing a head-on collision with a couple of nuns in a battered Mini, and parked the Volvo next to a dead Fiat in what seemed, apart from its vast size, to be a perfectly ordinary car park, probably the main car park, in fact.

He got out and looked across to what appeared to be the central campus. Only about, what, a mile and a half away. Never mind, the walk would do him good. He locked the Volvo and set out, his spirits high and tremulous.

Fifteen minutes later he was in the central campus all right, but no nearer to finding the medical centre, though he was well briefed on the location of the Meditation Chapel, the Sociology of Music Lab, and the Women's Crisis Centre. Part of the trouble seemed to be that there was not another living soul about, except for a figure dressed in vest, jeans, and overcoat, crouching under a broken coffee machine at the far end of a vast bombsite that might well have been the Students' Union Lounge. When Stephen had approached this figure, he or she had rolled

8

into a foetal position and started to weep quietly. Now he was trudging along yet another concrete walkway, or waterway, which was puzzlingly six inches deep in water though it hadn't rained for days, and which seemed to be going nowhere useful at all.

He turned a corner, and immediately bumped into a tall, fit and cheerful looking girl in a tracksuit. She bounced off him, said wow and sorry in an amused sort of way, and started to jog off out of his life.

"Excuse me!" said Stephen.

She stopped.

"You couldn't possibly direct me to the medical centre, could you?"

"Yeah, right," she said. "Hey, you don't look too good." She had a pronounced South London accent.

"No, honestly," said Stephen. "I'm quite all right."

"You sure?" She sounded unconvinced. "Right, well see that walkway there, follow it all the way round to the right till you see the signs. Can't go wrong. OK? And don't let them give you McCannon!"

She jogged off and Stephen stared after her. What a healthy person. What a nice, straightforward, un-self-pitying smile. But Stephen had promises to keep, and the healthy person clearly had miles to go before she slept, and in any case he was one of the walking wounded so far as that sort of thing was concerned. He followed the walkway to the Medical Centre.

The waiting room was reassuringly typical, except that there were only two people in it. One of them was a sad-looking African glumly twiddling his thumbs on a hard chair. The other was a person with whose type Stephen was all too familiar.

"Yes?" said this person, whose name was Mrs Kramer.

"Er . . . I'm Stephen Daker."

"And?" One had to admire the pitying, patient contempt of it.

"Well," said Stephen. "Here I am."

"Yes, here you are," said Mrs Kramer. "And?"

"Perhaps I should see Dr McCannon first?"

"You have an appointment with Dr McCannon?"

"Er, no, but . . ."

"I assume it's some sort of emergency. Please take a seat."

"Look," said Stephen. "I think you might have misunderstood, I'm . . ."

"Please take a seat!" snarled Mrs Kramer with sudden savagery, and went out of the room.

Stephen took a seat opposite the African, who was now sitting absolutely still. Stephen watched the big tears rolling down his cheeks. After a while Mrs Kramer came back.

"You're in luck," she said to Stephen, ignoring the sad African. "Dr McCannon will see you now."

Dr McCannon's room was very large, its institutional quality softened by a large number of paintings and prints (Landseer, Klee and Klimt seemed to be his favourites), photographs featuring McCannon with various raves from the grave, one of whom looked suspiciously like the Maharishi, a lot of Edwardian furniture, some half-eaten sandwiches, some whisky bottles, by no means all of them empty, and a truly disturbing quantity of stuffed things: owls, badgers, and so on. The owner of all this junk rose from behind his desk with a spasm of shagged-out bonhomie, and pressed Stephen down into a smelly old horsehair sofa.

"My dear man," he said. "Daker, was it?"

"Stephen Daker, yes."

"And you're new here."

"Well, yes," said Stephen. "Naturally."

McCannon frowned and clicked his tongue. "And you're not feeling too bright. Tell me all about it."

"No, really," said Stephen. That girl had said the same sort of thing. Maybe he was. . . . "No, really, I'm fine."

"Yes," said McCannon, taking longer over this monosyllable than Stephen would have thought possible. "Are you a married man, Stephen?"

Stephen panicked. "Yes. Well. In a sense. My wife didn't want to come down here with me. Not straight away. Well, er, perhaps not at all. Trial separation."

"Yes," said McCannon, with what seemed to be deep

10

satisfaction. "And there's a lot of pain there, yes? Any physical symptoms? Nausea? Panic? Terror?"

"Yes . . . no," said Stephen. "Look, I mean, isn't all this getting a bit, well, personal?"

"Illness *is* personal, Stephen. We're not machines."

"But I'm not ill," said Stephen.

McCannon smiled. "Of course you're not. Of course you're not. You're just experiencing a lot of pain. And my guess is that we're suffering *deep sexual* pain . . . I'm right, aren't I? We *cannot cut the mustard*."

"Look," said Stephen, staggered by the clairvoyance of this diagnosis. "Look – you think I'm a patient, don't you?"

"Just another human being feeling pain, Stephen." The clear blue alcoholic eyes were brimful of understanding. Any more of this and Stephen would be sobbing on his shoulder.

"No," he said firmly. "You think I'm a patient, and I'm not, I'm a doctor."

"Well, of course you are!" said McCannon indulgently. "This university is full of doctors!"

"No." How long would it go on? "I'm a real doctor. A medical man. And I've come to work here. As a doctor. At this University Medical Centre."

Jock McCannon had met plenty of psychotics in his long career. His manner was if anything even more gentle and compassionate as he leaned forward and asked: "Tell me now, Stephen. What makes you think that?"

"Well. Um . . . my letter of appointment. From the University Registry."

"Excuse me one second," said Jock, walking to the desk.

"Daker, you said." He pressed the button. "Bob. This new man. Blair-Athol, wasn't it? High flyer from Edinburgh?"

Bob Buzzard's voice came loud and clear over the intercom. "Didn't you get the VC's memo? Blair-Athol welshed on the deal, got a better offer from Princeton. No, they gave it to one of the also-rans. Some dim GP from Wolverhampton or somewhere. Dick Dado, or some such name."

"Stephen Daker?"

"Yes, that's the chap."

"Well," said Jock. "He's here."

"My dear man, I'm most frightfully sorry, that was really very embarrassing," said Jock, not looking a whit embarrassed as he shambled to the drinks cupboard. "Welcome to the team. Would you care for a wee drop of something, Stephen?"

"Bit early in the morning for me," said Stephen, looking at his watch, which said nine fifteen.

"Very wise, I'm delighted to hear it. As a matter of fact, your predecessor gave some cause for anxiety there. Oh, he gave the vodka bottle a most tremendous pummelling."

Stephen watched respectfully as his new leader filled a squat tumbler to a depth of an inch and a half with Bell's. Here he was, actually sitting down with a living legend, Jock McCannon, pioneer of radical community medicine, the man who wrote *Sexual Anxiety and the Common Cold*. "Total abstainer, eh?" said the living legend, tossing off rather more than half the contents of his glass. "Very wise."

"Well, no, not a total . . . abstainer," said Stephen. McCannon grunted, and made a brisk and thorough job of what was left in the glass.

"Glad to have you aboard," he said hoarsely, heading back towards the cupboard.

"I'm really very grateful for the opportunity," said Stephen, making a big effort. "I've read so much about your work here. Treating the patient as a whole person . . . ten minute standard consultations . . . the campus as village . . . time for research . . . the concept of the therapeutic community. It's all exactly what I dreamed about in Walsall."

McCannon's face darkened.

"All over now," he said grimly. "This is the Eighties. Come here, Stephen." The great ruined face loomed close. "This University is a swamp of fear and loathing. It's the cuts. The UGC has both its hands on the University's throat. Early retirements. Involuntary redundancies.

12

Savage competition between colleagues . . . even in this medical practice. You're not joining a happy team, Stephen. They're trying to get me out, and no doubt they'll try to get you out. Early retirement, mental instability, malpractice even. We have to stay one jump ahead of them."

"Er . . . who?" said Stephen carefully, hoping to God he wasn't going to hear anything about Venusians or death rays.

"Your colleagues, of course. Black Bob and the bonnie wee lassie. You realise that you come into the practice as technically senior to both of them. They are seething with bile, Stephen. It's a mercy that they hate each other so much, God knows what they'd be like if they ganged up."

"Thank you for taking me into your confidence, Dr McCannon," said Stephen, who was beginning to wonder if there might not, after all, be something to be said for Walsall.

"Jock. All first names here. And you are right," whispered the living legend, actually glancing over his shoulder, "my remarks are entirely confidential between the two of us."

"Er . . . of course."

"I can count on your discretion and loyalty then, Stephen."

"Yes, of course."

"Your *personal loyalty* to *me* as *head* of *this practice*."

Stephen wondered whether he had ever heard so many words stressed so heavily in a single sentence. "Well, er, yes. Naturally."

"Good."

After all that, Stephen was mildly surprised when McCannon called Black Bob into his consulting room, greeted him with every appearance of affability, and entrusted him with the task of showing Stephen round the medical centre. Black Bob did not at first sight seem to be seething with bile or anything else. A dark, brisk man of about Stephen's own age, dressed very neatly and correctly in a dark suit, white shirt, tie that obviously indicated membership of something or other, his manner was alert and sincere with a hint of well-controlled aggression, suggesting an extremely intelligent, bespectacled dog of the short-coated retriever type. Bob began by very decently making no bones about the fact that he'd been in for the job too but there were absolutely no hard feelings. Then he gave Stephen the tour.

First of all there was the Waiting Room. The sad African was still there, but seemed to have stopped weeping. Stephen was properly introduced to Mrs Kramer, who became alarmingly flirtatious, told Stephen that he was very naughty pretending to be just a patient, and promised proper welcomes from now on. Pausing in the new brutalist corridor (tastefully exposed concrete, low ceiling, strip lighting, no pictures) Bob reassured Stephen that Mrs Kramer saw it as her mission in life to keep the patients away from the doctors, and confided his opinion that women like that were worth their weight in gold.

Next came the Dispensary. Here Stephen was introduced to the nurse, Maureen Gahagan, and informed by Bob in her presence that Maureen was a simple colleen from the bogs, thick as six short planks, bone idle, and a total waste of space. Maureen sat silent throughout most of this, staring stonily at Bob with patient but quite probably homicidal hatred. Bidding Maureen the top of the morning, Bob ushered Stephen back out into the corridor.

"Not a bad girl really," he said. "Likes to be jollied along, teased a bit. Expect you noticed that."

They had stopped outside another door. Here Bob seemed to hesitate. "Rose Marie next, I think," he said. "Some people find her a bit prickly. Don't see that myself. Just another woman." He raised his hand to knock on the door and paused again. "My personal view is that there's nothing wrong with Rose Marie that a damn good rogering wouldn't sort out. Come to think about it, you might be the very man."

Before Stephen could disqualify himself from this duty, they were in a tastefully decorated room with a lot of greenery about it. A very good-looking woman of perhaps

14

thirty, wearing a white coat with apparently nothing underneath it, rose from behind her immaculate desk and smiled pleasantly at Stephen.

"Here he is," said Bob. "Rose Marie. Stephen Daker."

They shook hands and said how d'you do. Her hand was cool and gentle, and she left it entirely up to Stephen when to let go, which, what with the white coat and its contents, left him not a little disturbed. Her smile didn't waver. A rather long pause began to develop. Both Bob and this Rosemary person seemed perfectly happy to let it go on for half an hour or so.

"Er . . . Rosemary what?" said Stephen eventually.

"Oh, dear," said Bob, without bothering to conceal his pleasure.

"Just Rose Marie," she said. "That's my full name. I'm not exactly into patronymics, Stephen."

"Oh, yes, right, I see," said Stephen, not seeing, quite.

"Going through the whole of one's life labelled as one man's daughter or another man's wife," said Rose Marie pleasantly. She was breathing deeply and steadily, as if to demonstrate the wonderful efficiency of the human respiratory system. The smile didn't waver.

"Oh, yes, of course. Sorry. Absolutely," said Stephen, whose breathing had unaccountably become shallow and rapid. "And you are . . ."

"Oh, lord," said Bob happily.

"You mean what do I do here? I'm a doctor, Stephen. Not a nurse. Not a physiotherapist. And I don't clean the fucking loos. I'm a doctor, Stephen, just like you."

Stephen felt a powerful urge to fall to the floor and bang his face on the smooth vinyl tiles. "Yes, of course you are!" he gabbled. "Look, I'm dreadfully sorry, I didn't for a moment mean to imply . . . I was just . . ."

"You mustn't feel you have to apologise all the time, Stephen. I know it's difficult to be a man, too."

"Yes, I do find that rather difficult," said Stephen humbly.

"I'm sure we're going to work together really well," said Rose Marie with great warmth. "I'm looking forward to

15

that, Stephen." She lowered her eyes demurely, seeming to focus on the part of her uniform Stephen had been trying for some time not to look at, then looking him full in the eyes again. Some seconds or hours went by.

"Come on," said Bob. "I'll show you where your consulting room is."

It was a shame, as Bob said, that Stephen's consulting room had DR BLAIR-ATHOL so unequivocally labelled on its door. According to Bob, it was only once in a blue moon that Establishments got their bloody fingers out, and Stephen was going to have to live with it for years. The room, when they got in it, was considerably smaller than Rose Marie's, and noticeably scruffier.

"Bit claustrophobic for my taste," said Bob, "but O'Hara liked it that way."

They both headed for the chair behind the desk, and both paused simultaneously.

"Ah, yes," said Bob. "Mea culpa. Your place. Quite right."

Stephen sat down. It was a comfortable chair. It swivelled. When he was alone, he promised himself, he would whirl round and round and round in it quacking like a duck. For the moment he contented himself with sliding open the top drawer of the desk. A random collection of exotic and multi-coloured drugs in shiny capsules rolled to and fro.

"Er . . . what was O'Hara like?" asked Stephen.

"Well, we try not to talk about him too much," said Bob.

"No, I mean . . . what was his speciality?"

"Poking patients, in point of fact," said Bob. "Bad medicine. One of the few things they jump on here. Something they can understand, you see. All at it themselves, of course. Just thought it was worth mentioning, in case you're that way inclined. You can always get the totty on someone else's list."

"Thank you, Bob," said Stephen. "I don't think that's likely to be a problem."

"Look, old chap, d'you think you could manage Robert? Silly really, but I've never liked Bob much, bit naff and lightweight. D'you mind?

16

"And I must say I agree with you about the other. No temptation whatsoever. The students here are a dreadful shower, thoroughly unsavoury, don't see a bath from one week's end to the next, thick as brick walls most of them. And the faculty are worse, if you can imagine. Most of them ought to be in Turkish jails, in my opinion." He paused. "Come to think of it, some of them are. Anyway, absolutely no temptation to dip the Buzzard wick. Some of the secretaries are marginally tolerable, I grant you. But I'm in love with my wife."

Bob Buzzard banged his hand on the desk and nodded several times. He seemed to be entering an introspective phase. Stephen waited, rolling the pills about. Bob looked at him searchingly, as if wondering whether it was worth the effort, then seemed to come to a decision.

"Let me tell you about this terrible place, Stephen. They call it a new university, but it's twenty years old now. Novelty value's worn off, it's way down in the pecking order. Concrete's crumbling, all those bloody silly flat roofs leak, tiles falling off walls on to people's heads, we've got a repair budget four times the total salary bill. . . . I'll tell you what it's like. It's like a very, very inefficient sector of British industry. The plant's an obsolete slum, top management's totally corrupt and idle, middle management's incompetent and idle, and the workforce are bolshy and idle. And, of course, there's no bloody product. No wonder people get ill here. There's nothing else for them to do."

He had been going on for some time as if it didn't matter whether anyone listened to him or not. Now he suddenly turned his great cruel spectacles on Stephen as if seeing him clearly for the first time.

"Look, have you unpacked yet?"

"No, it's all in the boot. I came straight here."

"If I were you," said Bob Buzzard, "I'd get straight back in your car and drive all the way home to Wolverhampton or wherever it is. It can't be worse than this."

There was a good deal more to come. Bob, or Robert, took his induction duties very seriously, and over the next twenty minutes Stephen was treated to a great many

17

facts, opinions, and passionately held prejudices. Lowlands University, it appeared, was a shithole, give or take one or two marginally respectable departments such as Maths and Cybernetics. The medical centre itself was a shambles and well known to be, indeed on the way to being a national scandal, largely due to the mad old fart, who should have been sectioned years ago, and Marie Celeste yammering on about gender instead of getting on with the job. The only hope, it seemed, was Buzzard's rationalisation plan: two-minute standard consultations, computerised self-diagnosis, sub-contracts for all home visits, which would put the team on a fifteen-hour week maximum and open up fruitful areas like sponsored research, commercial consultation, and some lovely lucrative private practice.

For good measure, Bob (for some reason it was hard to think of him as Robert) threw in his track record, which turned out to be Shrewsbury, Trinity, Guy's, Royal Durham, ICI, Saudi Arabia, and then the fatal mistake: Lowlands. And Stephen confided his own less colourful CV: Birmingham, Birmingham, Birmingham, and Walsall, which had, as Bob remarked, a certain grim coherence, if nothing else. And before long Stephen found himself confessing without the benefit of alcohol that he actually liked being a GP, and not only because it was the only thing that he was any good at, but because he liked making people better, or at least better than they were before, and that despite all Bob had told him he was still very excited about being in Lowlands, because here surely at last he would be able to do the job properly, give time to his patients, explore the thing in depth; that here, if anywhere, he would really get it all together at last, because here there wouldn't be any excuse for not being a bloody marvellous doctor, which was all he wanted to be.

Bob was very patient about letting him say all that. "That's very moving," he said, when Stephen had finished.

"Sorry," said Stephen, who had embarrassed himself. "Boring."

"No, no," said Bob. "Moving. I'm not such a hard bastard as I seem, old chap. You're an idealist. And you've landed up in what's probably the worst practice in the British Isles. I'm sorry for you."

Just at that point the buzzer on Stephen's intercom buzzed. Bob leaned across and pressed the button.

"Oh, Dr Daker," said the desembodied voice of Mrs Kramer. "We have a couple of patients in reception. I wondered if you might be free to . . ."

"Doctor Daker's in a meeting," said Bob briskly. "So am I. Get the . . . I'm sure Dr McCannon or Dr Rose Marie would be able to help you."

"Look, I don't mind . . ." said Stephen.

"Bloody face," said Bob obscurely. "Come on. Let's get out of this place. Come and have a look at my word processor."

"And Dr Buzzard's been prescribing you these, has he?" asked Dr Rose Marie, smiling pleasantly. "Over how long a period?"

"Let's see. It must be about four months," said the patient, a slim, dark woman in her thirties, who was wondering, as everyone did, what, if anything, besides the doctor herself, lay beneath the white coat.

"I see," said Rose Marie. She reached for a thick buff file with BUZZARD on the cover, and made a note or two. "And did Dr Buzzard explain why he's been prescribing that particular drug?"

"Well, the first time he said it would just sort things out."

Rose Marie nodded and smiled encouragingly.

"And, well, recently he just sort of looks up as I come through the door and starts writing."

"Yes, I see," said Rose Marie, making another note. "Well, Antonia – it is all right if I call you Antonia, isn't it? – I think we'd better get you off these. They're quite strong, really, quite a few side-effects. In fact it's quite possible they're causing your present symptoms rather than alleviating them. I'd like you to make an appointment for a longer consultation next week, Antonia, say half an hour, will you do that?"

The patient had gone rather pale.

"Absolutely nothing to be alarmed about," said Rose Marie with warm conviction. "Really all I want to do is help you understand what's going on with your body so that you can take charge of it yourself. How does that sound?"

In Rose Marie's thrillingly low musical tones it sounded like a free holiday in the Bahamas.

"Well . . . fine," said the patient, feeling better in herself, as she would have put it, than she had done for a long time. "Thank you very much."

"It's a pleasure, Antonia. Tell me – your husband works here too, doesn't he?"

"Yes, he's a Reader in the German Department."

"And you're a secretary in the VC's office. There's one little thing I'd like you to think about between now and the next time: what we call 'illness' is one of the things that men do to women. That may mean something to you or it may not."

"Oh, yes," said the patient. "That does mean something to me."

"Good," said Rose Marie. She laid a sisterly hand on the patient's wrist. "I'll look forward to working with you, Antonia."

After the patient had gone she spent some time writing in the Buzzard file.

Always a problem, these overseas students, thought Jock wearily. Very popular with the University, of course, since someone in the Government had the bright idea of quadrupling their fees; the place was swarming with them, never mind whether they could speak English or not. Homesick, confused, apt to go suddenly berserk – well, what would you and I be like if someone picked us up and dropped us in Tibet or Sarawak? And now here was this heartbreaking little blossom from Hong Kong; arrived a week early, no friends, hardly any English, nothing to eat except the dogshit in the Refectory: no wonder she had a bellyache.

"And who paid all those enormous fees?" he asked gently, holding her little hand between his two great paws.

20

"I pay them myself," said the patient. "Do two jobs. Work in a shop, work in a bar. And school. It was quite hard." She smiled. Jock seethed with rage on her behalf: all that suffering to land up in this hell-hole.

"And now you're here, you miss your family and friends?"

"Oh, yes. Very much."

"Yes," said Jock. "Now listen carefully to me. In many languages the word for pain is the same as the word for sorrow. And there's a very good reason for that. Very often, much more often than people think, we feel our sorrow in our bodies, as a pain. It's quite normal. Do you understand me?"

"Yes," said the patient. She was trying to understand. She was sure she would be able to understand this kind old man if it weren't for the awful pain in her belly.

"This university," said Jock, "is a very long way from Hong Kong." His face darkened and he stared out of the window at the dull grey sky. "Sometimes it seems a very long way from anywhere. And here you are. You're lonely. You're very tense. Perhaps a little bit frightened. And all these feelings are coming out as a pain. It's a real pain, but it's caused by the feelings. Now do you understand?"

"Yes, I do understand," said the patient.

"Good girl," said Jock. "And I'd guess it's a little bit better already, am I right?" His great yellow teeth grinned at her out of his rumpled face. Why were old Europeans so ugly?

"Well, doctor," she said bravely. "Maybe a little bit." She was now feeling dizziness rather than pain, and the old doctor's breath was so strong.

"Good," beamed Jock. "Now I'm going to show you a way of relaxing the muscles that are causing the pain. Perhaps you'd just like to lie down for me for a minute."

After Bob had thoroughly mystified and daunted Stephen with technology, he offered to walk him back to his car and point out the general lie of the land. They emerged into the reception area to find the head of the practice hand in hand

21

with a Chinese girl about a foot and a half shorter than himself, who was gazing up into his eyes in an obedient and trusting sort of way.

"And the thing to do," he was saying, "is to relax, my dear. Relax, relax . . . walk around the lake, pick a flower, think a quiet thought. And you know if you need us, you can telephone any hour of the day or night, someone is always here."

"Thank you," she said, biting her lip. "You are very kind, Doctor."

"Yes, yes," said Jock vaguely, "away you go." He watched her walk rather stiffly out of the glass doors.

"Poor little thing," he said. "Poor wee lass." He turned. "Ah, Stephen." His yellow teeth flashed in a carnivorous grin. "Had enough already?"

"Er, no, not at all. Bob's very kindly offered to show me where my flat is."

McCannon frowned. "Ah yes. Don't be too, ah . . . it'll likely be something of a rather temporary nature, but I'm sure you'll be. . . . or indeed if not . . . something I had to tell you. What was it? Drinks! Drinks at the Vice-Chancellor's Lodge this evening! You're invited, my dear man, so am I. What a treat for both of us! Eight o'clock, on the dot, don't be late."

"Oh, thanks very much," said Stephen, pleased to be plunged into the dolce vita of Lowlands so soon.

"Very informal indeed, dress down," said Jock severely. "Something else, what was it? Ah, yes, of course, the wee lass reminded me, now as I intend to drink a very great deal indeed this evening, and you're a total abstainer – "

"I'm not a total abstainer," said Stephen.

" – and Doctor Buzzard and Doctor Rose Marie have previous engagements, I know you won't mind being on duty this evening." The carnivorous grin again.

"On duty? But, er, what about the party?"

"Oh, it's purely a formality, my dear man, term hasn't started, nobody here to be ill. You can take my bleeper, Mrs Kramer will fix you up."

Waving a huge vague paw over his shoulder, he shambled

purposefully in the direction of his noxious den. "Work to do, work to do. . . ."

The door slammed behind him.

Bob Buzzard walked Stephen briskly across the huge and almost empty car park, skirting the larger puddles. It was very quiet, except when two nuns in a battered Mini roared in past a NO ENTRY sign and soaked Stephen's trousers with spray. Neither of the doctors noticed a small scruffy man in his forties squatting by the dead Fiat, examining its rotting panels with glum resignation. (But you will, you will, you arrogant, overpaid, incompetent bastards, you'll find out who's really in charge before this thing's over.)

"That's where you're heading for," said Bob, pointing towards a large block in the distance. Even from where they stood it was clear that the architect had been after a sophisticated rendering in concrete of the cave-dwellings of Altona. "It'll be a shithole, of course, but at least it's handy. My advice is get off campus as soon as you can and save your sanity. Listen, d'you play squash at all?"

"Yes," said Stephen cautiously. "A bit. Do you?"

"Let's have a game this afternoon then."

"Really? I mean, isn't there some work we should be doing?"

"God, no," said Bob. He stared in a puzzled way for a moment or two at the wire coat hanger that served as aerial on Stephen's Volvo. He had clearly never been a GP in Walsall or anywhere like it. He shook his head briefly and went on.

"God, no. Plenty of that on Monday, when term starts. They'll all come shambling back with their manky throats and their athlete's foot and their bloody sea urchin spines and their Portuguese man-of-war bites and their . . . Legionnaire's disease and their scabies and impetigo and new varieties of clap. . . . and that's just the academic staff."

Stephen laughed, amused by this witticism. Bob turned his head and stared at him grimly. "I'm perfectly serious, buddy. Ask anyone. Buzzard rarely jokes. Look, get

23

yourself settled in, then shamble over to the University pub, you can't miss it, it's in what's laughingly called the Piazza, looks like the gents on Euston Station, smells like it too. See you there about half one. Right? Fine. Oh, and bring your bathers. We'll have a swim after the squash."

Stephen had managed to find the right warren of caves with surprisingly little difficulty, and had taken only two trips to haul his luggage up the winding staircase (witty translation in concrete from some French dungeon, no doubt). Now he stood at the front door of Flat 127, having trouble with the key. He had never been brilliant with keys, locks, in fact getting anything to fit smoothly and surely into place and do the job it was supposed to do . . . stop that, Stephen, he told himself. They've probably just given you the wrong key.

Suddenly the door opened from inside and Stephen found himself looking at a rather beautiful young man of oriental appearance dressed in what looked like a high fashion judo suit.

"Altered priorities ahead," said the chap, smiling sweetly. "All keys in this university work in reverse, two turns anti-clockwise. I think you must be my new flat mate."

He spoke English fluently, with a slight American accent, as if he derived great pleasure from forming the sounds of every word.

"Yes, I think I must be," said Stephen. "I didn't realise I was sharing," he added, realising immediately how unsociable, arrogant and racist that probably sounded. He needn't have worried. His new flat mate seemed wholly delighted by everything about him, to judge by the widening of his smile.

"Come in, please, let me help you. Make yourself at home. My name is Chen."

The cave, once he was inside, was rather a pleasant surprise. Most of the walls seemed to be curved like the walls of a cave, but unlike the walls of a cave they were covered in green blackboard material, a good deal of which was filled with mathematical hieroglyphs. The furnishings, low, simple and sparse, were mainly green and white. Chen led Stephen into a small bedroom, most of which was occupied by a low bed wide enough to sleep at least two people. Unnecessarily generous for present circumstances, thought Stephen sadly. Unless he was expected to share this too with Chen.

"I didn't realise myself until this morning, that we are sharing," said Chen. "They told me temporary, did they tell you too?"

"Yes, they did."

"Here I think temporary always becomes permanent." He paused for a moment. "Other way round where I come from. What do you think of it?"

The green walls snaking their way round the bed, undulating out into the hall, a glimpse through the doorway of a low green table with a bowl of flowers, green and white curtains shifting gently in the breeze.

"I think I'll like it."

"Good," said Chen, smiling happily. "You're a mathematician, I guess, Dr Daker?"

"Good God, no," said Stephen. "I'm a doctor. I mean a medical man."

"Typical cock-up I think," said Chen. "They make these flats for mathematicians, like me. I come all the way from Burma for this."

"Really," said Stephen. "They, ah, they seem to encourage a lot of overseas students here. I mean, that's nice," he added hastily.

"Oh yeah, big fat fees. That's very nice. Actually, with me, it's the other way round. They give me a big fat research scholarship."

"Why's that?"

"Because I'm so clever," said Chen simply. "Nobel prize soon, no hassle. All these boards, they're for the mighty calculations. Mostly I don't use, Stephen, I sit and think in my head. Sometimes I use a lot. Maybe sometimes I spread into your room a bit . . . how'd you feel about that?"

"Er . . ."

"Just the boards. No funny business. I'm so straight you wouldn't believe." So that was one question answered. "Anyway, Dr Daker, what do you say? Could you hang loose?"

25

"Stephen, please. Yes, Chen. I think I could hang loose."

Chen laughed aloud, looking at Stephen as if he were a longed-for but hardly expected birthday present. Stephen hadn't gone down so well with anyone for years.

"Shit hot, Stephen. Shit hot. And in return for hanging loose about the boards, I'll cook you great Burmese meals. Brilliant. You like to eat Burmese?"

"I'm sure I will," said Stephen with confidence.

"That's great. I think we're going to be ace flat mates, Stephen."

Bob Buzzard knocked on Rose Marie's door and went in. She was writing something in a file which she closed and put away in an unhurried manner, but not unhurried enough for Bob to be able to make out the name on the cover. She took off her glasses and gave him the smile.

"Well," she said. "How's our new colleague?"

"Pushover," said Bob, sitting down heavily in the patient's chair and averting his gaze from some silly balls on the wall about if this woman were a car she'd run you over. "Pushover. Birmingham, Birmingham, Birmingham and Walsall. I mean, I ask you, Rose Marie. What are they bloody well up to?"

"He did get a First at Birmingham, Bob," said Rose Marie thoughtfully. "Or so his CV says."

Robert, Robert, why couldn't she call him Robert, he thought, waiting gloomily for the next bit.

"What did you get, Bob? Wasn't it a third?"

"Lower second," he said sulkily. "Look, I thought we should work together on this one."

"Well, I really can't think what you have in mind, Bob."

"The point is," Bob said seriously, "that you and I have been shat on. After carrying the mad old sod for three years . . . I mean, I think you should have got the job, as you know."

"Well, thank you, Bob. That's very sweet of you."

"No more than you deserve, and I mean that absolutely seriously," said Bob. You smug, devious, smooth-faced little cock-teaser, he privately added.

"But honestly, Bob, it's done now, and it's hardly Stephen's fault, is it?"

"Oh, no, it's not his fault," said Bob savagely. "It's not his fault."

"But that's no reason why one shouldn't make the sod suffer for it; is that the general line of thinking?" said Rose Marie gently. No need for her to make it sound beastly; no doubt she had plans of her own along those general lines, though naturally Bob wouldn't get to know about them.

"Well, yes," he said. "Broadly speaking. In the best interests of the practice, of course. Thought I'd start him off with a game of squash."

Bob started Stephen off with seven games of squash, winning all of them. The great thing about squash, thought Bob, finessing in a nice little drop shot, is that you don't have to be all that much better than the other guy to give him a real seeing-to. He had spent nearly the whole forty-five minutes with his sturdy legs planted firmly on or around the T, sending Stephen scurrying backwards and forwards, all round and quite frequently into the walls, whose gleaming white was subtly softened by a piebald of black and green and the odd smear of dried blood. Stephen just managed to get to the drop shot, flicking it up feebly. Bob took a single step forward, and whacked the ball low and hard to the back right-hand corner. The light went out and Stephen slumped against the wall, gasping.

"That's it," said bob cheerfully. "Bang on schedule. Seven games to Buzzard, no games to Daker. Thanks very much, Stephen. You've got some nice strokes but no game plan at all. You let me dominate you."

"Yes, I suppose I did rather," said Stephen. It would be rather nice, he thought, to slide down the wall and lie on the cool wooden boards for a day or two.

"Swim now," said Bob. "Six quick lengths and out."

"Do we have to, Bob?"

Thrashed to within an inch of his life, and still the uppity oik was calling him Bob.

"Course we have to. Swimming's good for the heart.

27

Anyway, we've hardly raised a sweat yet. Hope you're not going to turn out to be a slacker, Dr Daker.''

This is something we're going to have to make a point of not doing regularly, thought Stephen miserably in the changing-room. They had drunk four pints of bitter each in the University pub, which had had no discernible effect on Bob, but had made Stephen first elated, then slightly confused, and was now swilling and heaving about inside him as he tried to make his weak and trembling legs behave themselves and get into his bathing trunks. Despite his physical condition he couldn't help noticing and being daunted by the length and thickness of his colleague's swarthy cock, and even more so by the black silky trunks with, surely that couldn't be the badge of a swimming club, which Buzzard was easing over his muscular buttocks. Breathing deeply, Bob pulled on a racing cap and a pair of streamlined goggles.

"Fit?" he said, and led the way to the pool.

Lowlands University boasted a beautiful swimming pool, Olympic size with all facilities. At one time there had been some sort of notion that Lowlands would lead the nation, ousting Loughborough and Carnegie in the pursuit of physical excellence, with honours degrees in things like judo and the triple jump, but all that, like so many grand schemes, had withered away, leaving only the splendid pool and a few artificial rockfaces as memorials. Bob and Stephen had the swimming pool to themselves.

Stephen watched with resignation as his colleague unhesitatingly launched himself in a flat racing dive and began forging smoothly up the pool at a speed which was probably not quite good enough to make him a serious contender for the British Olympic squad. Stephen was strictly a two-length man at the best of times, and no sort of diver at all since he had hit his head on the bottom at the age of twelve and had to be fished out with a boathook. He looked up towards the deep end. Bob was already turning, flipping his legs over in an unnecessarily flashy way. Beyond him, at the end, was a neat little glass-fronted office place. Someone was moving about behind the glass. This wouldn't do. Bob was halfway back already. Stephen lowered himself into the pleasantly tepid water, and struck out for the deep end. It was fine! It was nice! He still knew how to swim! His legs felt a bit floppy, and his arms weren't doing quite the right things, but he was moving in the right direction, and everything was under control. Whoever was moving about behind the glass was probably thinking, yes, couple of jolly good swimmers there, couple of fit chaps.

After not all that long he reached the far end, grasped the rail, firmly denied himself his usual rest, and pushed off vigorously back towards the shallow end. The second length was fine, though not quite so fine as the first length. There was something slightly amiss with the connections between his brain and the muscles of his right leg, which made his progress rather lopsided. After a while both his legs developed an obstinate tendency to sink towards the bottom, and his ears began to sing insistently. But he was near the end now. Four more strokes would do it. Well, eight then. He grabbed for the rail and clung on, panting.

Bob hauled himself out of the pool in one smooth muscular motion.

"Right," he said. "That's my six. Have to love you and leave you now, Stephen. Golf date in twenty minutes. Only four to go. Don't weaken."

He disappeared into the changing rooms and Stephen pushed off again. He might not be able to do four more lengths, but he'd bloody well do one more. Build up his power, one more each day, make it part of the new life. . . . Almost immediately he knew that the third length was not going to be a doddle. It was somehow extremely difficult to get his arms clear of the water, and whatever his legs were doing, they weren't moving him forwards very much. A little later he realised that he probably wasn't going to reach the other end at all. He put his feet down and found that he was well out of his depth. Coming up gasping, he struck out again. But his feet kept wanting to sink, and his whole body felt sleepy. He found that he was under water again. It was quite pleasant apart from the pain in his chest. This was silly. No one can breathe under water. Rising to the surface again, he caught a glimpse of what looked like a beautiful woman behind the glass panel. He must be hallucinating. Perhaps it would be easier if he swam under water for a while. . . .

Then something very rough and fierce grabbed hold of him under the chin, twisting his head round. He struck out at the thing, but it was stronger than he was. He gave up. What a way to go, attacked by a madman under water. Then he found that he was on his back, gasping on the surface. His head was resting on something soft and comforting and someone was telling him to relax because he was OK now. He allowed himself to be convinced, and closed his eyes. Someone was making him feel very safe and cared for, a feeling he hadn't had, he realised, for a long time. He tried to say something about this but his voice wasn't working right and this made him laugh.

"Take it easy," said whoever was looking after him, right in his ear, so he took it easy.

After a while he opened his eyes. He was by the side of the pool now, and someone was supporting him gently by the rail. He turned his head. It was a big girl in a soaking wet T-shirt. He had seen her before somewhere.

"It's all right," he said stupidly. "I wasn't really drowning."

"You were never going to get to the other end though, were you?" she said. She had a pronounced South London accent. "You OK now?" she said. Stephen nodded and she hauled him out of the pool. He sat on the side with his feet in the water. His chest still hurt but otherwise he felt fine.

"Didn't we meet this morning?" he said. She peered at him.

"Oh, yeah!" She frowned. "Hey, you shouldn't be swimming in your condition. You're not safe to be out on your own, you're not."

She still had her wet arm round him and her face, he found, looked just as nice frowning and wet as it did smiling and dry.

"You saved my life," he said.

"Yeah, right, that's what it's called. It's OK. I get paid for it."

30

"Oh, I see, you work here," said Stephen brilliantly.

"That's it."

A short, gorilla-like young man came out of the men's changing rooms.

"That's my relief," she said. "Shit, is that the time? Got to go now." She stood up and headed off towards the Ladies and out of his life again.

"Sure you'll be OK?" she asked, turning.

"Yes. Er – I wonder if I could . . ."

She grinned.

"I'll see you around."

And went.

Later, Stephen went for a slow walk round the lake. The pale, late-afternoon sun shimmered on the water, and reflected dazzlingly off the windows of the fortified rabbit-warren in the distance. A white dog and two black dogs were romping cheerfully on the grass by the water.

"I'm alive," said Stephen aloud. "I'm alive. And this is a beautiful university."

"I'm really sorry to lay this on you, Chen," he said later that evening.

"I wasn't going anywhere," said Chen. "No hassle. I like it."

"Well, it seems ridiculously complicated. If there are any calls, they get transferred automatically to this phone. You take the call, then you dial the number on the card, and that automatically bleeps me. Sounds crazy, but apparently it works."

Chen yawned and stretched. Stephen had heard of people yawning like cats before, but this was the first time he had seen anybody do it.

"Look, would you like me to go through it again?"

"No, no, please don't do that. Very low boredom threshold, and I know how to live in the twentieth century, Stephen."

Stephen wondered what it must feel like to be able to say that with so much confidence.

"Anyway, look," he said. "They promised faithfully

nobody gets ill in the vac, so there probably won't be any need of it."

"Oh, I hope there will. Then when I go home and they ask me what I did in UK I can say I was a doctor's wife."

"Well, thanks a lot anyway," said Stephen. "Suppose I'd better be off now."

Chen's eyes widened.

"You're not going to change?"

"I have changed." For the fifth time that day, in point of fact, but who was counting? Clean blue jeans, checked open necked shirt, blue cotton sweatshirt. "Very informal, they said. Thought this seemed about right."

He looked at himself in the mirror. He looked a bit of a prat. The shoes, that was it. Black polished shoes look silly with jeans, but his loafers had somehow gone astray, or perhaps Angela had kept them for sentimental reasons, or maliciously hidden them or ceremonially burnt them. Well, he would have to do as he was.

"Hm," said Chen non-committally. "Not like the Overseas Students Reception, then. I think my flat mate must be in with the in-crowd."

Stephen had never been very good at parties. Student parties had never been what they were cracked up to be: too many people and not enough to drink, stoned strangers wandering round with their own personal bottles clutched firmly under their own personal elbows for their own personal use, and always heaps of arms, legs, voices and furniture between him and any nice-looking girl he might have talked to. Walsall parties had tended to be edgy neighbourhood affairs, with an apparent agenda consisting of dogshit on the pavements, vandalism in the shopping precinct, and the latest moves in the swimming pool controversy; but there was also a subtext involving moody solo drinking in the vegetable gardens and lengthy sobbing in the bathrooms, which Stephen had never been able to get the hang of, somehow. Doctors' parties were more straight-forward affairs, involving nothing more demanding than getting ratted as arseholes and dropping one's trousers towards the latter stages; Stephen, unlike most doctors,

32

had never derived really deep and lasting satisfaction from either of these activities.

This party was different, but just as bad, if not worse, in its own way. A boy of about fourteen had taken Stephen's coat at the door, given his jeans a funny look, and jerked his head towards the snarling roar at the far end of the hall, as if to say: get in there, you poor bastard. The first thing he had noticed was that most people had interpreted the dress instructions much less liberally than he had. Very informal at Lowlands obviously meant something short of full evening dress with decorations, but not all that far short. The second thing he noticed was that there was plenty of alcohol about, almost enough for a doctor's party, though less of the hard stuff and more of the wine. Good. Then he remembered that this was no use to him tonight. On duty. Bad.

People were standing about in little groups, yammering and snarling away at each other with savage desperation, and there was enough hardeye and furtive measuring-up going on to qualify the event for a Walsall suburban special. No sign of anyone who might be his host or hostess. He took a glass of orange juice from a waitress, and wandered round the edges of a few groups. No one took any notice of him except for the odd glance of amused contempt, sometimes mingled with what looked like mild relief. New face. Obvious nonentity. Forget about him.

He listened to a thin woman telling a fat man that Paxos was absolutely vile and Antipaxos even worse; and to the fat man telling the thin woman that he'd never had much time for Antipaxos, what he swore by was ouzo and kaolin in equal measures, with an imodium chaser. Then he listened to a woman in a grey flying suit telling a woman in a black cocktail dress that the only solution for women was to learn to speak a new language. The woman in the black cocktail dress replied with a stream of rapid and impenetrable Italian. Stephen laughed. Both women turned simultaneously and looked at him in an offended way. He moved on, gathering that something called matrix credit was the bottom line, that someone called Grossman had done something very shortsighted and that someone called Furie had done something that was both disgusting and dangerous.

Then he came face to face with a very small but extremely well-fed looking man in an expensive suit, who actually seemed to want to talk to him.

"Jolly good!" said this chap heartily. "Jolly good!" He didn't look like an academic at all. More like a rather successful but not very trustworthy merchant banker. "Blair-Athol, am I right?"

"No, er, Stephen Daker I'm afraid," said Stephen.

"Of course, of course! Remember now, last-minute substitution. And a very shrewd one, I'm sure. My name's Ernest Hemmingway."

Stephen tried very hard indeed not to sink to his knees convulsed with hysterical laughter, and more or less succeeded.

"I know, I know," said the little man. "Can't be helped. Hasn't done me any harm in point of fact. I'm the Vice-Chancellor. Come and get a proper drink."

He led the way to the drinks table, where Jock McCannon wavered into view, clearly well on his way to fulfilling his earlier promise.

"Nothing alcoholic for Stephen Daker!" boomed Jock. "This man is a total abstainer!"

"I'm not a total abstainer," said Stephen.

"All this man needs is love! That's all any of us need!"

"Yes, yes, absolutely, Jock," said the Vice-Chancellor wearily. "The Scotch is over there." He handed Stephen another orange juice, grasped him by the upper arm – his grip was surprisingly powerful, no doubt he'd strangled a few elephants in his time like his namesake – and steered him into a relatively quiet corner.

"You'll have gathered that you're joining a bit of a problem team, Daker. Plenty of talent there, but all pulling in different directions. And of course," jerking his head briefly in Jock's direction, "the captain's one of the walking wounded." He lowered his voice but turned up the intensity. "You could do very well indeed for yourself, Daker. If you like a challenge."

He narrowed his eyes and stared up at Stephen for four or five seconds, making it perfectly clear that the challenge would involve nothing more taxing than piloting a stricken destroyer up the Yangtze or commanding the garrison at Rourke's Drift. Then he turned and said, or rather shouted: "Deirdre! Come and meet the new doc!"

The VC's wife turned out to be about a foot taller than her husband, and alarmingly upper-class.

"Oh, how marvellous of you to make it!" she said. "So brave! Now don't tell me, all your luggage is going round on a carousel at Helsinki Airport!"

"Er, no, it isn't."

"Rio then? Osaka? Prestwick?"

"No," said Stephen, puzzled. "I came by car."

"And now you can't find the key to your trunk!"

"I'm sorry, I don't quite . . . oh, I see." He felt his face going red. When, when, was he going to grow up and stop blushing? "Bit of a misunderstanding. Dr McCannon said it would be very informal."

"And so it is," said Deirdre severely.

"I do have a suit," said Stephen wretchedly.

"My dear, I'm sure you have a *lovely* suit! Don't give it another thought. Do please mingle, Docter er. It's easy come, easy go, you know!"

After a while Stephen did find someone to talk to, a gloomy, bespectacled psychologist who explained to him in great and closely reasoned detail why the new car parking regulations were an infringement of basic human and legal rights. There was some sort of disturbance over by the drinks table and they both turned. It was Jock. He was swaying, waving both arms about, and shouting at the Vice-Chancellor.

"It's cynical exploitation of the most contemptible kind!" shouted Jock, making quite a good job of the polysyllables but spraying a good deal of brownish spittle about.

"Now, steady on, Jock." Hemmingway seemed quite used to this sort of thing.

"I will not steady on! We take these young people from

35

all over the world, half of them don't even speak English, but we don't care, do we? We want their money, shove them into courses they can't follow, let them sink or swim, let them suffer, let them turn their faces to the wall and die, we've got their Deutschmarks, we've got their Hong Kong dollars!"

"Difficult times, Jock," said Hemmingway mildly. "They're helping us through the cuts. Helping to pay your salary, Jock."

Jock grabbed him by the arm. A bottle rolled off the table. Nearly all the other conversations had stopped now, and the party had a focal centre at last.

"But at what cost?" hissed Jock. "At what cost?" Tears filled his eyes. "You should have seen the wee lass that came in this morning, like a little broken flower! Presenting a bellyache, poor wee thing, and any shag could see she had a broken heart. And you broke it, Hemmingway, you and your kind!"

Stephen noticed Hemmingway turn his head and nod to a couple of heavily-built bearded men from Mechanical Engineering who were hovering nearby.

"This University is emotionally bankrupt!" said Jock loudly and passionately. "And you are a vile wee man!"

"All will look different in the morning, Jock," said the Vice-Chancellor cheerfully.

The two bearded men took Jock gently by the arms, as if well used to this task, and steered him towards the door.

"I'll never drink with you again!" said Jock over his shoulder, and then he was gone.

"Oh dear," said Stephen to the gloomy car parking enthusiast. "I wonder if I should, you know . . ."

"I shouldn't," said the psychologist. "Standard routine, I gather. Actually, our professor's exactly the same. Done all his best work by the time he was thirty, all downhill after that."

There was something very uncompulsive about his conversational style. As he embarked on a lengthy critique of his professor's achievements and character, Stephen let his eyes wander round the room. Good God. It couldn't be.

36

Back view, but he was almost sure, he'd seen a lot of the back of that head jogging away from him . . .

"Why should we have to put up with him for the next twenty years?" the gloomy man was saying. "Tell me, as a medical man, where d'you stand on the euthanasia issue?"

"Bit tricky," said Stephen. "Look, I'll tell you later. I've got to, er . . ."

Getting through the people between him and that lovely head seemed to take three-quarters of an hour or so, but he made it. Just as he reached her, she turned and smiled. It *was* her. His very own swimming-pool attendant.

"Hello," she said. She even looked pleased to see him.

"How . . . how long have you been here? I didn't see you."

"Not long," she said. "Saw you. I was sort of saving you up."

"Well, look, um . . . what are you doing here?" Nothing about the Hemmingways had suggested enthusiasm for worker participation, everybody else he had met seemed pretty high up in the academic hierarchy . . . what was she doing here?

"Same as you, I s'pose," she said.

"But look – I mean, you work at the pool, don't you?"

"So?"

Suddenly the conversation wasn't going so well.

"Oh, Lord," said Stephen. "You're not, you're not Hemmingway's daughter or anything, are you?"

"No."

"God, that's a relief. Well," he went on happily, "this place must be a lot more democratic than I thought it was."

She looked at him levelly for a few seconds. She was not smiling any more.

"That's a pretty shitty thing to say, don't you think?" She gave him some more of the level look. It made his ears buzz and he could feel himself blushing again. Horribly, terminally.

"Oh, God," he heard himself croaking. "Look, I'm sorry. I didn't mean it like that."

"I'm not good enough for the likes of you," she said in

a pleasant conversational tone. "What else could it mean? I thought you were a nice man."

"I am a nice man," he said desperately. "Well, I try to be. Look, I meant I'm delighted to see you here. I can't talk to all this lot."

"Not doing too well with me, either."

"Look," he said. "Could we start again, please?"

She gave it some thought. "OK," she said eventually.

Stephen took a breath.

"The thing is, I'm very nervous and tense and that makes me blunder about a lot, especially when it's important. Um . . . let me try and get this right . . . I went for a walk by the lake this afternoon. And it came to me that being life-saved by you this afternoon, I mean apart from saving my life, was just about the nicest thing that's happened to me for. . . ." He stopped. It wasn't just that he couldn't remember how long; it was rather that something odd was happening to his throat and his voice wasn't going to be able to finish the sentence. All he could do was stand about waiting.

The smile came back.

"Well, that's a whole lot better," she said. "Even if you're pissed and don't mean it."

"Not pissed," said Stephen. It was all he seemed to be able to manage. Something was the matter with his face too.

She took his hand. She took his hand! This wonderful life-saving person was holding hands with him, right there in the Vice-Chancellor's Lodge!

"Hey, you are tense," she said. "You're shaking."

"I know."

"Come on, relax. You're doing fine now."

Jock's bleeper went off suddenly and ridiculously loudly. She dropped his hand.

"Blimey, what have I done to him?"

"Nothing. Honestly," he gabbled. "I've just got to find a phone. Look, I don't – look, how can I see you again?"

She smiled.

"I'll see you around."

*

"Now, I know the whole area will be very tender," said Stephen, "but it is particularly here . . ."

The Chinese girl gasped.

". . . rather than here."

"Yes, I think." She was soaked in sweat and her eyes were dull and frightened.

"OK, that's fine," said Stephen. "All over now."

It was half-past ten in the evening. He went out into the corridor where Chen was waiting.

"Chen, would you dial 999, give my name and the University Medical Centre. Give them her name, age twenty-three, and sex, and where she is on campus. Tell them it's acute appendicitis."

He went back into the little concrete cell. The walls were quite bare. She hadn't done anything to impress her personality on it except bloody near die in it.

"We're going to take you into hospital," he said.

"I'm sorry, I'm a nuisance."

"Not at all," he said. "You were quite right to phone. But it's all right now. We know just what's wrong with you and we know just what to do about it." If we're in time, he thought. "Now you say you felt it last night for the first time. Dr McCannon examined you this morning, didn't he? Like I did?"

"No, he didn't do that," she said. "He talked to me."

Jesus, thought Stephen.

"And he showed me how to breathe. To make the pain go away."

"Yes, I expect that would help a bit."

He made himself smile at her.

"You are very kind, sir. You and the other doctor."

"Not at all. We're just doing our job."

The taxi-driver dropped Stephen off by the Piazza at half-past one. "This do you, John?" he said. "Go any further into that tangle I'd never get out, know what I mean?"

The taxi chugged away and Stephen stood wondering which way his flat was. He glanced up at the windows of the medical centre. There was a light on. The corner window.

Jock McCannon's. Stephen hesitated. He was going to have to do it sometime. Tomorrow morning, if not now. Now would be best, while he was still angry. He went in and walked up the stairs.

"You didn't examine her, did you?" said Stephen.

Jock was lying collapsed in his dreadful leaky horsehair armchair, with an empty bottle of Bell's lying on its side at his feet. The reading lamp shone down on his head. Stephen couldn't see his eyes: they might as well have been empty eye sockets.

"Of course I examined her," muttered the pioneer of student health.

You bloody old liar, thought Stephen.

"Halsey at the hospital," he said diffidently, "told me that in his opinion the appendix was about to rupture. He rather wondered what the hell we were playing at here when she told him she'd been seen by a doctor this morning with severe pain."

Jock suddenly lurched into life, gripping the arms of the chair and thrusting his head forward.

"Then he's damned impertinent and so are you. Don't you see what happened? That poor girl's psychic pain was so acute that she worried herself into an inflamed appendix!"

"Jock," said Stephen carefully, "you know that's nonsense. That girl came in with acute abdominal pain and you didn't even examine her. I'm sorry to have to say this b-but it's a clear case of negligence."

There. He'd said it. He had been a doctor for eight years without needing to say it once, or even think it, and now he had said it, on his first day at work, to the most distinguished man in his field. He suddenly felt very tired. The muscles in his left leg were fluttering.

"So it's you," said Jock very quietly.

"What?"

"I thought it would be Rose Marie, you know. Or that black-hearted bastard Buzzard. They've both tried to get rid of me before." He didn't seem angry, or frightened; his voice was full of senile wonder. "But it's you, is it? Have you come to this University to destroy me, Stephen?"

"No, of course not," said Stephen. "I was simply saying . . ."

"Yes, yes, I know," said Jock, with wonderful understanding and forgiveness. "I confess my error, of course I do. I should have examined that poor wee girl. But, Stephen, it was a small error of judgement. Not negligence." His voice had become high and wheedling. The old sod wasn't asserting himself; he was pleading.

"You're not like them. You have compassion. And you're a good doctor. You saved that poor wee girl. You wouldn't destroy old Jock, would you? Would you?"

He seemed on the verge of tears.

"No," said Stephen. "I wouldn't destroy old Jock."

"Thank you, Stephen. I knew you had a heart in you."

"But look . . ."

"I know, I know. Mea culpa." My God, the old sod was grinning at him like a naughty schoolboy. Suddenly he was quite sprightly again. "I've been going through a wee bad patch, Stephen. Life in tatters, eh? Withered ego. Libido like a guttering candle. Eh? Eh? But you'll help me through it, I know you will . . ."

He stopped as if struck with a sudden and brilliantly original thought.

"Eh . . . will you take a wee dram with me, Stephen?"

Stephen shook his head slowly.

"Ah. Of course. Total abstainer."

"No, I'm not," said Stephen savagely. "But I'm still on bloody duty, aren't I?"

Rust

Rust is the name of the Arts Council Fellow in Creative Writing. Ron Rust. Yes, you think you've heard the name but you can't quite place him, can you? Actually he hasn't always been Ron Rust. At one time he was Ronald Rust; that was in the very early days when he thought of himself as a poet, and so, to be fair to the poor sod, did the *New Statesman* and the *Listener* and *Encounter*. Unfortunately he had the bad luck to attract the favourable notice of

41

F. R. Leavis, so that was that, as far as Rust the poet was concerned. Cutting his losses, he became R. G. Rust the novelist, and wrote five bloody good novels, even though he says so himself. Published, too, and not by any old slag, either; in 1965 Frederic Warburg gave him sixty quid to get himself done at a flashy photographer's for the back cover of *Spinal Tremors*, Rust's third. In retrospect, that was probably a mistake. Rust isn't exactly hideous to look at, but his face does tend to put people off things, and so it proved with *Spinal Tremors*. Secker and Warburg soldiered on with R. G. Rust for two more, *Clap Hands* and *Neural Spasm* (both remaindered), and then decided to call it a day.

You probably don't remember Ronnie Rust the playwright. Well, whether you do or not, Rust has been there too. He even has a Broadway flop to his credit, which as he will tell you is a sodding sight better than a hit at the Theatre Upstairs. Rust has been met at Kennedy with the limo and the flowers. Rust has made nasty scenes in places that wouldn't let you through the doors. Rust has lived like a king on his hundred bucks per diem right up to opening night. And Rust has been told to get the fuck out of New York any way he likes on the morning after opening night. Yes, Rust's been there. Sodding right he has.

All through that time, Rust was an Author, and people used to ask the Author's opinion and have to get the Author's consent for things. Rust liked being the Author. He even joined the Society of Authors, though he didn't keep up his subscription. But for some time now he's been a writer. Ron Rust the writer. Let's get the writer in and get a complete rewrite. You know my rule, I never let the writer on the set. All that. That sort of writer. To make no bones about it, Rust is, has been so long that he has to think of himself as, a series writer. For television. A reliable one, too. Time you fifty minutes' worth to within fifteen seconds, every time, and that's what it's all about. The thing is, the commissions have been a bit sparse lately. Rust's getting on a bit. He's forty-eight. Mid-career for a novelist, right. Not for a writer. Most writers are dead by the time they're forty-five, dead or in homes for alcoholics. And the young ones keep coming up. See them on TV getting their BAFTA awards, about fifteen some of them look. But Rust is hanging on. Rust is tenacious. Some people call him the Pubic Louse, only partly because he looks a bit like one.

Rust knows he is lucky to be here on this Fellowship thing. He wasn't the Selection Committee's first choice. The sod who was, a bad-tempered gay minimalist poet called Tom Tarr, has welshed on the deal and taken a residency at Cornell for five times the money Rust is getting. But now Rust is here he is taking his post very seriously, particularly the work with the students. He is going to run three creative writing workshops a week. It's hard work, but Rust believes in it. Someone has got to take on the burden of discouraging new writers. The ones without talent, obviously. Nobody wants to read a lot of crap. But the ones with talent even more so.

The world is quite full enough of writers twenty or more years younger than Rust, getting all Rust's commissions, writing their postmodernist fictions or whatever they call them that make Rust's stuff look old-fashioned, getting all Rust's women . . . anyway, he can't discourage the lot of them, but he can certainly permanently cripple the literary ambition of any of the sods who happen to be students at the University of Lowlands. Rust believes so passionately in this work that he is prepared to devote two whole days a week to it. Sod mingle. Sod be part of the scene. Rust is a man with a mission.

And then there's his own work. Oh yes, he's certainly going to get on with that. And he's going to make this one stick. Nobody's done this one right before. Amis, Bradbury, Lodge, Sharpe . . . that other sod . . . what are they, frightened of telling the truth or something? This place is a madhouse, and Rust is going to do justice to it. Just needs writing. That's all.

At moments like this, in the violet hour, when the typist etcetera and the taxi throbbing waiting etcetera and the sad African focuses his tearstained eyes on Rust's trusty Olivetti, Rust is apt to review his life and achievements so far, with a view to fuelling his anger for the night's work. Rust has always been a night writer. What has Rust got out of it all? What does he own? He used to own a perfectly decent little house in a leafy suburb of Wolverhampton. Yes, Wolverhampton does have the odd leafy suburb, and Rust had some very tolerable times there with his first wife, whom he loved very much but didn't treat very well. Anyway, she's got that house.

Then he used to own that great big flat in Weymouth Street, a bit flash for Rust really but dead handy for Broadcasting House and Bertorelli's, and loads of doctors just round the corner in case one felt not quite the thing. Doctors. Yes. Anyway, his second wife's got that one. You know, the actress. You've seen her on the box. Rust loved her very much but she didn't treat him very well.

He still does, in theory, own the flat in Muswell Hill, a bit out of it some would say, but perfectly all right for Rust, if it weren't for Carol and her sodding chum. Rust loved and perhaps loves her very much too, but they seem to be renegotiating their relationship in a direction highly un-favourable to Rust. Anyway, Rust doesn't much feel like going back there. Rust has always been one for getting out fast and travelling light: a sort of boat person of the emotional life. Sometimes he regrets this.

What else does he own? He doesn't own a decent suit. He wouldn't mind having a decent suit. Suddenly he wants a suit very badly, not just a decent suit, but a real flash suit, four-hundred-quid job. Deep Throat has got a four-hundred-quid suit. Got it off a drug rep. Rust does quite unequivocally own that rotbox of a Fiat, which coughed itself to death almost immediately after arriving at Lowlands University, as if trying to tell Rust something.

Rust owns his body, such as it is. He owns his experience. Such as it is. He owns his talents and his skills, such as they are. He owns the next ten hours. Yes, it's getting near the time. This one, he promises himself. Sodding BAFTA award for this one, no messing. The trusty Olivetti squats silently on the work table. Yes, he's ready. He gets off the bed, goes over, and switches on.

44

2

WE LOVE YOU: THAT'S WHY WE'RE HERE

The Volvo was bucking and weaving in the most disconcerting way. He was trying to keep the gear changes to a minimum and steer into the skids, but the water inside the car was over his knees now and his feet kept slipping off the pedals. The road signs were coming faster: keep left, no entry, altered priorities, ABSOLUTELY NO VOLVOS GO BACK GO BACK. Suddenly a nun loomed up, frighteningly close to the windscreen. He swung the wheel over. Another nun. No chance of avoiding this one. He let go of the wheel and put both hands over his face. There was no impact. He opened his eyes again.

Bob Buzzard was in the passenger seat, telling him to get back in the car and go straight to Wolverhampton without passing go. He tried to explain that he was in the car already and that it was Walsall anyway and not Wolverhampton. Then the water came up over his head. It would be all right if he didn't panic. He would simply open the door, glide up to the surface and go to the party. But Bob Buzzard was holding him back. He said it was stupid to go now because he was making a cup of tea on his word processor . . . Stephen tried to explain that he was drowning and wouldn't be able to drink the tea, but his voice was too slow and gurgly. And a crab had got hold of one of his toes, and the whole situation was getting a bit beyond him. Chen was squatting at the end of his bed. Nice Chen. Reliable Chen.

"I've made you some tea," said Chen.

"Oh, thank you," said Stephen.

"Sugar?"

"Two, please."

"Very bad."

"I'm the doctor," said Stephen firmly. And then, "Oh, God." He took the mug and sipped.

"You were growling and squeaking in your sleep," said Chen. "Like a little dog."

"Sorry," said Stephen. "Just, you know . . . panic and terror."

"First day of term," said Chen. "Think of all the little freshers. Think of their panic and terror."

"Yes, all right. I know."

Chen was quite right. He could do it. He was a good doctor. But it was all the other stuff, stuff like walking into rooms with other people in them, touching anyone in a non-medical context, talking to them . . . what on earth could one say in a ten-minute standard consultation? That was six hundred seconds. How was he going to fill all that silence? And this morning there was going to be a group meeting. What was a group meeting? What did you wear for a group meeting? When the head of the practice wore odd socks, what options did that leave for Stephen?

"Chen," he said. "I'm really sorry. Forget it. I'm fine, really. Absolutely fine."

"No," said Chen seriously. "You have a problem, and I'd like to help you. Would you like a bit of Burmese psychology?"

"Yes, thanks very much," said Stephen gratefully.

Chen looked at him intently for a few moments. Then he said: "Get up and go to work or I'll cut your feet off."

Conventional wisdom has it that we spend our second year at university trying to get rid of the friends we make in our first year. Angie and Megan had been room-mates for one night, and were sick of each other already. Angie was extremely pretty in an out-of-control jail-baitish sort of way, while Megan had always been regarded as a bit of a

46

sour-faced boot even by Trethomas standards. There was, of course, a lot more to both of them than that – isn't there to everyone? – but we won't go into it now.

They were standing outside the pub on the Piazza at half-past nine on the first day of term, watching the seething throngs of posers and wankers crisscrossing the square, screaming at each other and embracing, giving each other hardeye, moving purposefully towards places they looked confident of being able to find, and generally behaving as if they knew what was what.

"I told you not to wear that scarf," said Angie. "Nobody's wearing them. Not a soul."

"I'm wearing one," said Megan stubbornly.

Angie was watching a tall, dark, powerfully-built man in his thirties in a black leather jacket moving through the crowd. He was attracting lots of glances and waves. Then a tall healthy-looking girl in a tracksuit jogged up to him and he seized her in a fierce bear-hug which just went on and on and on.

"My father," said Angie wistfully, "says in any university there'll only be about a dozen people really worth knowing. Find them, and there's your education."

"Your father sounds a bit daft if you ask me," said Megan. She had one of those Welsh accents that makes the speaker sound slightly offended whatever they're saying. In fact Megan often did feel offended, messed about, and generally taken liberties with. She was feeling like that now, and not only with Angie. There was a small, scruffy middle-aged man sitting on an empty barrel no more than ten yards away, who had been leering intently at the two girls for some time now. Nasty little pervert. (Quite unfair, you censorious little Welsh prig. He has other plans for you. Watch out.)

"Megan," said Angie, "you don't understand anything, do you? Good job you've got me to look out for you."

"Very grateful, I'm sure," said Megan. "You coming to the bookshop or not?"

"Well, now," said Jock, flashing his horrible yellow destroyed grin round the room. "The item of pressing

47

importance would seem to be the Induction Week Spiel."
He paused to allow himself a lengthy coughing fit. The
weekend did not seem to have done him much good. His
hands were shaking and there was a large bruise in the
middle of his forehead. "Are you with us, Stephen?"

"Well, no, I . . ."

"Freshers Induction Week," said Bob Buzzard briskly.
"Various nobs get up and give the new first years the official
propaganda. Wonderful university, new realistic climate of
the Eighties. Lucky to be here, ha ha. Work hard, join a
club, keep your nose clean and watch out for falling tiles.
And Jock does a thing about the Medical Centre. Where it
is, who we are, what we can do, what we can't. All right?"

"There is rather more at issue than that," said Rose
Marie gently, smiling at Stephen. She was quite as beautiful
as he remembered. Empathetic, too. He felt sure that here
was someone who shared his ideals, someone he could
really work with, maybe even . . . stop it. All over, all that.
Remember?

"Indeed there is," Jock was saying. "We meet these
young people at what is perhaps the most impressionable
moment in their lives. The chord that is struck in our initial
address to them will resonate profoundly in their wee
souls."

Bob groaned softly.

"That is why I am soliciting your views. We are, after all,
a true collective, isn't that so, Rose Marie?"

"Well, yes," she said pleasantly, "if we ignore a few
blatant inequalities of power, status, gender and salary,
you could say that."

"Teasing again," rumbled Jock roguishly. "You're a
wicked wee lass. And so unfair. Because this year I am
minded, like King Lear in the play, to surrender some of
my symbolic power. I feel as if my roots are covered with
snow, my dear chaps. I feel that the Freshers – such a
precisely evocative word – should hear a younger voice. A
voice with sap in it."

"You mean you want one of us to do the spiel?" said
Bob.

"Precisely."

"OK, I'll give it a whirl," said Bob. "Next business?"

There was a short silence.

"I would like to know what's being said on my behalf," said Rose Marie silkily.

"Quite. Quite," said Jock. "Last year, if you recall, I stood before them, and I said, quite simply: 'We love you. That's why we're here.' I was minded to say more, but when I heard those words reverberate, they seemed to be enough."

"You might have told them what the surgery hours are," said Bob.

"So what would you be telling them, my dear chap?"

"Quite obvious. Tell 'em where we are and so forth. Then I'll point out that a hell of a lot of capital's been invested in them, mistakenly in my view, but there we are. We could have a word processor or an MG Maestro for the money that's spent on every one of them. So it's their duty to look after the machinery and keep it on the road. Students run on good food, hard work, early nights and exercise. Absolutely no excuse for drug and alcohol abuse, VD, anorexia, piles or pregnancy. We can help, but we're not magicians. We're more like mechanics. That's all."

"Perhaps you'd like to get them undersealed?" said Stephen, surprising himself, and winning a warm and serious smile from Rose Marie.

"Wouldn't be a bad idea," said Bob. "Technology's there."

"Well," said Jock. "If that's the future, it terrifies me, I must confess. What says our dearest Regan?"

"It's not a joking matter, Jock." She was still smiling, but much more clearly in a part-of-the-job sort of way.

"Ah, God, these women!" shouted Jock, throwing both arms above his head. "Nothing's a joke any more! Go on, go on, we're deadly serious, lovely girl!"

"Why don't you call Stephen and Bob your lovely boys, Jock?" she said pleasantly.

"They are my lovely boys. I'm sorry, I'm sorry, please do continue, er, *Doctor* Rose Marie!" He didn't seem in the

49

least embarrassed or perturbed. Neither did she. Perhaps, thought Stephen, it's one of those games they both enjoy.

"Well," said Dr Rose Marie. "First of all I would outline the kind of care this practice offers to every member of the University. Then I would invite them to consider the idea that the University, like other phallocentric hierarchies, like this practice itself, is a structure which consciously or unconsciously sets out to oppress women. And does it very well. Just as fewer women proportionally get Firsts, or senior academic posts, so more women proportionally become ill."

"More than one reason for that," said Bob, grinning at Stephen. Stephen lowered his eyes and studied Jock McCannon's socks. One green, one purple. Nice stroke, Jock.

"Yes, of course, Bob," said Rose Marie compassionately, "but I know you'd agree with me that the central reason is that women are a colonised race. And they should think about that in terms of their mental and physical health. Whether it's a good idea to distort their body chemistry and threaten their life expectancy to suit their boyfriend's convenience, for example."

"By going on the Pill, you mean," said Stephen.

"Good, Stephen." Another pat on the head for Dr Daker.

"Damn sight more reliable than the alternatives," said Bob sturdily.

"I shouldn't think you've considered the alternatives I have in mind, Bob," she replied sweetly.

There was a short silence during which Stephen, though not the other two men, wondered what those alternatives might possibly be.

"Right, well thank you Rose Marie," said Jock, who had visibly aged a decade or two during her exposition. "Think we get the general drift. Stephen?"

They were all looking at him. Oh, God. The meeting had been fine so far. Oh, well, it had to come.

"Well," he tried hopelessly, ". . . I don't really feel that I should . . . being new to the practice . . ."

"Come, Stephen." Jock's grin was positively wolfish. "Nothing will come of nothing."

"Well," said Stephen. "Though I was enormously impressed with what Rose Marie's just said – and Bob's thing of course . . . I think if someone could say something that takes into account how they're all feeling, the boys as well as the girls . . . that it's all right to feel lonely and frightened, it's part of being human. And that we're dealing with people, not symptoms. That we're here to listen to them and pay attention to them as people."

He stopped. This was horrible. It didn't sound like him at all, it sounded like one of those dreadful men on *Thought For the Day*. He was aware of Rose Marie's patient condescending gaze, of Bob Buzzard wincing at every second word. And now something was making him go on: "And . . . and that if they feel they need us . . . well, here we are. I mean, they don't have to wait till they're bleeding from the rectum."

He stopped again. This time he really would keep his mouth shut.

Bob clapped his hands together slowly three times.

Rose Marie uncrossed her legs, then crossed them again on the other side.

Then more silence.

Then Jock said, with deep emotion: "We love you. That's why we're here."

"I suppose so," said Stephen. "Sorry."

"Speak for yourself, buddy," said Bob Buzzard. "I love my wife, my boys, and my car. Full stop."

"Stephen," said Jock. "The job is yours."

"Oh, look –" said Stephen desperately – "I didn't mean I wanted to do the speech!"

"That's the feeling of the meeting," said Jock heavily. "Next business."

As soon as the meeting was over, Stephen went to his room, shut the door, sat in O'Hara's swivelling chair, and whirled round and round in it quacking like a duck. This made him feel a little better than before, but it wasn't quite

51

enough. He got up and went over to the wall and hit his head on it two or three times, whimpering quietly. Then he felt ready to go back to his desk and work on his draft for the Freshers Induction Spiel.

This went pretty well, considering. There were one or two snags, of course. Virtually everything he could think of to say looked absolutely fatuous when written down on paper, worse than *Thought For the Day* now he thought about it, more like that chap who sorts people's sex lives out on that phone-in programme. Nauseatingly smug and somehow transparently fraudulent at the same time. Well, no doubt another six or seven drafts might sort that problem out. What was worse was the certain knowledge that he would faint, vomit, or go into hysterical paralysis within thirty seconds of actually standing up to deliver the thing.

It was quite a relief when somebody knocked on the door. Working on the speech had punished his linguistic resources so severely that for the moment he couldn't think what it was you said to get people to open the door and come in. But he didn't have to worry about that for long. Rose Marie came into the room, sat uninvited in the patient's chair, crossed her legs in a leisurely manner that afforded him a rather more generous view than he wanted of her not-to-be-thought-about legs, and gave him, for the second time, her most disconcerting smile.

"May I?" she said. "I just wanted to congratulate you on your performance in the meeting."

It was impossible to tell if she was being nice or nasty.

"Oh . . . look," he said.

"And wish you the best of luck with your speech. I think I've been underestimating you."

"No, you haven't!" No. That sounded wrong. It was the legs, that was the problem. "I mean I know it must have looked as if . . . but really I didn't want the job."

"And yet you got it. Quite a performance." Oh, dear.

"No, really. Look, I'm honestly getting nowhere with it," he tried. "I was hoping, well I wonder if you'd help me with it. I was very impressed with your ideas."

She looked at him thoughtfully.

"I feel as if I'm being seduced," she said. What? She felt what? How could she feel that? For a wild moment Stephen thought of checking his zip, but that would only make matters worse. Something of this must have shown in his face, because she added: "I was using the phrase as a political metaphor, of course."

"Ah, yes, of course," said Stephen. Suavely, he hoped.

"And I'm afraid I must refuse, Stephen. I know it isn't easy to be a man these days, particularly if you happen to be intelligent and well-meaning. But you'll have to find your own solutions. For me, you see, you're part of the problem, I'm afraid." Part of the problem? In what way? What problem? What part? And what was she smiling at now?

"But I'll certainly come to your talk," she said. "I'm looking forward to it *very* much."

Half an hour later Bob Buzzard breezed in without knocking at all, and slammed a file on his desk.

"Just off for a game of squash," he said. "I do love to thrash a sociologist. Speech all sewn up?"

After Rose Marie had gone, Stephen had crossed out everything he had written so far, swivelled and quacked for five minutes, and then sat down and written a whole different talk. Seeing Bob now made him realise, he wasn't sure why, that he'd have to cross that one out too.

"I can't do it, Bob. It's hopeless."

"Not my problem," said Bob genially. "Shouldn't have greased so hard for it, should you? I honestly thought you were going to crawl right up Jock's, still, no skin off my nose, I'm off back to Saudi Arabia first chance I get. What's the matter anyway?"

Stephen told him.

"Well, well," said Bob delightedly. "You're right up shit creek then. How ever did you manage in Wolverhampton?"

"Walsall. There wasn't much call for oratory there. I'm going to have to back out."

"Oh, no," said Bob. "You can't do that. Your whole reputation's on the line here. It's make or break time, buddy."

"Bob. Robert. Will you do it? Please?"

Bob shook his head, grinning. "Not a chance." A thought seemed to strike him. "Tell you what though. Try a couple of these." He produced a little box of pills from his waistcoat pocket. "Two hours before the off."

"What are they?" asked Stephen. "Stelazine?"

"Good Lord, no. These are the new things. Prophylanx. State of the art. Trial run was in the Falklands with the paras. They were popping 'em like Smarties."

"Really," said Stephen, impressed.

"Home straight in on the anxiety centre, apparently. No fear, no pain, no broken heart. You'll probably feel like jumping off the stage and strangling a few of 'em. Seriously, though, these'll crack it for you. Er . . . not too good with booze."

"I'll remember," said Stephen. "Bob, this is really kind of you."

Bob looked embarrassed, just for a second.

"Well. You know. Anything to keep the wee lassie off the platform. Now I really must go and humiliate that sociologist. Cheers."

Stephen dreamt that he was lost in the University, late for his talk, running down walkways knee deep in water. He turned a corner. Two nuns were barring his path. He ran between them. A tall fit-looking girl was jogging ahead of him. "Help me, I'm lost!" he called, but she couldn't hear him. Then he was battering at a plain wooden door that had no visible means of opening. He couldn't get through. Just as he was starting to cry the door gave way, and he stumbled onto the stage.

The auditorium was packed with students. They were all very pale; that was because they were dead. Jock McCannon was on the stage, pointing grimly towards the lectern. Stephen took a faltering step forward. If he kept very calm, no one would notice he was in his pyjamas. What he needed was a drink of water. But the water jug was made of some sort of bendy plastic. It evaded Stephen's grasp and tumbled silently onto the floor. The audience were laughing at him now. He was struggling to speak. He was speaking. "I love you," he said. "That's why I'm here."

"Absolute balls!" shouted Bob Buzzard.

"Sexual harrassment!" hissed Rose Marie.

The students were on their feet now. They were coming for him. The girl in the tracksuit got up and started jogging out of the auditorium.

"Save me, please!" yelled Stephen.

"I brought you some tea," said Chen.

"Oh. Thanks," said Stephen. Chen was squatting at the foot of the bed looking at him with mild concern. "Er . . . growling and squeaking again?"

"Worse than that," said Chen. "You were howling like a wolf."

Stephen looked at his watch. Half-past seven. Bob's pills lay on the bedside table next to it. Two hours, he'd said. Just about right. He took two of the pills, and washed them down with a mouthful of tea. Christ.

"Good?" said Chen.

"Chen. What did you put in it?"

"A little Scotch whisky," said Chen. "For bravery." He put his finger and thumb together and showed Stephen a gap of about a millimetre. Then, smiling, he slowly widened the gap to about an inch and a half.

"Not so good?"

Oh, what the hell, thought Stephen recklessly. He took another big swallow. "Just what the doctor ordered," he said.

Two hours later, Stephen was actually standing on the stage in the main lecture theatre, giving his talk. He had sat through three other platitudinous but highly competent lecturettes from the Registrar, the Dean of Arts, and the Librarian. Now it was really his turn, and it was going terribly. Bob's pills were absolutely no use at all. It must have been the whisky; somehow it must have neutralised the pills instead of accentuating their effect; that's why Bob must have warned him off the booze. Anyway, the auditorium, despite its vast size, was remarkably short on oxygen, and the audience looked far away and out of focus, though not so out of focus as to prevent him being uncomfortably aware of two nuns who appeared to be playing noughts and crosses in the front row, Rose Marie looking pained and disappointed in the second row, and Bob Buzzard leaning back in the third row with his arms folded and a sarcastic grin on his face. The three distinguished gentlemen on the platform were clearly not only bored out of their minds but something else as well; anxious, or annoyed. Perhaps that was because the Freshers, from whom awed and respectful silence could reasonably be expected for the first six weeks or so, were shifting in their seats, turning round to talk to each other, and even in some cases eating quite substantial lunches.

". . . and outside the normal surgery hours, it's always possible to get in touch with one of us . . . by ringing . . ." His voice seemed to be coming from a long way away. What was he saying? "By ringing . . ." Now he couldn't find the number. He knew he had written it down.

Someone in the audience groaned quite loudly.

There it was. Over the page.

"Five one oh one," he said limply. Nobody was writing it down. He took a deep breath.

"Other services offered by the Medical Centre include . . ." It was no good. This was it. He couldn't manage another word. It was faint or vomit time. The only question was whether he would be able to stumble into the wings or whether he was going to do it where he stood.

"Look," he said. "This is terrible, isn't it?" Something was happening. That was his voice. And it was coming out of the front of his face. He crumpled up his notes and put them in his pocket. At least he had the strength to say sorry before he died.

"Look, you can read all that stuff in the handbook," he said. "Who needs it here? You've sat and listened to three boring talks already . . ." (the chaps on the platform all involuntarily turned their heads towards him at the same moment, causing a few giggles in the audience) ". . . and what right have I to add insult to injury? You didn't come to university to be bored, did you?"

This was better. They had stopped talking to each other. They were listening to him. He was also feeling a great deal better in himself. Really quite energetic and strong. What was he doing clinging to the lectern? Feel much better if he strode about the stage a bit while he talked.

"Silly question!" he said, striding about. "Course you didn't. You came here to . . . to find yourselves, develop yourselves, fulfil yourselves, and . . . all that stuff. At least I hope so. That's why I came here."

Someone in the audience cheered. It sounded a bit derisive, but he was getting across. He was doing fine. He was a great success.

"And to have fun. Right!" he shouted, stabbing his index finger in the air. He had seen union leaders doing this on television and often wondered if it felt good to do. It did.

"Having fun. Yes. That's all right. In fact it's essential. A university isn't just a degree factory, even in the Nineteen-eighties! I'll tell you what it's all about, it's all about people! Intelligent, lonely, nervous, cheerful, talented, vulnerable, nice'n'nasty . . . infinitely varied 'n'uniquely valuable people!" Steady. Moving about a bit too fast. Nearly off the stage then. But it was going down well. Some people were even clapping.

"Now," he said fiercely. "What's all this got to do with the Medical Centre? I'll tell you what it's got to do with the Medical Centre!" He stopped. He couldn't for the life of him remember what it had to do with the Medical Centre. Then it came back to him.

"We care for you as whole people," he said. "We're not mechanics. I mean we can do the job all right. We'll prescribe the Pill for you, and treat your symptoms with the highest level of professional skill 'n'competence. But you're not just a set of symptoms to us. You're you. And we care about you."

He was stabbing his finger again. Why had he ever been frightened of public speaking? Public speaking was bloody good. He'd give a lecture every week.

In the audience, Angie turned to Megan.

"Isn't he wonderful?"

"I think he's drunk," said Megan.

"One last thing," said Stephen. "There's one big snag about being a doctor. People only come and see you when they're ill. When they're down. That can be really depressing, I can tell you. But look, it doesn't have to be like that. You don't have to be ill to come and see us. Come and see us when you're feeling fine!"

He paused again. He was feeling tired. And the slight suspicion was growing in his mind that he might have gone just a teeny little bit over the top. Never mind.

"Listen," he said. "We . . . care about you. That's why we're here."

Then he sat down, suddenly and heavily. The applause was tumultuous.

"Angela Fry for Dr Daker, please," said Stephen four hours later. He drank from a glass of water and tried to get his face ready. The door opened and a pretty girl came in. That was all right except that her colours were too bright.

"Hello, Miss Fry," he said. "How are you?"

"Angie, all right? And I'm fine. Just carrying out my orders, you know, come up and see us when you're feeling fine?"

"Oh, yes," said Stephen, putting his hand to his head. Her voice was a bit bright too; she was very nice but he wished he could turn her down a bit.

"Hey, you OK? Shall I go away and come back?"

"No, no, I'm fine," he said. "Slight headache."

"D'you want a head massage? I used to do that for my father."

"No, no. Really. Thanks. Well, Angie."

Stephen was good at getting people to talk, and listening to them when they did. Angie told him that his talk was terrific, and she'd asked particularly to be on his list, that she was loving it at University, that she wasn't homesick at all, because home was a real pain with her mother and her

58

stepfather and her really gross little half-brother; her real father was all right, in fact wonderful, but she didn't see much of him, and was pinning all her hopes on this place, which looked very promising so far. In fact, ace. Well, her room-mate was a real downer, but you couldn't win them all. Then she paused a bit, and smiled a rather nice shy smile.

Yes, actually, she said, there was something that she wanted: she wanted to go on the Pill. Again. She couldn't for the moment remember the name of the one she was on before, but when Stephen suggested one or two she remembered it was Logynon. No, she hadn't discontinued because of any problems with it, it was just that there hadn't been anyone to make it worth her while. Here she smiled a rather less shy smile at Stephen.

People assume that doctors never get embarrassed, but some of them do, and to cover his blushes, as well as because he had to, Stephen took her blood pressure and asked her the usual stuff about jaundice and epilepsy and blood-clotting problems in the family, getting the usual answers. Then he wrote the prescription.

"Aren't you going to ask me why I'm starting again?" she said.

"Well . . . one could hazard a guess. It's not really any of my business."

"I don't mind talking about it," said Angie. "I've fallen in love with someone."

"Someone here?"

"Mm. I'm crazy about him actually. He teaches drama here."

"Look," said Stephen, who was in fact a little shocked, "I really think perhaps you shouldn't be telling me this."

"I don't mind," she said. "You're not shocked, are you? I've been into older men for yonks." Something about the way she said it indicated clearly that was what she thought Stephen was.

"I see." God. He was blushing again. "Er . . . are you sure you've thought about this enough?"

"Oh, yes," she said cheerfully.

"And he . . . I know it's none of my business . . . he feels the same way?"

"He will do," said Angie. "He doesn't actually know yet. I only met him yesterday."

Not long after this, Megan came to see him as well. Not from choice, as she made quite clear. She was supposed to register. Mrs Kramer had assigned her to Stephen, and here she was. No, there wasn't anything wrong with her and there wasn't anything she wanted to talk about. But she still sat there. Stephen waited.

"Why did you have to go on about sex in that talk of yours?" she demanded eventually.

"Did I?" said Stephen, surprised. He couldn't actually remember, but it didn't sound like him.

"'Go on the Pill,'" she said. "'Fulfil yourselves.' Just encouraging people."

She went on to tell him that it wasn't just him, that English at Lowlands was all about sex, the girl she was sharing a flat with couldn't think or talk about anything else, and that it wasn't herself she was worried about, it was the rest of them.

"Don't you think it's irresponsible," she said, "going on about sex and Freud and that, at people who haven't got anything to protect and sustain them? No, I don't suppose you would think that, you're just as bad as the rest of them."

"And you have got something to protect and sustain you?"

"Yes, I have," she replied in an offended tone. Of course she had. He had come across that tone in Walsall too, and he knew that she was quite prepared to sit there waiting as long as he liked: he'd have to ask her in the end.

"D'you mind if I ask you what it is?" he said eventually.

"The love of Jesus Christ." Well, of course it was.

Once started, she found a lot more to say. Education and Religious Studies, she was supposed to be doing, but Education was all Freud and Marx as far as she could see, and Religion was all curry and marijuana. The Students'

Religious Society was even worse: transcendental meditation, and trips to Stonehenge and Avebury. She had a really splendid line in universal contempt, a fluent delivery, and a voice like a knife scraping a plate. After she had said all she had to say, which took about twenty minutes, and stumped off, Stephen laid his head gently on the desk, too exhausted even to swivel and quack.

He still hadn't got the hang of the bloody lock. He stood there fumbling and muttering to himself, until he heard Chen's voice from inside.

"Other way round, remember? Altered priorities here!"

He got through the door and trudged into his bedroom.

"God, what a day," he said. "I feel like a battered baby, Chen." Maybe a shower would be the thing. He took off his jacket, and started to feel a tiny bit better, so he took off his tie, shirt, trousers and shoes as well.

"Chen!"

"Yes, Stephen?"

"You haven't cooked yet, have you?"

"Not yet."

"I can't face eating tonight. All I want is two quiet pints in some bar, then bed. D'you fancy coming? Er, just the bar, I mean. I hate drinking on my own."

He went into the living room. Chen was sitting on the floor with the girl from the swimming pool. They looked as if they knew each other very well indeed. Stephen found that this made him feel sad.

"Oh. Sorry," he said.

"Hello," she said, smiling.

"Didn't realise," said Stephen. "I'll . . . I didn't know you two knew each other."

"Ah, we're old friends, Lyn and me," said Chen. "As for the drink, sorry, next time maybe. I think I'm going to be working all night."

"Yes, of course." On her, thought Stephen. Some guys get all the luck.

"Take Lyn," said Chen. "She likes a drink."

"Oh, no. I wouldn't dream of it. No, it's all right. I'll

just . . ." Why couldn't he just get out? Why did he have to hang about irresolutely looking a prat no doubt in his socks and Y-fronts?

"What's the matter?" said Lyn, grinning at him. "Don't you want to?"

She seemed to mean it.

"Really?" he said.

"My pleasure, Doc."

In the bar, Stephen began to feel a lot better. It wasn't simply that a little judicious bitter drinking seemed to make just the right connection with the morning's pills and Scotch. He was finding Lyn very nice to talk to. So nice that after half an hour or so, he felt ready to risk the dodgy area, the bit where things had gone so disastrously wrong at the VC's party.

"Lyn," he said. "D'you mind me asking, um, what you do at the University. I mean I know you work at the pool, but that's not all, is it?"

"Well, no, s'pose not. What do you want to know for? Don't you like mysteries?"

"I'm not sure," he said.

"I mean, what d'you want to do, put me in a category? I don't like that stuff." Same sort of words as last time, but this time she wasn't looking at him like a piece of shit on her shoe.

"No, really not that," he assured her. "You're, um . . . unique."

She smiled. "OK, Doc. You smooth talking bastard. I'm a policewoman."

"I don't believe you."

She sighed. "Well, I am really, but I haven't done much of it lately. Joined the force after A-levels, but I didn't like arresting people. They sent me off to do this psychology degree. Sort of scraped a starred First . . ." She glanced up at him for his reaction; what she saw made her grin. "Then I went back and worked in intermediate treatment for a bit. Alternatives to custody. I'm here on a research scholarship. PhD in body language. OK?"

He simply couldn't think of anything to say. How old was

she? Twenty-five, twenty-six? How could she have done all that? How could he cope with it?

"See?" she said. "I knew I shouldn't have told you. You're scared of brainy women, aren't you?"

"No! No, really. I'm just scared of women!" God, he was going to have to do better than this. "I mean that's really interesting. A PhD in body language?"

"Yeah. It's dead good, body language. Um . . . let's see. That girl over there. The fair one."

Stephen hadn't noticed the bar filling up. Now as he looked around he noticed that all the tables were full, people supping the stuff as if there was no tomorrow, laughing and shouting and falling about. How had it escaped his notice? There was a large group round the big central table. The focal point seemed to be a big, swarthily handsome guy in a leather jacket who was talking quietly and intently, making the group of girls round him lean forward to catch every no doubt mind-expanding word. As an adolescent Stephen had fantasised about being one of those sorts of guys. What a hope. Then he realised that the fair girl Lyn meant was his new patient, Angie Fry.

"That's a dead easy one," said Lyn. "Everything turned to him, everything open. She's even turning her palms up, you hardly ever see that. She's making a present of herself to that bloke."

Stephen wouldn't have noticed all that himself, but as soon as Lyn said it, it was glaringly obvious.

After a moment Lyn added: "She's almost certainly a virgin too."

Oh, is she, cleverclogs, thought Stephen, feeling irrationally pleased.

"What are you grinning at?"

"Nothing. What about him?"

"Oh, that wouldn't be fair," she said. "I have inside knowledge. I'm a friend of Carl's." Chen, Carl. All the goodlooking men. How could he compete? He couldn't compete. He couldn't even cut the mustard.

"Your body language is very interesting," she said. Oh, God.

"You've got very expressive hands, but you're sort of scared of them. That's really odd, cos I don't think you're violent. Here, let's have a look."

She took his left hand in both of hers. Her hands were warm and her fingers felt very strong and confident. She uncurled his fingers, smoothed them out, and waggled them one by one. He reached for his bitter with his free hand.

"How does that feel?"

"Very nice."

"No, it doesn't. You hate it. You've got a touch taboo." She gave him his hand back and he resisted the urge to sit on it.

"How d'you manage, being a doctor and that?"

"Oh, I'm all right with patients," said Stephen. "It's just people. Female people in particular."

She frowned. "Where d'you get your cuddles then?"

"I don't get any cuddles, Lyn."

"Your wife doesn't cuddle you?"

"My wife doesn't even hit me any more," he said. "She's working on becoming an ex-wife."

"That's it, then," she said triumphantly. "You've just done a bit of dodgy learning."

"You're a behaviourist!" he accused her.

She grinned. "Isn't everyone?" She leaned back and looked at him, not exactly fondly, rather as if he were a lucky find, a pair of shoes, say, that just went with that particular shirt.

"Well, blow me down, Doc. Touch taboo. D'you want to do some work on it?"

"Er . . . what sort of work?" he said cautiously.

"You could help me with my research. I'm doing a little paper on touching permissions in social groups. You could come along and keep me company."

"What sort of groups?"

"Oh, you know. Hells Angels . . . karate clubs . . . lesbian discos . . . is he going to faint? I'm joking, Stephen. Nothing too scary, promise. And at the same time I could sort you out a little learning programme. How about that?"

64

It would be a way of seeing more of this extraordinary person, but . . .

"Couldn't I just do seven years in analysis instead?"

"I haven't got that much time, Doc. I'm a woman in a hurry. How do you feel about tin churches?"

He had imagined massed fat black ladies with uniforms and tambourines, but Lakeland Road Gospel Hall was very small, corrugated iron rather than tin, and as far as he could see an all-white outfit. It was like being in a time warp. The women, who predominated, tended to wear what his mother used to call tailored costumes, and there were more hats on view than he could ever remember seeing. In the fourth row he noticed a girl wearing a new University scarf. Odd, that. He hadn't seen anyone wearing one, except Yellowbelly Fred, the University mascot. Ah, well, more time warp, he supposed. Her back view seemed vaguely familiar, though.

Nothing odd had happened so far, except for two hymns of quite extraordinary length. There didn't seem to be any vicar or vicar-substitute at all, and nobody, thank God, had done any touching that he could see. The seventh verse of "What a Friend We Have in Jesus" was staggering to a close. As it did so, a curly-haired young man rose to his feet and faced the congregation, singing the last two lines in an offensively beaming sort of way, directing the words at individual worshippers in the practised style of a cabaret singer. Lyn nudged Stephen.

"That's him. Lay preacher. They don't have ministers here. This one's called Colin. S'posed to be the state of the art. Does laying on of hands on a good night."

Everybody went amen, and they all sat down except Colin, who continued to beam at them affably. Unlike anyone else in the hall, he was rather fashionably dressed, in a light blue suit that went with his eyes.

"Jesus loves us," he said eventually. He had a broad but pleasant sounding Lowlands accent. "Jesus loves every one of us. He even loves me!" he grinned roguishly. "And I'm a sinner. Yes, I am. We're all of us sinners. And you know the wonderful thing? Jesus doesn't mind. He doesn't mind.

He says it's not important!" He treated the congregation to another of his cheeky grins, then went immensely serious.

"Just so long as we can feel the power of his love."

"Amen!" barked a woman at the front, sudden as a belch.

"Amen!" agreed Colin enthusiastically. "And I can feel it tonight. Oh, yes. Tonight is one of the good nights. It's so strong in this room. I know there are those among you feeling it as strong as I am."

Lyn nudged Stephen. All right for you, he thought, this is all material for you, but what am I doing here?

"Don't fight against it," said Colin, smiling directly at Stephen. "Let it flow through you," he said to the girl in the scarf. "As I'm letting it flow through me. I can feel it in the soles of my feet. Flowing up through my spine. And into my heart. All through my veins. Surging through my blood. The love of Jesus, quivering at my fingertips like electricity."

He stretched out his arms so that everyone could see his fingertips, which were indeed quivering. What a cheap trick. It was disgusting. It was embarrassing. It was also, come on, admit it . . . a little bit frightening.

"Who will share it with me? Who wants to feel the love of Jesus? Yes, now, while it's flowing strong?"

Stephen felt Lyn tense beside him. No, don't. Please don't, Lyn, I couldn't bear it.

An elderly woman got up from an aisle seat and moved towards Colin. She stretched her hands out, he took them in his and clasped them both. In the sudden silence her little sigh of pleasure was shockingly audible.

"The love of Jesus," said Colin, like a garage mechanic confirming that she had indeed got genuine Michelins. "Yes, that's the love of Jesus."

The woman, trembling now, allowed herself to be detached, and went back to her seat.

"And it's still there," said Colin. "That's the beauty of it. It doesn't go away. It's inexhaustible. It's waiting for you. Yes. You. Come on. You've been waiting such a long time."

Someone else was getting up. It was the girl with the scarf. As she stepped awkwardly out into the aisle, Stephen recognised his patient. Megan. The Welsh girl. She stumbled awkwardly towards the lay preacher, and he reached both hands forwards, cupping her face between them and drawing it towards him.

"The love of Jesus," he whispered. "Shutting out the pain of the world. Like the gentle rocking surge of a mighty ocean."

Megan started to weep softly. Her face was pressed into his chest. His arms were round her. He smiled peacefully and dreamily round at the congregation. Now he was looking at Stephen, in a friendly but controlling sort of way.

"The love of Jesus," he said. "It's so strong tonight."

"OK," said Carl Pierce. "So now you know something about energy." He had taken off his leather jacket and looked very good in a sweaty, heavy-metal way: black T-shirt full of big muscles, strong cheekbones glinting in the low light, all that. The thing about Carl Pierce was he really took charge in his Movement Workshops. He looked at his watch. "Right, we'll just finish up with a couple of trust things."

Not liking the sound of this, Stephen edged carefully towards a darkish corner. He knew far more about energy than he really wanted to know now. With luck he'd be able to get his breath back and watch the final throes without attracting attention. No such luck.

"One," said Carl. "Nobody sits in and watches. Either you're in or you're out. Two. Trust means you trust me. Get in there, right?"

Stephen got in there. He tried to get Lyn for his partner, but she had gone way out of reach. He was claimed by a bad-tempered girl weighing not more than twelve or thirteen stone. He noticed that Angie Fry had chosen to trust Carl.

The first trust exercise involved standing opposite your partner, holding hands, leaning outwards to take the weight, then slowly going down to floor level. Everybody managed fine except Stephen and the fat girl. And it seemed to be Stephen's fault.

"Lean back," she hissed.

People were looking.

"I'm trying, honestly," he said. He was trying. But his body wouldn't let him. She'll drop you flat on your back, said his body.

"Like this!" she growled, taking the risk his body wouldn't let him take.

The sudden weight was enormous. There was nothing he could do about it. He collapsed on top of her. Somehow his whole arm had gone down her T-shirt. He panicked.

"Keep still. Stop that."

Carl came over and gazed down contemptuously at Stephen.

"OK, Sandra, let's swap."

Sandra glared at Stephen, then went over to Angie and glared at her.

"Relax, OK?" said Carl quietly to Stephen. "This one's easier." Then he raised his voice without taking his eyes off Stephen, as a lion-tamer might instruct his apprentices.

"Face your partners. This one's about empathy. Make contact fingertip to fingertip. One partner leads, the other is the mirror image. Don't speak. Don't make any conscious decisions. Discover who's who. The aim is total co-operation, total empathy. Do it."

This one was easier, or perhaps doing it with Carl made it easier. Stephen began to forget the strangeness of it, and notice things, such as the huge size of Carl's hands and feet.

"Don't look at your partner's hands and feet," said Carl, in a friendly but controlling kind of way.

"Look in your partner's eyes."

Yes, he was right. It was easier like that. It was really rather pleasant, being taken charge of like this. Not as good as lifesaving, but still. . . . He found that he was beginning to like Carl.

"And finally," said Carl, "make the moves really small. Concentrate on the eyes. That'll help you. Imagine you're an eye doctor making a diagnosis. Look very deep, and very close. And reach a point of stillness."

Stephen obeyed. He looked very deep and very close. Wait a minute. The light wasn't good enough really, but he knew he'd seen something like that before. Yes. He was sure of it.

"Fine. Relax," said Carl. "Not bad. You're getting there," he added to Stephen.

"Look, could I . . ."

Carl had turned away. "That's it for tonight, group. See you next week." A man in his twenties, wearing a denim jacket and thick hornrims, was standing by the door.

"Be right with you," said Carl to this man.

"Er, just a second – " said Stephen, but Angie Fry had got there before him.

"You haven't forgotten, have you?" she said eagerly, clutching Carl's arm.

"What?" said Carl, amiably enough.

"You said you'd come back for coffee."

"No, Angie, *you* said that. Sorry, I've got something on."

"Chuck him. Please?"

Carl seemed to hesitate for a moment. Then he took Angie by both elbows and said deliberately: "Three things you ought to know. One, I don't mess around with my students. Two, I'm in a long-term relationship. Three, I'm gay. OK?" He patted her shoulder. "You were working well tonight, Angie. OK, night, everyone."

Angie started to cry.

"Look, I'm awfully sorry, this won't take a minute," said Stephen.

Carl turned angrily.

"What?"

"Could we just have a brief word in private?"

"Look," said Carl. "It's late, I'm tired, I've got a date. What is it?"

"I just thought I should make sure," said Stephen. "You are getting treated for glaucoma, aren't you?"

"For what?"

69

"Er . . . glaucoma. It's an eye disease. It was when you asked us to imagine we were . . ."

"I know what I said. What do you know about it?"

"Well, er . . ." said Stephen apologetically, " . . . I am a doctor."

Carl's front collapsed abruptly. His face looked very young and frightened.

"Christ. Is it serious?" he said.

"Look, I'm not sure," said Stephen. "I'm not an eye specialist, and the light's not good in here. Come in and see me tomorrow, and if it's what I think it is, I'll fix you an appointment with a consultant."

Carl grabbed Stephen's arm.

"You didn't answer me. Is it serious? Could I go blind?"

"If it's glaucoma, yes, it's serious, but it's completely treatable, and you won't go blind. That's a promise."

"You OK, Stephen?" said Lyn as she walked him back to the flat. "Look a bit nackered, you do."

"Oh, Lyn," he said. "I don't think I could stand another evening like that one. I mean it was nice of you to try, but really . . . bit of a hopeless case, don't you think?"

"Oh, I wouldn't say that," she said. "Thought you stood up to it quite well, considering. Even making a bit of progress on the learning programme too."

"What d'you mean?"

"Well, what's all this then?"

"What?"

"We're holding hands, Doc."

"Oh, yes."

Two days later, the consultant confirmed Carl Pierce's glaucoma: twenty-per-cent loss of field in the left eye, right eye affected but undamaged so far, and a good prognosis. Carl was so moved and relieved that he bought Stephen a bottle of Glenfiddich and went round telling his friends and acquaintances that the weedy new doctor was one, a nice guy, two, a fucking genius who's saved his eyesight, and three, not a total abstainer at all. Unfortunately Jock McCannon was not among Carl's friends and acquaintances.

On the same day, Angie Fry came smiling bravely into Stephen's consulting room. After telling Stephen that everything was fine and great, and that as her father said, once you got your sex life sorted out everything else fell into place (this last Stephen could have well done without), she fell uncharacteristically silent. Then she cried for a while, and told him that she wasn't doing anything with Carl at all, or anybody else; that she was in fact a virgin (one up to cleverclogs, thought Stephen ruefully) and didn't Stephen think she was useless and pathetic. Stephen assured her that he didn't, and managed a few more convincing things along those lines. Quite soon she stopped crying and told him one thing hadn't changed; she was still into older men.

The day after that, Megan Price paid him an unexpected visit. Fixing him with a stern glare, she told him that she was engaged to be married, and that she wanted to go on the Pill. She had even brought her fiancé along as supporting evidence. His name was Colin and he was a lay preacher.

Rust

Rust is in a restaurant eating a big steak. Not just any old restaurant, either; Rust is in Julie's Restaurant. That's Julie's *Restaurant* we're talking about, not the wine bar upstairs full of literary agents falling off the silly cushions dropping food off their knees. No, this is the proper place with the pink tablecloths and the full menu. Rust is having a good time for once.

He is sitting at a table with two men called Jonathan Powell and Ken Riddington. Jonathan Powell is eating frugally and drinking Perrier. Ken Riddington is eating substantially and drinking moderately. Rust is shovelling and swallowing down all the food and drink he can get his hands on.

This is par for the course. Powell and Riddington understand this and indulge Rust's greed. They know, as Rust knows, that he'll only get one shot at Julie's. Even if the thing does a bomb, it'll be all downhill from now on as far as creature comforts are concerned. People who go on about BBC waste and extravagance ought to be condemned to five sodding years in Series and Serials, that's what Rust says. One decent meal at the start, to set you up for the treadmill, then forget it. Series and Serials likes lean, hungry writers.

But Rust is getting ahead of himself. He still hasn't sold his idea, not for definite. They must have faniced the pilot script a bit though mustn't they, or we'd be in Threshold House drinking lukewarm coffee out of plastic cups in Riddington's slum of an office.

Oh, it looks good all right but they still need to be nailed down. Rust is going to have to talk in a bit, he knows that. Reluctantly he turns down the cheese. Doesn't want to spatter the Head of Series and Serials with bits of Gorgonzola while he's making up his mind. Riddington orders an enormous slice of some gigantic tart or other. (How does Ken stay so thin? Must consult Deep Throat about it.) Jonathan Powell shakes his head. The waitress goes away. Here we go then, thinks Rust.

"Well," says Jonathan Powell. "I think it's heaven on wheels." Little pause. "Are you sure you can write it, Ron?" Sod me, thinks Rust, he's trying to finish it in the first round, what's the matter with him, train to catch or something? Of course, he knows what Powell means. This one's a bit classy, BBC2 all the way, not Ron's usual line of country, feel a bit happier if it was Malcolm or Freddie or even that other fellow, Ron being more your bread and butter man, besides being a bit, well . . . old for a writer?

Rust holds his glass of Fleurie up to the light. He studies it carefully, turning the glass round and round. He has often wondered why sods do that; to create pregnant pauses and make time to think, probably. That's why he's doing it anyway. It looks quite nice actually, just like a big glass of red wine. Right, that'll do. He puts the glass down carefully on the table, and looks Powell right in the eye.

"Listen," he said. "*Nobody's* done this one right. And I know just how to do it. I've got it all in here. Just wants

72

writing. It's very important to me, this one. If I don't write this one, I don't want to write anything."

Jonathan Powell smiles.

"Fine," he says. It's fine, but it's not final, of course. Still, he's not shitting on it. Rust is beginning to get excited. Now it's Riddington's turn. (The tart has gone already. How does he do it?)

"Well, as you know, Ron, I think it's a brilliant idea. A lovely idea. But I'm not quite sure I've got the feel of it yet. Let me put it this way, we know it's not *Dr Finlay's Case Book*, but are we talking about *Doctor in the House* or are we talking about *Hill Street Blues*?"

"We're not talking about either of them, Ken. This is something new. Something unique. We're going to find a new language. And when they see it, they're going to say, oh, yes, that's what it's like! OK?"

Ken looks worried. He likes things to be like things. Well, everybody does. And this one of course will probably finish up being more like this than like that, but what the hell, thinks Rust, you might as well sodding well try. Anyway, it's Powell that he's really worried about. Powell is the Head of Series and Serials, after all. He's the one who needs something new.

"It's not going to be just a tiny bit like, er . . .?" says Powell. Rust knows exactly what he means.

"It's not going to be remotely like that," he says firmly. "Seventies show. This is the Nineteen-eighties. It's a whole different world."

"And this one has doctors," Riddington remembers.

"And not just any old doctors," says Rust. "This one has really dreadful doctors, almost as bad as real doctors." Rust has been supping it a bit, but suddenly he knows it doesn't matter.

Jonathan Powell takes a sip of coffee. Puts his cup down.

"Let's do it," he says. Then smiles at Rust. "Heaven on wheels. Just needs writing."

3

WIVES OF GREAT MEN

A clear, sharp late-October morning. The still surface of
the lake reflecting a cloudy sky. In the middle of the lake, a
small rowing boat. In the rowing boat, two nuns. One rests
on her oars, the other expertly casts for trout. Around the
perrimimeter of the lake, two figures are jogging. One is a
woman and the other is a man. The woman, a tall healthy-
looking person in a tracksuit, is about thirty yards ahead of
the man. When she reaches the bridge, she stops and waits
for him. As he struggles towards her, she smiles at him
fondly.

"Well, now," said Jock McCannon. "Our second group
meeting of the term. We survive, we survive. And how nice
it is to see you all together. Our little team." Jock bestowed
a paternal pat to the head of the stuffed owl at his elbow,
and beamed cadaverously round at his little team.

"Doctor Daker looking very pink and well. Early
morning sexual intercourse no doubt?"

"No, no, really!" said Stephen, embarrassed. "Er,
jogging."

"Too bad," said Jock. "Well, we have an innovation
today. Maureen is with us."

Maureen Gahagan blushed. She hadn't wanted to come,
but Rose had gone on and on so much about it being so
important, creative transgression of gender-based con-
structions of reality or whatever, that she hadn't had the
heart to disappoint her.

74

"We didn't have the chance to consult you, Bob," Jock went on, "I think you were called away urgently to the . . . golf course, but Rose Marie, supported by Stephen here, proposed that our little meetings should include the nurse, as a matter of courtesy."

"Democracy," said Rose Marie.

"And *keen personal pleasure*," said Jock, leering horribly at Maureen. "Now. We have weathered the October crisis, and Bob has some figures for us culled from his rinky-dinky little computer. Bob?"

"Thank you, Jock," said Bob, opening a brand new plastic folder. "Er . . . d'you think you could manage Robert?"

"I'll try, Bob. Old habits die hard."

"Right," said Bob, gritting his teeth. "Well, the only statistically significant element relates to the new intake, the freshers. No suicides. No nervous breakdowns requiring hospitalisation. And withdrawals are down by twenty-five per cent."

There was a short silence.

"Are you sure, Bob, that your little computer's quite well?" said Jock.

"Absolutely. Ran it through the Registrar's Epson to check."

"Well, that's really good!" said Maureen.

"Hm, yes and no," said Bob. "As you all know, I believe in weeding out the no-hopers right from the word go, but you could look on the bright side and see it as a productivity gain."

"Indeed you could," Jock beamed. "A gain in human happiness. I wonder where we should look for the explanation."

Another rather longer silence. Then Maureen could contain herself no longer. "Well, it's obvious, isn't it? Dr Daker replacing Dr O'Hara."

"Oh, no," said Stephen, embarrassed. "I'm sure. . . ."

"A little simplistic, perhaps?" Jock murmured threateningly.

"I don't think you're aware of all the factors, Maureen,"

75

said Rose quickly and gently. Maureen was a heroine of the struggle, but, awfully, well, *emergent* in her relation to phallocentrism.

"I think I am," said Maureen sturdily. "The factors are, they were all asking for him after that talk he gave. And he's got a nice way with him."

"O'Hara had quite a nice way with freshers too, remember?" said Bob.

"Yes," she said darkly. "And we all know what way that was."

"Eh . . . Maureen," said Jock. "When we invited you to join our meetings, we didn't envisage your taking them over completely." Maureen blushed, glared, and fell into a sulky silence.

"Now," said Jock. "The Vice-Chancellor is already baying for more cuts, more economies, more redundancies. How do we respond?"

The responses were as follows: Dr Rose Marie was for total resistance to any cuts at all. The practice should indeed press for expansion, particularly in the areas of cervical smear tests and body awareness groups for women. Nurse Gahagan supported her. Dr Buzzard proposed that the wives and families of academic staff were a suitable group for economy cuts. He produced figures showing that wives and families of senior academic staff in particular took up more surgery time than their husbands. Dr Buzzard moved that family medical care should be withdrawn forthwith, making an exception for the VC's own disgusting brood. Dr McCannon observed that it was a terrible fate to be the wife of a Great Man.

Dr Daker suggested that Dr Buzzard's proposal implied a rather narrow view of medical care. Dr Buzzard saw his point: wives as support services, need to keep them ticking over or the whole thing collapses, but pointed out that if that argument were followed through the medical team would be looking after their bits on the side, their dogs and cats, servicing their typewriters and cleaning their cars. The line, felt Dr Buzzard, had to be drawn somewhere.

Dr Rose Marie argued that not only were the wives more

interesting and intelligent people than their husbands, they needed more help, because their husbands quite literally made them sick. Here she was warmly supported by Nurse Gahagan. Dr Daker would have liked to say something at this point, but was unable to get a word in edgeways.

Dr Buzzard then proposed a second area of cuts, closing the Sick Bay and dispensing with the services of Nurse Gahagan. Nurse Gahagan pointed out that she had a patient in sick bay now, which was why she was unable to stay and listen to any more of Dr Buzzard's stupidity. She reminded Dr Buzzard that he, like the rest of them, needed people to be ill, otherwise he wouldn't have any job, and then she informed the medical team that she would not be attending any further stupid meetings. She then left the conference, which continued in her absence.

"Right, Mrs Kramer," said Maureen, striding into the crowded waiting room, "I'll take anyone who's here for jabs or dressings, with or without an appointment." She turned to the patients. There were no more than twenty of them. "And the rest of you might as well go home for all the joy you'll get this morning!" She marched out, very pink in the face.

A big, fierce-looking man of about fifty got up and walked heavily to the counter.

"Yes," he said, "I'd just come to the same conclusion. Would you present Professor Furie's compliments to Jock McCannon and tell him that his practice is a bloody shambles!"

"You should have made an appointment, Professor Furie," said Mrs Kramer, unmoved.

"Like these poor bastards, you mean? Good day to you!" He walked out, slamming the door. Mrs Kramer placidly crossed his name off her list, and the waiting room settled back into gloomy silence.

Professor John Furie drove home very fast, narrowly missing a head-on collision with two nuns in a battered Mini. He switched on the Commodore in his study and ran up the draft of the article for *Nature*. Ten-minute job. Well, twenty, better say. Bloody screen was too bloody bright. They were supposed to have fixed that. Why could nobody do their jobs right except Furie? Bloody doctors. Get the whole place closed down, make a clean sweep. See how they liked that. Now. The door opened and his wife Helen came in. For a moment Furie experienced the odd feeling that he didn't know who she was, but then he remembered. Yes. And the rest.

"I'm just off, then, John," she said. She stood in the doorway, a slim, gentle-looking woman whom Furie had once found very beautiful. Then not. And now, oddly, did again.

"What? Off where?"

"Shops. And I'm having lunch with Chris and Mary in town. I did tell you."

"Hilary," he said. "You said Hilary."

"No, Chris and Mary," she said patiently. "Don't you remember, I told you we were going to Nico's and you said don't have that bloody moussaka."

"Yes, that sounds like me. Right. Right. Not Hilary then. Well, off you go. Don't worry about me, will you?"

She lingered. "You look busy."

"Oh, it's nothing much," he said savagely, "two articles late on deadline, Promotions Board at two, I'm giving consultancy on the transatlantic hookup at four, and I've already wasted twenty minutes in that bloody shambles of a surgery. I was rather hoping you could handle the telephone for me today: I thought that might not be too much for me to ask."

"I've put it on the answering machine," she said.

"Oh, fine, that's taken care of everything, well have a lovely time, enjoy yourself," said Furie, baring his teeth.

When she had gone he turned away from the keyboard, and put both hands up to his head, as if trying to hold his brains in.

Jock McCannon kept Stephen back after the meeting.

"You were very quiet there, my dear chap," he said, pouring himself a quarter of a pint or so of Bell's.

"Still feeling my way, I suppose," said Stephen. "Look, er, haven't we got a lot of patients to see?"

"No, no, my boy," said Jock, waving this irrelevance away. "I felt the power of your silence, Stephen. We are kindred spirits, you and I. We are men, Stephen. Rose Marie, for all her brave intelligence, is just a wee lassie at heart. And little Robert is a schoolboy, and always will be, with his rinky-dinky computer activities. But you and I: we bear the terrible burden of manhood."

"Yes, it, er, does sometimes seem a bit of a burden," said Stephen uncertainly.

"Yes," said Jock fervently. He stared into his glass thoughtfully for a long time.

"Look, if that was all," said Stephen, "perhaps I'd better be getting back to my . . ."

"No. Wait!" said Jock, fixing Stephen with a terrible glare. "What I was going to say is this. That while we care for the plight of the wives of great men, it is to the great men themselves that our hearts go out."

"Is it?"

"You know it is. It's a kinship of the loins. They cry out to us, the great men, as they thrash about in the maelstrom of middle life. And we cannot but respond."

He sank into thoughtful silence again. Or perhaps it was a coma. It was hard to tell.

"Yes, er, right. Well, perhaps I'd . . ."

"Let me tell you how the crisis will present itself, Stephen. In walks a man of some distinction, riding high on the ocean of his fame. And he'll ask you for something to stop him feeling tired all the time. The problem is, of course, that he is simultaneously experiencing the decline of mental powers and a failure of libido. And libido is king, as we know. Libido rules OK. Search out the deep sexual anxiety, Stephen. That will unlock the secret. I speak to you as a father to a son. Some day, this kingdom may be yours."

"Well, um . . . thank you, Jock."

Jock looked at him severely. "Your patients are waiting. This will not do. You'll never achieve greatness if you fritter your time away in idle speculation and morning whisky-drinking. Go to it, my boy. Go to it."

Stephen went to it, and cleared up his backlog of patients by half-past twelve, so that he was only half-an-hour late for his swimming lesson. Lyn wasn't cross with him. Unlike his ex-wife Angela, in fact unlike any of the rather small number of women he had been involved with, she never seemed to get cross about anything.

It was early days yet, of course, as she kept telling him. He saw her about two or three times a week, most of their meetings involving some punishing physical pursuit or other. She made it quite clear that she saw several other people as well. Seeing Stephen meant, of course, rather more than seeing him: she swam with him, ran with him, talked with him, ate and drank with him, and held his hand sometimes. Seeing the other people, he deduced, meant other things as well. She didn't tell him who the other people were or which bits of them she saw. Stephen found that he could cope with all this quite comfortably, though in his dreams she was still always jogging inexorably away from him.

He managed four whole lengths this time, impressing himself no end and pleasing his teacher. While he clung gasping to the rail, unable to defend himself, she took him by the ears and kissed him firmly on the mouth. He experienced a pang of deep sexual anxiety, but he didn't faint or scream, and later, towelling himself in the changing-room, he was invaded by an unaccustomed sense of great physical well-being. This was just as well, because he was in for a tough time.

"Professor Furie for Dr Daker, please," he said into the intercom. He reached for his notes, but before he'd had time to glance at them the door was flung open and a big, fierce-looking man came in and plonked himself on the chair opposite him.

"Daker, right?"

"That's right."

"You're new here."

"Yes, I am."

"Well, I won't waste too much of your time or mine," said Furie. "I want you to prescribe me some Dexedrine tablets. Month's supply should do it. All right?"

In will walk a great man, thought Stephen. Extraordinary. "Dexedrine," he said encouragingly. "You feel the need of a stimulant?"

"Yes, I do know what Dexedrine is, Daker. And I'd be obliged if you'd get scribbling."

Stephen, like some, but by no means all doctors, didn't much care for being used as an automatic drug-dispenser.

"I'd like you to tell me why you think you need them first," he said mildly.

"You think that's your business, do you?" growled Furie, thrusting his great square jaw at Stephen's face.

"Yes, I'm afraid it's precisely my business," said Stephen, wishing it didn't sound so prim. "I wouldn't prescribe a dangerous drug without making sure that it was indicated. Any doctor would tell you the same."

Furie emitted a brief bark of contemptuous laughter. "You'd be surprised. Still, fair enough, even a GP has his pride. The thing is, I've got a tremendous log-jam of work on, not enough hours in the day, crucial that I deliver on time. Ten years ago I never needed more than three hours sleep a night, now it seems to be more like six. Losing concentration, tired in the mornings. All right?"

"And you normally see Dr McCannon, is that right?"

"I don't normally see any doctor, because I'm never ill. I haven't lost a day's work through illness since I was sixteen."

"Really," said Stephen. "That's very impressive."

"Yes it is isn't it, now d'you think you could just get on with the prescription? If I had the time there's nothing I'd like better than a jolly good gossip with a nice young medical man, but I've got work to do, even if you haven't."

"You seem very anxious to get away, if you don't mind my saying so." He was sure that he was on to something here, some unexplained surplus of intensity.

"Oh, you've grasped that, have you?" The man's sarcasm was ferocious. "Yes, yes, I'm anxious to get away!"

"Could you tell me why that is?"

"My God!" cried Furie to the ceiling. "I can't believe this! Because I have *work to do*!"

Stephen was feeling quite frightened by now, but his sense that something else was going on was growing surer with every moment.

"It isn't that there's something you're anxious to avoid discussing?"

Furie stared at him. "And what might that be?" he said quietly and dangerously.

"I don't know," said Stephen.

Furie suddenly stabbed a finger at him. "Tavistock Institute!" he roared.

"I beg your pardon?"

"Don't deny it! You've been trained at the Tavvy, or got at by some half-baked Tavvy lunatic, haven't you?"

"No, honestly," said Stephen. How did this man know about the Tavvy? And why did it make him so angry?

"Birmingham, Birmingham, Birmingham and Walsall, really."

"I don't believe you," said Furie a little more quietly, though he still looked ready to leap over the desk and strangle Stephen. "You're a half-baked post-Freudian, aren't you?"

"I'm honestly not a post-Fruedian," said Stephen. "I'm eclectic."

"Stand your ground, Daker. I hate wafflers. How were you going to proceed?" Furie folded his powerful arms and grinned sadistically. Stephen was suddenly reminded of his final viva voce, and started to stammer and blush.

"Look, I really don't think we should pursue this line of . . ."

"Come on, man! I'm your patient! I need help!"

"Well," said Stephen carefully, "I find it very interesting, what you said about being tired all the time."

"And? And?"

"I was wondering whether you felt 'tired all the time' in

any other aspect in your life." There. He'd said it. He'd been brave enough to seek out the deep sexual anxiety. Now, if Jock was right, the poor man's façade would crack, and out would tumble all the fear and misery and pain, and he would beg his doctor to help him out of the labyrinth of fear.

Furie sat quite still. Then his hands began to tremble, and his face grew red.

"You insulting little bastard!"

"What?" This wasn't the right response.

"Are you suggesting that I'm impotent? Is that it?"

"Not at all," said Stephen, trying to keep his voice from flying into the upper register. "But it's quite possible that there's some central physical cause underlying your feelings of, er, lassitude."

"Oh, there is, is there?" snarled Furie threateningly.

"And I really think it might be a good idea if you could come in for a full examination."

"Oh, yes, you'd like that, wouldn't you? Feel a bit more in control of the situation if you had me naked and bent double with two rubber-gloved fingers up my arse! Yes, I follow your reasoning very well, Daker! By God, I thought McCannon was the worst doctor on earth, but you take the bloody biscuit, Daker, you really do! Now write that bloody presciption!"

"Look," said Stephen very bravely. "I'll tell you what I'll do. I'm not going to prescribe Dexedrine for you. There's something else which is more sophisticated and more specific for what you need, which I take it is a short term high without any side-effects like impairment of judgment. It's called Cotinac. I do think you should have a full medical sometime soon. The feelings you describe might just be temporary strain, normal ageing processes, but they might indicate diabetes or thyroid problems, or any one of a number of things. You don't have to come to me for that. Go to BUPA and pay for it if you wish." He paused. "And I must say that I sense there's something upsetting you very much, that you can't talk to me about. I think you should consider talking to someone. Really."

83

"Write the prescription, damn you," said Professor Furie quietly.

"Don't drink alcohol when you're taking these," said Stephen, trying to stop his hand shaking as he wrote. "They'll last you a fortnight. If you need any more, come back. If you get any side-effects, get in touch straight away. But you should be fine." He slid the piece of paper across the desk.

"Thank you very much," said Furie. "You must have enjoyed humiliating me."

"No, honestly," said Stephen. "Nothing was further from my . . ."

"You don't know me, Daker, but if you ask around they'll tell you that John Furie is a powerful friend to have on your side and a dangerous enemy to have against you. You're going to be sorry you ever met me, Daker."

Report on Group Case-Conference: Patient J.F.

Present: Dr. J. G. McCannon (Chair), Drs Daker, Buzzard, Rose Marie. No apologies.

Dr McCannon opened proceedings by expressing pleasure at this rare treat, reminding the group that there had not been a case conference since Professor Machonochie's sex change. Dr Daker then outlined the case.

The patient was a man of forty-nine, and a professor, who was asking for stimulants while paradoxically being in a state of high nervous excitement. Patient also complained of being "tired all the time". Dr Daker had tried to explore the nature of the tiredness, but the patient had accused Dr Daker of suggesting that he was impotent. Dr Daker then suggested a full medical check-up, which the patient reacted to in a negative way, fantasising it as a homosexual proposal of the sado-masochistic variety.

Dr Buzzard observed that Dr Daker certainly seemed to draw the loonies. The patient was clearly some old has-been who could not get it up any more mentally or physically. Patient should be given a placebo, booted out, and a hint dropped to the VC about early retirement.

Dr McCannon thanked Dr Buzzard for his contribution and invited Dr Rose Marie to comment. Dr Rose Marie declined on the grounds that she was not interested in boys' games.

Dr Daker reported that he had prescribed a mild course of Cotinac, but that the patient had been dissatisfied, and had made unspecified threats against Dr Daker and the practice as a whole.

Dr McCannon then enquired the name of the patient. On learning it he remarked that this put a different complexion on things. Dr Daker had taken exactly the right lines in normal circumstances, but Patient J.F. was not a normal circumstance. Patient J.F., besides being an internationally famous professor of biochemistry, was also Pro-Vice-Chancellor and Chairman of the Finance Committee. A powerful political operator, he had already been responsible for closing down the departments of Film Studies and Media Research. Moreover, having studied medicine before moving into biochemistry, Patient J.F. really had it in for doctors.

Dr Buzzard concurred with this view, adding that the patient was handy with his fists too, having put last year's Creative Writing Fellow in hospital with a broken jaw. Dr Buzzard added that in his opinion Dr Daker was up shit creek without a paddle.

The case was referred back to Dr Daker for further consideration and the meeting closed at 3.45 p.m.

After Stephen had seen the last of his patients at evening surgery, Rose Marie knocked on his door, came in, sat down, and regarded him thoughtfully.

"Stephen, I feel rather bad about my lack of input in the case conference this afternoon," she said. "I wouldn't want you to think I wasn't interested."

"Oh, thank you," he said. He had spent all the intervals between patients peering nervously out of the window in case Furie was hanging about outside with a set of knuckledusters. Now, no doubt, Rose Marie had some further titbit for him. Furie's prowess with a shotgun, perhaps, or a crossbow.

"I think you were right to confront the patient in this case, Stephen," she said earnestly. "You've got integrity. And you're surprisingly courageous."

"No, actually I'm not," said Stephen sincerely.

"I hope you weren't influenced by Bob's childish remarks. Typical weak male response to the phallic bully. Bob sees himself as a hard man, but when he finds someone stronger than himself, he rolls on his back like a puppy. I don't find that very attractive in a grown man, do you?" Something in the way she used the words attractive, grown and man, coupled with the remarkably audible crossing and recrossing of her legs, conspired to give Stephen another fierce twinge of his old trouble.

"Furie, of course, is the same type," she went on.

"Oh, you know him then?" said Stephen.

"His wife used to be a patient of mine, Stephen. I hope I was able to help her. John Furie is a bully of the crudest kind. But he lacks any inner certainty. I like to picture him as a hollow plaster phallus. Do you see what I mean?"

"Yes," said Stephen, swallowing. "All too vividly."

"So you see it's essential that you continue to confront him with his own contradictions. If you do that, I'm sure the plaster will crack."

"Yes, I see," said Stephen, who had privately decided that confronting Furie with anything, including his, Stephen's presence, was probably not a very good idea.

"You'll have to fight him, of course. Perhaps even physically. But when he sees your determination, he'll capitulate. I'm sure of that." She smiled. "And in any case I'm sure you know how to look after yourself."

"No, no, really," said Stephen. "Violence isn't my thing at all."

"I don't confuse gentleness with weakness," she said. "And in any case, there's no alternative. If you show him any weakness, he'll destroy you."

*

86

Stephen arrived home to his nice, safe Furie-free flat to find Chen hard at work. Every blackboard in the place was covered with what his Burmese friend called the calligraphy of desperation. Stephen made him a cup of tea.

"Chen," he said. "Do know anything about self-defence?"

"Of course. I practise self-defence."

"Really?" said Stephen, delighted. Perhaps there might be time to learn some of it before Furie got to him.

"Oh yes," said Chen. "I come to England. Very safe country. That's my self-defence."

"It's not a safe country, Chen," said Stephen with heartfelt sincerity.

"Try Burma," said the mathematician.

"Actually, what I was thinking of was, well . . . unarmed combat, that sort of thing."

"Not popular in Burma. Armed combat, yes. Carry a sharp sword. Always strike the first blow. Do you want to kill someone, Stephen? I could get behind that. I could hang loose. I want to kill my professor. You could help me do that. I could help you kill your enemy. What do you say? Could you hack it, Stephen?"

"No," said Stephen regretfully. "It's . . . unrealistic. Thanks all the same, though."

"Well, you're a barrel of laughs tonight," said Lyn in the bar that evening.

"Sorry Lyn. Problems at work." The swing doors banged open and he glanced round nervously. Two rugger types. Might come to his rescue if Furie . . . stop it Stephen, why should Furie come looking for you here? He sighed.

"Lyn, do *you* think it's a terrible burden being a man?"

"Not a man, Stephen. I'm a girl." Well, yes, that was both true and nice, but it wasn't a fat lot of help. The swing doors banged open again. Two big girls in sweaters advertising Guinness made their way to the bar and demonstratated their loyalty by ordering pints of it.

"Look, are you all right, Stephen?"

"Fine. Fine. Just a bit . . ."

The door banged open again and Professor Furie marched up to the bar and banged on it sharply.

"Let's go," said Stephen urgently.

"I haven't finished my drink yet, Stephen."

"That man at the bar. Don't look. I don't want him to see me."

"Barman!" Furie was shouting. "Do you think you could manage to get me a large whisky, if you've quite finished your chat?"

"Oh, do drink up, please Lyn," muttered Stephen. "I'll tell you about it later."

"Too late," she said. "He's looking over."

Without any conscious thought in his head at all, Stephen found himself on his hands and knees under the table.

"Oh, Stephen. What are you doing?"

"Dropped my, er . . ."

"Daker!" It was like the knell of doom. Stephen struggled up, a fixed and terrified grin on his face.

"I want you, Daker!"

"He wants to beat me up," said Stephen through his teeth. "I'll try and get between you," said Lyn, grasping the situation commendably quickly. "If that doesn't work, fall down with the first punch and stay there."

Furie banged his empty glass down on the bar, and came straight for Stephen, his head down. As if watching a slow motion film, Stephen was vividly aware of the huge shoulder muscles moving under Furie's Harris tweed jacket. He threw up a despairing hand to ward off the expected blow, then let out an involuntary cry as Furie seized his hand and pumped it up and down.

"Daker!" shouted Furie, "You're one hell of a doctor! Those pills are magic! Especially with whisky!" He sat down heavily on the empty chair. His eyes were glittering oddly. "Here's looking at you, Daker!" he said, picking up Stephen's half-full glass and draining it.

"You – you're not supposed to take alcohol with them," said Stephen. He was still trembling violently.

"Don't worry, I'll buy you another," promised the professor.

"Two double Scotches here, three double Scotches! Sorry, my dear. This man is one hell of a doctor. Did you know that?"

"Well, I thought he might be," said Lyn. "I'm not one of his patients myself. Never ill, see."

"Neither am I, neither am I!" he turned round and bellowed in the direction of the bar. "Come on, Fido, where are those whiskies?"

Hypomania, thought Stephen. Oh God.

"Well, this is very pleasant," said Furie, beaming at Lyn with what looked like undisguised lust.

"D'you know Lyn Turtle, Professor Furie?" said Stephen in a high nervous voice. "Lyn, this is Professor . . ."

"Of course I know Lyn! Everybody knows Lyn! Hell of a bright girl, even if she is at the soggy end of social psychology. We all love her little articles!"

The barman arrived with the tray of drinks, moving faster than Stephen had ever seen him move before.

"Thanks very much, about time, keep the change," said Furie, throwing a fiver on the tray.

"Well, cheers," said Stephen. He was beginning to recover a little. "Thank you very much." He watched Furie drain his glass. "You know you really shouldn't drink with those pills, especially if you're going to drive."

"You're driving tonight, Daker. I've elected you. And you can lay off the good advice, you've been a hell of a doctor all day, it's time to relax. Now. I've shifted more work today than I've done in months, and I feel like celebrating. What I propose is that I buy you and this lovely young woman a bloody big steak in the Grill Room, then we all go back to my house for a gang-bang! Might even get the wife to join in!"

All this was delivered at a volume which would have done very well at a large open-air rally, and produced a respectful silence throughout the bar.

Furie threw back his head and roared with laughter. "Just my little joke!" He leaned forward earnestly, all traces of levity gone. "Seriously, though, we have got to get beyond the puritan work ethic. Now, what about that steak?"

"Er, look, Professor Furie," Stephen began.

"John! John! Call me John! John Thomas Furie, that's my name! Now there's a funny thing."

Suddenly Furie lapsed into an introspective stare, his eyes wide and unblinking, his body so still that he might have been dead. Lyn looked anxiously at Stephen, then tried to line her face up with Furie's eyes. Nothing. She waved her hand tentatively. Nothing.

"Hey John."

He snapped instantly out of his trance, leaning bearishly across the table at her. "Yes, my lovely creature?"

"I'll have to leave that steak for another night, John. I'm running a workshop at eight. Sorry."

Disappointment flooded his face. For a moment he seemed about to burst into tears. Then he drew his lips back from his teeth and grinned savagely.

"No matter! Don't worry about it! Another time! Something to look forward to!"

"Er, yes," said Stephen, "and I . . ."

Furie turned on him and grabbed his arm in his huge fist. "Not you, Daker. You're my man for the night." He picked up Stephen's glass and drained it. "You're in the driving seat, Daker." He stopped and looked puzzled.

"Ah. Knew there was something. Got to have a piss. Wait there." He stood up briskly, knocking the chair over. "Funny things these pills," he said as he marched towards the door unbuttoning his flies, "you don't go all day, and then all of a sudden it seems as if there's nothing more vital . . ."

The rest of his words were lost on Stephen and Lyn, as Furie crashed through the swing doors, knocking down and breaking the nose of a small scruffy-looking man in his forties who happened to be on his way out at the same moment. This too went unnoticed by Stephen and Lyn, and by Furie himself, since the man went down without a sound and lay quietly on the floor well out of Furie's eyeline.

"Lyn," said Stephen. "You're deserting me."

"You'll be all right," said Lyn. "He didn't want to beat you up at all. He thinks you're great."

"He's hypomanic," said Stephen. "It's not a rational condition. He could switch at any moment."

Stephen experienced a strong urge to take Lyn by the hand and run very fast out of the bar. But, oh hell. He had prescribed the pills. Professor Furie was his patient. And frightening as Furie was, there was something oddly touching about his plight. Yes, even that old maniac McCannon had his moments of searing insight. Here, if anywhere, was a great man, thrashing about in the maelstrom of middle life, and calling out for help. And it was clearly Stephen he was calling to, bugger him.

"I think I've got to stay with him," said Stephen.

Lyn took his hand. "You are a good doctor. It'll be all right, Stephen. He thinks you're wonderful. You are, too, in a way."

The University Grill Room was a place where academics could gobble down steaks, escalopes, avocadoes and prawns, and guzzle bottles of indifferent wine at heavily-subsidised prices. The subsidised prices were made possible by the large profits made by the University caterers on the dogshit they served to the students in Refectory.

It was a fairly quiet night, apart from Furie. On one table sat four serious-looking men in dark suits, at another a reader in Social Administration and his research assistant, who were kissing each other with passionate intensity and getting food all over themselves. In the corner sat a small, scruffy man with a swollen nose, picking at a paella in a dazed sort of way. And right in the middle of the Grill Room sat the Professor of Biochemistry and his personal physician; and the Professor of Biochemistry was on excellent conversational form.

"University catering is absolutely appalling, even at the so-called quality end, don't you think?" said Furie, upending the second bottle and banging it on the bottom like a bottle of ketchup to get the last drops out. "Look at this bloody house wine. 'Don's Delight'! What don would delight in this? Eh? Donald Duck? I suppose Don Bradman might have used it to oil his bat with! Eh! Eh! Never mind, let's have some more of it!"

Two of the dark-suited men turned round.

"Yes?" roared Furie. "Can I help in any way? Enjoying your *meal*?"

Chastened, they turned back.

"That's the Philosophy Department and their external examiner," Furie confided in ringing tones. "Three half-wits kowtowing to a nonentity!"

"You're shouting, John," said Stephen gently.

"Am I? Am I?" shouted Furie. "Good Lord, wouldn't want to offend anyone. But old Marlowe-Spence there hasn't had an original thought in his life. Still annotating Austin, are we Geoffrey?"

Wisely, the man referred to decided not to have heard.

"Deaf as a post too," Furie went on. "I think we'll chop the Philosophy Department, make that next year's little project. Reprieve for the Medical Centre, because of this excellent new doctor, eh?"

"Really," said Stephen, "you're too kind."

"No, no, any spark of intellect in this desert of mediocrity is to be cherished. Well," he went on, putting his knife and fork down. "That was the worst steak I've had in years. Where's that girl? Over here, Toots!"

The waitress came over, taking her time. She was a tall good-looking girl of about twenty. Stephen thought she looked very tired.

"Did you call, Professor Furie?" Neither her voice nor her face betrayed any expression at all.

"Indeed I did. That steak was terrible. It was roughly hacked by an incompetent butcher from the wrong part of a third-rate animal, it was badly hung, and then grilled to a frazzle by an idiot!"

"Why did you eat it, then?" she asked, with admirable acuity.

"Because I was starving! Don't bandy words with me."

"Well, no one else is complaining," she said. "Was your steak all right, sir?"

"Er . . . yes! Fine!" said Stephen. "Sorry," he added to Furie.

"This man," said Furie powerfully, "is too tender-hearted to complain. Those men over there know nothing about food or anything else. Those two," indicating the lovers with a stab of his fork, "don't care about food. They're eating each other. My compliments to the chef, and would he care for a fist fight with Professor Furie?"

"OK, Professor Furie, I'll pass the message on," she said, rather as if he'd asked for the vinaigrette, and went back to the kitchen, taking her time.

"Look," said Stephen. "Is this wise?"

Furie leaned across the table. "My father was a butcher," he said. "I know meat. Intellectual honesty is an absolute value. And I can look after myself in a fist fight."

"Yes, so I've heard."

"That waitress was a cool customer, wasn't she? Sure I've seen her somewhere before. Ah, here she comes. Well?"

"Chef says he doesn't fancy a fist fight," said the girl. "He's just popped out to the car park to let your tyres down."

Furie gripped the edges of the table. Stephen prepared himself for violence. Then Furie roared with laughter.

"Very good! Very good!" Then he narrowed his eyes and peered at the waitress. "Look here, don't I know you? Are you a member of this University?"

"That's right," she said. "My name's Alison Blair. You're my personal tutor, actually."

"Well, there you are," said Furie triumphantly. "Never forget a face. Look, what time do you finish?"

"When we get rid of you lot," she said wearily.

"Fine. How about coming back to my place with this chap? We can all – "

"Could we have two black coffees please?" said Stephen quickly and sharply.

"Yeah, all right," she said, looking at him with mild dislike, and went away.

"You interrupted me, Daker."

"I was afraid you were going to invite her to a gang-bang," said Stephen.

"So I was. No harm in that. Just my little joke."

"John," said Stephen earnestly. "Women don't find that sort of thing funny these days."

Furie's fists clenched again.

"Don't they. Odd." He was breathing heavily through his nose. "My wife finds that sort of thing funny. She finds it bloody hilarious!"

He leaned forward and brought his face close to Stephen's. "I'm a bit out of control, aren't I?"

"Yes, you are, a bit."

Furie considered this judiciously. Then he said, quite quietly, "I *feel* absolutely fine . . . but objectively, I think I'm going crazy."

Stephen was sitting on the old leather Chesterfield in Furie's study, listening to Furie talking about women. He felt very tired and not quite sober. He had managed to get his patient out of the Grill Room without incurring charges of assault, slander, or sexual harassment, and had succeeded in driving the professor's vintage Rover home without hitting anything, though there had been a narrow squeak by the porter's lodge with two nuns in a battered Mini. Furie was still drinking; it seemed futile to stop him now. Surely, thought Stephen, counting just the drinks he had seen Furie put down that evening, surely he would pass out soon. But Furie, though he must be very drunk indeed, was neither staggering nor slurring as he paced about the room.

"More whisky," said Furie.

"No, I won't thanks . . . oh, why not. I'll have to get a cab home anyway."

"That's the spirit," said Furie, filling his glass. "It's the women, Stephen. It's what we do to the women. We love our work. We let it take us over. We ignore the women. We blind ourselves to their needs. And when we realise what we've done, it's too late."

"Yes, I know," said Stephen. Yes, he thought. I do know.

"But do you? Do you?" cried Furie passionately. "You're not giving me that Tavvy shit again?"

"No," said Stephen. "I was thinking about my own marriage."

"But you're a moderate man. You do things moderately. I do things to extremes. I've eaten that woman like a piece of meat, Stephen. When I think about what I've done to her I can't bear it, you know? So what do I do? I shut it out! I come in here and whack off another brilliant bloody article!"

He picked up a few sheets of what might well have been a brilliant bloody article, and threw them across the room. "I've got an international reputation! Have you got an international reputation?"

"No, I haven't got an international reputation," said Stephen.

"It's not worth having, take my word for it," said Furie sombrely. "I've got to go to Brazil next week. Who wants to go to bloody Brazil? Eh?"

"Well, I wouldn't mind," said Stephen.

Furie suddenly went very still.

"Ssh," he said.

Stephen heard the front door open and close.

"Helen?"

"Hello," called a woman's voice.

"In here."

Helen Furie came into the study. She seemed surprised to see Stephen there.

"This is Stephen Daker," said Furie. "He's one hell of a doctor."

"Oh, the man with the marvellous pills," said Helen, smiling pleasantly at Stephen. "Nice to meet you, Stephen."

"One *hell* of a doctor," said Furie, and sat down heavily at his desk.

"Are you all right, John?" She glanced at Stephen rather nervously. Furie turned to her abruptly.

"Good film?" he said, very fiercely indeed.

"Mm. Yes," she said mildly. "Not quite what it was cracked up to be."

"Details?" he said in the same tone.

She took that in her stride too.

"Well, the sets were a bit Brigadoon, I thought. And the wolves were a bit of a disappointment, just like a lot of fusty old Alsatians, I thought. Still, maybe that's what wolves are like."

"Hmmm," said Furie thoughtfully.

"Look, I'm going to put the kettle on," she said. "Anyone else want coffee?"

"Oh, yes please," said Stephen.

As soon as she had gone out of the room, Furie rushed over to the coffee table, grabbed the handbag she had left there, and rummaged furiously through the contents. "She could have read that in the bloody *Courier*," he muttered. "bloody . . . bloody . . . I'll . . ." Growling, he turned the handbag upside down and shook it.

"Look, er . . . what's the matter?" said Stephen.

Furie was on his hands and knees, his eyes staring blindly. "I can't . . . I can't. . . ."

He put his hands over his eyes, moaning. Then his great body slumped to the floor. He rolled from side to side, weeping loudly, as if in unbearable pain. Stephen felt the tears prickling at his own eyes. Helen Furie came back into the room and looked down at her husband.

"Oh, Lord," she said. She didn't seem too surprised. "Come on, John," she said gently. "It'll be all right. Let's get you up."

Furie stopped rolling, and, after a few moments, sobbing. His hands were still over his eyes.

"I'm sorry," he said. "I'm sorry. It's just. . . ." Then he took his hands from his face and stood up slowly. He was quite steady on his feet.

"You'll have to excuse me, Daker," he said. "I am very tired. I am going to bed now." He walked slowly and steadily towards the stairs.

"I'm sorry," Helen Furie said to Stephen.

"It's happened before?"

"Oh, yes." She hesitated. "Look, d'you think I could come in and talk to you about it? That's not unethical, is it? I'm . . . rather worried about him."

"Yes, of course. Can you come tomorrow at eleven thirty, after normal surgery hours?"

"Yes, fine." She smiled, then bit her lip. "Look, I'd better get up to him now."

"Yes, sure."

When she had gone upstairs, Stephen crawled across to the phone and ordered himself a taxi. He looked at his watch. It said half-past one. There was something odd about that; but he couldn't think what.

Stephen checked Helen Furie's file before she came in. She had been quite a frequent visitor, complaining of headaches, insomnia, mild depression, as well as the usual colds and throat infections. But all that seemed to have stopped a year ago; and six months ago she had left and registered with a doctor living nearer to her home. Nothing remarkable there. Stephen had often noticed how married couples seemed to take turns at being ill, the turns lasting sometimes weeks, sometimes years. Helen Furie appeared to be a well woman now.

At half-past eleven she came in, quiet and composed. Stephen, feeling rather guilty, confessed that he'd been looking at her old file; and she seemed to be equally embarrassed, and very anxious to assure him that she had no fault to find with the University Medical Centre, it was just that now they weren't on campus it was such a long trek in, and any way she'd been fine lately, and Dr Parker round the corner was very good with the children.

"Please," said Stephen. "You don't have to apologise. Anyway, it's not about you, all this, is it?"

"Well, it is, really." She paused and looked up at him. "I'm having an affair with someone. And it's made me really happy. It was bliss for a while, I felt so, you know, strong, confident, all that. I could cope with all John's . . . stuff."

"Then he found out, yes?"

She sighed. "He asked, and I told him. I didn't think he'd mind, I mean, he'd never seemed to notice, and he'd had lots of you know, flings himself. Well, he sort of fell apart. He can't think of anything else. He's not really getting any work done. He follows me around, he keeps going through my . . . well, you've seen him."

"Yes," said Stephen. The tears were starting to prickle again.

"You see, I haven't told him who it is. I have said I won't give it up, because I don't think I can. And I've told him it's not something I'm doing to him, it's something I'm doing for myself. And he can't grasp that. He knows I won't leave him." There were tears running down her cheeks, but her voice was steady. "I don't want to leave him. I still love the old bastard. Well, you know."

She wiped her eyes and smiled at him. "What a long face! It's not that bad, you know. Come on," she said, opening her bag. "Cheer up. Let's have a cigarette."

"I don't smoke," said Stephen, wiping his eyes. "Well, yes, I will. Thanks."

She leant over and lit it for him. "You are a funny man. No wonder John likes you."

It was, as she said, such a relief to confide in someone. Stephen wouldn't believe it, the interest John took in her these days. Night after night of psychoterror, waking her up every half hour, who was that chap she was talking to in that coffee bar in 1964, in a way it was all quite flattering. Then he would get out of bed and drive his car furiously round the estate, or do other weird things like digging this big hole in the back garden and trying to make her get in it with him. On that occasion she had managed to get him inside and run a bath for him, then she had had to get in that with him as well. Really desperate for it, the way he had been when he was twenty.

"Poor man; poor man," said Stephen, deeply moved.

"And then the next night he'll be complaining he's impotent. I mean look, John, I said to him, we were at it till half-past four last night, you're bound to be a bit tired. 'No, no, my sexual life is over!'"

"It must be really awful for you both," said Stephen sadly.

"Mmm, it's hell," she agreed enthusiastically. "And the violence!"

"He's violent with you, too?" said Stephen, stricken.

"Oh, not with me. It's all right, Stephen. Don't be upset. Just with things."

"Things?"

"Mmm. Just yesterday he got a hammer out and gave his filing cabinet a frightful battering. It's awful to say this, but it's quite exhilarating in a way. I mean, he's such a performer. Biggest biochemical research lab in Europe, longest list of publications, now he's got to have the biggest nervous breakdown in history!"

"Mrs Furie," said Stephen.

"Helen, please."

"Helen. I think your husband needs specialist help. I'll try and get him to agree to my referring him to a consultant psychiatrist."

"I'm sure he'll go if you say so. He really trusts you, Stephen." She paused and smiled at him. "You know, I think you're a hell of a doctor, too. You've done me so much good today. D'you know, I feel really cheerful now?"

"Well," said Stephen inertly. "Thanks very much, Helen." He felt as if he had just been beaten up.

It is dawn. A large, black, vintage Rover is parked by the side of the lake. A tall, heavily-built man gets out of the car and stands in his overcoat watching the first swifts skimming over the surface of the water. Then he takes off the overcoat and wades steadily in.

Later that morning, Mrs Kramer was presiding over the usual full house in the waiting room. The door burst open, and Professor John Thomas Furie, immaculately dressed in a dripping wet suit, strode up to the counter.

"I've come to see Daker," he said.

"But you have no appointment, Professor Furie," she said sweetly.

99

"Bugger appointments! Daker!" he roared. "I want you!" He disappeared down the corridor.

"But Professor Furie, you are too wet to see Dr Daker!" called the receptionist after him.

"Right, Daker!" said Furie. He stood dripping on the carpet and breathing heavily through the nose.

"John, how are you?" said Stephen, rising. "You're all wet. I'm glad you came in because . . ."

"Glad, are you?" Furie looked wildly round the room.

"Do sit down, John. I was hoping we could have a chat."

Furie didn't sit down. His shoulders were heaving and he kept clenching and unclenching his fists.

"About my wife, perhaps?" Clearly his condition had deteriorated dramatically. Keep calm, Stephen. He likes you. He trusts you. You're one hell of a doctor.

"No . . . er . . ." he began cautiously. " . . . I did, er have a talk with her yesterday, I hope you don't mind."

"In bed, no doubt, while you were shafting her, no doubt. Typical of you cold-blooded Tavvy men. Yes, I do mind very much indeed, does that surprise you? By God, I thought of Buzzard, I even thought of McCannon, but it was you, Daker, it was you all the time!"

It wasn't so much what he was saying, it was the way his eyes were ranging wildly round the room as if in search of something to smash. Stephen pressed the intercom button, leaving it open.

"Er, help," he said quietly. And then: "John, let's talk about this sensibly. How could it have possibly been me? I've only been here four weeks."

"Modern transport, you conniving little bastard! This is the twentieth century! Oh, I've been over that Volvo with a fine tooth comb, I've smelt the smell of your adulterous couplings on the cherry-red upholstery! I'm going to get you struck off, Daker, make no mistake about that, but first I'm going to kill you!"

His words carried over the intercom with perfect clarity. The massed patients in the waiting room, more used to routine announcements about Miss So-and-So for Dr So-and-So, listened in awed silence. Bob Buzzard looked up from his desk, where he was writing a valium prescription for the sixth time that morning. Rose Marie looked up from an entry she was making in a file marked "STEPHEN DAKER", and smiled slightly to herself.

"John, that's illogical," said Stephen, "if you'd just sit down and think about it. Er, help."

"Illogical? Illogical? Haven't you ever heard of catastrophe theory?" Furie picked up Stephen's desk and threw it aside, growling deep in his throat. Stephen let out a shrill involuntary cry. Bob Buzzard walked briskly into the room.

"OK, Stephen, leave this to me."

"Et tu, Buzzard!" growled Furie, turning and knocking Bob senseless with a punch to the side of the head.

Jock McCannon hovered in the doorway in an understandably tentative way.

"Now, John," he said, "we've had our differences, I know. . . ."

"And you, McCannon? So it *was* a gang-bang after all!" He picked up a typewriter and raised it above his head.

"Rose Marie!" gasped Jock. "For pity's sake!"

Rose Marie came into the room and watched coolly as Furie advanced on Jock.

"Please!" whimpered Jock.

Rose Marie walked up to Furie, then slipped behind him and did something very sudden and neat that caused him to sink to the floor with a surprised expression on his face. Then she forced his arm up behind his back and sat on his head.

"Trouble?" said Maureen, coming in.

Furie was still growling horribly, his face contorted.

"Just sit on his legs, would you Maureen, love?"

"It's a pleasure, Doctor," said Maureen cheerfully.

Furie's growls began to subside. Maureen looked up at Stephen, who was still standing paralysed against the wall with his arm across his face.

"No need to worry, Dr Daker," she said. "All in a day's work for me, this is."

"And would you be kind enough to phone the ambulance, Stephen? I think we'd better section him, don't you?" said Rose Marie.

"Er . . . right," said Stephen.

"Daker. Daker," said Furie, twisting his head so that he could see Stephen. "I want you to know that this is just personal. I still think you're one hell of a doctor."

Bob Buzzard, regaining consciousness, began to moan softly.

A week after that, Stephen was down by the lake, sitting on a little bridge and throwing pebbles into the water. Nice cool sunny day, just getting a bit chilly as the sun went down behind the fortress blocks. Two dogs playing down by the water, woman walking on her own round the perimeter.

"Hello, Stephen," said the woman as she reached the bridge. He turned. It was Rose Marie. Out of her white coat and in jeans and a leather jacket, she looked quite different; very much like a human being, in fact.

"Hello," he said, throwing another pebble in.

"Heard about Furie?" she said. Oh, God. Just like her to spoil everything.

"What?" he said apprehensively.

"By all accounts he's making a splendid recovery. Still in the secure ward, of course, but he's working again, apparently he's got a really promising new line on the brain chemistry of hypomania."

"Well, bully for him," said Stephen. Rose Marie smiled, and seemed about to move on.

"Rose," he said. "I never got a chance to thank you properly for what you did the other day."

"Well," she said. "I must confess I felt a strong temptation to let things run their course. Boys' games, you know. Why not let them get on with it?"

"I'm glad you didn't," said Stephen.

"Well, I did feel a certain obligation," she said. "I was, after all, involved." The way she said it made it quite clear that she was talking about something more than a professional involvement.

102

"With Furie?"

She smiled. "Oh, no."

He stared at her blankly for a moment. "Helen?"

She returned his gaze levelly. "I must get on," she said. "Surgery at six. I'll see you Stephen."

Rust in the Hat Shop

Rust is in the Hat Shop and he is in a bad mood. Not about being in the Hat Shop; the Hat Shop is not a hat shop but a quite reasonable pizza place that serves wine and cocktails, by no means Julie's Restaurant, but a sodding sight better than the Bush. No, Rust is in a bad mood about Carol and her chum. He came up last night thinking he might stay at the flat, and after making the journey from Liverpool Street to Muswell Hill in no more than a couple of hours, he had found that Carol and the chum had gone away somewhere. That was all right: Rust is quite happy to spend the odd night alone in the flat, playing with Carol's cats, watching Carol's telly and drinking Carol's whisky. He has also been known to sleep in Carol's nightie.

Then he discovered that they had changed the lock. Altered sodding priorities there, with a vengeance. Rust wandered round the garden for a bit, saying hello to the cats, who ignored him and went in through the cat flap. Where was the Rust flap? he asked himself. Then he noticed that they'd replaced his vegetable patch with some sort of lesbian rockery. Well, no joy for Rust there, clearly. He has spent the night on Deep Throat's sofa, and very grudging Deep Throat was about it, considering the consultancy money he is getting from Rust's own personal budget.

This woman business is getting serious. Not only are these sparky young fifteen-year-old playwrights getting Rust's women, or women otherwise theoretically available to Rust; now he is having to contend with the lesbians. Not content with being unavailable to Rust, they are now competing successfully with Rust for the few other women left available. Women seem to be catching on to each other in a big way. Not that Rust blames them of course. He has always preferred women himself, and been slightly puzzled as to why they weren't at each other all the time. Now they are. Added to that, of course, is the fact that Rust isn't getting any younger. Now Carol has so devastatingly renegotiated the relationship, who's going to look at Rust? Well, we'll see. Rust is, after all a writer. There are still some strokes a writer can pull, even an old one.

"What?" he says. He realises that Riddington has been talking for some time, besides demolishing a whole deep dish pizza of his own, half of Rust's, and three-quarters of the script editor's.

"You don't feel the girl's a wee bit idealised?"

"Not a bit of it," says Rust stoutly. "I've known plenty of women like that. You just don't know the right women, Ken." Well, of course she's idealised. All the best bits of Carol plus dollops of extra intelligence and tolerance. Rust is dying to see who they'll cast. Last time Rust wrote himself a bit of wish-fulfilment, they cast a real cracker: soft, sensitive, witty, tender, you sodding name it. Rust fell in love on the spot. Unfortunately, on location she got into a real thing with one of the actors, the one based on the best bits of Rust plus extra dollops of height, looks, and general niceness. Ah, well. Mustn't weaken.

"You know," says Rust, "with the right casting . . ."

"Mmm . . ." says Riddington gloomily. "After that last business I don't think I know what's sexy any more." He calls for another large salad with blue cheese dressing. He thinks Rust likes blue cheese dressing as much as he does. He is wrong. Rust thinks blue cheese dressing smells and tastes of vomit, but he has never been able to tell Riddington this. Great creative partnerships have foundered on such tiny points of difference.

"What else is there?" says Riddington.

"The two girls?" says the script editor. She is sipping some sort of blue drink through a straw. The script editor is supposed to be the writer's friend, helping him fully to realise his grand design. This script editor is on Rust's side in getting Riddington out of the Bush and into the Hat

104

Shop (no blue drinks in the Bush) but not, on the whole, otherwise.

"Ah, yes," says Riddington. He assumes his tactful expression. That's putting it mildly: his whole body goes so tactful he might be doing it in a game of Adverbs. "We felt, Ron, that there might be a little more depth there . . . more light and shade . . . a bit more to be discovered . . . hard to put exactly what we felt . . ."

"You feel they're flat characters that don't develop," says Rust.

"Well . . ." says the script editor, who is studying tact with Riddington.

"Meant to be flat," says Rust with his mouth full. "Not meant to develop. Characters don't develop in two days, do they? Has your character developed much this week, Ken? Course is hasn't. Neither has mine." He glances at the script editor, who lowers her eyes and smiles, having had a formative experience just the night before last.

"Anyway," he goes on, "we're trying to do something new here, and that includes the way we approach character. We're moving in the direction of the postmodernist text: the postmodernist TV series!"

Riddington abandons tact. "Listen, Ron," he says. "I don't know what a postmodernist text is. You don't know what a postmodernist text is. She doesn't know what a postmodernist text is." The script editor, who is writing a postmodernist novel for Brilliance Books, remains silent.

"I mean, come off it, Ron. Fuck," says Riddington, clinching his argument. "Two nice young actresses are going to be pestering the balls off the director asking for their reality base or whatever it is they ask for these days."

Two nice young actresses. How has Rust forgotten about that? But a difficulty remains. He decides to come clean about it. "The thing is," he says, "I don't find anybody under twenty-five interesting."

"Know what you mean," says Riddington gloomily. The script editor, who is twenty-four, remains silent.

"I wish you'd have another look, Ron," says Riddington, who is thinking of having a pudding or two. "You know the sort of thing I mean, and you're so clever at it, just a couple of tiny little scenes would flesh them out. . . ."

"I'll see what I can do," says Rust generously, privately resolving that in the book version at least those two girls are going to be as flat and clear as a couple of sodding Mondrians.

"Thank you very much, Ron. Know you'll come up with something wonderful. By the way, what's happened to your nose?"

"Walked into a door," says Rust truthfully. It's something he's always wanted to say, and he can tell that they don't believe him.

"Nuns?" says the script editor.

"Ah, yes, these nuns. Er . . . what are the nuns *for*, Ron?"

"They're just there," says Rust. "I can't explain. You've just got to trust me on the nuns, Ken. All I can say is . . . those nuns are terribly important to me."

Ken knows inarticulate passion when he sees it, and he respects it. But he is also a bugger for his budget. "Why do there have to be *two* of them?" he asks keenly.

"There are always two nuns," says Rust firmly.

4

BOB'S HAMBURGER SUIT

Bob Buzzard was a bloody good bloke. That was Bob's view of the matter, though not everyone shared it. Basically, all Bob wanted to do was get on with his life. Nothing wrong with that. Daphne wanted him to get on with his life. The boys needed him to get on with his life, if they were going to get to Winchester. The thing was, his life had got a bit stuck lately. Not Bob's fault. Coming to Lowlands had looked like a bloody good career stage on paper. To be brutally honest (Bob preferred brutal honesty wherever possible) he didn't have the academic clout for a teaching hospital or anything like this, but the intellectual prestige of a university ought to rub off in some sort of way. Unfortunately he hadn't grasped at the time what a shithole Lowlands would turn out to be, and he hadn't at that time met the mad old fart, the uppity dike, or the new chap. Dick Dado. Little Miss Blue Eyes. Bit of a Herculean task, carrying that shower and getting on with his life all at the same time.

This morning had been pretty typical. First of all, Daphne had been frightfully sorry, but no way would she risk her life in that Datsun till Bob had taken it in to Wheelie Boy for two new tyres and *not* remoulds this time, darling. That meant that Bob had had to take the boys to Cecil Lodge. The sprogs had whinged most of the way, about how the boarders duffed them up and called them the double-glazing reps, and why did he have to take them so early, and why did they have to go to Winchester anyway.

107

Bob had explained with reasonable patience that the pillocks from the boarding kennels didn't know a double-glazing rep from a hole in the ground, that the hours between seven and nine were when you got ahead of the opposition, and that they were going to Winchester because they belonged to an evolutionary bloody species. That had shut the sprogs up, so that he was able to concentrate on carving his BMW (yes, all right, a BMW, but only a three one bloody eight) through the other early morning road users, most of whom had the traffic sense of suicidal frogs.

Bob was unusually early this morning because he had a working breakfast at the George with Jimmy Partington. Jimmy was a bloody good man. He had been at school and university with Bob, and now he was a Hamburger man. He'd been able to put one or two little things Bob's way. In fact the suit Bob was wearing now had come like that; token of gratitude for a little bit of help Bob had been able to give. It wasn't a four hundred quid suit, but it was a bloody good suit all the same, and Bob looked bloody smart in it. And this breakfast looked like leading to a little thing or two.

"More I see of medical practice," said Jimmy, wrestling with one of those silly little mousetraps they put marmalade in these days, "more I'm convinced that it's a simple matter of some people knowing how to live in the twentieth century, and some who just haven't got a clue about the way it's going."

"Absolutely, Jimmy," said Bob with his mouth full.

"I mean, correct me if I'm wrong. You're the guy in the surgery. I haven't had my hands on a patient since I was a houseman."

"Not much hands-on experience about it these days, Jimmy," said Bob, who never touched a patient if he could help it, never know what you might pick up. "Just a question of which slot you put the penny in. Here, pass that over, let's have a go."

"I remember this place when they had proper pots with silver spoons," said Jimmy Partington wistfully. "Chap would wake you up with a real pot of tea. Got to go to Thailand for that these days. I say, steady on!" Bob, always quick to anger, had lost patience with the marmalade carton. He was stabbing at it savagely with the point of his knife.

"Damn!" he said. Knife, carton, and marmalade had all finished up nestling in his crotch. He mopped furiously at his parts with a napkin.

"That the suit?" said Jimmy.

"Mm, yes," said Bob, licking his fingers. "Wasn't any trouble about that, was there?"

"Lord, no. Couldn't put it through the books, of course, had to take it out of the tea money, so to speak. Next time we'll make sure you get a proper Hamburger consultancy facilitation."

"What's that, Jimmy?"

"Little cheque," said Jimmy, smiling. "Well, quite a middling one, to be fair. In any currency you like, within reasons. Multinationals have their uses."

"Yes, I see, Jimmy," said Bob dreamily. "God, I wish I'd got into pharmaceuticals when you did. No more eyeballing with runny-nosed depressives, no more spotty adolescents shaking their tattered tools in your face before you can say Special Clinic. I should have been a Hamburger man."

"Lot of anxiety in our job," said Jimmy. "Whereas you've got security. You can freelance from a solid base. Best of all worlds."

"I'm not supposed to moonlight, Jimmy," said Bob primly.

Jimmy wasn't having that.

"Nobody is, but everybody does. Everybody who's got something to offer. And we don't call it moonlighting, we call it giving consultation. Sexier, don't you think? . . . How's Daphne, by the way?" he added, going off on a different track, or perhaps not. "Wonderful girl, that."

"Funny, I never seem to think of her like that," said Bob. "Oh, she's fine, I suppose. Full of beans. Getting on with her life. Banging on about next summer already. Tenerife, she says. Out of the question, of course. School fees, cars . . . though of course there's nothing I'd like more than to bring a smile to her face."

"Oh, I think you might manage that," said Jimmy.

"Really?" said Bob.

"We're having the Easter conference in Bermuda this year. Think Hamburger might be persuaded we need you along to give us a bit of head. Especially if you were giving a paper."

"But Jimmy, what the hell could I give a paper on?"

"Ah," said Jimmy. "That's the nub of this little working breakfast. He opened his case and slid a thick glossy folder across the table. "Confidan."

While this momentous meeting was taking place, Stephen Daker had been working on his problems. He had managed four circuits of the lake, actually keeping up with Lyn for three of them, and been rewarded with a chaste kiss (but on the mouth and lasting for several seconds). He had taken this like a man, and Lyn had pronounced it not bad at all. This had made him feel absurdly pleased.

Now he was lying on his bed in his tracksuit, listening to the sound of the shower, and on the whole succeeding in contemplating without panic the fact that Lyn was standing under it with no clothes on at all. His learning programme was a very gentle one: he had progressed beyond the equivalent of imagining a very small spider fast asleep in another room, but he was still a long way from the equivalent of letting a great big fat spider crawl about all over him.

The sound of the shower stopped, and after a few seconds Lyn came out. She was wearing one towel wrapped round her, and was rubbing her head with another one.

"Hello," she said.

"Hello." His voice sounded almost normal. Good.

"It is all right, this, me using the old facilities and that?" she said.

"Yes, of course," he said, sincerely. "It's a pleasure." It was a pleasure, so far, but he felt he was about to move to another learning stage, and he wasn't sure whether he was ready for it.

"Your place is so much handier than mine, see. And also, it gives you a chance to get used to my body in a non-threatening context."

"Yes, I do understand, Lyn."

She went over to the corner of the room where she had dropped her clothes. Then she took off the towel she had been wearing and rubbed herself briskly with it, just like someone getting dried after a shower. She did it awfully well, too, seeming to be quite preoccupied with getting really nice and dry and absolutely nothing else. Then she turned and smiled at him.

"See? Just absolutely ordinary stuff, Doc."

"I, er, wouldn't say that," said Stephen faintly.

"Couple of mates, been out for a jog," she said. She was pulling on pants and T-shirt now. Stephen found himself able to breathe relatively normally again.

"You can handle it."

He cleared his throat. "I, er. . . thought that came later on."

"Jokes, now," she said. "You are doing well. Yes, you're right, that comes later on. Whenever you're ready. The client's in charge all the way."

She walked over, sat on the bed next to him, and ruffled his hair. He found that he didn't mind that at all. "O.K.?"

"What's the next stage?" he felt bold enough to ask.

"Um . . . let's see. You and me. In bed. No clothes. But no sex. How does that sound?"

He thought about it carefully. "Very nice indeed," he said.

"Good," she said, pleased.

"It really is extraordinarily kind of you, all this, Lyn."

"You reckon?"

"Why d'you bother?"

"Pure disinterested research project."

"Oh. Yes. I see."

"Your face," she said. "Because I like you very much, you prat."

"I think I'm in love with you," he said. It had come out without his meaning it to.

She frowned. "Oh, dear. Very bad, that."

"Is it?" he asked, apprehensive.

"Well of course it is," she said impatiently. "Part of your problem, isn't it? Faulty learning. What sort of behaviour d'you associate with love? Functional impotence, for a start."

"Getting plates thrown at me. Bad sleep patterns, gastric disorders, nausea and vertigo, banging one's head on the bathroom wall, letters from the solicitor, yes I do see what you mean, Lyn."

"Right," she said, smiling. "So we'd better think of some other word for what we've got."

"Lyn," said Stephen. "I feel really good. I think I'm a very lucky man."

She nodded. "This is true."

From: The Vice-Chancellor's Office
To: Dr J. G. McCannon, University Medical Centre.
Dear McCannon,
We on the Academic and Research Committee feel that it's time that the Medical Centre's contribution in the research field should have its proper recognition within the University, and also nationally and internationally. Perhaps you'd like to drop in for a chat about this next week, and in the meantime let me have a memo of published, ongoing and proposed research initiated in your group.
As ever,
Ernie

Minutes of Group Meeting held at the Medical Centre.
Present: Dr J. G. McCannon (Chair) Dr Daker, Dr Buzzard, Dr Rose Marie.
Dr McCannon opened the meeting by reading aloud a letter from the Vice-Chancellor (copy attached). Dr McCannon offered for consideration the opinion that the Vice-Chancellor was a malevolent back-biting dwarf. He

and his gang of Machiavellian cronies were trying to treat the members of the medical group as if they were an academic department, like engineers or philosophers. Publish or die was the message, and if the doctors didn't publish, Ernie would kill them.

Dr Buzzard felt that that was coming it a bit strong. Dr McCannon became distressed, but generously offered refreshments to the meeting. The other members declined, but Dr McCannon himself took advantage of his own generosity. Dr Rose Marie supported Dr Buzzard in the opinion that the situation was not too bleak. She commented that Dr McCannon had published, that all the group had published. Dr Daker said that he had not published.

Dr McCannon reminded the meeting, that his two works, *Sexual Anxiety and the Common Cold*, and *The Therapeutic Village*, major works though they were, lay fifteen years in the past, and could be purchased remaindered for fifty pence each in the University Bookshop. He feared that he himself would be remaindered, for little more than fifty pence, unless the practice could jump to the crack of the Vice-Chancellor's whip.

Dr Daker said that it all seemed rather unfair, as caring for the patients was a full time job if it was done properly.

Dr Buzzard said that that would not wash. Dr Daker might as well say that the lecturers were there to teach their students.

Dr Daker said that he thought that was what they were there for.

Dr Buzzard explained to Dr Daker that while that might notionally be the case, in reality the lecturers were there to avoid contact with students as much as possible; this enabled them to write books and articles nobody would ever read, and swan off to conferences to give papers that nobody would listen to. The more of that they did, the more time off they were granted, until they got so eminent there was no danger of them ever having to see another student.

Dr Rose Marie commented that some of one's colleagues

were quite successful at avoiding student contact without being eminent at all.

Dr Buzzard asked Dr Rose Marie if she had anyone particular in mind, but Dr Rose Marie declined to reply.

Dr Buzzard said that if that was the way the trend was going, why not go with it: close down the Sick Bay, let the ancillary staff go, and put in for two nice young research assistants.

Dr McCannon said that he hoped the practice would be able to survive this difficult period without major restructuring. In his opinion, Ernie's cruel searchlight would eventually swing round on to someone else. In the meantime, he would be grateful to colleagues for anything they might be able to fudge up for the memo. He had himself embarked on a new work of some length entitled *The Sick University*, which he believed would have some little greatness about it.

Dr Rose Marie submitted a list of recent articles and conference papers to the meeting (see document 3/85/RM), mainly relating to women patients in a world of male doctors. She was also contracted to Virago to write a book entitled *Massive Insults to the Vagina*.

Dr Daker regretted that at present he had nothing to offer, though he hoped to in future. At present the actual general practice was taking up all his time.

Dr Buzzard advised Dr Daker to learn how to live in the twentieth century; Dr Daker should realise that there were people out there who were after his balls.

Dr McCannon asked Dr Buzzard if he had any little schemes going.

Dr Buzzard said that he had.

Dr McCannon complimented Dr Buzzard on his new suit and enquired if the stains on his crotch were marmalade stains.

Dr Buzzard said that they were.

Dr McCannon asked whether Dr Buzzard had anything else to offer the meeting besides a decorated suit.

Dr Buzzard said that he had. What he had to offer was a full-blown research project: an in-depth intensive study of the new Hamburger tranquilliser breakthrough, code name Confidan.

Dr Rose Marie said that she was sure she had read something about that and asked Dr Buzzard whether there had not already been some user trials in the United States. Dr Buzzard explained that that was just a preliminary hiccup, and that this was the real thing, with intensive user trials, Hamburger funding, personal consultancy fees, and a real chance of endowments for the University if the thing could be got right.

Dr McCannon observed that the dwarf loved the smell of an endowment.

Dr Buzzard generously offered to let Dr Daker in on the project, as his own work had not yet got under way, and Dr Daker accepted.

Dr Buzzard made the same generous offer to Dr Rose Marie, who declined.

Dr Buzzard said that that was no skin off his nose. Any fool could see that Confidan was the paddle that would get the University Medical Centre out of shit creek.

There was no other business.

"The beauty of it is," said Bob to Stephen in the University Pub, "the beauty of it is that we can get a really big sample, because Confidan has so many indications. It's bloody wonderful stuff, Stephen."

"Good for exam nerves, that sort of thing?"

"Absolutely," said Bob. "Reduces anxiety without turning you into a cabbage. Be spot on for your panic and terror, Stephen, fancy a couple now?"

"No thanks," said Stephen. He looked around the bar. The usual knot of obsessives playing the machines, a few Neanderthals from the Rugby Club flipping beer mats, little Angie Fry in the corner gazing deep into the eyes of a man who was definitely not an Older Man, but might well be a Younger Man. None of it worried him. He wouldn't even be frightened if John Thomas Furie came in. Furie had made a spectacular recovery, published a flurry of articles on the brain chemistry of hypomania and was going round the university telling anyone who would listen that

Stephen Daker was one hell of a doctor. Stephen was, he realised, feeling pretty good.

"Actually, Bob," he said, "the panic and terror have been on the retreat lately."

"That tottie of yours?" asked Bob, doing his intelligent gun-dog face.

"She's not my tottie, Bob," said Stephen patiently, "but, well, yes."

"Fair enough," said Bob generously. He stared into his pint and then drank some of it. "If you ask me, a woman's only a woman, but a good drug's safer in the long run. Anyway, this stuff. Exam nerves aren't the half of it. Post-flu depression, nausea and diarrhoea, male menopause, menstrual gloom, general undefined shitty feeling, you name it, Confidan's the answer. It's compatible with alcohol too."

"You make it seem like a patent medicine, Bob. Haven't thought of flogging it off a barrow in the market, have you?"

"Let's be serious, Stephen," said Bob, demonstrating seriousness with a gun-dog-getting-told-off face. "This is the one that's going to put us on the map. It's not an analgesic, but the mood management factor's so good I'm even going to try it with minor sports injuries. Raises the pain threshold, you see. If I popped it into a few of those big chaps over there you could hit 'em with a goal post and they wouldn't care."

"Well," said Stephen, "I hope you're right."

"Look, buddy," said Bob. "I wouldn't be sticking my neck out unless I was sure. If Hamburger International are going all the way for it it's got to be good."

Stephen thought about it. It certainly sounded good. Hamburger were absolutely enormous, everyone knew that. There couldn't really be a snag, so what was that nagging doubt? "Um, Bob," he said diffidently. "Why have they picked us?"

Bob smiled complacently. "Bit of luck, really. Old school friend of mine. Jimmy Partington. Always kept in touch. And now he's a big Hamburger man."

116

"I see," said Stephen. So that was it. Old boy network. Answered all the questions. And now, it seemed, he was in on it too. It was really very kind of Bob. He was really all right, old Bob, in his way.

"Right then," said Bob. "Starting tomorrow, we'll push the stuff out. It's strictly a short-term job, pilot study, show 'em what we can do, and then they'll give us the really big job. We should get all the data we need in a couple of weeks. I'm going on to three-minute consultations to get the numbers up, and I'd advise you to do the same. God, Stephen, I haven't felt so cheerful for years. We're really going somewhere at last."

"Look, um, Bob. I'm really awfully grateful, but . . . I mean are you saying we should get the patient in, hear the symptoms, prescribe Confidan, and shoot them out again?"

"Exactly," said Bob. "And 'where indicated' means just about every single bod who walks through the door. Then check 'em out in six and ten days. Bingo."

Oh, dear. "I . . . I don't think I can just do that, Bob. I mean, they come to us for more than that, don't they? Really?"

"I'm not going to poison them, buddy. This stuff is going to do them good. Thing is, if you're going to let them cry on your shoulder, or mop their fevered brows, or whatever it is you do, it's not only going to take up time, it's going to fog the issue. What made them better, Confidan or Doctor Daker's doggy eyes?"

Stephen sighed. "I know. But there it is. Sorry, Bob."

"Fine! Fine! Won't press you," said Bob with unusual restraint. "Just do the best you can. You know, if this goes well, buddy, this time next term you could be walking round the University in a suit like mine!"

Anyone who knows Bob Buzzard will tell you that when he's got the bit between his teeth he doesn't fart about. That night he cleared the Commodore for action, phased in a new disk drive, and dry ran the printer. All systems went. By ten o'clock next morning he had seen ten patients. Their

117

complaints had varied from mild tonsilitis to anal warts. He prescribed Confidan for all of them, referring the anal wart man to the special clinic at the hospital as well. Bob Buzzard wasn't put on this earth to peer up buggers' bums, after all.

His research colleague found himself unable to keep up with this formidable rate of throughput. Stephen was seeing a patient who had been coming over a number of weeks, a third year student with claustrophobia. He liked her very much, identified with her feelings, and couldn't bear to give her the Buzzard treatment.

"I think you're coping with it very sensibly," he said. "It *is* a daunting experience, reading a seminar paper. I used to dread it. But you got through to the end this time."

"Well, more or less," she said. "About halfway through the floor started coming up and tilting, and I had this very strong suggestion that Professor Elgin was slowly turning upside down. Quite funny, really. Well, seems funny now."

"Sure he wasn't turning upside down?" said Stephen.

"Some pretty funny characters in the Philosophy Department." They had got to this stage now, risking the odd joke.

She was sitting quite calmly opposite him, smiling as if she meant it, and the door was closed. On her first two appointments she had not showed at all, being unable to make it through the waiting room.

"Not him," she said now. "He's a very upright man. So anyway, I remembered what you said, managed to mutter 'any questions so far?' and of course there weren't, so it gave me a chance to do your breathing thing, and the floor kind of got itself under control, and my professor very slowly turned all the way back again, and I got the thing finished."

"Well, that's fine," said Stephen enthusiastically. "We're winning, slowly."

"I was sick afterwards though," she said. "Wish we were winning fast."

Why did he hesitate? Why did he have this faint guilty

feeling? The symptoms, after all, constituted a precise indication. She was a prime target.

"I'm going to prescribe you something this time, Sarah," he said. "I think it'll help in the short term, and reinforce your own efforts. It'll relax you generally, and that'll help you control the hyperventilation." He wrote the scrip. Somehow, he'd have liked her to do it all on her own. What sort of doctor did that make him? Maybe Bob was right and he didn't know how to live in the twentieth century at all.

Stephen's throughput took another dip. Half an hour later, Rose Marie dropped in for a chat, sitting very close to him and alarming him considerably. Any progress Stephen had made in the panic and terror sector soon seemed illusory in Rose Marie's presence. However, he congratulated himself, his body was much more under control now: however panicky he felt, he was able to conduct himself with suave aplomb, even when she sat so close that he could feel her breath on his cheek.

"Don't be alarmed, Stephen," she said. "I want to confide in you."

"I'm not alarmed."

"I'm afraid I alarmed you when I confided in you last," she said, smiling.

"No you didn't. Really."

"Yes, I think I did, Stephen." She couldn't really have nothing on under that white coat, could she? What was she doing, leaning forward like that? Did she want him to think about the unthinkable?

"I told you I'd been having an affair with Helen Furie, and you've not been able to look at me without blushing ever since. Now why is that, I wonder?"

"I haven't told anyone else, you know," he said, blushing.

"I'm sure you haven't," she said warmly. "Not that I'd mind if you did. My sexuality disturbs you, doesn't it?"

"No, of course it doesn't," he croaked. Unconvincing. Try harder. "I mean it did, er, surprise me at the time, but then when I thought about it . . . well I find women more attractive than men. Women are more attractive than men.

So, um, I mean it shouldn't be surprising if they're attracted to each other." Not bad, Stephen. It made sense and he'd said it without squeaking once.

Rose Marie gave him a long look of gentle amusement. "It's very sweet of you to say that, Stephen. You're trying very hard to understand, but you still can't look at me, and you're blushing as much as ever. What is it, Stephen?"

"Well," he said, coming clean. "I just don't know how to take you."

"As a colleague and a friend, I hope. That shouldn't be too hard. Should it?"

"No," said Stephen, immensely relieved. "That's fine. I mean I really admire your work and everything, and I respect your judgment about all sorts of things . . ."

"But you're still bothered because you find me attractive, and you can't reconcile that with your stereotype of the lesbian woman. That's it, isn't it?"

That was so clearly it, or at any rate a very large chunk of it, that Stephen could find no way to respond except opening and closing his mouth a few times.

"And being bisexual, like eighty per cent of the population," she went on (he wished she would stop fiddling with the top button of that white coat), "I can empathise with that. And yes, your instinct is right. I find you attractive too. You and I could easily have a relationship which would be a valuable learning experience for both of us."

"Er . . ." said Stephen.

"But we're not going to of course, because we're adults and we're capable of exercising our options in a rational way. Aren't we?"

"Er, yes," said Stephen. "Yes, of course we are."

"I'm really impressed with the way you've thought this through," she said. "You're absolutely right, it's best to get the psychodynamics of the thing out into the open. I really feel much better about the whole relationship, thanks to you, Stephen."

"Well, thanks very much, Rose Marie," said Stephen. He was pleased to have been of assistance, yet couldn't

120

help feeling that he might have been just a tiny bit, well . . . managed.

Rose Marie breathed deeply in and out, demonstrating rather more than the marvellous efficiency of the human respiratory system. "You know, I'd made up my mind to leave it all undiscussed," she said smiling. "I came in to talk about something quite different!"

What she had come in to talk about was the Confidan study. As a colleague and friend she was rather worried that Bob (who was of course himself a dear friend and valued colleague) might be, without meaning to of course, taking advantage of Stephen. Had Stephen made quite sure that he would be credited with joint authorship of the report? No? Then surely he must see that he was being used as an unpaid and unrecognised research assistant. It wasn't really any of her business, but as a colleague and a friend she just wanted to make sure that Stephen got all the credit that was due to him. Stephen had not thought about this at all, but took her point immediately. He was touched and grateful. When she went away he found that he was thinking about his friend and colleague very warmly.

When Rose Marie was back in her room, she placed a transatlantic call to her friend Lois in San Diego. Her memory had been correct. San Diego had done the pilot study, she even knew a guy who was on the team, but for some reason the report had been shredded. Lois thought she knew where she'd be able to get hold of an outline, though. Rose Marie put the receiver down, unlocked her drawer, and took out the files marked Buzzard and Daker. Yes, it was very important that both of them got their names clearly associated with this one.

"Um . . . what do we have to do now?" said Stephen. It was half-past four in the afternoon, the quiet time of the day in between visits and evening surgery, and he was lying in bed with Lyn. Neither of them had anything on, and both of them were eating bananas. There was nothing significant about the bananas: Lyn was a behaviourist, not a Freudian. She didn't half like bananas, though.

"Nothing, Doc," she said with her mouth full. "Absolutely nothing. Just relax and eat your banana. That's the programme."

"That's really all?"

"That's really all."

Stephen shut up and ate bananas for a while. It was all right, being in bed with Lyn with nothing on. Getting undressed and getting in had been a bit traumatic, even though he'd reminded himself she'd seen his body lots of times before. Well, nearly all his body. She hadn't seen his cock before though. Well, it was perfectly all right, his cock was; Stephen knew, as only a doctor can, that it was quite dramatically average in size and shape, and he also knew, as all of us do, that (within reason) it's not how big it is, it's what you can do with it, but that wasn't much help because he hadn't felt able to do anything with his for quite a long time, and all in all it had been quite a relief when she'd given it a friendly glance, and not rolled about the floor clutching her sides with laughter helplessly pointing at it, or anything like that.

He had, of course, seen Lyn before with nothing on at all, and this time that had been quite unequivocally nice. He couldn't quite believe that they were actually there together, all that bare flesh under the duvet; but he could feel that they were, because they were touching at various points. And, feeling that they were, he couldn't quite believe that he was taking it all so calmly. But he was. There was absolutely nothing going on down there. Well, that was all right, because there wasn't supposed to be anything going on down there. All the same, he wouldn't have minded a few hints that something might, a few wayward stirrings to master and subdue.

"Lyn," he said. "What if we get bored?"

"It's all right to be bored," she said. "Just so long as we're comfortable."

He turned and looked at her face. She had finished her banana now and she was licking her fingers. He thought what a nice clean pink tongue she had. It was a long tongue, too, and very pointed. When she had finished licking her

122

fingers she licked all the way round her mouth. When she noticed that he was watching she grinned and showed him how she could lick her nose as well. Now the fair down on her upper lip was damp, and caught the light slanting in through the window.

"Lyn," he said. "Um . . . what if we want to . . . I mean what if we happened to . . . what if we found we felt like . . . ?"

"We just don't," she said. "We just lie there enjoying it."

"Enjoying what?"

"Wanting to, but not. Knowing we could if we felt like it, but not. That's the rule."

"Yes, I see."

"Have you had all the bananas you want now?"

"Yes, thank you, Lyn."

"Turn over, then."

He did as he was told. It was nice to have someone else in charge of him. Like being lifesaved. It would be nice to have someone in charge of him all the time, to tell him what to do about all the awkward things, like whether Rose Marie was right about Bob's ruthless ambition, and whether he ought to be combative and thrusting himself, and seize his share of whatever was going, and . . . oh, all sorts of things.

"You've got a nice warm back," she said. She was stroking it, long slow firm strokes, from the nape of his neck to the base of his spine, heavy steady pressure all the way down. When Angela had stroked him, in the days when she had, it had always been a light feathery sort of business, insubstantial and ticklish. It suddenly occurred to him that perhaps Angela hadn't ever touched him in the right way, either.

"I've been thinking about that research project of yours," she said. "Why don't you ask Bob if you can run a control group? Match the symptoms, but different treatment. Bob's get the wonder drug, yours get the usual."

"Lyn, that's brilliant," said Stephen into the pillow.

"No, it's not, it's standard practice," she said. "Why

isn't he doing it already? You don't think he's just faking something up to please the company?"

"Mm. Might be. Mm. Mm."

"Have you switched your brain off, Stephen?"

"Mm".

"Are you all right?"

"Yes," he said. "Fine. In fact . . . I think I'm surprising myself."

"Oh, yes?"

"Lyn. How long does this stage of the programme last?"

"About six months."

"Oh."

"Your face."

Bob was very decent about the control group idea. Bob was very decent about everything. Bob was on cracking form. He had rigged up his consulting room as a small-scale Ops Room, and had enough hardware and software to send a gundog into space, probably.

"Damn good idea," he said, punching a few figures into the keyboard. "No need to worry about numbers, I scored thirty-three yesterday, and they're all in the memory bank. Don't worry, Stephen. Even if you're just monitoring the control group there should still be a suit in it for you. Seen Jock today? Think we should keep the old fart up to date with progress."

"No," said Stephen. "I'm a bit worried about Jock. He seems to have stopped going home. He just crouches in his room muttering into a cassette recorder. D'you think he's all right?"

"Working on his book, buddy," said Bob confidently. "He's fine, never better. At least it's keeping him out of mischief." Suddenly sheaves of printout started to spill out of one of the machines. Bob dodged nimbly round to rake it in.

"Oops. Always takes me by surprise. Well, there it is. Shape of the future. Look, buddy, we've got a heavy day today. I'm aiming to shift forty of them. Come round to lunch on Sunday, we can talk things through then. Daphne and the boys are dying to meet you. You can bring that tottie of yours if you like."

Jock McCannon was working on his new book, and it was going well. The creative sap had not dried up after all. Image after fruitful image for the Sick University rose up in his mind: the constipated administrative structure, the clogged and flooded walkways, the puny stature of its leader, even the nuns picking over the rubbish skips, all, all, seemed charged with resonance. Jock liked to dictate his case histories while the patient was actually present: it gave the prose immediacy and vitality, and it saved a hell of a lot of drinking time. The patients didn't like it as much as Jock did, but they put up with it; there was not much to do with Jock except put up with him.

Jock sat, or rather lay as if thrown there, on his leaky old chair, while his patient, a swarthy and slightly smelly male student, stared back at him with suspicion and fear.

"A typical consultation in the Sick University," said Jock into the recorder. "Always the same. Always new. One face, one body taken at random from the long procession of pain." He flashed a yellow grin at the young fellow to set him at his ease. It was not an unqualified success.

"This is a young man," said Jock. "The unlined, greasy, pustular skin denotes innocence and ignorance. But then the eyes of the patient meet the eyes of the doctor. And everything is changed, changed utterly, in that moment of acknowledgment of a shared mortality, in which each symptom inscribes itself as an ideograph of the inevitable death that is all we humans share. A terrible beauty is born. The existential bond has been forged. And now it can begin."

He leaned forward in his chair and drew his lips back from the dreadful old teeth. "So what's the matter with you, my dear chap?"

"Er . . . piles?" said the patient.

It was getting towards the end of the day. Bob Buzzard had been working like a Trojan, popping pills into trampolinists with broken necks, sad girls with herpes, suicidal education lecturers. They came in with symptoms and they went out with Confidan. Bloody good. Didn't have to talk to them, didn't have to touch them, hardly had to look at them, and it was all in the cause of scientific advancement. Not to mention cars and holidays. This one looked quite straightforward, rather a clean neat sort of tottie, not your typical Lowlands type, must be a secretary. Headaches, probably, they all had headaches. He scribbled on his pad.

"Two of these three times a day," he said. "You should notice the difference by tomorrow, but come back and see me on Tuesday in any case."

"But I'm not ill," said the tottie. "There's nothing wrong with me."

"Sorry?"

"You put in for extra secretarial assistance. Well, here I am."

"Oh, I see," said Bob. "Oh, right. Fine. Jolly good!"

He gave the tottie a brief searching glance. "You do look a bit peaky though. Have to do something about that."

He produced a little bottle of Confidan tablets from his waistcoat pocket. "Tell you what. Have one of mine."

Daphne Buzzard was an absolute whiz in the kitchen. Bob Buzzard knew that and so did all his pals. Say what you like about Daphne, they all said, old Daphne can get the old grub on the table, and very good grub it was too. Bit on the fancy side for some of them, of course, but Daphne knew what was what. Never at a loss, Daphne. Old Bob had been known to turn up with some old chum or other ratted as arseholes at one in the morning, and she'd come up with the goods. Oh, she'd give them hardeye, all right, but then she'd whack out the wok and come up with something really tasty, just what the doctor ordered.

Bob was feeling very fond of Daphne as she rattled about the kitchen putting the finishing touches to her salade composée, dealing out the kiwi fruit slices as fast and accurate as the Bunnies dealt the duff hands at the Playboy Club, where old Jimmy Partington had once taken Bob.

She was in a pretty filthy mood, of course, but she didn't let that slow her down. That was the thing about old Daph; she knew how to get on with her life.

"I can't quite think why I'm going to all this trouble, darling, can you?" she said, ripping up the radicchio in a fine frenzy. "I don't suppose any of them have even heard of nouvelle cuisine, they wouldn't know a kiwi fruit from a goosegog. That person in dungarees will probably ask for salad cream on it. I mean why can't they all stay in their bedsits with their pot noodles and let us get on with our lives?"

"We are getting on with our lives, my darling," said Bob.

"Oh, yes, we are, my darling – darling do get out of the way – entertaining your drunken no-hope friends again. Honestly Robert darling, if any of them falls face down into the pudding today, that's it. No more. No way."

"They won't do that, my darling. Working lunch."

She stopped what she was doing and turned round. She didn't exactly put her hands on her hips, but she did give him third-degree hardeye.

"Working lunch?" she said. "Working lunch? If it's a working lunch, why has Daker brought his tart?"

"She's not his tart, my darling, she's his tottie," said Bob mildly.

"But what's she doing here? And why are they so early? Don't they know what time people have lunch?"

"Good practice for the boys," said Bob. Daphne snorted.

"Daphne," said Bob.

"What?" she snapped. The salade was finished, perfect, complete, as composée as any salade could ever be.

"You do love me, don't you Daphne?"

"Robert?" she said. "Are you all right?"

"Been a bit of a fraught week," he admitted.

She softened instantly. Some chaps would never be able to credit the way a woman like Daphne could soften. Bob couldn't credit it himself, sometimes. But there she was, suddenly soft as butter. Amazing woman. Amazing.

"Oh, Robert," she said. "I didn't notice. Yes, of course I

love you, and I'm sure this pill thing's going to be absolutely the cat's pyjamas. It's just that sometimes one wonders, you know, what it's all about, that's all."

"Let's have a fast gin," he said tenderly. "Just you and me. Let them stew for a bit."

"Get ahead of the opposition," she said.

"That's it, my darling. Ah, not unrelated to Tenerife, this lunch," he added.

Daphne's eyes sparkled. Bob got a real buzz out of making her eyes sparkle.

"So we *are* getting on with our lives!" she said. And then, with just the merest trace of hardeye, "Not before time, my darling."

The boys got in some very good practice entertaining Lyn and Stephen. They didn't like entertaining either Mummy's guests or Daddy's guests very much, but Daddy had made it quite clear that that was what they bloody well had to do, so they did it.

"Mummy and Daddy are having a row in the kitchen," said Ollie for openers.

"How d'you know?" said the lady in rompers. "I mean they might be making love for all you know."

"You don't do *that* in the kitchen," said Ollie contemptuously.

"Right," said the lady in rompers, "I'll try to remember that, Ollie."

Simon felt that things were already beginning to get a bit out of hand, and they'd only just started. "Anyway," he said. "I think it's rather rude to talk about that sort of thing."

"What sort of thing do you like to talk about?" said the lady in rompers. The man was just staring about as if he'd just woken up. It was often like that with Daddy's guests.

"We've got nineteen computer games," said Ollie. "We're going to make one of our own up soon."

"What have you got?" said the man. Probably a complete wally, but Daddy had said talk to him.

"Packman," said Ollie, "Batman . . ."

"Flatman . . ." said Simon.

"Vatman?" said the man. Maybe he was all right.

"Crapman," said Ollie, giggling.

"I'll give you a game if you like," said the lady.

"Girls are no good with computers," said Ollie firmly.

"After lunch," said the lady. "For money."

"You'll never beat us," said Ollie, and was then struck by a moment of doubt. "Well, you might possibly beat me, but no one's ever beaten Simon. Not even our Daddy."

"Our Daddy's a doctor," said Ollie to the man. "Are you a doctor too?"

"Yes, I am, actually," said the man, which only went to show you. People who look like wallies can sometimes be quite important. Daddy was always saying that.

"Our Daddy hates being a doctor, you know," said Ollie. "Because of the patients, you know."

"And his colleagues," said Simon. "He has these awful colleagues, you see."

"The mad old fart," explained Ollie.

"And the uppity dike," said Simon. "Actually, I'm not sure what an uppity dike is."

"They have a lot of them in Holland," said the man.

"And Dickie Dado, the wet liberal," said Simon.

"He's so wet you could shoot snipe off his back," said Ollie.

"Sounds a useful character," said the lady in rompers.

"Yes, if you wanted to shoot snipe I suppose he would be," said Ollie seriously.

Then Daddy came in from the kitchen with a tray of bottles and glasses. "Stephen! Lyn! Drinks!" he shouted in a very loud voice. He must have been having one in the kitchen, Ollie thought.

"Thank you, boys," said Daddy, "you can bugger off now."

Hours and hours later, or so it seemed, lunch was finally happening. The salade had been very thoroughly decomposéed without one single word of appreciation, but the person in dungarees had not asked for salad cream. One had, one supposed, to be grateful for small mercies, thought

129

Daphne. On the other hand, the person in dungarees had had far too much to say for herself already. Anyone would have thought that someone with an accent like that would have had the sense to smile a lot and say nothing, but there you were, all the old certainties were vanishing. Jimmy Partington, predictably, seemed to find it all quite fascinating. Well, it was all a bit of a debacle as far as Daphne was concerned, and no way would Daker or his dungareed tart darken her doors again.

"Honestly, darling" she said sharply to Robert, who was carving, "you are making a dog's breakfast of it."

"Awkward swines, these saddles of lamb," said her husband. "Chap doesn't know which way to come at them." Chap was ratted out of his mind, that was the only problem. Chap didn't know when to stop.

"Jimmy," she said, "could you be an angel and pour the wine?"

"No problem." No one rather imagined that would be the case. Oh, well, Jimmy P. wasn't so bad in his way. In fact he could be rather a sweetie . . .

"Damn," said Bob. The knife had slipped and the juice had gone all over that suit of his he was so keen on.

"Oh, really, darling!" she couldn't help saying.

"I think he's doing fine," the dungareed tart or tottie took it upon herself to say.

"Oh, that's all right then," said Daphne. "Lyn thinks you're doing fine, so there's nothing to worry about. Of course, I was terribly spoilt as a girl, Daddy was an absolutely wonderful carver. And still is. Isn't he, boys?"

"Yes, Mummy," said the boys. In unison. Bless them.

"Daddy, she would have you know," said Robert, in the sulks again, "is an obstetric surgeon. A really fast man with the knife. First time I saw him going to work on a turkey I fainted dead away."

Jimmy Partington was laughing fit to bust. Daphne could have killed him where he sat.

"Well, at least he didn't throw juice all over his suit," she said.

Robert said oh God and started mopping away, which

gave Daphne the chance to get some meat on people's plates and start the whole thing moving again.

"I mean let's just try and have a nice quiet civilised lunch," she said. "D'you think we could possibly do that now, darling?"

Jimmy P., who to do him justice did have some sensitivity to one's moods, took it upon himself to spread a little sunshine.

"Well, cheers," he said, raising his glass. "Here's to us. Confidan!"

"Oh yeah," said the person. "How's that going?"

"Well, Bob's the man to ask," said Jimmy. Nobody except Daphne ever seemed to call him Robert. That, Daphne thought, was symptomatic of the whole business.

"Absolutely fine," said Robert. "Not a hitch, not a hiccup. Mind you, it's next week we're going to see the first proper results. But I'm very confident." He was too, the poor darling. You could see that.

Then, would you believe it, Daker's scrubber said: "What sort of method d'you use for dealing with the whatyoucall, the data?"

"Well, it's all a bit technical, Lyn," said Jimmy P. "Bit hard to explain to the layman."

"Layperson, Jimmy," said Robert roguishly.

"Yes, indeed, layperson, well said," said Jimmy P. "D'you see yourself as a layperson, love?" Jimmy P. seemed altogether too much taken with this person in dungarees.

"Yeah, now and then, Jimmy," said the person. "Not in this context, though. I mean, crudely speaking, your problem would be matching the controls and knowing how much to allow for the Hawthorne effect. Well, that for a start."

Daphne thought that Jimmy P. had gone a bit blank for a second, but dear old Jimmy could always bounce back. "Hey, hey, hey! You're not just a pretty face, are you?"

"No," she said, "my bum's usually reckoned to be my best feature, Jimmy. How about you, eh?"

That was clearly quite enough. The boys were giggling

behind their hands, quite obviously thinking that things were well out of control and that anything went, but they were in for another think.

"Stop that!" said Daphne sharply. "I hope I'm not going to have to ask anyone to leave the table!" And that seemed to have the desired effect on everyone, even the person in dungarees.

Later that afternoon, Jimmy Partington stood by the window watching Lyn playing football with the boys in the back garden. She feinted to the left, wrong-footed Ollie, and got her shot in. Simon took it in the midriff, and collapsed winded. Jimmy turned from the window with a sigh.

"Plenty of energy, that tottie of yours, Stephen."

"She's not a tottie, Jimmy," said Stephen patiently. "And she doesn't belong to me."

"I think you'll find she does, old chap," said Jimmy.

"I did, er, tentatively test the hypothesis on the landing earlier on. No dice. Awfully nice about it, but no dice. I belong to Stephen. That's what her lovely eyes said."

"What did her lovely mouth say?" said Bob, who was slumped on the sofa next to Stephen. All three men had been drinking Californian brandy for some time.

"Well," said Jimmy. "I think her lovely mouth said something like: 'don't let's make prats of ourselves, Jimmy'. So there you are. Belongs to you."

"There's a logical flaw in your experiment," said Stephen carefully. "Just because she didn't fancy you . . . you follow? Nobody belongs to anybody else."

"I belong to Daphne," said Bob with utter conviction.

"Where is Daphne?" said Stephen.

"Out with the dogs," said Bob. "Think it's best. You know I'm very glad I got you both over here. Like old times."

"Absolutely," said Jimmy Partington.

"You and I didn't have any old times, Bob," said Stephen.

"No, but from now on we can," said Bob. "Important point in history, this. Start of something getting done. Feel as if I've started to get on with my life again. Not bogged down."

"Well," said Jimmy Partington, "if we can get a good result on this one, Hamburger's going to be very happy."

"And what exactly is a good result?" asked Stephen.

"Stephen," said Bob, "you know what a good result is. It's the one that gets us the consultancy retainers, and the elegant research profiles."

"Not to mention the suits," said Stephen.

"No, not to mention the suits," said Bob. "Actually," he added, dabbing away at his crotch, "I wish you hadn't mentioned the suit just now."

He reached for the brandy and refilled his glass and Jimmy's. Stephen shook his head, then wished he hadn't. Not changing his mind about the brandy; just wishing he hadn't shaken his head.

"*And* the university endowments," said Bob. "We could go the way that Salford's going. Get so much private investment we could go independent. Eh? I'd like to be part of that. That's a breakthrough Robert Buzzard could spearhead."

"Daphne would be very pleased," said Jimmy. Jimmy was looking a bit pie-eyed. Perhaps he was drunk. How odd. Stephen felt perfectly all right so long as he kept his head still.

"Daphne would be very pleased," said Bob. "She's given me the best years of her life. At least, one could hazard a guess that they were the best years of her life. She's been very patient. You know . . ." He paused, and stared into his brandy with furrowed brow, suddenly a first cross beagle/bloodhound, not too bright but go all day for you, ". . . everyone in my family except me is a company director, and everyone in her family except her is a consultant at the very least. And here she is. Married to a general practitioner in a holiday camp. I've seen it in her eyes: when's he going to get on with his life? Well: I think this is really going to be it." Bob nodded a few times.

"That's really moving, Bob," said Stephen. "I hope it all works out for you."

133

"Thank you, Stephen," said Bob. "And I'll tell you another thing: I won't forget your help and encouragement."

Lyn came in through the French windows.

"Hello, my lovely girl," said Bob. "Come and have a brandy with us."

"No thanks, Bob," she said. "I've come to take Doctor Daker away. Think you've made a bit of a dog's breakfast of him."

Most people would have said that Doctor Daker was a total write-off as far as the rest of Sunday was concerned, but Lyn was optimistic. She was also determined and practical. She sat him in the passenger seat of his Volvo, drove him back to his flat, refused to let him get into bed, got him into his tracksuit, forced him into five circuits of the lake, jogged him back to the flat, refused to let him lie down, drove him into the shower, followed him in, gradually turned the heat down until he was gasping, and then let him come out. Then she watched him dry himself. Then she watched him clean his teeth. Then she let him get into bed, and got in it with him. It was now eight o'clock on Sunday evening.

"What are the rules?" said Stephen. He felt deliciously drowsy.

"Well," she said. "I'm going to stay all night. If that's all right with you."

"Yes it is, Lyn. Er . . . anything else?"

"Nothing else. I thought we might just see how it goes. How about that?"

Suddenly he felt much less drowsy.

"Oh, Lyn."

"And, um, if we do feel like doing something, well, we might as well get on with it, that's what I thought. Cos it's not as if it's ever any good the first time, is it?"

"No," he said, his mind whirling. So this was it. This might be the first time, or it might not, and if it was, there was going to be at least a second time . . . and there weren't any expectations . . . this thing might actually be possible.

"There is something else I've got to say to you," she said.

134

He looked at her. Her face was very serious. He realised that almost everything she'd said to him before had had a laugh somewhere at the back of it, had been part of a game. This was different.

"Um, look . . .," she said. She seemed almost embarrassed, something else he realised he'd never seen before.

"It's all right," he said. "Say it."

"Well . . . if this turns out to be a great success, you're not going to go all funny on me, are you?"

"How d'you mean?"

"You know. The way people in love go on. Obsessive. Possessive. Nasty. Jealous. Sulky. All that."

"No," he said fervently. "I've done all that, Lyn."

She bit her lip. There was more to come. "Because when I'm with you, I'm really with you, but I like to be in other places too. Is that OK?"

"Yes, of course," he said.

"And other people," said Lyn. "I really fancy quite a lot of people, Stephen. And I go to bed with quite a few of them. And I don't think that's going to change."

Stephen found he wanted very much to make her smile. "It's all right, Lyn," he said. "I do realise all that. It's OK. I mean, if you didn't fancy a lot of people you probably wouldn't fancy me, would you?"

She did smile. Her whole face went happy and relaxed. "That's nice," she said. "OK, Doc. You've passed the viva."

She snuggled down into him. "Let's sort of give it a whirl, eh?"

What they gave a whirl was not exactly it, but quite a number of things, all of which turned out to be very nice. Some of the things were things he had never done before with Angela, in the days when he and Angela had done things; and some of them were; but even those things were quite different with Lyn, so different as to seem not the same things at all. There was also a lot of laughing and talking, which there had never been with Angela. After a rather long while Stephen began to feel deliciously drowsy again.

135

He woke in the early hours of the morning to find that he was somehow inside her, and that was very nice too. He had no idea how she had managed this, but, well, there they were. Giving it a whirl. When she realised that he was fully awake, she reached behind her and switched the bedside lamp on so that he could see her smiling.

"Hello, Doc," she said. That was all either of them said, but she smiled at him the whole time. And it was all, all of it, very nice indeed.

When it was light he woke again. She was sitting up on her heels, looking down at him, and she was still smiling.

"Hey. You," she said. She leant down very carefully and kissed his chest. "Not bad. Not bad at all."

Jock McCannon was in a bad way. He had not been home for six days. His consulting room was littered with empty and half-empty bottles, forgotten takeaways, cigarette ends; all the detritus of despair. It was the book; it was the book. It was not that the book wasn't going well. The book was going all too well. Its conclusions were inescapable. The University was sick. It was sick unto death. Each day death triumphed: each day they came, the patients, demanding to be made better, knowing that no one is ever made better; we are simply kept going for a little longer. Each day the Sisyphean therapist pushes his boulder up the mountain; each day it rolls back. Each day he ponders the alternatives of cynicism and despair. And so the sick university, emblem and icon of the dying planet, shuffles towards the end of the century.

Jock stood by the window, watching the nuns scurrying away from the rubbish skips as the lorry approached. He spoke into his cassette recorder.

"Two glossy crows blown on the wind across the dead campus," he said. "And the doctor has come full circle again. To despair. Morning has broken. The bottle is empty. The book is written. No . . . spoken. No. Better 'written'. Who fucking cares?"

He raised his eyes to the ceiling, where two stuffed owls hung from a stout hook. Yes. It was time. Time to be at one with the stuffed owls; rolled round in earth's diurnal course with rocks, and stones, and bits of loose concrete.

Bob Buzzard, breezing in to work at eight thirty, heard a crash as he passed the old fart's consulting room. Old fart must have fallen out of his chair again reaching for the trusty Bell's. Oh, well. Pop one's head round the door, give him the progress report.

When he opened the door, the old fart was crawling round on his hands and knees muttering to himself, which was more or less par for the course. What wasn't par for the course was that Jock was cursing away quietly at what looked like the torn half of an old MCC tie. Bob hadn't realised that the old fart was interested in cricket at all.

"You all right, Jock?" he said chirpily.

"No, I am not all right," said Jock. "I am trying to hang myself, and it's proving extraordinarily difficult. Would you be kind enough to go a long way away, Bob, and leave me to destroy myself in peace?"

"Er, right," said Bob. "Fair enough. Sorry, Jock."

He shut the door quietly and went out. Half-way down the corridor he stopped, sighed, and turned back. When he went in Jock had clambered back on the desk again and was trying to do something with the light flex.

"No," said Bob. "Sorry. Not on. I just can't let you go through with this, Jock."

"Indeed," said Jock. "You surprise me."

"Well," said Bob, getting out his bottle of Confidan, "think you ought to try a course of these first, anyway."

Later that morning Stephen was going down the corridor when Maureen Gahagan stuck her head round the door of the dispensary.

"Doctor Daker, will you just come in here for a minute?" Stephen went in and she closed the door.

"Anything wrong?"

"What's Doctor Buzzard been doing to his patients?" she said.

"What d'you mean?"

137

"Well, it looks to me as if he's been clipping them round the earhole," said Maureen.

"Oh, no," said Stephen. "Oh, no, Maureen, that's not like Bob."

"He doesn't like patients, you know."

"Yes, I know he doesn't like patients, but he doesn't hit them. He doesn't even touch them if he can help it. You know he doesn't like examining them."

"Well, you look for yourself," said Maureen. "I swear I've seen six of them this morning coming out of his room. Ears red as beetroots!"

"I'm sure it's just a trick of the light," said Stephen. Odd, though, he thought. By the time he got back to his room he had forgotten about it. Any spare thinking time he had that morning went on thinking about very nice things, and he spent quite some time staring into space with a vague smile on his face.

"Really?" said Dr Rose Marie on the telephone. "You're quite sure? Any disturbance in the sense of balance? Yes, I see. Well, thanks a lot, Lois, that's just what I needed to know."

She put the receiver down.

"Well," she said. "What a shame."

She was smiling.

Stephen's nice claustrophobic philosophy student was a changed woman. She came into his consulting room with a spring in her step, she closed the door herself, and she sat down straight away without fidgeting.

"It went fine!" she said. "I, well, I actually enjoyed it. Professor Elgin kept me back afterwards and congratulated me on my presentation. Not the content, the presentation. How about that? And he stayed the right way up all the time."

"I'm delighted," said Stephen. "We've cracked it."

"The only thing is . . . I hate being a drag . . ."

"Go on," said Stephen.

"If it's not one thing it's another," she said. "I seem to have picked up some sort of ear infection or something."

When she had gone away, Stephen went along to Bob's

room. Data was pouring out of the printer, and Bob was scanning it feverishly, muttering and groaning to himself while absent-mindedly rubbing at his left ear.

"Sorry to disturb you, Bob, I can see you're busy," said Stephen. "It's just a thought that occurred to me about Confidan."

Bob turned a haunted face to him. "If it's anything about ears I don't want to bloody well know, all right?" Then Rose Marie leant round the open door.

"Can I come in, Bob," she asked gently.

"Why not?" yelled Bob. "Why not?"

"I've been talking to a friend in San Diego, California," she said. "Did you know they did a trial there of something that sounds just like your latest thing?"

"Oh, yes?" said Bob warily.

"Well, the buzz goes, they ran into a few odd side-effects. Ear inflammation, of all things."

"Really," said Bob.

"Mm. Startling frequency. Eighty-one per cent. With impairment of balance in twenty-seven per cent."

"Really," said Bob.

"I . . . well, I just felt you ought to know. As a friend and a colleague."

Bob put his head in his hands. "Thank you, Rose Marie," he said indistinctly. "I'm getting seventy per cent and twenty-one per cent."

"Oh, dear," she said. "I am sorry, Bob."

You could often see people scratching in the University Pub, and it was by no means unknown to see people falling over. But by Stephen's reckoning, just under a third of the drinkers were scratching their ears, pulling at their ear lobes, or shaking their heads irritably, and every five minutes or so, someone would fall down, or lurch into a table and send glasses flying.

"Bob," he said. "You do actually realise how appallingly irresponsible it was?"

"But it was a *Hamburger* product," said Bob. He was avoiding Stephen's eyes.

"You knew about that Californian research, didn't you?" said Stephen.

"Well . . . vaguely."

"And you didn't check it out."

"No, I didn't," said Bob sulkily. "What are you going to do? Gate me for a month? Haul me up for a prefect's beating?"

Stephen sighed.

"It's not fair," said Bob. "Jimmy Partington swore they'd modified it."

"Not enough, it seems."

"I mean," said Bob, "it's not as if it's a *dangerous* side-effect."

"No," Stephen conceded.

"And it is a bloody marvellous trank, you've got to admit that."

"Yes, it does seem to be. But you know what you've got to do though, don't you?"

"Stop prescribing it," said Bob tragically. "Tabulate the evidence. Make a cautiously negative report. It's not a good result, Stephen."

"It is a valuable piece of research, Bob."

Bob stared moodily into his pint.

"No Tenerife for Daphne," he said. "No Bermuda. No giving consultation in South American pleasure resorts. No BMW Mark Seven. No bloody fun, no bloody games. Back to square one."

Over by the bar, a chap in a red sweat shirt staggered, swayed, grabbed at a stool for support, and brought down the chap who had been sitting on it.

"Shall I tell you something, Stephen?" said Bob, pulling at his left ear. "I hate being grown up. When I was fourteen years old, I was head of dormitory. I could slipper anyone I liked. I think of those days with increasing frequency." He seemed near to tears.

"Come on, Bob," said Stephen.

"And that's another thing," said Bob. "Nobody calls me Robert. I don't like being called Bob. It's not a serious name."

140

"Oh, yes," said Stephen. "Sorry, er, Robert. It's just that we keep forgetting."

"No, it's not," said Bob. "People don't see me as a Robert. They look at me and they think, yes, there's one of the Bobs of this life. And you see, I'd thought, with this Confidan thing . . . ah, well. Mustn't be maudlin. At least I have my suit. Popped it into one of those two-hour cleaners this afternoon. Good as new, eh?" He grinned at Stephen, a cheerful doggy grin. One thing about Bob Buzzard, he always bounced back.

Jock McCannon loomed up, a rare sight in the pub. Not that he was an unsociable man exactly; it was just that he had never been able to come to terms with the minuscule size of pub doubles.

"Ah, Bob," he wheezed hoarsely.

Bob looked up in a resigned sort of way.

"Robert." Jock was swaying lightly on his feet, holding a double Bell's in each hand. "I want to thank you. I'll say no more. You know what I'm talking about." Then a puzzled expression came over his face.

"Odd," he said. He lifted his left hand towards his ear, apparently unaware that he was pouring whisky in a thin stream on to Bob's shoulder. "I feel a bit . . ." He lurched suddenly, and grabbed at the table for support. In so doing, he knocked Bob's pint glass of beer into his lap.

"Oh, my dear chap!" he said. "I'm frightfully sorry. That isn't your new suit, is it?"

"That's all right, Jock," said Bob. "Don't give it another thought."

Rust and Deep Throat

Rust is in a Greek restaurant off Charlotte Street. No, not *that* one. Way out of Rust's bracket. And anyway, Rust is paying the bill. Mind you, it's not one of your regular salmonella kebab joints either. It's just a nice little Greek restaurant where they know Rust. Quiet, too, with a bit round the corner out of the way. Rust is in the bit round

141

the corner out of the way. That's because he is with Deep Throat.

Deep Throat is a tall, handsome, well-fed sod in his forties, wearing a four-hundred-quid suit. Deep Throat does more than a little bit of moonlighting. And he does like a nice suit. Rust likes a nice suit too, but he hasn't got one. Rust is in his usual scruff. Either you wear a four-hundred-quid suit, or you look as if you don't give a fuck, that's Rust's philosophy of dress. If we were all like Rust, Alison Lurie's *Language of Clothes* would be a sodding thin book.

Alison Lurie is one of the few writers Rust really admires. He would like to meet Alison Lurie, though he doubts whether she would like to meet him. Still, why shouldn't he meet Alison Lurie, instead of having to meet his dreadful creative writing students, and Riddington, and Powell, and Deep Throat? He knows why. The Arts Council pays him to meet his dreadful creative writing students. The BBC pays him to meet Riddington and Powell. And Deep Throat is his Deep Throat.

"Well, we made that chap look pretty silly," says Deep Throat, referring to the second bottle of Retsina. "Have another, eh?"

"OK." Rust tries not to sound reluctant. Not that Rust is a stingy sod, not any more than the rest of us. It's just that he knows that on the third bottle of Retsina he's liable to pour out a load of maudlin stuff about Carol and her sodding chum and related subjects. Deep Throat is a wonderful listener, and Rust is not surprised that rich nutters pay Deep Throat to listen to their stuff. But with Rust it's supposed to be the other way round. He is paying Deep Throat to listen to Deep Throat's stuff.

"Well," says Deep Throat, lighting a cigar, "the main thing to bear in mind is that they're all fucking crazy. That's the main thing to bear in mind."

"Yes," says Rust. "I think I've grasped that, actually."

"Well, fine," says Deep Throat. He must be joking if he thinks he's getting away with that.

"I'd like a few specifics really," says Rust.

"Well, let's see. Broadly, you're doing fine. You got trank all right in the last one, and you know it's STD these days, not VD?"

"Yes, that's all right. What I had in mind was well, you know, stories."

"Thought that was your job," says Deep Throat.

Rust gives him a bit of hardeye. He is, after all, paying.

"Oh, yes," says Deep Throat. "Here's a nice one. Guy comes into the surgery, this is just last week. Little Chinky chap, think he was a Thai. Anyway, you know the sort, small but perfectly made. Well, it turns out he's worried about the size of his todgebar."

"His what?"

"His todgebar, you know, his dick."

"What did he call it?"

"How the fuck can I remember what he called it? Anyway, I chat to him a bit first, you always do that, doesn't really matter what you say, I told him about the amazing variation you get, and how they're all perfectly normal, and how the ladies don't mind what fucking size it is so long as you can get it in, you know, all basic warm reassuring stuff, and then I say, well now, why don't we get it out and have a look at it and I'll set your mind at rest. Get it out? He could hardly fucking find it! Fuck knows what my face must have looked like, smallest thing I've ever seen in my fucking life!"

Deep Throat is shaking with hysterical laughter, spilling Retsina all over his four-hundred-quid suit. Rust, who has had many moments of anxiety about his own todgebar, thanks Christ he never went so far as to take it to a GP.

"Any good?" says Deep Throat, when he has recovered.

"Wonderful," says Rust. "Shame I can't use it."

"Why not, man?"

"Well," lies Rust, "this is the BBC, not me, you understand, but I think they'd see it as racist for a start . . . and then you see the punch line is really a visual one . . . it's a million to one they wouldn't let you show it, and even if they did, we'd be into one hell of a casting problem."

"Ah," says Deep Throat. "See your point. I never watch the box myself." He thinks for a while.

"Here's a nice one," he says. "No ethnic minorities, not a todgebar in sight. You couldn't make a whole episode out of it, but there's a nice little sequence there, sort of light relief. It's very funny indeed. I'm seeing this heroin addict, right? Third year psychology student. Nice girl, but a bit unreliable; you often find that with heroin addicts."

"Yes, I thought that might be the case," says Rust rather wearily. Deep Throat has a very shaky grasp of what the layman can suss out for himself.

"Right," says Deep Throat. "So she's turned up for her appointment, but she's down in the waiting room. I'm running ten minutes late. Get rid of the girl I'm with, send down for the junkie. Just as I do that, the phone rings. I take the phone call, wonder what the fuck I'm supposed to be doing next, then I remember. The junkie hasn't come up. Call her up again. Nothing. Fuck, I think, I know what she's fucking done, she's gone to the bog and O.D.'d. Race down the fucking stairs and into the Ladies, got some funny looks too. Bend down and look underneath, there she is, on the floor, knickers round her ankles, spark out. Jammed against the door too. Can't get it open.

"So I climb over, and of course I have to slip and put my foot down the boghole. Fortunately she hadn't thought to take a shit before topping herself. Get the door open, drag her out. No pulse. Call the receptionist to get an ambulance, then I start the mouth to mouth resuscitation. After about five minutes, she starts breathing. And puking. All down the sleeve of my suit. This very suit, as a matter of fact. D'you like it? Took it into one of those two-hour cleaners, good as new, eh? Where was I? Oh, yes, feeling very good, quick action saves girl's life, all that. Then I remember what she was coming to see me about. Only viral hepatitis! Christ. You can die of that, you know, Ron.

"So I race up the bloody stairs again, into the dispensary for the Listerine. Take a big swig out of the bottle. Bloody funny Listerine. I call the nurse. What's the matter with this mouthwash? What mouthwash? This fucking mouthwash.

Oh, that, she says. That's not mouthwash. That's a urine sample, chap brought it in this morning. What's the urine sample for? Gonorrhea, she says with a winning smile. Like it?"

"Very much indeed," says Rust. It has everything. Pace, medical detail, humour, brutality, no extra sets, it could serve as a plot pivot; but he knows he can't use it. "I think, though, it might be a bit rich for the viewers' blood."

"Bit rich for my blood too," says Deep Throat. He lifts his glass of Retsina to the light, chuckles reminiscently, and drinks deeply. Somehow Rust doesn't fancy any more Retsina.

"I was thinking of something, well, a little more low key than that, actually," says Rust. "Sorry to be a bore."

"It is supposed to be funny, this thing?" says Deep Throat.

"Oh, yes," says Rust.

"Well, I don't know," says Deep Throat. "Have you ever thought you've got a bit of a problem, Ron?" Rust has many problems. Which one could Deep Throat be thinking of?

"Medical practice," says Deep Throat, "it really isn't very funny, not very often. Most of it is boredom and routine, and seeing a lot of people when they're not feeling quite the thing. Not much fun at all."

"Yes," says Rust. "I've got that."

"Oh, good, I'm glad you've got that," says Deep Throat. "Well, d'you think you could get this too? The rest of it is even worse, like telling pretty girls you'd like to fuck that their bone marrow is all rotted to buggery, and telling well set-up young fellows like you and me that they've got malignant growths the size of fucking footballs in their stomachs, and there's absolutely fuck all you can do about it, thank you doctor for being so honest, well good afternoon, next please. Sorry."

"It's all right," says Rust. "I knew there was that problem; just hadn't encapsulated it so vividly."

"What are you doing about it?"

"Evading it," says Rust honestly. "Skating round it.

I never mention it, and neither does anyone at Series and Serials because it scares us all shitless."

"Yes," says Deep Throat. "That's what I'd do if I had the chance. Glad we've cleared that one up, Ron. I'd been wondering about it a bit."

Rust feels terrible.

"How's life, anyway?" says Deep Throat. "Getting much?"

"Not a lot," says Rust. This, as we know, is an understatement. Circumstances of life, the Lowlands air, and thinking about illness have so combined to work upon Rust's libido that he hasn't even had a wank in weeks.

"Wise man," says Deep Throat. "Lot of nasty things about these days." Deep Throat is silent for a few moments, then he says: "I know, Ron. Think this might be a poignant little plot for you. Do you happen to know anything about contact tracing?"

5

CONTACT TRACER

Jock McCannon had come through. Strange, strange, the capacity for the human psyche to heal itself. The doctor had seen the dark night of the soul, and almost surrendered to it. Now it was morning again, and faint messages were beginning to hum along the frail tendrils of Jock's battered nervous system. There was hope; there was hope. And Black Bob's pills had certainly helped a bit. That nasty new bruise on his forehead would soon subside. He was alive again. That was the main thing. He stood at his window looking down at the early morning scene and realised that he had another chapter in him after all.

The nuns were at the rubbish skips again, and now Jock looked down on them with something like affection. Perhaps he had been wrong: perhaps they weren't symbolic Shakespearean crows at all. Perhaps they bore witness to the indomitable tenacity of the human spirit. He cleared his throat, pressed the start button, and began to speak.

"The Sick University: Part Two. A new morning. A new beginning. McCannon was sick unto death, but now he lives again. He's on his feet. He is sober. He even feels stirrings of the old creative sap. He looks down on the sick university, and sees it transformed before his eyes. Everywhere he looks, he sees the germination of creative contact."

Below him, the rubbish van had arrived. Instead of fleeing before it as they had on previous occasions, the nuns were standing their ground. They were shouting at the driver and shaking their fists. The driver was shouting back. The nuns would not be moved. The rubbish van was moving off slowly. The nuns stood on the skips and threw bricks at it. Jock turned from the window, his eyes alight.

"Tendrils of human communication reach out to each other," he rumbled. "A spark jumps a gap . . . contact! And the fragile, infinitely powerful link is made. New insight is born." He collapsed heavily on to the sofa.

"And that is the germ of my message to you, Vice-Chancellor," he said. "Seek out and foster the creative human contact, and your University will bloom again!" Good. That would do for a little while. It was always a mistake to rush things. Jock McCannon closed his eyes. It was time for a little nap.

Ernest Hemmingway, Vice Chancellor of Lowlands University, was jogging round the lake in a bright red tracksuit. This was a new departure for him, but one he intended to pursue with vigour and determination. Furie had been bending his ear with a lot of very convincing stuff about the biochemistry of creativity, and if there was one thing a VC had to be these days, it was creative. Lowlands had survived the first round of cuts when other places had been hacked to pieces, but only through a bewilderingly Machiavellian restructuring plan and some highly creative accounting. But the second round of cuts was looming up already, and that would take something extra. Ernie didn't know what that would be, not yet. But apparently pounding round the lake would stimulate the blood flow to the brain, or something. Unless Furie was playing a cruel practical joke. But that didn't bear thinking about.

He panted to his secretary, Dorothy, who was standing on the lakeside well wrapped up in scarf and coat. She clicked off the stopwatch.

"Seventeen minutes dead, Vice-Chancellor."

"Are you sure?" He couldn't actually be getting slower, could he?

"Sorry Vice-Chancellor," she said.

"Right," said Ernie. "Give me the memotape." He strode away from her towards his looming fortress, dictating as he went.

"Sir Roy Krafft-Ebbing, S.M. Electronics. Dear Roy, I was very shocked to read your remarks about the indifference and hostility of the Cambridge establishment, and I wondered if you'd be interested in coming down to Lowlands and giving us the once-over . . ."

Stephen and Lyn were in bed in Stephen's flat. Their early morning run had been rescheduled to the early evening; now they had something better to do in the early mornings.

"Hey, you," she said.

"Mm?"

"It gets better. It really does."

"Yes, I think so too."

"Good," she said, snuggling into him. "Be awful if one of us thought so and the other one didn't. And I'll tell you another thing. You're my very best client."

"Really?"

"Really. Who would have thought that Doctor Daker once had a touch taboo? You are going to figure very prominently in my research report."

He struggled up. "What?"

"Don't worry, Doc," she said. "Names will be changed to protect the innocent."

"Lyn," he said, after a bit. "Your . . . other clients. Do you . . . I mean do you employ the same therapeutic techniques?"

"I never discuss my clients with my other clients, Stephen."

"No, no," he said. "Of course not." She moved away to get a better look at him. Her hair was a mess and her face was pink and blotchy from his stubble. She looked wonderful, but also rather stern.

"You're not getting jealous, are you?" she said.

"No. Really."

"When I'm with you, I'm with you."

"Yes, I know."

149

"Yeah," she said. "You bloody well ought to." She sat up and stretched. "Hey, you know when you were in school, did you have to read all those Shakespeare plays and things?"

"One or two," said Stephen.

"Where the bloke's after the wrong girl, so some wise Duke or something slips another girl into bed with him after dark, and he can't tell the difference?"

"I don't think anything like that happened in *Julius Caesar*," said Stephen.

"Well, the point I'm making is, Shakespeare was a wally. Everyone's totally different like that. Everyone's got a sexual idiolect. I'd know you anywhere. Straight away. With you . . . I dunno. It's like *listening* to you. I mean, it's like listening to *you*. Someone really ought to do some work on sexual idiolects. I think I might have a go at it myself in fact . . . what's the matter?"

"Nothing, really," he said. "It's just that, occasionally . . . I mean don't get me wrong, I feel tremendously lucky and grateful, and all that, but just now and then I do feel, well, a bit like one of those smoking beagles."

"An experimental subject."

"Well, yes."

"We're all experimental subjects, Stephen."

"In life's cruel laboratory," he said. "That's the sort of thing that Jock says." Suddenly he felt depressed for the first time in weeks.

"Hey," she said. "Listen, you. I was trying to tell you you're special."

"Oh," he said.

"I'd say more," she said, "only it's against the rules."

Stephen had to get up quite soon after that, because he had an early morning meeting. Not the usual ramshackle group practice meeting in Jock's cave, but a rather dauntingly high-powered affair in the VC's office, and God knew what it was all going to be about. It certainly called for a good suit and a close shave though. The trouble was, he didn't have a good suit, not having been able to provide Hamburger with a good result. Still. He had his integrity,

150

and that, surely, must count for something with Ernest Hemmingway.

At half-past eight they were all sitting round in the VC's office, waiting for the great man to appear. Stephen had never been there before, and gazed round with interest. Everything in it looked as if it had cost a great deal of money about twenty years ago. There were several paintings of stripes, which seemed to Stephen as fine as any of their kind, and a number of not all that small sculptures with very sharp edges, sharp enough to constitute a safety hazard. The vacant desk was curved, and not more than ten or twelve feet across.

He didn't have time to notice much more, because Dorothy came in with a trolley of drinks. The selection was much sparser than in the Vice-Chancellor's Lodge; in fact just about as sparse as it could be.

"Apple juice?" said Dorothy. Dorothy was good at keeping a straight face.

"Thank you," said Dr Rose Marie, taking one as if it were her usual tipple, which it might be as far as Stephen knew.

"Oh, er, yes, thanks," said Stephen. He took a sip. It was all right, actually. Jock McCannon refused with a pained look and a feeble wave of his paw.

"Apple juice?" said Bob Buzzard crossly. "I'm not a hippy."

"Sorry, Dr Buzzard," said Dorothy. "It's his new thing. You know. Health."

"Oh, yes, that," said Bob gloomily.

"He's in another meeting at the moment but I think it's nearly over. He's only three minutes behind schedule, his morning work-out overran a bit."

Jock sighed noisily.

"Are you all right, Dr McCannon?"

"Oh, yes, my dear," said Jock, treating her to the old cadaverous grin, "just a little weary from my weight training, you know."

The door from the inner office swung open rather violently, and the Vice-Chancellor bounced in, vivid as a little hummingbird in his red tracksuit. He had somebody with him. A rather glamorous-looking woman of perhaps forty, in dark glasses.

"Morning, excellent, good of you all to come along," he said. "You won't have met Dr Theodoulou. Our most recent appointment. Reader in Interdisciplinary Studies. This is our medical team, Daniela."

Daniela Theodoulou smiled a warm intimate smile at each member of the medical team. "Nice to know you," she said. Her voice was husky, with a strong Italian accent, and the way she spoke suggested infinite possibilities.

"Inter what was that?" said Jock.

"Interdisciplinary Studies," said Daniela Theodoulou. As if that said it all.

"Daniela's opening up some new lines of investigation along the interfaces between subject disciplines," said Hemmingway briskly. "Microbiology and Business Studies. Anthropology and Electronics."

"Anywhere we see a growth potential," she said, smiling. "I like to think of myself as a catalyst, you know. See a possibility, make something happen. And now I must excuse myself. I have to go and talk about cell cultures to the Law Faculty. See you around, maybe."

"Well," said Ernest Hemmingway when she had gone, "I've had a look at your research profiles, and by and large they stand up pretty well, some could do better. Need more projects like your Hamburger thing, Buzzard, pull in some overseas funding. How's it coming along?"

Bob was magnificent. "Er, coming together, Vice-Chancellor, and I think I've got something else that might be very viable."

"Good, good. What?"

"Er, ah . . ." Bob's face was blank for a moment, but only for a moment. "A simple diagnosis, indications, storage-and-retrieval programme for seventeen minor ailments. All on a floppy disk. We could market it under the Lowlands University Software Imprint."

The Vice-Chancellor blinked once or twice. "That's rather good, Buzzard. That's the kind of thinking we need.

You see? Hard-nosed research-based packageable product. What we're looking for are new developments that'll involve the new technologies, bringing together creative research insights from the University, and harnessing them to the new industries. Your floppy disk's an example of that, Buzzard."

Bob beamed ecstatically. "Thank you, Vice-Chancellor."

"A very small example," said Hemmingway severely. "I'm looking for some large-scale breakthroughs, and my instinct is that they'll happen along the interfaces. Creative contacts. Interdisciplinary networks. New paradigms. That's why I'm seeing everybody. New ideas can happen anywhere."

The Vice-Chancellor paused to draw breath. Some of the words and phrases he had been using had only very recently entered his vocabulary, the word paradigm, whatever that might be, only five minutes ago, but Daniela Theodoulou had made paradigms sound damned exciting, and if she could, so could he. She was only a woman, after all. Damned exciting woman, though. However. Time to wake them up a bit.

"One short-term thing," he said. "Last year, the *Sunday Times* published a slanderous piece called 'Frank Profiles of British Universities.' You'll remember what it said about Lowlands?"

"Ah, yes," said Jock maliciously, "I think I can remember the very words, Ernie."

"Good for pure maths," said the little man in the red tracksuit, "good for cybernetics, otherwise forget it, and by the way the roofs leak. Not very inspiring is it? Any positive thoughts on how to enhance our profile?" There was a short pause.

"We do have a very high standard of care and counselling," said Stephen tentatively.

"Do we?" said Hemmingway, obviously astonished. "I'm delighted to hear it. Where's your evidence?"

"Er . . . very low drop-out rate . . . and we have one of the lowest suicide rates in the country."

"Not *the* lowest?" said Hemmingway keenly.

"Not quite, no," said Stephen apologetically.

"Well, work on it, Doctor, er . . . anyway it's something. I think we should get it in the press, don't you? High profile it. The Caring University. Fine note to end on." He glanced at his watch. "Thank you all very much."

"Eh, my new book, Ernie . . ." began Jock.

"Another time, Jock. Well, very good to see you all," he said, beginning to shoo them with little goose-girl gestures towards the door, "and don't forget the interfaces. Seek out the creative contacts!"

Back in his cave, Jock McCannon thought long and deeply. The transcript of his tapes had come in from the typist. He leafed through the eloquent pages, every one pregnant with painful insights. Then he turned back to the title page.

The Sick University

by

Jock McCannon

Sighing heavily, Jock struck out the word "sick" and replaced it by the word "caring". Then he added:

Dedicated, with affectionate
admiration, to Ernie Hemmingway,
true forger of creative contacts.

Then he put his pen down.

"Oh, the things that we do," he said, "the things that we do!"

"Jeannie McAllister?" said Stephen.

"That's right," she said. She had big spectacles, an intelligent face, a confident smile, and a Glasgow accent.

"We don't seem to have seen much of you, Miss McAllister."

"You can call me Jeannie. No, I'm never ill. So, I thought I'd come and see you anyway."

"Well, that's nice," said Stephen, rather puzzled. The "Come and see us when you're well" invitation had inspired a good number of visits from neurotic or simply lonely students in the first three weeks, but the number had dwindled now, and Jeannie McAllister didn't look either neurotic or lonely.

"Actually, it's a bit cheeky," she said, not looking embarrassed at all. "I'm doing this for low life."

"Low life?" said Stephen, thrown for a moment. "Oh, *Low Life!*"

"That's right."

Low Life was the student newspaper, an aggressively downmarket weekly tabloid produced to very high, indeed practically professional standards.

"I'm on the staff," said Jeannie McAllister. "Well, I more or less am the staff." She smiled shyly.

"Oh, er . . . well done."

"Thank you, Dr Daker. We'd like to do a feature article about you actually, sort of in-depth interview. You've made ever such a good impression on the students."

"Oh, no," said Stephen, embarrassed. "Really."

"Oh, come on, you know you have. I was hoping I could find out what the secret is. You know, how you put the patient at her ease, the little clues you look for, how you get the rapport going, all that. It would be fascinating."

Stephen felt desperately flattered, and tried very hard not to show it. She was very sweet, this girl, very naïve, he had to remember that and let her down lightly.

"I'm afraid it would be unprofessional, Jeannie. Really, I'm sorry, but it would cut across the confidentiality of the doctor/patient relationship."

"Ah, well," she said, smiling. "Worth a try. I'm sorry, Doctor Daker, s'pose I just didn't think about it."

"And honestly," said Stephen, "there isn't any secret. Except that all of us in this practice believe in longer than usual consultations, and we're committed to treating the patient as a whole person. And that, we think, contributes to the extremely low suicide and drop-out rate in the

155

University. One of the lowest in the country." That was it, of course! He could do his bit for the VC here and now, he could begin the high-profiling of the Caring University!

"Really?" she said. "That's smashing. Just let me get that down, shorthand's terrible . . ."

Stephen benevolently watched her scribbling. She raised her head.

"Don't happen to know who's got the highest suicide rate, do you?"

"Er . . . I don't think it would be fair to tell you," said Stephen.

She put her pencil down. "You're very discreet, aren't you?" She seemed so eager. It was a shame to disappoint her. But he was going to.

"Doctors have to be, Jeannie," he said, feeling very mature, and wishing he had a snuff-box.

"Yes, of course," she said. "What's your biggest problem, then? VD?"

"Sorry?" he said, alarmed.

"I didn't mean you personally, Dr Daker."

He attempted a middle-aged chuckle, with only partial success. "No, no, of course not. Well, it's not really a problem in the University either, Jeannie."

"You mean you don't get any cases at all?"

"Well, naturally," said Stephen uneasily, "in a community like this one, preponderantly young adults living away from home, and a high level of social interaction, it would be very surprising to find a complete absence of STD."

Jeannie McAllister was scribbling again. "STD?" she said. "And that's . . . ?"

"Sexually transmitted diseases, but the point I was making was the very low incidence here. Er, in fact I really don't think it's worth mentioning it, Jeannie."

She really was scribbling quite a lot, but eventually she stopped, to his mild relief, and looked up. "No," she said. "I shouldn't think we will."

As soon as she had gone, Rose Marie came in and sat down. "That wasn't Jeannie McAllister, was it?"

156

"Yes, it was."

"Stephen, you know I wouldn't pry into anything confidential . . ."

"Oh, she wasn't ill," said Stephen. "She wanted something for the student paper, so I told her all the good news. Care and counselling, all that. Bit of luck, really, her coming in just after what the VC said. I think we might have done ourselves a bit of good."

"I hope so," said Rose Marie.

"Intelligent girl, I thought," said Stephen. "Sorry. Woman. Person. You know. What's the matter?"

"She is bright, yes," said Rose Marie. "Not very scrupulous, though. You do know she's a stringer for the *Sun*?"

"Good Lord, really?"

"Still," said Rose Marie, "I'm sure you were very discreet."

"Yes, of course I was," said Stephen. "I simply told her what an excellent practice we run here. More or less."

The headline said:

HERPES? NO HASSLE, SAYS DR BLUE-EYES

Below the headline was a photograph of Stephen and Lyn smiling at each other sitting at a bar table. The message was clear: Dr Daker and his girl friend were herpes sufferers and proud of it; yet somehow none of the words actually said that. Jeannie McAllister *was* a bright girl. The copy below managed to suggest that suicide and the contraction of sexually transmitted diseases were the chief leisure occupations on the Lowlands campus, and that the medical team regarded these manifestations with cheerful insouciance. Though the words didn't actually say that, either.

"This is terrible," said Stephen. He was sitting with Lyn at a table in the bar, but he wasn't smiling.

"When could they have got that photo?" said Lyn.

"God knows."

"It's really nice of you," she said.

"But it's a complete distortion of what I told her!"

She took his hand. "Relax, Stephen, it's not really that bad. If you read it carefully, you can see it's saying there *isn't* much VD and there *aren't* many suicides."

"Who's going to read it carefully though? I mean look at that. 'Dial STD for Doctor Blue-Eyes.'"

"Come on, Stephen, it's quite funny really. Doctor Blue-Eyes, that's nice."

"D'you think the VC will find it funny?" said Stephen gloomily.

"He won't mind," she said. "He'll probably cut your picture out and put it in his wallet. Everyone likes Doctor Blue-Eyes." She grinned at him. Yes, maybe he was exaggerating. And there were, after all, more important things in the world than what Ernest Hemmingway thought about him.

"I think what Doctor Blue-Eyes needs tonight is a good steak and rather a lot of red wine, and a bit of tender loving care," he said.

There was a bit of a pause. Then she said: "Ah. Snag."

"What?"

"Well, I can't. Sorry. Promised someone."

Somehow he couldn't make himself smile reassuringly. "Yes, all right," he said.

"You're usually on duty on Thursday evenings."

"Yes, I know. Don't worry. It's fine. Honestly. I'll do some work."

"Oh, dear," she said. "Your face. I can't stand this. Look. After I've finished with the someone, would you like me to come round and creep into your bed? Might be a bit late, mind."

"Oh yes, Lyn, I'd like that very much."

Roy Krafft-Ebbing's reply was disappointingly vague, but Ernie Hemmingway had other fish to fry. Sakamoto Corporation had shown a very lively interest in the feelers Ernie had put out; such a lively interest that here he was, down by the lake with six of their top executives at eight

158

o'clock in the morning. Sakamoto executives liked early morning starts just as much as Ernie Hemmingway did. Dorothy, his secretary, didn't like early morning starts, but he didn't have to consult her wishes, did he? This morning, which was only a shade on the nippy side, oops, she was making her point by dressing as for an Arctic expedition. Hm. If it wasn't that she knew too much he'd jolly well let her go, see how she liked that.

"And here, gentlemen," he said heartily, "is where we shall be having our new Science Park." There he had to wait while the interpreter johnnie did his bit, and one of the inscrutable chaps responded.

"Science Park yes," said the interpreter. "Woburn Abbey, Lions of Longleat, very nice to visit. Mr Sakamoto asks particularly will there be crocodiles in the lake here?" All the Japs rolled about laughing. God, foreigners.

"No, no, gentlemen," he said, forcing a chuckle. "A Science Park is a dense concentration of high-technology research and development labs. Not crocodiles, gentlemen. Portakabins!"

"Ah, we see now," said the interpreter johnnie. "In Japan we call that Industrial Estate or Row of Factories."

"No, no, not the same thing at all. Well, not quite. Are there any more questions?" The little woman in black said something that made them all laugh. God, this was tedious. He'd want a knighthood at least if this came off. "Yes?"

"Miss Hitomi asks when will we be meeting Doctor Blue-Eyes?"

"Ha, ha, very good!" laughed Hemmingway, who was very close to rage. "I'm afraid our schedule's a bit too crowded for that, ha ha. We'll be going over to Cybernetics next, and then you can meet our new Reader in Inter-disciplinary Studies.

"I, eh, I do have a patient with me, Ernie," said Jock, winking at the Indian student who was crouching nervously next to a stuffed badger on the horsehair sofa. "Well, of course, I realise the importance of the matter, Vice-Chancellor. Yes, yes, I do see that. Did she really, I must tell him that. No, no, you're quite right, it's not a joking matter." Jock took the receiver away from his aching ear and muffled it inside his hairy old jacket.

"I shan't keep you waiting long, my dear chap," he said to the patient. After a moment or two he took the telephone out again and waited for a momentary pause. "But Ernie, if you read it carefully you'll see that it's very complimentary about the practice, and indeed . . ." He was cut off by another long jabbering stream of complaint from his leader. He put the receiver down on the floor.

"Would you care for something to read, old fellow?" he said, indicating a pile of medical journals on the coffee table. The student smiled gratefully, and opened one of them. The article was about cancers of the penis. He replaced it on the table.

"Yes, Vice-Chancellor, I'll make absolutely sure," said Jock. "Ah. He's gone. Vile wee man. Now then, my dear chap. Tell me all about it." But the patient seemed quite unable to speak.

"Sore throat?"

'No.''

"Well, what, then?"

"I'm sorry," said the patient. "I'm . . . too ashamed."

"My dear fellow," said Jock, "you mustn't be. Whatever it is, you can be sure I've seen many cases before, and if it's the kind of thing I think it is, I've had it myself as a young man, and look at me now! Fit as a flea!"

The student looked rather doubtfully at Jock. It wasn't fatal, then, but it looked as if it was pretty serious.

"Well, come along," said Jock. "Don't be shy. Out with it like a man, eh?" The student obeyed.

"Eh, what are you, ah, didn't quite mean it like, oh well. Saves time," said Jock. "Ah, yes. *Yes*. I *see*. Yes, *indeed*."

The patient was thin, pretty, shy, pale, and scared out of her wits. And she had completely run out of things to say about her common cold symptoms.

"Well," said Stephen, "They *are* very irritating, these colds that won't go away. Not really an awful lot we can do,

160

but I will prescribe you something to relieve that sinus headache."

"Thank you," she said. No preliminary shuffles. She had something else to talk about all right.

"Everything else OK?" he said. He found it best to start while he was writing, then look up with the last question.

"Life in general?" He looked up at her. "Anything else you'd like to talk to me about?"

"Well, um, yes, there is actually. I mean it's probably nothing, but . . ." she tailed off.

"You've probably noticed something unusual," said Stephen encouragingly, "and you'd like your mind set at rest."

'Yes."

"And?"

"Um . . . it's a bit embarrassing."

Bob Buzzard was lumbered with a truculent oik who looked as if he hadn't had a bath for a week. Ah, well. Get it over with as soon as possible.

"So it's a bit embarrassing, is it?" said Bob. "Below the waist, I take it."

"That's right, yes."

"Front or back?"

"Er, front."

"Front only. Sure?" said Bob, giving his Deputy Dawg, full strength.

"I do know the difference," said the truculent oik, truculently.

"You must be one of our more able students," said Bob. "So we've got a bit of trouble with the old trouser snake, have we? Well, well, well."

"And how long is it since you noticed the discharge?" asked Rose Marie gently.

The patient, a plump girl with a blotchy face, had obviously been crying, and was sniffing now. "About a week. I was hoping it would just go away, but it won't."

"Yes, I see. And you were very sensible to come in when

161

you did. Now, d'you feel anything else? Any burning sensation when you go to the loo?" The girl nodded. Not bad. She had quite an interesting bone structure under those puffy cheeks. All she needed was to take charge of herself and learn to be a woman. "And that's been going on for about the same number of days?"

The girl started to cry again. "You know what it is, don't you? It's something awful, isn't it?"

Rose Marie's heart went out to this victim of the phallocracy. "Listen to me, Clare," she said. "The chances are it's nothing to be frightened of, and nothing to be ashamed of. It does sound from what you say as if you've got a little infection there. And it's likely to be the sort of thing that we can pass on when we're making love." Her manner was quite excruciatingly sisterly.

"You mean VD, don't you?"

"That's an awfully emotive word, don't you think? I'd like you to think of it as something like a throat infection, a bit irritating, a bit painful, but very minor, and easily treatable." She smiled encouragingly. "Anyway, let's find out something for certain first. Do you know how to examine yourself, by the way?"

"No, I don't."

"Well," smiled Rose Marie, "I can show you how to do that at the same time. It's really very easy."

Stephen, like most doctors, was terrified of accusations from neurotic patients, and he always asked a nurse to stand by when he was making a full examination. Not that this patient was likely to be difficult: just very, very shy, upset, ashamed, and guilty. And there just wasn't any way of making it a pleasant experience for her. As Bob Buzzard said, give them a reassuring smile and they think you've got a hard-on like Cleopatra's bloody Needle. Stephen would have liked to have seen Bob's version of the reassuring smile.

"OK," he said. "Fine. All over." It was all right to smile now. "If you'd just like to get dressed now?" He walked over to the sink to wash his hands. "Well, you were absolutely right to come in. There is something there, we'll know for certain in a couple of days. It's just a minor infection, nothing to get upset about, and you'll be rid of it completely in a couple of weeks. I think we ought to have a urine sample and do a blood test to be absolutely on the safe side. Maureen will take care of that for you."

Maureen came over and stood by him. "NSU, is it Dr Daker?" she said in an undertone.

"Yes, I think so. Why?"

"Just that Dr Rose Marie has another one the same next door."

"Non-specific urethritis," boomed Jock grandiloquently. "How very curious. Yes."

His patient had gone very pale.

"Oh, don't be alarmed, my dear chap, it's a fine phrase to roll around the tongue, but it's a trivial ailment. One of the minor penalties exacted on us by the goddess Aphrodite. And all it requires of you, my dear fellow, is that you take four tetracyclin a day, abstain from carnal pleasures for a fortnight, and tell your ladylove – tell *all* your ladyloves – that they should abstain likewise, and come and have a chat with me. Mmm?"

"I've only got one ladylove, doctor," said his patient.

"I admire your restraint," said Jock.

"And we only did it once."

"My dear fellow," said Jock, "what absolutely rotten luck!" He paused, and frowned. "I wonder." He went over to the intercom. "Bob, do you have the records of the last day or two on your wee machine?"

"Got mine on floppy disk, as you know. Haven't looked at the others yet, still in note form," said Bob's voice.

"Just bundle them all up like a good chap, would you, and drop them in before you go?"

"Nothing special, was there, Jock?"

"No, no, no. A little light reading for the wee small hours, that's all."

Dawn in the Sick University. The head of the practice was standing at his window. He had been up all night, calling on those strange reserves of energy that lie deep within us all. And by God, he needed them now. This was a time for greatness. He switched on his recorder and spoke.

"Seek out creative contacts at the interfaces! Ah, Hemmingway, Hemmingway, you troubled midget, how your own words mock at you! Mine too, mine too. Oh yes, tendrils of human communication are reaching out to each other all right!" He crossed the room to the huge sheet of paper he had pinned to the wall. Large scrawled circles depicted the various sub-divisions of the University: Arts, Social Sciences, Admin, Physical and Engineering Sciences, Catering. Here and there he had planted little red drawing pins. "Tendrils of human communication. Yes." He picked up a thick marker pen and began to draw lines connecting the scrawled circles.

"From Arts to Social Sciences, from Sociology to Catering, the feelers go out; a spark jumps a gap . . . contact! Proof, if we're seeking it, that God does indeed exist, and that he has it in for each and every one of us! The enemy is amongst us. The little foreign bodies are in our midst. But Jock McCannon won't lie down without a fight!" He switched off the recorder, went over to the telephone, and dialled.

Stephen rolled over in bed and picked the phone up. "Hello. Lyn? What? Dr Daker speaking . . . oh, it's you, Jock." Oh, God, he thought. Jock was apt to ring up in the small hours of the morning, just for a little chat, or to tell him some story he'd remembered about Ronnie Laing, or read him a bit of his book. Quite touching, really, but it did tend to get in the way of one's dream life, and more recently one's sex life too.

"What?" he said. "*Another* early morning meeting? Is it the VC again? Oh. What is it then, Jock? It's not something I've done, is it? What d'you mean you hope not? Right, yes, of course. No problem, Jock. See you at eight thirty then."

Bob Buzzard was late for the emergency meeting. Not like Bob; hated to be late for anything, liked to get ahead of the opposition. But the bloody traffic had been unbelievable, suicidal frogs weren't in it. By the time he got to Jock's room, there they all were waiting for him, little Miss Blue-Eyes, Marie Celeste, the colleen from the bogs of Shannon, and the old fart himself, striding moodily about with a stick behind his back, for all the world like Bob's old TA major.

"Take a seat, Buzzard," said the old fart. Then he spoke into his tatty old recorder. "Briefing began at . . . eight forty-two."

"Have you seen the waiting room?" said Bob. "I could hardly get through. Place was full of bodies."

"Live ones, I trust," said Rose Marie.

"Think so," said Bob. "Hard to tell in this university, of course. What's the matter with the appointments system? Why doesn't old Carmen send them all away?"

"I think you'll find they're all emergency cases," said Jock heavily. "I believe this practice may be facing its greatest crisis since 1974 . . . yes, the enemy is amongst us. He turned to the window again, and stared out over the stricken campus.

"He's flipped, hasn't he?" said Bob to Stephen in an undertone. "He's gone gaga. Seen it coming, of course."

"Bob," said Stephen. "You didn't happen to see anyone with NSU symptoms at evening surgery, did you?"

"Yes, I did, oddly enough," said Bob. "Chap from Cybernetics, and that rather jolly little thing who runs the tea bar in the SCR."

"Maureen!" said Jock without moving. Maureen went over and put a red drawing pin on Cybernetics and another on Catering.

"Ah," said Bob. "I see. Snakebite."

"Thirteen cases in two days," said Jock, "two of whom have cheerfully owned up to a surprisingly large circle of intimate friends. Ladies and gentlemen, we have an epidemic on our hands!"

"Aren't you dramatising this just a little, Jock?" said Rose Marie. "Thirteen cases hardly constitutes an epidemic."

"But when you take the contacts into account," said Stephen, "and the contacts of the contacts . . . "

"And the contacts of the contacts of the contacts," said Jock darkly. "Will the line stretch out to the crack of doom? A university is a network, a community of interacting scholars, a multiplicity of interfaces. Consider how a new intellectual concept spreads and gathers strength within the academic community. Well, it's very much the same with non-specific urethritis, except it spreads a damn sight faster than post-structuralist poetics. And it falls to us. The five of us in this room today. To meet this challenge head on. Without publicity, without assistance. And to win." His shoulders were back. The clear blue alcoholic eyes were blazing. It was a Churchillian moment. "Any questions?"

"Jock, if it's really that serious," said Rose Marie, "don't you think we should make use of the special clinic at the City General?"

"They do tend to be a bit brutal there, Rose," said Stephen.

"And quite right, too," said Bob. "Students who waste the taxpayer's money thrashing about in the pit are asking for a bit of brutality. And in any case, I for one did not enter this profession to become a pox doctor. Yes, absolutely, Rose Marie. Let's pack the lot of them off to the Special, and get on with our lives."

"Dr Buzzard, I am surprised at you!" Jock McCannon was shaking with anger.

"What's the matter?" said Bob, alarmed.

"Where is your Falklands spirit? We are a Task Force, man! This is our war, our struggle, the honour of the practice stands or falls by the way we handle this crisis. We must go it alone." He had brought his face very close to Bob's and spoken very loudly indeed.

"Yes, I see. Right. Fine. Sorry, Jock," said Bob, wiping the flecks of spittle off his cheeks.

"There are also questions of policy involved," said Jock more moderately. "I have not been up all night for nothing. Imagine the publicity if the Special Clinic were suddenly to be inundated with Lowlands University

166

students. The local press would pick it up. And then the national press."

"The *Sunday Times* guide," said Rose Marie.

"Oh Lord, yes," said Stephen. "Lowlands University. Good for mathematics, cybernetics, and non-specific urethritis."

"Exactly," said Jock. "If we handle it within the confines of the practice we'll be able to follow up the contacts much more quickly. And operate a policy of absolute secrecy."

"You'll never keep a thing like this quiet," said Maureen.

"No defeatists on my team. Absolute secrecy. Nobody must be informed."

"Not even the Vice-Chancellor?" asked Stephen.

"Especially not the Vice-Chancellor! If we can win this battle, we shall have saved his University for him and he'll never know. Our only reward will be that when the chips were down . . ." He put an arm round Maureen's shoulders. ". . . we did it our way! Any questions? Right then, let's go to work on this!"

An epidemic of any sexually transmitted disease is not much fun for the doctor. It starts with a trickle of tongue-tied, anxious people; the key phrases are "a bit embarrassing" and "rather personal"; and there is plenty of time to reassure and educate the patients and send them on their way relatively happy and secure. Then the trickle gradually develops into a flood, or as Bob Buzzard put it, whole departments going down like dominoes, and there's not time to do anything but look at the symptoms, treat them locally, prescribe, and get the contacts; then the contacts come in, puzzled and innocent, as often as not with no symptoms at all, and you have to tell them no, they haven't won the Irish Sweepstake after all. After two or three days the doctor's dreams are full of tubes and tunnels and journeys to the centre of the earth, huge looming toadstools and crumbling pillars, floating sentence fragments: little grey card, back for a check-up, just squeeze hard on this. . . .

By half-past eight on Friday evening Stephen was grey-faced, exhausted, drained, washed out, done for. He pulled on his coat and walked like a somnambulist down the corridor. He had seen them all already, seen them all, and he didn't want to see any more of them. Rose Marie's door was open, and he looked in. She seemed as calm and composed as ever, sorting out her notes on the day's work.

"Come in, Stephen," she said. "I've just finished. What about you?"

"Yes, just now."

"You look tired," she said. "It's been quite a week, hasn't it?"

"Yes it has. And it's not just the extra work, is it? It's really . . . well, it's quite distressing, some of it."

She looked at him curiously. "You find examining all those vaginas distasteful?"

"No, no, it's not that," he said hastily. "That's not the problem . . . though it can get a bit disorientating after a while. You know, the way a word becomes absurd if you repeat it often enough. But not distressing."

"What, then?"

He walked over to the window. It was dark outside. They were all out there, all the patients he'd seen that week. "It's the emotional reactions," he said. "Like the girls with one steady boy friend. They can't understand how it's happened. They don't *want* to understand how it happened. And then they do understand how it happened. And you can give them tetracyclin to make them better, but it doesn't make them feel better inside. And that's, well . . . really sad."

"Illness is one of the things men do to women," said Rose Marie lightly.

"It's not always that way round," he said. "It's sad whichever way it happens. I keep thinking about all those painful conversations that must be going on out there."

Rose Marie took her glasses off and turned right round to look at him.

"You're such a bleeding heart, aren't you, Stephen? Don't you ever get angry?"

"What about?"

"Well, it's obvious," she said briskly. "This NSU thing is

168

a classic demonstration of the University as a phallocentric hierarchy. The professor and his female research assistant, the catering manager with droit de seigneur over his waitresses, third year men and first year women, the steady boyfriend with a bit on the side. And, of course, they all have to be on the Pill, because that's the way the boys like it. More comfy for them and less hassle. D'you realise that if the sheath came back into fashion we wouldn't even *have* an epidemic?"

She was right, of course. Well, he supposed she was right. It was just that none of it seemed to relate to him. The catering manager had been as scared and as sad as his waitresses; more than once, it had been the steady girl-friend who had turned out to have not one but several bits on the side. Yes. And out there in the darkness, all those awkward, fumbling conversations, darling I think we ought to have a talk first; but I don't understand what we're talking about; why do I have to go, there's nothing wrong with me; you do still love me don't you . . . Yes. All that. He turned from the window. "I suppose total chastity would be even better."

"Well, I don't think I'd propose anything quite as radical as that," she said smiling.

He didn't answer.

"You were joking, weren't you, Stephen?"

"I'm not sure. It's . . . a bit of a downer, as Bob would say."

"Yes, it is." He was sure she knew exactly what he was thinking.

"Ah, well. Better get along, I suppose," he said. "Jock seems to be thriving on it, anyway. You know, I wish I could get rid of the feeling that absolutely everybody in the University has got it."

As he was going down the corridor Jock's door opened, and two nuns came out. Jock came out with them.

"No, no, no, dear ladies," he was saying. "You really mustn't feel guilty about it. It's always a pleasure to see you!"

He noticed Stephen, who was standing pressed against

the wall like a man about to be shot. "All right, my dear fellow? Standing up to the fray?" Stephen found himself incapable of answering.

"You look a bit peaky, my dear boy." Jock patted his shoulder. "You get yourself home and have a good night's sleep. McCannon will be at his post. All will be well!"

"Well," said Lyn. "This is very nice." They had eaten one of Chen's brilliant Burmese meals, they had played Scrabble with Chen till midnight (so embarrassing for Stephen coming last all the time) and now they were in bed, lying side by side rather formally, like . . . well, like patients.

"Are you all right, Doc?"

"Yes," he said. "I'm fine. Bit tired. You know. Er . . . are you all right, Lyn?"

"I'm all right," she said.

"Good."

There was a pause.

"So how's your sexual idiolect tonight then, Doc?"

"Um . . . bit reticent, Lyn."

"Yes, I thought it might be."

There was another pause. Stephen found himself wishing he had a banana or two about his person.

"Er, actually, Lyn, I was wondering if we might go back to Stage Two for a bit."

"Yeah, all right," she said. "If you like." She was frowning. Puzzled.

"Just for a bit."

"Yeah, sure, that's fine with me. You really liked Stage Two, didn't you?"

"Yes, I did," he replied gratefully.

"I thought you liked Stage Three even better, though."

"Yes, I did! I mean I do. It's just. . . ."

"Look," she said. "It's not anything to do with other people, is it?"

"No," he said. And then, "Well, in a way."

"When I'm with you I'm with you. You know that."

"Yes, and when you're with other people you're with other people."

"Well it stands to reason, doesn't it?" She sat up abruptly. "Oh, *Stephen*. You promised me you wouldn't get into that possessive jealous bit."

"I'm not. It's not that. Really."

"What is it, then?"

He just could not think of any way to tell her. "Look, really," he said. "It's only for a little while. Think of it as a sort of phase I'm going through."

A grin slowly formed itself on her face. "Here, you haven't been sneaking off and getting yourself a crafty dose of herpes or something?"

"No!" he was shocked. "No, really."

"Oh." She thought for a bit, then said slowly, "But you think I might have."

"No. No, I don't."

"Yes, I can see how you might think that. I haven't, though."

"I'm sure you haven't."

"Stephen. I'm a body language person, remember? You're looking at me the way people look at tax inspectors."

"I've never been to bed with a tax inspector, Lyn." Nervous. Feeble. Pathetic. Oh, bugger it all, medical confidentiality had never been a problem before. But it wasn't just that, either. Something about those journeys to the centre of the earth, those nodding toadstools, had got to him.

"No," she said. "I'll believe that. But you wish you weren't in bed with me now."

"No honestly, I love being in bed with you. It's just I don't feel . . ."

"Yeah. I know."

"Stage Two would be fine."

"Yeah. I know."

"Trust me, Lyn."

She managed to raise a smile. "Yeah. All right. Stage Two it is." She switched the light off.

*

171

Jock McCannon's chart was a forest of red markers. The members of the medical team stared at it gloomily. But Jock still had the light of battle in his eyes. He hadn't looked so well for years.

"We are holding the enemy," he announced. "But only just. The next two days of the campaign should be crucial. I'll hand you over to Bob Buzzard for the detailed analysis."

"Thank you, Jock," said Bob, moving to the chart. "Well, I've run the figures through the computer and I have the feedback. Arts Faculty produced the largest number of cases, predictably. Idle sods, too much time on their hands. Modern Languages don't seem to have heard of French letters. Similar pattern with the secretaries and the younger porters, and Communications Studies have lived up to their name. Never let anyone tell you that they're just a lot of wankers. Waitresses and bar staff were a problem till we sewed up the Catering Manager's trousers with cobbler's thread. Sociologists appear only to do it with each other, and we've got control there. Engineers, you'll be interested to know, have a very low rate of sexual activity. Singing about it in the bar would appear to be their only outlet. And Physical Sciences hardly troubled the scorer. So far, so good."

"What about the nuns?" said Stephen. He had woken in the night thinking about the nuns.

"Sorry?" Bob looked baffled.

"The nuns."

Jock's yellow fangs flashed briefly. "Ah! My dear fellow! They were merely inviting me to open the Poor Clares' Annual Bring and Buy Sale!"

"Oh. Sorry," said Stephen. "Been getting a bit jumpy."

"Well," said Rose Marie. "That all sounds as if we're practically home and dry."

"Unfortunately not," said Jock. "Bob, would you be so kind?"

"We should be getting only referrals from the contact tracing now, but there's a small and steady stream of new

172

cases with no discernible pattern to them. Except that they're all baffled, and spin you a lot of old cobblers about anything from sharing the communion cup to bugs in the air conditioning."

"I think we might have an asymptomatic carrier," said Jock sepulchrally. "Or more than one."

"One would be enough," said Rose Marie.

"Some Speedy Gonzales type," said Bob. "Rogering his way round without a care in the world."

"But surely," said Stephen, "if there is such a person . . . he'd have had a referral? Why hasn't he come in for a checkup?"

"Because he hasn't had the symptoms himself, and he simply can't be bothered," said Rose Marie pleasantly. "You've got too much faith in human nature, Stephen."

"But we'll get the bastard," said Bob grimly. Bob had lost a bit of weight in the past week. His face was leaner, sharper, fiercer. Could he be turning into a Dobermann?

"Um, look," said Stephen. "I can't help thinking . . . isn't this just fantasy?"

"It's our only hope," said Jock. "If we don't pin this down in the next day or two, we could have another escalation, and then it's curtains. Call in the City General. Inform the Vice-Chancellor."

"And read all about it in the paper," said Bob. A gloomy silence hung about the cave. Then the door opened and Mrs Kramer came in.

"Awfully sorry to interrupt," she said, "but they are queuing down the stairs, you know. Would you be inclined to see any of them, or shall I send them away? Oh, and that Jeannie McAllister person is being most persistent about seeing Dr Daker."

"Jeannie McAllister?" said Stephen numbly. He had forgotten about her. If she was on to it, forget about the next day or two, it would be on local radio by midday.

"Let me see her, Stephen," said Rose Marie. "I think this might be a suitable job for a woman."

"Come on." Bob addressed his computer screen. "Come

on. You crafty little swine. I know you're hiding in there somewhere." He ran the search again. The screen said:

  INSUFFICIENT DATA NICE TRY ROBERT
  SPEEDY GONZALES

Stephen was talking to Dorothy, the Vice-Chancellor's secretary, and both of them were finding it dreadfully embarrassing, while trying their level best to pretend it wasn't.

"How long since you first noticed the symptoms?" said Stephen. He had spoken that sentence forty-five times in the last seven days.

"Oh . . . about a fortnight, I suppose," she said.

"Yes, I see. It's . . . rather a long time to wait before coming to see someone about it."

"Yes, I know. It was really stupid of me. I just couldn't believe it at first. And then our GP's a personal friend, and I sometimes do a bit of voluntary work at the City General . . . you know."

"Yes, I do understand." Stephen thought how brave she had been coming to the Centre. Would he have done the same in her place?

"I . . . suppose I'll have to tell my husband about it."

"Yes, I'm afraid you will," said Stephen. "Actually, you'll probably find that he'll be very relieved to be able to talk about it himself."

"Oh no," she said. "Oh no. You don't understand at all. It's me, you see. I'm the one who's to blame."

"Now, Miss McAllister," said Rose Marie. "First of all I assume that you don't mind talking to me instead of Dr Daker. He has a very heavy case-load this morning." Her manner, while not exactly hostile, was very far from the warm sisterly approach she usually adopted with her female patients.

"No, that's all right," said Jeannie. "It's very good of you to see me at such short notice."

"All right," said Rose Marie. "Now I'd like to establish some ground rules for our conversation."

"Yes?"

"The first one is that it'll be completely confidential. Do you agree?"

"Oh, yes, Dr Rose Marie," said Jeannie, nodding fervently.

"That means confidential not only in terms of not being published, but also that you don't talk about it to anyone. Anyone at all."

"Yes, I understand that."

"And while you are free to ask me anything you like, I'm not necessarily prepared to answer all your questions. All right?"

"Yes," said Jeannie. "Um . . . it isn't so much a matter of me asking questions, actually Doctor."

"Oh? What is it a matter of, then?"

"Oh, dear," said Jeannie McAllister. "Well . . . it's a bit embarrassing and personal."

"Ah," said Rose Marie. "I see now. I'm so sorry, Jeannie." Her manner was warm and sisterly. She couldn't believe her luck.

"Well, take your time and tell me all about it."

"No. I'm sorry. I can't," said Dorothy to Stephen.

"But . . . I mean, it must be someone you know," he said helplessly.

"I'm sorry," she said. "I know it must seem ridiculous and stupid to you. And it is."

"I can absolutely guarantee it'll be completely confidential. We're really anxious not to intrude into anyone's private life. It's simply that contact tracing has to be done. If it's . . . if it's someone you don't want to see again, for example, we can make the contact without involving you. Anywhere in the country. If you could perhaps just give us a telephone number."

She was silent. Such a sensible person: it was easy to see that she could see the point, and she wanted to help. What was it? Holiday fling? Husband's best friend? Someone out of a silly film, a milkman or window-cleaner?

"Believe me," he said, "I hate this part of it. It's awful.

175

Makes you feel like Special Branch or something. I don't mind telling you, it's done my personal life no good at all. That's just between the two of us."

She hesitated. "If I . . . if I just write down a name," she said.

"That's all. You won't hear any more about it."

She decided very suddenly. "Oh, what the hell. Give me a piece of paper." She took the slip, scribbled, folded it, and passed it back.

"Thank you very much, Mrs Hampton," said Stephen. "You've been most helpful."

When she had gone he opened the folded slip of paper, and found the need to whirl round and round in his revolving chair, whimpering. Then he got up and put his coat and scarf on. He pressed the button on the intercom. "I am going out, Mrs Kramer," he said. "I may be some time."

"Daker," said the Vice-Chancellor. "When someone says they want to see me on an urgent and personal matter, I make a point of finding time for them."

"It's very good of you, Vice-Chancellor," said Stephen. His voice didn't sound too bad, only about half an octave above what it should have been. He was glad that Hemmingway wasn't wearing the red tracksuit today, though the four hundred quid suit he was wearing looked daunting enough.

"I also usually find that when people say the matter's private and confidential, it means they want to confess something. My advice to you is: think before you speak. It may not be possible for me to respect your confidentiality. This University is not in the cover-up business. We've all learnt the lesson of that student files kerfuffle in seventy-six. And if it's the kind of thing your predecessor got up to, I shan't be able to support you. All right?"

"I . . . have thought it over, Vice-Chancellor," said Stephen.

"All right," said Hemmingway, looking at his watch. "Fire away."

"Well," said Stephen, wriggling on his chair, "it is really rather delicate . . . I wish there was some other way. . . ."

"Yes, yes, yes, we'll take that as read. Come on, let's have it straight, shall we?"

Taking a deep breath, Stephen let him have it straight. "Your name's been given to me as a sexual contact by a patient suffering from a sexually transmitted disease." In his effort to sound firm and confident, he had almost shouted it. The words didn't just hang in the air: they bounced off the walls, they boomed back from the hard-edged abstracts, swung jabbering from the thorny metal tangles of the sculptures.

Hemmingway was sitting very still. It was impossible to tell what was going on in his mind. Stephen waited. Then the Vice-Chancellor looked up at him, his little eyes sharp, dangerous, almost murderous. "Are you trying to black-mail me, Daker?" he said quietly. "Is that what you're here for? Because if you are. . . ."

"I'm telling you so that you can have a check-up and get the condition treated, if necessary. It's possible that you might be what we call a symptomless carrier."

Hemmingway thought for a few moments. "Who else knows about this?"

"Only me," said Stephen. "And the other patient."

Another few moments.

"What are the chances of keeping this quiet?"

"They're excellent, Vice-Chancellor. I can put you in touch with a consultant who'll treat you privately in London, I expect you'd prefer that. There won't be anything in our records. And *I'll* certainly respect the confidentiality of this conversation."

"I see," said the Vice-Chancellor. "Thank you." He shuffled about a bit inside his four hundred quid suit, which was beginning to look a little large for him. He seemed to be preparing himself for something very difficult, something that he'd never picked up along the way. He cleared his throat. "Daker," he said, "I'm sorry I reacted hastily. Can't have been easy for you, this."

"No, it wasn't," said Stephen fervently.

"Um . . . care for a drink?" Hemmingway sprang up, seeming to find relief in movement, and went over to the cupboard. He was, Stephen noticed, walking rather stiffly. Symptomless carrier my arse, thought Stephen.

"What'll you . . . oh, no, you're a teetotaller, aren't you?"

"No, I'm not," said Stephen.

"Never forget that sort of thing. Mind if I have one?" He poured himself a neat Scotch, modest in size by McCannon standards, but quite a drink for a man of five foot two in the middle of the morning. "Um . . . I suppose you find all this . . . um, how shall I put it, slightly scandalous, man in my situation, that sort of thing?"

"No, not at all," said Stephen eagerly and unconvincingly.

"Of course you do. But I am a man, Daker. What's your first name, by the way?"

"Stephen," said Stephen.

"I am a man, Stephen, a man as other men." He paused for thought. "Perhaps more so."

"There really isn't any need to explain," said Stephen. Over the last week he had heard so many confessions, so many rationalisations, so many excuses, so many genuine and faked-up hard-luck stories, so much sadness. He didn't think he could bear to hear the Vice-Chancellor's.

"This can be a very lonely job, Stephen. Nobody knows the struggles I've had to keep this University viable through a world recession. And sometimes, when the battle's been a bloody one, a man needs . . . well a man needs comfort. Reassurance. Validation. Can you understand that, Stephen?"

"Yes, of course I can," said Stephen. "But are you really sure you want to talk to me about it?"

"You're a doctor," said Hemmingway. "Who else could I talk to?"

"Well, er . . . your wife, perhaps?"

"My God! My wife doesn't need to know anything about this does she?"

"Well," said Stephen. "That depends."

178

"Depends on what? Daker, you *are* trying to blackmail me!"

"It depends on whether you've, er, enjoyed marital relations in the last six weeks or so," said Stephen.

Relief flooded the Vice-Chancellor's face. "Daker," he said, "I've never enjoyed marital relations very much, and I haven't practised them for years."

"Then no, she doesn't need to know," said Stephen.

"Daker, you're a good fellow. I've got a lot to thank you for."

"Not at all," said Stephen. "I'm just doing my job."

"No, you're a good fellow. It's really a shame."

"Er . . . what's a shame, Vice-Chancellor?"

"Well, of course, I shan't be able to look you in the eye after this, shall I?" said Hemmingway reasonably. "Much too embarrassing. No, I'm afraid that one of us should really start looking round for other posts quite soon. And you do know which one of us I mean, don't you?"

"Yes," said Stephen. "I think I do."

"That's a good man," said Ernest Hemmingway. He held out his hand for Stephen to shake. "Your references, of course, will be excellent."

"Thank you," said Stephen numbly. He was about to turn and go when he remembered. "Er, there is just one more thing."

"Yes, Stephen?" The Vice-Chancellor was beaming benevolently now. Nothing would be too much trouble.

"Are there any more contacts we should know about, Vice-Chancellor?"

The day after that, Daniela Theodoulou paid Jock McCannon an unexpected visit.

"How very nice to see you again so soon," said Jock in a macabre parody of courtliness. "Tell me, how are the new initiatives getting on? All those developments along the interfaces?" She smiled at him behind those tantalising glasses. Ah, the mystery of womanhood. Damned attractive creature, too. In the days when he had sap . . . ah, well.

179

"I find the University very interesting," she said, "I'm developing some nice connections. I think we can make some good things happen, you know."

"And now you've come to visit us. Have you come to make something happen here?"

"Who knows?" she smiled. "Perhaps I spark something off with you, Dr McCannon. But mostly I'm here because of these mysterious little grey cards people push through my letter-box. She opened her bag, took out the cards, and spread them. Jock stared at them dumbfounded. She could have discarded two and still held a winning flush.

"You mean," said Jock shakily, "they all arrived this morning?"

"I don't know," she said, "I don't think so. I think maybe they've been, how d'you say it, piling up a bit? You see I haven't been home so very much lately."

"No, well," said Jock, "I can imagine that."

"Do you know what it can mean, all this?"

"Yes, my dear," said Jock. "I rather think I do."

"We have come through!" boomed Jock. "We have saved the University! Interdisciplinary Studies! What else could have linked Philosophy with Weightlifting, Cybernetics with Ancient Greek? And she was an asymptomatic carrier!"

"But who put you on to her, Jock?" asked Rose Marie.

"Stephen did," beamed Jock.

"And who was the link, Stephen?"

"I'm afraid I can't say," said Stephen. "Sorry."

"What a gentleman!" barked Bob, disappointed. Speedy Gonzales was still hiding in the depths of his computer. He would never get the bastard by the short and curlies now.

"You look tired, Stephen," said Jock McCannon. "You look as if you have been through a formative experience."

"Yes, I rather think I have, Jock."

"Will you all take a wee dram with me? Not you, of course, Stephen, I know you're a total abstainer."

180

"No, I'm not, Jock."

"Here we are, then," said Jock, hefting a brand new bottle of Bell's, the first for a week. "We few. We happy few. We band of brothers. And sisters, saving your presence, Rose Marie." He filled his glass and raised it, leaving his team to help themselves. "First this week," he said. "And not, by God, the last. D'you know, I think it's time old Jock went to pieces again!"

"Well, you're full of surprises, you are," said Lyn. They were in bed again, and things were all right again. "I did say it was only for a while, Lyn."

"You're very unexpected sometimes, you are."

"Is that all right?" Luxury question. He knew it was all right.

"Yes, it's good," she said. Then thought for a bit. "Look, what was it anyway?"

"Nothing," he said. "I mean, nothing to do with you or me. Not really. The thing is I still can't talk about it."

"Professional etiquette?"

"That sort of thing."

"Doesn't matter," she said. "The old sexual idiolect is OK again. You're a bit on the wonderful side, you are." He lay there and thought about that for a while with a daft smile on his face. He didn't think he was all that wonderful, but he thought she was, and if she thought he was he wasn't going to quarrel with her about it. Then he started thinking about the other thing.

"Look," he said, "there's something I ought to tell you. I think I've screwed up my career prospects here."

"How d'you mean?"

"Been advised to apply for other posts. No hurry, no hassle, good references, but all the same."

"Who is it?" she said. "I mean, who advised you?"

"Someone quite high up. Well, very high up, actually. I didn't do anything wrong. It was just . . . bad luck."

"Well, fight it," she said.

"I'm not sure that I can."

"Well sod them then. You're an ace doctor. Everyone

181

knows that. You could make it anywhere. I'd give you a testimonial anyway." He smiled wryly. "You really like it here, don't you? You daft bugger."

"Yes, I do," he admitted.

"Well, stay, then. Tell them to get stuffed. Be difficult."

"Yes," said Stephen. It was so simple. "Yes, I bloody well will."

"Look," she said. "I've got something to tell you too. It's a sort of a confession. Can you stand one?"

"I don't know," he said.

"It's about being with other people."

"Yes?"

"Well," she said. "Oh, dear. Well, the thing is, I haven't been with other people lately. I've sort of, you know, gone off it, being with other people. I've only been with you."

"Oh," he said.

"Is that all right?" she said anxiously. "Do you feel threatened? I mean, it's nothing heavy, it doesn't mean you have to see me every night, or anything, I haven't gone dependent, honest. It's just, well, maybe it's a phase, I don't know. I didn't like to mention it the other night, you seemed so tense."

"Oh, Lyn," he said, "I wish you had."

"You mean you can cope with it? A one-to-one relationship?"

"Yes, Lyn," he said. "I think I could make a stab at it."

Rust in the Bush

The Bush is, must be, thinks Rust, the worst pub in London, and here he is in it again. Its staff are surly, its drinks are expensive, and its clientele is disgusting. Rust does not except himself from this judgment. Who would want to drink in a pub where the likes of him could regularly be seen? He has just paid a pound for a pint of dreadful Australian lager, and Christ knows what for a pint of Guinness for Riddington. All around him the doomed and seedy denizens of Series and Serials are making their shabby deals, interspersed with dangerous Irishmen and what might well be distinguished actors, supping the stuff like there's no tomorrow and smoking like beagles.

Upstairs is some sort of dreadful little theatre to which Rust has never been, on principle, where plays by sparky fifteen-year-olds are presented, with great acclaim, to people like Carol and her sodding chum. Thank God there isn't a lunchtime show today. It's bad enough waiting for the favour of the misanthropists behind the bar, without having to compete with a lot of shrill sods baying for their St Clements and their Perriers. That is something to be thankful for, yes, but apart from that Rust is touching rock bottom.

It shouldn't be like that. It should be the most exciting time of all. Series and Serials have committed themselves, so long as their nerve holds. Rust is into rewrites on the early episodes already, and Riddington is into directors and casting. This is where it should all spark off, this is where the creative contacts should be bouncing off the interfaces. But it never happens like that. It's a time of suspicion and gloom, a sense of having committed oneself to a totally unreliable enterprise, a bit like a honeymoon, really.

"Who d'you fancy for the girl, then, Ron?" says Riddington. Rust mentions the names of two actresses he has worked with before, and then a third that he has often longed to work with. In fact, Rust thinks he would faint from pleasure if he just could get to sit opposite her in the caterer's tent on location.

"That girl," says Riddington with certainty, "has got about as much sex appeal as that radiator over there." He points with a quivering finger to make sure that Rust doesn't associate her with the wrong radiator.

"Oh, come on, Ken," says Rust.

"The camera doesn't like her, Ron." That's not the point. Rust likes her. Or he thinks he would like her if he got to meet her. And if she likes him, who cares whether the sodding camera likes her or not. Sodding cameras are spoilt for choice, anyway, thinks Rust. I'll have the ones the camera doesn't like.

"Think we should see her, anyway," says Rust.

183

"Oh, we'll see her," says Riddington gloomily. "We'll see them all."

Rust thinks, not for the first time, that Riddington's job should be taken away from him and given to someone who would appreciate it. That's the trouble with jobs. Riddington is really, Rust has to admit, quite good at his job, but he doesn't seem to get much fun out of it. Rust would be terrible at Riddington's job, but he wouldn't mind having a crack at parts of it. Similarly, he keeps meeting people who think that being a writer is a wonderful job. Rust hates writing; he hates it passionately, but it's the only thing he can do. No, not quite the only thing he can do. He has turned out to be really quite good at discouraging students from taking it up. Only the other day he had a major breakthrough when the most talented man in his creative writing group threw it all up to go and work on an oil rig. Rust encouraged him earnestly, but he fears he'll be back in six months with some post-modernist masterpiece called "Swell" or "Slick" or something. Still.

Riddington has syphoned up two foot-long sausages and a few pounds of mashed potatoes. He doesn't seem to be gorged or sated, but a little colour has come into his cheeks. "Tell me, Ron," he says, "how's it all going to end?"

Rust is not used to metaphysical inquiry from this source. "Er, how d'you mean, Ken? The world and that? Well, my feeling is that the human species is a bit of a freak, far too developed in some directions, not enough in others. As for example, sexual hangups and the sodding Bomb, right? We're just a sodding hiccup in the vast unfolding scenario, that's what I reckon, human beings might be interested but we're not relevant in the long run."

Riddington listens carefully to this, then shakes his head. "Not what I meant, Ron," he says.

A man drinking alone on the next table has been listening to them. Rust has been noticing him ever since they came in. He feels that he knows this man, though he can't quite place him. Tall, craggy, powerfully built,

184

with a Yorkshire Moors complexion and a deep, considered seriousness about him, he looks very much like photographs Rust has seen of Ted Hughes. Perhaps it is Ted Hughes. What's he doing in the Bush, in that case? He must have come down in the world. Anyway, he seems deeply interested in what Rust has just said about the fate of the human species.

"What did you mean, then, Ken?" says Rust. He feels as if he is on *The South Bank Show*, or one of those dreadful public wanks at the ICA.

"What I meant was," says Ken, "How do you see the series ending? Should we leave it open for a possible fowwup, or close it off?" Those Guinnesses must be better than they look, thinks Rust, succeeding eventually in reading follow-up for fowwup. Ted Hughes is nodding sagely on the next table, obviously keen to hear Rust's thoughts. The trouble is, Rust doesn't have any. He would dearly like to see all the doctors and their rotbox university off in some extremely expensive Chromakey holocaust, but he knows he might regret it later when the cheques stop coming.

"Fuck knows, Ken," he says honestly. "Fuck knows." What an odd phrase that is, he thinks. He has said it two often, that is the trouble. He feels like a doctor who has been peering down too many vaginas lately: things tend to lose their fundamental whatness. Perhaps the Australian lager is better than it tastes as well. Fuck knows. Fucknose. Fucknose? Now there's a thought. That reminds Rust of his dead Fiat. Not long ago he tried to get hold of a part for his Fiat, and the girl at the spares counter told him that they were out of genuine Fiat parts, but she could fix him up with a quick nasal. This seemed to Rust an unconventional but very agreeable suggestion, try anything once, until he realised that she was referring to the highly reliable parts manufacturer called Quinton Hazell. This will never do. Ted Hughes must be getting very frustrated, waiting for Rust's views on closure, surely the central comtemporary literary issue.

"What I'm really looking for, Ken," he said, "and

you may feel that this is being, oh, over-ambitious, self-indulgent, throwing away the baby with the bathwater, is some sort of ending that challenges the viewer with his or her viewerliness, foreground the fictionality of the whole undertaking, while still, and this is the most important thing, still maintaining the authenticity of the primal narrative drive, the old inescapable. You know. *What's going to happen next?*"

"That's what I was fucking well asking you," says Riddington sourly, getting up to buy more drinks. Rust is deeply disappointed. He thought he was getting through to Riddington, taking him on a heady journey from the shores of naturalism to the wild seas of deconstruction, where catastrophe theory is the only theory, and the ship sails best upside down. Ah, well. Ted Hughes still looks keenly interested. He raises his great craggy head, and meets Rust's eyes. He is clearly acknowledging a fellow artist of his own giant stature. Rust holds his breath. Ted Hughes rises, a little unsteadily, and comes over to sit by him. He is clearly so moved and excited by Rust's ideas that he can hardly command his limbs. He grasps Rust's arm in his great fist. He looks earnestly into Rust's eyes.

"I've never heard so much fucking shit in my whole fucking life," he says to Rust in a thick Dublin accent; and then abruptly he vomits over Rust's trousers.

6

THE HIT LIST

It was cold waiting in the Piazza for the nuns to come, but it couldn't start until they were there. They had to get the parcel out of the rubbish skip. Nobody would talk to him and nobody would look at him. It was all a misunderstanding and there was almost certainly a way to explain but he didn't have the right suit for explanations. He realised now that it had been a terrible mistake to wear his pyjamas. Everybody else was in four-hundred-quid suits. Bob Buzzard was supposed to be bringing him a suit but it had to have something cybernetic done to it first. He was trying to tell Ernest Hemmingway about this but Hemmingway kept turning round and going into the cupboard by the Piazza fountain. It wasn't any use asking Rose Marie to help because she was a barrister and for her he was part of the problem. He couldn't understand what his mother was doing there; she was wearing her old yellow coat, but she didn't look cold. Perhaps that was because she was dead.

Now the nuns were coming with the big parcel. The parcel was nearly as tall as the nuns but it seemed to be very light to carry. They were coming straight towards the centre of the Piazza. When they were a few yards from Stephen they stopped. Then they unwrapped the parcel. It was Angela, and she was in her wedding dress. He understood now that they had all come here to kill him. A long way away he could see a girl in a green tracksuit jogging. It was Lyn. He called out to her but she couldn't hear him. She jogged away from him, out of sight. They

187

were all coming closer now. There was a curious scraping, swishing sound. He didn't know what it was. It was the nuns, he realised suddenly. They were sharpening a big axe on Angela's leg. That was what they were going to kill him with. He tried to cry out. He tried to run. He could not move. He could make no sound.

"I'm sorry," said Chen. "I'm disturbing you."

Stephen sat up, rubbing his eyes. Chen was in his room, scribbling mathematical symbols on the blackboard that formed the wall opposite his bed and snaked in all the way from the shared living room.

"Big thoughts," said Chen. "Need all the boards. Make a mess, make a noise. Just for a wanky old Nobel prize. Sorry."

"Not at all," said Stephen. "It's a pleasure to see you. I thought two nuns were going to execute me."

"Nuns again," said Chen, writing some more.

"They had a big axe. What are you doing?"

"Nearly finished," said Chen. "I needed the space, you see, to find out what I was going to say. There. Isn't that beautiful?"

Stephen looked. It looked like a lot of maths to him. "Is it?"

"Beautiful, original, elegant. And it's never been said before."

"What does it say?"

"What do you care what it says?" said Chen, squatting on his heels. "It's beautiful, and no one can understand it. Well, maybe six people in the States. Two guys in France. Viola Slawek in Katowice, she'd like it. Nobody here. Oh, I'm such a clever boy."

"Chen, doesn't your professor understand it?"

"He pretends he does, but he doesn't," said Chen darkly.

"If he really understood it he would steal it, get himself a Nobel prize. Well: now you see it, now you don't." He picked up a cloth and started to rub it all out. "It's OK, Stephen, it's all in my head. Like your nuns."

"Yes," said Stephen.

188

"Why don't you dream nice dreams, about that big girl of yours?"

"She was in it," said Stephen, "but she went away."

Chen sat on Stephen's bed and inspected him carefully. "Panic and terror," he said eventually.

"Just a twinge."

"What's been happening?"

"Oh . . . nothing really. My wife's petitioning for divorce. The VC's advised me to apply for other posts. I've got an overpowering feeling of impending doom. How do you cope with life, Chen?"

"I hang loose. Like our national poet. Would you like to hear what he says?"

"Yes, please, Chen."

Chen closed his eyes and swayed for a moment. Then he said:

> "Live in the moment as the leaf falls in the wind,
> Float like the feather on the foam,
> And when they come to your door with the big axe,
> Kick them in the goolies, run away fast."

"And is that what he did?"

"No," said Chen. "When they came to his door he was too fat to run very fast."

Ernest Hemmingway was dictating a letter to his secretary, Dorothy. He would have rather not have been doing this; dictating to Dorothy made him feel rather uncomfortable these days. In fact he would be very happy to let her go altogether. Trouble was, he didn't dare let her out of his sight. Knew too much. Let him know that she knew too much. Anyway, he couldn't get by without her. So that was that. Ernie Hemmingway didn't believe in wasting time on insolubles. He'd just thought of one of his best administrative strokes in years.

"As you know," he said, "it has been a matter of policy within the University since August 1971 that all new appointments to the academic and administrative staff should have a full medical examination before the appointment is confirmed. I was lying in the bath last night, you know, and suddenly a vision shot into my head of old Skinner-Joyce at last year's Convocation falling off the stage because he'd somehow managed to tie his shoelaces together. Absolutely gaga. Tragic, too, in a way, of course, but still . . ."

Dorothy Hampton looked up from her notebook. "Is this all part of the letter?"

"No, of course it isn't. Er . . . full medical examination before the appointment is confirmed. This as you also know has become standard practice throughout the British Isles. A delicate question thus arises regarding the situation of academic staff appointed before that time. The present stringent economic climate means that this University is being subjected to the sharpest scrutiny. I am sure that you will agree that we owe it to these senior colleagues to ensure that their security of tenure is unassailable on medical grounds. Rather a neat one, don't you think?"

"Wouldn't that include you, Vice-Chancellor?"

"No, it would not."

"Oh, yes," she said, "you had that plushy BUPA screening, didn't you?"

"Quite."

Dorothy had a new smile that she was trying out with increasing frequency. Sardonic was probably the right word for it. He would definitely have to find some way of wiping it off her face. For the meantime, all he could think of was to ignore it. He cleared his throat.

"I am therefore requesting the University Medical Centre to move ahead on this one without delay."

"He wants us to move ahead without delay, the vile wee man," said Jock. The letter was shaking in his hand.

"But there must be scores of people appointed before 1971," said Stephen.

"Most of the senior academic staff, yes," said Jock.

What was the matter with Jock? It was going to be a hell of a nuisance, obviously, thought Stephen, but nothing to get upset about. They'd bumble through it the way they bumbled through everything else, wouldn't they?

"I don't see how we're going to find the time to fit them all in; a full medical's very time-consuming," said Rose Marie.

"Ah, wee lass, he's thought of that," said Jock in hollow tones. (Where had the horrible yellow grin gone? Stephen found he was missing it.) "I don't think you've appreciated the devious wiles of our midget leader." He read some more of the letter:

"As the whole exercise will be of necessity a time-consuming business, and I am anxious that the efficiency of the medical service should not be impaired by these extra duties, I am asking the Senior Registrar to furnish a confidential list of those colleagues whose security of tenure is a matter of special priority to the University in this transitional period."

"Well, that's very thoughtful of him," said Stephen. He looked round. They were all staring at him.

"Oh, Stephen," said Rose pityingly.

"You mean . . . he's picking out his special cronies for priority treatment? He wouldn't do that, would he?"

"The list I've had from the Senior Registrar isn't a list of Ernie's special cronies, Stephen," said Jock. "Rather the reverse."

"You mean it's a hit list?" said Bob eagerly.

"I fear so, Bob."

"Brilliant!" said Bob. "Who's on it?"

Jock pulled out a crumpled sheet of paper which showed clear signs of having been through rough and passionate handling, and bore stains of whisky and what might well have been tears. He smoothed it out and read from it, Remembrance Sunday style:

"Leo Architrave from Social Psychology; *both* Professors of Education; poor old Perry Skinner-Joyce from Philosophy; James Glans, Scrote Reader in Classical Civilisation; Canon Pottle . . ."

"Canon Pottle," said Stephen. "Who's he?"

"Warden of Kennedy Hall," said Jock doomily.

"Very strong on tucking his charges up in bed and wrestling with their souls," said Bob. "He's had it coming. Who else?" Bob was practically rubbing his hands.

"Lilian Hubbard," said Jock. "That's a little rough, I must say."

"It's outrageous!" said Rose Marie. "And inexplicable, surely. She's the one really distinguished name on the list. Students actually come to do history here just because of her. She's got an international reputation!"

"All the work was done a long time ago, though, wasn't it?" said Bob. "Anyway, who needs history?" He folded his arms, leaned back and stared round the room challengingly, like a dog who's stolen the Sunday joint but knows you can't pin it on him. "Sorry, have I said something crass and philistine again? Well, it's true, isn't it? Anyway, her dog bit Hemmingway's wife."

"That, I should have thought, would predispose him in her favour," said Jock.

"So what has he got against her then?"

"She's a woman," said Rose Marie simply.

"Oh, Lord, gender on the agenda again," groaned Bob.

"She's also a Hall Warden. Fairlie Hall. The only all-women's Hall in the University."

"Of course!" said Jock. "How astute of you, my dear. It's the *building* he wants. With Lilian Hubbard out of the way, he could convert it into a rest home for rich crooks, or whatever else takes his fancy. Poor Lilian."

"March of progress," said Bob cheerfully. "Nothing we can do about it."

"But look," said Stephen. "We're being used, aren't we? I mean if what you say is right, the VC's proposing to use medical examinations to get rid of a few inconvenient people, and reduce his salary bill at the same time."

"Exactly," said Jock.

"Well, I'm not sure that we should go along with that."

"I think we have to, Stephen. The little red dwarf's motives may be vile, but his logic is impeccable. Everyone appointed since 1971 has had a medical. He's simply eliminating an anomaly."

192

"And he's absolutely right," said Bob. "I've got a lot of time for old Ernie, he has some bloody good ideas. And he's put together a good hit list for starters. We'll be a leaner, fitter organisation with some of that lot in the geriatric ward, won't we? I mean in any sane world, old Skinner-Joyce would have been put down and gone to pussy heaven years ago, be doing him a kindness. Don't look at me like that. I mean, what have they got to fear? If the poor old buggers get through the medical, they're laughing! If not, let's get 'em on the front at Bournemouth with the old rug and wheelchair where they belong, eh?"

"How delicately you put things, Bob," said Jock. Jock's shoulders had drooped; his voice held a terrible resignation in it. "Yes, we have heard the true voice of the Eighties. Yes. Eh, as a matter of fact, I didn't quite reach the end of hit list stage one. There was one other name on it."

"Who?" said Rose Marie.

"J. G. McCannon, MD."

"Oh," said Bob.

"I don't know," said Stephen. "I thought I really liked this University."

"Come on," said Lyn. "You still do."

They were sitting in the coffee bar. The usual straggle of haunted looking students in their T-shirts and Oxfam overcoats, two nuns who had somehow managed to extract a genuine pot of tea from the surly management, a small, scruffy looking man in his forties savagely scoring lines through a large pile of typescripts.

"It's funny," said Stephen. "When I first arrived Jock told me the place was a swamp of fear and loathing. I didn't believe a word of it then. But I do now."

"It's just a place, Stephen," she said. "Lots of people like it here. Look at them. Look, some of them are actually smiling."

He looked round. He couldn't see anyone smiling except the nuns, and he didn't like the way they were smiling at all.

"Look," he said. "I'm worried about those nuns."

"They're all right, honest."

"Not opening parcels or sharpening axes?"

"They're sitting very quietly drinking their tea and nicking the sugar lumps."

"Why are they nicking the sugar lumps?" he said, panicking slightly.

"I don't know," she said. "Maybe they know a horse."

"It was a very vivid dream, Lyn. You were in it, but you ran away."

She sighed. "Yeah, I know, you told me. Look, what is it? You haven't been like this for ages. Is it the divorce?"

"Partly, I suppose," he said. "I mean it's absolutely the right thing for her to do. I was never really any use to her, Lyn. But, you know, six years of your life officially written off as failure."

"You're not here to satisfy people's expectations, Doc. You're here to have a good time."

"Yes." Behind him he could hear the nuns getting up from their table. He didn't dare to turn but he knew they were coming for him. Then the rustling black habits swished past him. Not this time, then. He watched them gliding up the aisle towards the door. As they passed the small scruffy man, one of them brushed against the pile of typescript, sending his coffee cup somersaulting into his lap. He rose with a little gasping scream; but they hadn't noticed. The swing doors juddered behind them and they were gone. Stephen caught the scruffy man's eye and momentarily felt a kind of kinship. They were after him as well.

"Look, I've been thinking," said Lyn. "This business of the medicals for the hasbeens, you can handle that. Maybe some of them want to retire early, they might have been waiting for the chance. If it's an official health job, they'll get a good deal on the lump sum and the annuity. And the ones that do want to carry on, well they must be fit enough, otherwise they wouldn't feel like it, would they? So you give them the medical report they want to get."

"Lyn, that's brilliant," he said. "But is it ethical?"

"You'll have to make your own mind up about that," she said. "Look, I've got to go now. Getting my research report

194

back from the binders. Don't have a relapse now, please, or I'll have to rewrite the last two chapters."

"I'll try," said Stephen.

Bob put his head round the old fart's door. "You said you wanted to have a word, Jock."

"Did I? Yes, I must have done if I said I did. Now what was it?"

Gaga. Absolutely gaga. And getting worse by the minute.

"If it's this medical business, no problem, Jock. I'd be delighted to give you the once-over, just for form's sake." Ruined smile from the old fart. God, he'd get the chop on teeth the gums alone, never mind the rest.

"Very kind of you to offer, Bob, I'm most grateful. But I think I must decline."

"Fair enough," said Bob, disappointed.

"No, my old bones need very gentle handling. In fact, I'm thinking of asking someone from Archaeology to pick over the remains."

"Ha ha, rubbish. You're as fit as a flea!"

"Rather an elderly flea, though. I may not hop as high as in former years, but I can still bite, Bob. Ah yes. Remembered. Our leader wants a representative from the practice on his Forward Innovations Team. The Lord alone knows what that is, but I thought it sounded right up your alley, Bob. Er, *Robert*."

Bob thought so too. Bloody good. Right on the inside rail. "Thanks very much, Jock, I'd be glad to."

"Not at all, my dear chap. Find out what's cooking, eh? Besides our goose."

"Not that bad, is it, Jock?"

"Rumour has it," said the old fart, "that the DES are thinking about a twenty-five per cent cut in funding. This Forward Innovations Committee may be old Ernie's last attempt to save his bacon before the axe falls."

Fairlie Hall was a large late-Georgian House built on a decent human scale. Part of the country estate which

195

had formed the site for the sick university, it had escaped the attentions of the new brutalist mandarins; its well-proportioned windows blinked mildly across at the fortified rabbit warren on the far side of the lake. Let's be honest. It was the only nice building in the whole sodding University, and everyone knew it, even the new brutalist architects. Ernest Hemmingway knew it all right, and he wanted it. Since even he couldn't think of a way of getting it for himself personally, he was going to do the next best thing and get it for Sakamoto Corporation.

"Well, there you have it, gentlemen," he said. "A pleasant building, I'm sure you'll agree. Very convenient, very salubrious."

"Fairlie Hall," explained the interpreter johnnie to the assembled Nips.

"Fairly run down in its present state of course, ha ha," said Ernie, "but with the sort of endowment we've been discussing, the interior could be quite transformed. Accommodation at senior executive level, redesigned ground floor to afford luxurious small conference facilities, and of course, we'd put in a bar and a restaurant with a first class Japanese chef. Raw fish direct from Grimsby, that sort of thing. Steam baths, jacuzzi. Everything to make you feel at home." One of the inscrutable chaps said something and there was the usual bout of giggling.

"Mr Kimura is interested that all the rooms are occupied by beautiful young women just now."

"Yes, well," said Ernie hastily, "it's being used temporarily as student accommodation, but we'll get rid of, find alternative accommodation for, all the young women, that's no problem." The Kimura chap put his oar in again. More merriment. God, this was hard work.

"Mr Kimura says he hopes not *all* of them!"

Filthy swine. "Yes, yes, jolly good, ha ha, well, of course, we'll thrash out all the details in committee. And we were considering that in view of the very generous benefaction, we might make some recognition by renaming the converted house: Sakamoto Lodge, perhaps, something like that."

196

While the interpreter johnnie was telling them all about Sakamoto Lodge, Ernest Hemmingway noticed a small figure approaching with a large dog. Oh Lord. Stand very still. Here he comes. Dangerous great brute.

"Morning, Lilian, ha ha. Er, your dog's, er . . ."

"Morning, Vice-Chancellor," said Lilian Hubbard. "*Leave* it, Caesar! *Leave*! *Heel*. Good boy." The slavering brute reluctantly abandoned the Vice-Chancellor's trouser bottoms and sat panting by its mistress, never taking its eyes off Hemmingway.

"Good morning, gentlemen," said Dr Hubbard. "Can I help in any way?"

"No, thank you, Lilian, we're just on a tour of inspection."

"Flogging my girls' rooms for the vacation again, no doubt. Well, I trust these gentlemen will conduct themselves more decorously than the last lot you foisted on me, International stuff-you-daub-on-walls or whatever they were. This does happen to be my home throughout the year, you know." The slavering brute, clearly picking up the aggressive vibrations, drew its lips back from its teeth and began to slink in Ernie's direction.

"Did I say *heel*, Caesar? International *paints*, that was it. You'll excuse me, I'm sure. Important work to do." And to Ernest Hemmingway's great relief, she stumped in through the front door.

"That was Doctor Hubbard," he told the interpreter johnnie. "She'll be retiring in the summer."

Bob Buzzard studied the new poster on Rose Marie's wall. "Bit deep for me, that," he said. "I mean, shouldn't it be like a boat without a rudder or an egg without salt, something like that?"

Rose Marie took off her glasses and smiled tolerantly.

"I mean," he went on, "I may be a bit dense, but fish don't actually *need* bicycles, do they?"

"No, they don't Bob."

"Ah!" he said. "Got it now! Yes, indeed, say no more! Really packs a punch, that one! And it's the sort of thing you can look at day in, day out, it never goes stale on you like, oh, Van Gogh's sunflowers or the Night Watch, or the Pirelli calendar. Satisfaction every time, as the bishop . . . ah, sorry, beg your pardon."

"Did you actually want anything, Bob?" asked Rose Marie sweetly.

"Ah, yes," he said, sitting down heavily. "Point of fact I did. What are we going to do about old Jock?"

"Well, we must do everything we can to help him, mustn't we?" So demure. Butter wouldn't melt up her, never mind that.

"I've done my best," he said. "Offered to give him the once over, but he turned me down."

"I made a tentative approach myself. He doesn't seem to trust us, Bob. It's such a shame. For such a distinguished career to dwindle away in incompetence and alcohol."

"Right. Absolutely."

"And it doesn't take much imagination to envisage what an impartial medical report on Jock would look like."

"Lord, no. Signs are there for anyone to see. Tremor memory loss, brain damage . . . you can practically hear his poor old liver howling for mercy . . . and God knows I wouldn't like to see those kidneys on my breakfast plate! Eh?"

Rose Marie winced. "Quite. You, or I, or Stephen, could fill in the spaces without even examining him," she said.

"No problem!" said Bob cheerfully. He stared at her. She looked back at him levelly.

"No problem," he said.

Stephen Daker was chosen to conduct Dr Lilian Hubbard's physical, and he found her a fascinating but rather daunting patient. She found "ninety-nine" far too boring to say, and substituted several stanzas of Horatius keeping the bridge, with comments on the unrealiability of Macaulay as an historian, a naïve hero-worshipper without an informing theory. Lungs, heart, blood-pressure were all in

198

excellent shape for a woman of her age. Stephen began to relax.

"Would you stand on the scales, please?" he said. She did.

"Eight stone four?"

"Yes, exactly."

"I never vary, Dr Daker. I have weighed the same for thirty years. I often wonder why I bother to get on the um tell-you-your-weight-thing. It's purely a matter of routine, like brushing one's . . . damn it . . ."

"Shoes?" said Stephen.

"Teeth. I'm rather . . . on edge, Dr Daker, I'm afraid."

"There's absolutely nothing to worry about," said Stephen.

"You're doing fine. Now if you'd just stand there for a moment or two. Just look at the print on the wall, if you would."

"Bit of a waste of my time, this," she said. "Not a very good print at all, wood round the outside's the best thing about it."

Stephen spoke very quietly. "What would you say it was worth, Dr Hubbard?"

"What?"

"I was just wondering if it had any value," he said, a little louder.

"None whatsover," she said, turning round. "Not that you're interested. You were attempting a crude test on my hearing, which is quite adequate for normal purposes."

"Yes, you're quite right," said Stephen. "I'm sorry."

"No need to be," said Dr Hubbard. "Just doing your job, no doubt. Now there's a phrase that resonates through history."

"Come and sit down, Dr Hubbard," he said. He watched her walk to the chair. Very upright, no stiffness, a tough old bird. When he sat down, he noticed that her hands were trembling slightly. That wasn't anything clinical. It was fear. There was no sign of it in her voice though.

"Ah, yes. So much for the physical; now for the senility check, eh?"

"No, really. Not at all. I can say, though, that you're in remarkably good physical shape." He was making a few notes in pencil on a rough pad.

"The world of scholarship is more concerned with my mental shape, I should imagine," she said.

"I was just wondering," said Stephen, "if there was anything else you might like to tell me about, or ask me about. You haven't consulted a doctor in ten years, you say. No problems at all?"

"Such as?"

"Well, say dizzy spells. Blackouts. Quite common."

"D'you think I'd tell the University if I had? You seem a very pleasant young man, Doctor Daker, but I can hardly afford to trust you. Moreover, I'm perfectly capable of reading upside down, and I do know that mild aphasia – thank you for the question-mark, by the way, very undogmatic of you – is a kind of speech loss caused by brain damage, often from a stroke, or a tumour. Am I right or am I wrong?"

"You're quite right, Dr Hubbard." What would be nice would be a lever to pull that would send him straight through a trap door. Oh God. He was blushing again.

"I haven't had a stroke, Doctor Daker, I'm eccentric, which is neither an illness nor a crime. I remember important things, and tend to forget trivial ones, especially when I am preoccupied or agitated, both of which I am now. So at the moment, no doubt it'll come back later, the name of that thing over there you stand on it and it tells you how heavy you are totally escapes me. Nor, now I come to think of it, can I recall the name of that thing you've got in your hand you can write things down with it and *cross them out as well*."

"Pencil," said Stephen. He drew a light line through "Mild aphasia (?)".

"Pencil, yes," said Lilian Hubbard. Her hands had stopped trembling now. "What a boring thing to have to remember! Am I to go on Ernest Hemmingway's scrapheap because I can't remember the word for . . . whatever it was? What was it?"

"Pencil," said Stephen, smiling.

"Very good!" she said, as if to a very dim student who had for once in his life said something bright. "I'll tell you what, Doctor Daker, I'll make a bargain with you. You can remember things like what to call a pencil and scales, there you are, told you it would come back, and I'll remember the hard bits."

"What are the hard bits?" said Stephen. He was beginning to enjoy himself.

"Well, for example, I could tell you the names of all the mourners at Eleanor Marx's funeral, exactly who said what, and what the political significance was to be in terms of European socialism and in terms of what they called in those days The Woman Question. That's a chapter I could write without recourse to notes. I could tell you about all the undergraduates in my charge, and write you a detailed reference for each of them without opening the file. I can also recall with perfect accuracy events in the short and inglorious history of this University which would make you jump out of your socks, Doctor Daker."

"I'm sure you could, Dr Hubbard."

"Come round to tea one day and I will. I'm not Old Mother Riley, you know. I'm the best damned historian you've ever met."

"I believe you," said Stephen sincerely.

"And I'm . . . really very worried indeed about the outcome of this medical. I just need five more years, you see, Doctor Daker. Four would do, at a pinch." As soon as she had gone, he filled in the form and sent it off to the Registry.

Report on a meeting of the Forward Innovations Committee Chair: The Vice-Chancellor. Representation from Finance and Development Committee, all major faculties, Medical Centre. Guests: representatives of the Sakamoto Corporation.

To receive: The Report on the Science Park Implementation.

The Vice-Chancellor introduced the report, and urged

immediate implementation. Before this was able to proceed, Dr Lilian Hubbard entered the conference room and announced her intention of monitoring the business. She was very interested in forward innovations and so was her dog. The Vice-Chancellor reminded Dr Hubbard that she was not a member of the committee and neither was her dog. Dr Hubbard pointed out that Senate regulations permitted non-voting observers, and said nothing about dogs one way or another. The Registrar confirmed that this was the case, and the meeting proceeded.

The Vice-Chancellor informed the committee that the Sakamoto Corporation had provisionally agreed to take up a substantial research and development facility in the new Science Park, working closely with the Electronics and Cybernetics Departments of the University. The level of funding was still confidential, but he was able to tell the committee that it would be substantial, allowing for a new Chair in Cybertronics. Dr Buzzard offered the full facilities of the Medical Service to all Japanese colleagues, and the Medical Service was warmly thanked for this facility.

Dr Hubbard then asked where it was proposed that all these Japanese scientists were going to live. The Vice-Chancellor said that this had yet to be ironed out, various options being under consideration. Mr Takishi informed Dr Hubbard that the Japanese colleagues would be living in Fairlie Hall, a very pleasant building. Dr Hubbard said she was well aware that Fairlie Hall was a pleasant building. Mr Takishi said that his people would be very happy to live there. The Vice-Chancellor said that this was just one of a number of options.

Mr Takishi said that the interior would, of course, be completely restructured with steam baths, jacuzzis and many other delights, and that it would be renamed Sakamoto Lodge in honour of the company president. Dr Hubbard told Mr Takishi that he had been seriously misled if not lied to, and that Fairlie Hall was and always would be a hall of residence for women.

The Vice-Chancellor moved next business and suggested to Dr Hubbard that the matter of Fairlie Hall might be discussed at another time. Dr Hubbard said there was nothing to discuss. The Vice-Chancellor was going to have to find somewhere else for his new friends. Mr Takishi informed Dr Hubbard that he was frightened of her dog. Dr Hubbard instructed her dog to get off Mr Takishi. Dr Hubbard and her dog then left the meeting, which went on to consider the urgent question of medical reports.

"It's a painful business," said Jock. "A painful business." The medical team, apprised of the urgency of the situation by Bob Buzzard, were reviewing progress on the first batch of medicals.

"Well, Jock," said Rose Marie, "not all of it has been too distressing. Leo Architrave from Social Psychology is quite keen on converting his slipped disc into a golden handshake. Apparently he has a nice little job lined up in Canada, where they'll let him lie on the floor all day."

"Poor old Perry Skinner-Joyce lay on the floor in my consulting room for a least ten minutes," said Bob. "Tripped over the rug as he came in, didn't seem to notice he wasn't upright. Anyway, there's another scalp for the bathchair brigade."

"Canon Pottle lay on my couch and wept," said Jock, who seemed near tears himself. " 'Pull yourself together, Pottle,' I told him, 'you're in better shape than I am!' 'No, no, Jock,' he sobbed. 'I am not a well man and I am not a good man, and my work here is over.' Poor fellow. He was weeping for his boys, all those generations of boys he cared for in Kennedy Hall. 'You know, Jock,' he whispered, 'they were all my sons.' "

"Good God, were they really?" said Bob. "About time he packed it in then! You had Lilian Hubbard, didn't you Stephen?"

"Yes," said Stephen. "She's fine. No problems."

"Apart from being deaf as a post, aphasic from a stroke she's not telling anyone about, and mad as a hatter in general?"

"What?" said Stephen. His ears buzzing oddly. Surely Bob couldn't have been rooting about in his waste bin?

"Where on earth did you get that from?"

"Oh, sorry, must have picked your rough notes up by mistake," said Bob, without turning a hair. "Well, she is, isn't she? All those things?"

"No, she isn't," said Stephen angrily. "Those were . . . they were tentative speculations, and I rejected them. She is very slightly deaf; after all she's getting on a bit . . ."

"Well, isn't that the point, buddy? We're supposed to be weeding out the geriatrics!"

Stephen found that something was making him shake, and it wasn't panic or terror. Struggling to keep his voice steady, he said: "She is very slightly deaf, Bob, but it is not a problem. She has a slightly eccentric memory and that's not a problem either. And she isn't as mad as a hatter, she is one of the sanest people in this University, which I admit is not saying a lot."

"What did she do," said Bob, "bung you a case of Scotch?"

Stephen was on his feet. "Look, um, Bob," he found himself saying, "I h-haven't hit anyone since I was in junior school . . ."

"Gentleman, gentleman!" boomed Jock. There was a short pause.

"Right, fine, sorry!" said Bob. "Take it back, no offence intended. It's just a bit of a snag, that's all. Ernie is very keen to get her out of Fairlie Hall, Japs have set their hearts on it, multi-million endowment swinging in the balance, and it would just about suit everyone, and keep us all in employment, if your tentative speculations turned out to have a bit of mileage in them."

"Well, they haven't, Bob. She's fine. I'm sorry to disappoint you." He walked out of the meeting and back to his room. Five minutes later, he was still shaking.

"Can I come in, Stephen?" said Rose Marie. He didn't answer. He didn't feel like answering. She always came in anyway. She closed the door with exaggerated care, as if he were dying or something, and sat down.

"You're very upset, aren't you, Stephen?"

"This place," he said bitterly.

"I know," she said. She waited patiently. She was good at waiting. He didn't want to talk about it, but he knew he was going to.

"This bloody awful place," he said. "I know there have to be cuts, and I ought to know what Bob Buzzard's like by now, I'm even quite fond of him in a way . . . but she's a person, Rose. Not some inconvenient obstacle."

"She's a very fine person," said Rose Marie softly.

"Yes, she is," he said.

"And I was very moved by your support for her. I was . . . quite disturbed by the strength of my response to your anger, Stephen."

"Afraid I rather lost control of myself," he said. He didn't want to look at her very much. She'd be doing her breathing, and her significant looking. It was all part of this place and things he didn't like about it.

"Perhaps you should lose control of yourself more often," she said. "I found myself . . . how shall I put it? . . . responding to you as a woman."

"Oh," he said. This was obviously very different from responding as a colleague and a friend, or a long-time member of the Labour Party, and no doubt very flattering, but he didn't want to have to cope with it.

"Yes," she said. "I don't think you fully appreciate the strength of the response you evoke in women, Stephen."

"Yes, I do," he said. "I've been a profound disappointment to women from my mother onwards."

"Oh, no," she said warmly. "You know, for a moment in there, I really wanted to see you fight Bob, physically. I felt that as a woman."

"Oh," said Stephen.

"I do want to see you fight, Stephen. But Bob's not a worthy opponent. You're going to have to fight with Ernest Hemmingway."

"What, physically?"

"If it comes to that. He isn't going to give up easily. He wants Lilian Hubbard out, and you have become her

205

champion. You're going to have to show him that you're not frightened of him."

"But I am frightened of him," said Stephen.

"No, you're not, Stephen. Not deep inside. Not in your essential maleness. I know this as a woman. Deep down, Ernest Hemmingway is frightened of you."

"Is he?" Stephen found that hard to believe.

"Yes, he is. But you're going to have to teach him that. And to do that . . . it might be necessary to lose control of yourself in a major way."

Jock was feeling much more cheerful. Suddenly the idea had come to him, in a flash, as all great ideas come. He would solve the problem of his medical examination by doing it himself. Was he not qualified to do it? Did he not know the patient better than anyone else? Of course he did! And no lesser person than the Head of the Practice could be entrusted with such a task . . . how convenient that that was he.

He wound the length of tubing round his stringy old bicep, humming a little tune. "Now just relax, Doctor McCannon," he said aloud to himself, "this is purely a matter of routine, you're a fine man for your age, a fine man . . ." After a while he risked a look at the dial.

"Hmmm . . . another piece of faulty equipment, can't rely on anything nowadays . . . let's see now, we adjust for the normal distribution curve, take away the number we first thought of, and that gives us a hundred and forty over ninety. Really? Well, Dr McCannon, that's very satisfactory, I do congratulate you. I think that calls for a little drink, don't you?"

He reached for his trusty bottle of Bell's. "And then we'll see if we can conjure up a little urine sample."

Bob Buzzard was right on the inside rail again, talking person-to-person on the blower to the great man himself.

"Yes, Vice-Chancellor," he said, "we've more or less finished the first batch, and you should have got the reports by now. Pretty much what we expected, by and large."

Hemmingway had indeed got the preliminary reports,

and had them spread out all over his enormous desk. "Yes," he said. "Two or three good scalps there. Shame about Jock McCannon. He'll take it hard. A fine career."

"Yes," said Bob. "We're all a bit cut up about it here."

"So much so that you forgot to sign it. Pop over here some time would you, and do that, Buzzard?"

"Well, er, yes, right, actually it was Doctor Rose Marie," said Bob, in a bit of a flap. He'd been hoping Ernie wouldn't notice the absence of a signature.

"Well, whichever one of you it was," said Hemmingway impatiently. "Now what about Lilian Hubbard?"

"Should be with you now, Vice-Chancellor."

"I haven't seen it."

"I'm afraid it's not very helpful, sir."

"Dorothy?" said Hemmingway. She was sorting out some personal files. She always seemed to be sorting out personal files these days.

"It's in your in-tray," she said wearily. She walked over and found it for him.

"I don't think Doctor Daker appreciated the situation in its broader context," babbled that fool Buzzard over the telephone.

Ernest Hemmingway spread the report out on his desk and skimmed it. Ernest Hemmingway had always been lightning at mastering a brief. "No, it doesn't look as if he did," he said. "I'm only a layman, but this looks like a rather sloppy bit of work to me. Well, too late now. We're moving straight ahead with the site inspection, got to show the Jap chaps we mean business, eh? I've got the University architects over at Fairlie Hall this morning. Must say I hoped for a bit more input from you on this one, Buzzard. Feel a bit let down. Good day to you."

"Not my fault," sulked Bob. "Did my best." The dialling tone hummed back at him sceptically.

"Right, Dorothy," said the Vice-Chancellor. "I'll see Architrave first, I think, and then Skinner-Joyce, assuming he can get up the stairs."

"Vice-Chancellor," she said. She was standing by the window.

"What?"

"I think there's something rather odd going on." She sounded rather pleased. That usually meant trouble, these days. He joined her at the windows.

"Good God," he said. "Pass me those binoculars."

Fairlie Hall was transformed. A huge banner was spread across the whole façade at first-floor level. The legend said:

FAIRLIE HALL FOR WOMEN ONLY

Half-a-dozen young women were standing chained together completely blocking the front entrance. They were dressed in dark colours, and their faces were serious and intent. In front of them stood Lilian Hubbard, in full academic dress, with Caesar crouched at her side. All the upstairs windows were open, with less formally dressed women leaning out. These students were taking the proceedings with more gaiety. Some were laughing and singing. From a second-floor window, two nuns beamed down benevolently, shelling peanuts and taking sips from a brown bottle.

Facing Fairlie Hall was a little knot of men, comprising the University architects, two men with surveying equipment, and two of the Sakamoto men.

"This is a charming ceremony," said Mr Takishi, the interpreter. "These fine young women in the chains, we like this very much. Could you explain the symbolism please, Professor Hubbard?"

"We are here to deny you access to our home, gentlemen," said Lilian Hubbard. "We who study history, we who live in history, must be prepared to play our parts in history. Gentlemen, I have nothing against any one of you personally, but I say to you in deadly earnest that unless you sling your hooks double quick, we'll set the dogs on you!" The architects, the surveyors and the Sakamoto men conferred briefly in whispers. Then they turned round and began to walk away slowly. Caesar growled.

They walked more quickly. Laughter, applause, and misophallic comments issued from the first-floor windows, and a brown bottle was hurled from a second-floor window, narrowly missing Mr Takishi. One of the surveyor's men began to run.

Bob Buzzard found it a bit of a bind, not only having to save the University, do his bit for Forward Planning, and process the Eventide Home Express, but also service his regular patients into the bargain.

"Well," he said, "I think we should carry on with these for another fortnight, don't you?"

"But what are they supposed to do, exactly, Doctor Buzzard?" said the patient, a bolshy type from, wouldn't you know, Fairlie Hall. Sooner that place filled up with steam baths and geishas the better it would suit Bob Buzzard.

"They're to make you better, Miss Stephenson, that's what they're supposed to do. I won't confuse you with a lot of technical jargon. What you've got to grasp is that I'm the doctor and you're the patient, and I'd hardly be prescribing these if they were going to make you worse, would I? Right? There you are, then, you toddle off to Boots with that, and all your troubles will be over." Through the years Bob had perfected the technique of delivering a speech such as this while walking round his desk, slipping a hand under the patient's elbow, and escorting her to the door. He felt tempted to give this one a bloody good shove into the corridor, too, but he restrained himself.

"But I did rather hope we could . . ."

"Fine, fine, see you in two weeks, then! Bye!"

"Have you got a moment, Robert?" Rose Marie, lurking in the corridor. He wished he had given the girl a bit of a shunt, could have killed two birds with one, still, fantasies of violence weren't his style, and real violence wasn't really on, not even in Thatcher's England, not in this bloody University.

"All the time in the world for you, Rose," he said. "Come

and sit down. Appreciate that. Calling me Robert." She sat down and smiled at him. Odd woman. Sometimes she really got on a man's tits, other times, soft as shit, gentle, pliable, in fact if he weren't in love with his wife, really quite . . . still, not on his own doorstep.

"I often feel that your contribution isn't really fully appreciated, Robert." She looked as if she might fully appreciate his contribution right there in his consulting room, what was the matter with him? Keep alert, Buzzard. "I was very impressed with the calm way in which you handled Stephen's little outburst. I responded to your strength and your dignity, Robert. As a woman."

"Oh, well," said Bob. "Can't take things too seriously, can you? Got quite a soft spot for old Stephen you know, even though he does carry on like a big girl sometimes, oops, beg your pardon, I mean we all get the old red mist now and then."

She was looking concerned about something. Real caring doctor-face. Didn't suit her. Still, he supposed, women feel they have to look caring, goes with the gender.

"I think it's rather more than that, Robert," she said. "I'm quite worried about Stephen. He came in to see me afterwards and talked in quite a hysterical way about how you were his enemy and Hemmingway was his enemy . . . quite disturbing."

"Really? Old Dickie Dado going round the twist?"

"I think he might be . . . heading for a little breakdown. I wonder if the Vice-Chancellor should know about it?"

"Yes. Well," said Bob. "Think he should, really. Only fair."

"Well, Robert, you seem to have his ear at present."

Yes, he did. For a moment it occurred to him how much more convenient it was to be a chap. Chaps did have chaps' ears, by and large. Must be a bit frustrating for totties like Rose who wanted to get on with their lives. "Yes, he does seem quite pleased with my input. Especially Jock's report."

Her eyes widened. "You persuaded Jock to let you examine him after all?"

"Well, no. I mean, as you said, any fool could fill in the gaps without actually examining him." He was beginning to get the sense that something might have gone a bit wrong.

"And you actually went ahead and did it?"

"Well, that's what I thought you . . . yes, I did."

"Oh, *Bob*," she said. "Don't you think that was a little rash?"

Ernest Hemmingway turned gloomily from the window. Nothing had moved on the Fairlie Hall front. The mad-woman wasn't always there with her slavering brute, but the suffragettes were still chained across the doorway day and night. They had worked out some way of changing the guard, which totally baffled him. It always looked like the same bunch of women, but even feminists must need a pee now and then. Of course, he could always call up Group Four or some less scrupulous bunch and shift them by force majeure, but politically that was a bit ticklish. So he'd been forced to laugh it off and explain it to his new friends as British folkloric theatre, but it was beginning to wear a bit thin.

Well, let's see what kind of a lever he had on young Dr Daker. He had left him sitting in silence for five minutes, and that was more than enough for most people, in Ernie's experience. "Well, now, Daker," he said, heartily. "Stephen, isn't it? I thought this might be a good time to have a little chat about your career prospects here."

"I didn't think I had any career prospects here, Vice-Chancellor," said the medico. Sounded pretty calm about it, too. Fatalistic. That was what it was. Like those Indian johnnies. When life's cheap, they don't give a toss, very hard to deal with. Got to give them something to aspire to.

"Situations can change remarkably quickly, you know: of course it's hard to keep brilliant chaps like you, but in view of Jock McCannon's early retirement plans I was hoping we might be able to tempt you."

"I didn't know Doctor McCannon was planning to retire." That had opened his eyes a bit.

"I think you'll find I'm right," said Ernie genially. "And that, you see, opens up some interesting possibilities. I just wanted to make sure that, how shall I put it, that you have the University's best interests at heart."

"Well, yes," said Stephen. "Of course I have."

"Good." And indeed it did sound promising. "This is a terribly sad business," he went on, laying it on as thick as he dared. "Poor Lilian Hubbard. She and I go back a long way, you know. Knew her at Oxford when she was just a young girl. Tragic business. I very much hope that we can deal with it humanely."

"I'm sorry . . . I don't think I understand."

"Lilian's mental breakdown, Stephen. This . . . bizarre behaviour: chaining girls to railings, setting dogs on the University architects. She needs help and support. Skilled psychiatric help and support." Fellow was looking a bit shocked. Well, he needed to wake up a bit. Whole thing was obvious, to anyone with an ounce of nous about him. But it seemed he needed to have it spelled out to him.

"I've done my best on this one, Stephen. I've tried to reason with her on the telephone, but I'm sorry to say she became quite abusive. Now I understand that she has a bit of a soft spot for you, and, oddly enough, for Jock McCannon. And what I thought was that if you and Jock could get in there and have a chat with her, you might be able to get her to co-operate."

"I'd certainly be prepared to go and talk to her," said the young chap. "And listen to her. And help her." Good. Now we'd get the shilly-shallying, cut him off quick. "But I don't think I'd . . ."

"Good man. Good man. And if she doesn't see reason, well I'm not too hot on the technicalities, but isn't there something called sectioning?"

"Sectioning?" Chap looked a bit taken aback. Odd. Surely sectioning was the right word?

"Something like that, isn't it?"

"Under sections two, three and four of the 1983 Mental Health Act, two doctors can commit a patient to a mental hospital without the patient's consent. Is that what you mean?"

"Exactly," said Ernie. Chap looked a bit bowled over, Lord knew why.

"You want us to commit Lilian Hubbard to a mental hospital because she's inconveniencing your plans for Fairlie Hall?" said Stephen.

"No, no, no. In her own interests. There's no stigma in mental illness; we all live in the twentieth century, I hope, and of course we'd all prefer it to be voluntary. But I fear she's too far gone for that." All that sounded perfectly reasonable to Ernie, but the medical man was beginning to look a bit wild-eyed. That other doc, one who looked like a dog, Buzzard, that was it, had tipped him the wink that Daker might be a bit unstable. Well, he was right, it seemed.

"Can't you see – can't you see that's a monstrous suggestion? Sectioning is only used in the most urgent and extreme cases, where the patient's actually dangerous. She's not dangerous. She's not even . . ."

"She is dangerous," said the Vice-Chancellor sharply. "She's endangering the viable future of this University, which includes your future as well as mine. I hope I make myself clear, Stephen."

"I won't do it," the fellow said. Now some Vice-Chancellors would put the boot in at this point, but Ernest Hemmingway was a flexible operator. There were other ways of getting the best out of people, and in any case one could put the boot in later.

"Don't say any more now," he said, in warm and reassuring tones. "You've been under a strain. As we all have, in this difficult time. And some of us bear up under the strain better than others. Go away, my boy. Think it over. Consider where your own best interests lie."

"And then it suddenly came to me," said Stephen. "*He's crazy.*"

"Well, of course he is," said Lyn. They were walking round the lake. Things always seemed better by the lake. Ordinary dogs fooling about in ordinary ways, the odd duck, the still, shimmering surface of the water. It should be possible to keep a sense of proportion by the lake; but now, on the north side, the banners of Fairlie Hall confronted the distant fortifications: the sky and the water themselves mirrored the fear, conflict and madness of the sick university.

"Well," Stephen went on. "Either he's crazy or I am."

"Oh, it's him," said Lyn reassuringly. "You're OK, you're just a bit neurotic."

"Thanks very much, Lyn," he said. "That's a great relief."

She stopped, took him by the ears, and gave his nose a quick suck. "Irish blow job," she said. "Like it?"

"Yes," he said. "Thank you very much. You *really* think he's crazy?"

"Yup."

"Well . . . don't you think someone ought to do something about it?"

"No point," she said. "He functions perfectly in his context. I mean, madness is a social construct, like ideas of who's pretty and who's a criminal. This University's a crazy place. That means that when you're in it, crazy's the norm. People like you and me and Lilian, we're the misfits."

Stephen thought about this for a bit, trying to find the flaw in the argument, but it made perfect sense. Though some things were normal, surely, even here. The dogs, the ducks, and over there two people taking a quiet walk through the trees . . . he stopped. It was the nuns. They seemed to have a sack of litter with them, and they were systematically distributing crisp packets, empty cans and other even less attractive things on the velvety grass. Twenty yards behind them, a small scruffy man was dodging from tree to tree, apparently tracking them, or hunting them down.

Stephen shuddered. "You're not really serious, are you, Lyn?"

"Only partly serious." She grinned. "I don't have to be really serious. I'm not going to be here for ever. I can have a bit of fun while I'm here, then get back to the real world. And . . . well, you know I've finished my research project."

214

"Yes." Panic and terror. Not crippling, not overpowering, but there, deep down, biding their time.

"Well," she said, "maybe now's the time to go."

"But I thought – don't they want to renew your Fellowship?"

"Yeah, they do. But I don't want to get sucked in. I've been getting a bit of . . . real world nostalgia lately."

"But this *is* the real world for Lilian Hubbard. And Jock McCannon. They really need it."

"Yeah, Stephen. I know."

"And, well, in a way . . . well it sort of feels like the real world to me."

"Yeah, I was afraid of that. It's got you, Stephen. The mad university has got you in its grip. You need it too."

"Right," said Stephen. "And it bloody well needs me."

"More than it needs a Science Park?"

"Much more than it needs a Science Park," he said firmly. "More than it needs Ernest bloody Hemmingway. What it needs is people like Lilian Hubbard and Chen and even Jock McCannon, and you, and me. I think I'm joining the opposition, Lyn."

"My hero," she said.

"And I wish you'd stay."

"Very good of you to come over, Jock," said Ernest Hemmingway genially.

"Oh, it's a pleasure, Ernie," said Jock. He did look rather pleased with himself. Two modest double Bell's ahead of the rest of the world, a spring in his step and feeling intimations that even the ancient sap might be stirring, he had put on his hairiest suit and his most horrible yellow tie especially for this occasion. "Eh, yes, indeed. I love my visits here. Drinking coffee out of fine china cups, the smell of raw power . . . Heady stuff, Ernie, heady stuff for a simple man like me."

"Of course," said the Vice-Chancellor, "it goes without saying I'm very sorry about this medical business."

"Oh, I don't think you need to be, Ernie. I think it's working out quite well."

"I was referring to your own case, Jock," said Hemmingway, assuming the serious tones of a really flash funeral director. That should take that vile yellow grin off his face.

"Really?" said Jock. The clear alcoholic blue eyes were wide with innocent surprise. "But you haven't seen the report yet."

"What? I've got it here in front of me." He held up the doggy chap's beautifully typed report. Nobody was going to wriggle out of that one.

"May I see that?" said Jock. "Thank you, Ernie." He skimmed through it, humming cheerfully. "Ah. Do I recognise the spoor of Doctor Buzzard's rinky-dinky little dot matrix printer? I see I do. Oh dear, oh dear. I think young Bobby Buzzard's been having a joke with you, Ernie. You see, he didn't examine me at all. As I'm sure he will admit, if pressed. No, Ernie, here is the official medical report on J. G. McCannon." He extracted the crumpled document from the hairy recesses of his jacket and passed it across the desk. The Vice-Chancellor took it between finger and thumb; it was disturbingly warm and, even more disturbingly, slightly damp as well.

"A much more encouraging prognosis, I think you'll find." Hemmingway leafed through it crossly. It was a terrible report. It said that Jock was well. That wouldn't do.

"I can't read the signature," he said.

"It's signed by the senior physician in the University," said Jock proudly. "J. G. McCannon."

Ernest Hemmingway opened his mouth and left it open for several seconds. Then he said, "You can't sign your own medical report!"

"Have your secretary search the University regulations, Vice-Chancellor," said Jock, winking caddishly at Dorothy, who was sorting through some personal files. "I don't think you'll find they have anything to say on the matter. And, eh, while she's doing that, you might care to glance at the text of this little book I've been writing through the long and sleepless nights. *The Sick University*, it's called. I think you'll find it interesting." From another recess of his noxious jacket, Jock pulled out a set of galley-proofs. "Don't bother with the whole thing, pages seventeen to twenty-two should give you something of the flavour," said Jock, lighting a crumpled Woodbine. Ernest Hemmingway skimmed through pages seventeen to twenty-two and whimpered under his breath.

"The publishers are quite excited," said Jock. "Only in proof at the moment, of course. Still time for a few emendations. I'd be grateful for your thoughts, Ernie, on both matters."

The Vice-Chancellor stared at the Senior Physician with fear and loathing. "You look a little peaky, Vice-Chancellor, if you don't mind my saying so. Perhaps you ought to see a doctor."

It was shit or bust time at Fairlie Hall, as Bob Buzzard would have put it had he been there. But the doggy chap had been called away urgently on family business until the heat died down a bit. Plenty of other people were there though. The serious young women were still chained to the railings, the less serious young women were leaning out of the first-floor windows haranguing the architects and the Sakamoto men, and a group of not very dangerous-looking University security staff were standing about in peaked caps pretending to be saying important things into their rinky-dinky walky-talkies.

Lilian Hubbard was not part of the scene. She was inside, in her study, entertaining Stephen and Jock to tea. Tea at Lilian Hubbard's was quite a flexible meal. She thought tea ought to consist of anything you might feel like having at tea time, so besides the tea itself, there were, a big fruit cake, some sausages, a lot of large Polish gherkins, tins of Kennomeat, dog biscuits, several pounds of ginger snaps, and bottles of whisky and red wine.

"Any new developments, Stephen?" said Jock to his colleague who was standing at the window.

"Hemmingway's arrived with the Registrar. A few new security men."

"Ah," said Lilian Hubbard. "Ernie's stormtroopers. Tell me Doctor Daker, have they got big black things?"

"Er . . . not that I can see," said Stephen carefully. "Oh, truncheons. No, I don't think so. They don't look very warlike."

"My splendid young women will be more than a match for them. Won't they, Caesar?" Caesar, who had the largest chair in the room to himself, made no comment either way. "And Hemmingway knows it. He'll be making up his mind whether to call the police."

"As a matter of fact, Lilian," said Jock McCannon, "he's waiting to see whether Stephen and I can persuade you to become a voluntary patient in a mental institution. That's what he thinks we're doing here."

"Ha! Hear that, Caesar? Doesn't the poor little man realise that we *are* voluntary patients in a mental institution? Come and sit down, Doctor Daker. Have some more of this with the red things in."

"Thank you," said Stephen, taking a piece of cherry cake.

"And Dr McCannon, would you be so good as to pour out a little more of the, er . . ."

"Amber fluid, yes indeed," said Jock, doing so. "I wonder if they had whisky and cherry cake in the days of the Paris Commune."

"Thank you, Dr McCannon," she said. "A pleasing image. It dignifies our little struggle." She raised her glass. "To history, gentlemen."

"Actually," said Stephen, "the only thing that sticks in my mind from school history is that history's always written by the winning side."

"Well, then, Dr Daker, we'd better *be* the winning side, hadn't we?" she said.

"Yes, we had. Um . . . how are we going to do that? I mean, ultimately Hemmingway's got all the big guns, hasn't he?"

"He wouldn't actually shoot us? How splendidly apocalyptic!" said Jock. "What a way to go!"

"You're a nice man, McCannon," said Lilian Hubbard,

"but you were always a bit of a noodle. Drink your whisky and shut up, there's a good chap. And as for you, Dr Daker, I'm perfectly aware that the VC could have me bodily ejected from Fairlie Hall. But at what cost to the reputation of the University?" She got up and began to dust cake crumbs off herself. "I'm very grateful to you both. You've been staunch in my support, at some little cost to yourselves. But I think I can take care of the final stage. And now, if you'll excuse me, I have a lecture to give. My students will show you out by the fire exit."

Stephen stared at her. "But surely, if you go over to the Lecture Theatre, they'll just take over the Hall when you're gone."

Lilian Hubbard smiled grimly. "I had considered that, Dr Daker. That is why I've arranged to lecture from the, um, it's over there with glass in you can see through it."

As Stephen and Jock came round the side of the building, they had to jostle their way through two or three hundred students with files and notebooks making their way to the lawn in front of Fairlie Hall, where they sat down in rows, looking up at the windows expectantly. Hemmingway pushed his way through the crowd.

"Well? What happened? What the hell's going on?"

"We, ah, had a long talk with Doctor Hubbard," said Jock solemnly.

"And? And?"

"She's . . . eh . . . agreed to make a statement."

"She's coming out?"

"She did say it was the final stage," said Stephen.

Hemmingway flung his arm round Stephen's shoulders. "Excellent. Excellent. Well done, the pair of you. Let's hope it's a short statement, eh?"

With a rumble and a squeak, the big sash window above the front entrance slid up, and Lilian Hubbard came into view. She looked calm and businesslike, just as if she were about to give a lecture, in fact. Some of the students started to cheer, but she shook her head impatiently and held up her hand for silence. As soon as she got it she started straight in. Her lecturing style was not flamboyant or charismatic. She had never needed it to be. What you got with Lilian Hubbard was the real stuff.

"This will be my final lecture," she said, "on problems in historical interpretation, and in it I shall be dealing principally with the vexed question of the value to be attributed to the evidence of the interested participant."

The students were scribbling already. Hemmingway was staring at her perplexed. Jock McCannon sat down on the grass and happily prepared himself for sleep.

"When I was a very young lecturer at Girton," she went on, "I was entrusted with the supervision of a rather backward M Phil student from one of the men's colleges: his dissertation topic was, if I remember it rightly, Machiavelli and the Medicis, and I'm sorry to say that it was never completed to the satisfaction of the University examiners."

Hemmingway clutched Stephen's arm. "Daker! What is she up to?"

"It's just a lecture, Vice-Chancellor," said Stephen soothingly.

"When I pointed out the shortcomings of his work to the young man, he explained his lack of application in terms of the distraction of his thoughts; he had fallen head over, what d'you call them, yes, *heels*, in love with me, he said; and proposed that we should have sexual intercourse, or, as he put it at the time, that he would take me through the Gates of Paradise."

"No," said Hemmingway quietly. "No, no."

"I decided that this might be a convenient opportunity to compare the pleasures of fornication with those of scholarship." She paused to check a reference in her notes. Stephen looked around, and saw the entire Sakamoto deputation approaching from the direction of the Science Park. They were wearing light mackintoshes and carrying little cases.

"Without going into detail," Dr Hubbard continued, "the event was something of a disappointment, except insofar as it confirmed me in my devotion to historical research. The young man's performance in the sexual field was no more inspiring than his performance in the sphere of scholarship. The problem was, I believe, in both cases, that he had such a very small, um, that he only had a tiny . . ." Two hundred mouths gaped up at the window. Two hundred pens were poised over notebooks. ". . . intellect."

"She's got to be stopped!" said Ernest Hemmingway.

"Now I don't propose, for the present at least, to name the young man in question. But let us suppose, as a hypothesis, that in later life he acquires a position of power, which he uses in an attempt to oust me from my job and my home."

Hemmingway abruptly lost his cool. "Section her!" he yelled. "Section her!" Heads were turning.

"In a situation such as that, you will readily recognise, the objective truth of my little anecdote is immediately called into question, in a way that highlights the problem which forms the the subject of my lecture."

"There!" yelled Hemmingway. "You see? She's mad! Why don't you section her?"

"Why don't you leave her alone?" said Stephen, shaking his arm free. Hemmingway turned a look of hatred on Stephen but before he could say whatever it was that he was going to say, the Japanese party had arrived.

"Ah, Vice-Chancellor!" said Mr Takishi.

"Oh, my God," said Ernest Hemmingway. "Er, come away, gentlemen, bit noisy here. Just, er, Dr Hubbard's farewell adress."

"Yes, that is what we must do," said Mr Takishi. "I am sorry, Vice-Chancellor."

"What?"

"We must come away, we regret very much. We have been in conference with Osaka headquarters. A dim view is being taken."

Hemmingway's jovial laugh sounded like the gasps of a dying creature. "But this is a, ha ha, just a temporary problem, I assure you, gentlemen!"

"No, no," said Mr Takishi gently, "permanent problem I believe. We regret very much, but not unusual in your

221

country. Very nice site, very compatible plant, but problem with labour relations."

The Sakamoto men began to move away, nodding, smiling and bowing. Hemmingway went with them, talking, gesticulating, tugging at their macs, twisting his sturdy little body this way and that in his efforts to make them stop, consider him, reprieve him, make things all right for him. It was quite poetic, Stephen thought, like a Japanese dance drama about tourists and beggars. They moved into the distance, and Stephen sat down on the grass next to Jock.

"It really is intolerable," said Lilian Hubbard severely, "when one can't conduct an academic lecture without suffering interruption and inattention. If we may continue now. My second example of the problem of the participatory observer is H. M. Hyndman's account of the internal disputes of the Socialist Democratic Federation in the year 1884." Lilian Hubbard had a great deal to say about Hyndman, and Stephen lay back on his elbows and settled himself for an instructive fifty minutes. Lyn jogged into sight round the corner of the building, saw him, and came to sit next to him.

"Good lecture?" she whispered.

"Very good," said Stephen.

"That's good."

Rust and the Novel

Rust is back in his room again. Not a lot has changed. He can still see the strip of grass. He can still see the strip of lake. He can still see the big sad African. He can see his trusty Olivetti waiting for him at the table. But next to the Olivetti are two huge piles of typescript, one on each side. They don't belong to his sodding Creative Writing students. Their stuff goes on the floor, or gets lost in bars. No, these piles of typescript belong to Rust. One is the serial and the other is the novel. He likes the novel best, because it is all him, and he hates the novel worst, because it is all him.

Rust has a problem. He doesn't know how to finish. This is not as bad as not knowing how to start, but it is bad enough. Why can't novels finish themselves off as straight-forwardly as cars do, just cough a bit and then die? Fuck knows. Fucknose. He has been to see his car again today. He goes to see it every day. He doesn't know why. It is always the same, or nearly the same, just a little more rotted than the day before. Like Rust. Not even the starving hordes of hollow-cheeked students trying to keep body and soul together in Thatcher's sodding England on £1,785 per annum or thereabouts have thought Rust's car worth cannibalising. This makes Rust obscurely sad. It will, of course, be the same with him. If he is run over in an accident no one will want his heart. Or his lungs. Or his kidneys. Or his liver: no, especially not that. No one will want his cock. No one wants it now.

When Rust has a problem with the work, he has a regular way of dealing with it. It isn't infallible, and sometimes it doesn't help at all, but it's Rust's way, and he perseveres with it stubbornly. What he does is buy a bottle of Bell's, and gets ratted. That is what he is doing now, getting ratted and working his way slowly towards the problem. No point in charging at it head on. A bit of displacement activity is what's needed. Ernest Hemmingway used to sharpen pencils, which goes to show what a prat *he* was. Rust has always had it in for Ernest Hemmingway. What did he think he was playing at, being so big, for a start? Rust likes only two things about Hemmingway, his short sentences and his wish-fulfilment women. I will be your good girl, I will be your little rabbit. Rust can get behind that. Apart from that, forget it.

In fact, Hemmingway appeared on his list of People For the Chop years after he had done the job himself. Rust just couldn't bear to let him go. That's an idea. He could revise the list. He gets it out of his case. Wogan, the entire staff of the British Film Institute, Tom Stoppard, Julie Walters, the guy who writes the Diary in the *New Statesman* . . . hundreds of them. Experimentally he crosses out Tom Stoppard and substitutes the Catering Manager of Lowlands University.

Difficult. Damned close-run thing. Have to think about that one another time.

He turns the paper over. On the other side is his list of names for characters. A series writer needs a lot of these because of Negative Checks. McCannon changed his name from Mackenzie not to escape the consequences of some early indiscretion, but because of Negative Checks. If it turns out that there are any other series writers called Rust, Rust will cease to exist, and he doesn't fancy that. Not many names left to play with. He's used up most of the best ones. Soames. Sodd. Prettiman. Could a guy with a name like Prettiman swing a plot? Depends what the plot is, and Rust doesn't know that yet. He would like someone called Prettiman to come and sort things out for him, Rust. Wait a minute. He's thought of another name. No. Riddington wouldn't let him call anybody Fucknose.

Rust had a dream about Riddington last night. (Well, why should doctors have all the dreams?) In this dream he was recycling paper for Riddington. This involved riding a bicycle into this enormous pile of shit, pedalling furiously until the wheels became clogged and wouldn't go round any more. Then he searched the pile for pieces of paper. There was paper there all right, not as much paper as shit, of course, but Rust managed to find some bits of light blue toilet paper. He put them in his bicycle basket and pedalled laboriously back to Riddington, who was waiting at the edge of the pile. Then he cleaned off the pieces of paper on his sleeve, and handed them one by one to Riddington, who seemed neither particularly pleased nor particularly disappointed. That was the dream. It would not take Sigmund sodding Freud to work out the significance of that one, thinks Rust.

The Bell's is beginning to do its work now. Something is beginning to crystallise in his mind. It's to do with the novel. It's only a feeling, but he hangs on to it. It's not fear, it's not loathing, it's . . . it's resentment. That's it. He resents the novel and everyone in it. Those doctors don't just have the dreams, they get everything. Money, suits, girls. And Rust doesn't get anything except a swollen nose.

It's not fair. After another couple, he starts to talk to the novel.

Look, says Rust. I want to be in the novel.

Why, this is the novel, nor are you out of it, says the novel.

Cheap trick, says Rust. I'm not in the real novel, am I? I'm only in these crappy little interlude things. Admit it. I'm marginalised in my own novel. Why can't I get some of the action?

I know what you want, says the novel. You want to fuck that girl Lyn. What on earth makes you think she'd fancy you?

She fancies a lot of people, says Rust sulkily. Anyway, I wasn't saying anything as crude as that. This is an artistic point I'm making here, I want to talk about what is foregrounded and what is absent.

Do leave off, says the novel. You're foregrounding yourself enough at the moment, aren't you?

Rust can't answer that. He changes tack. Another thing, says Rust. Why can't I get out of the present tense? It makes me feel temporary and vulnerable.

You ought to be flattered, says the novel. Present tense is dead fashionable. Everybody's doing it. Gets you out of history, lets you float like a feather in the wind, none of that awful draggy feeling that everything's been settled in advance.

Look, says Rust. Those doctors are in the past tense, I want to be *in there*.

Listen, says the novel. Everyone gets to be in the past tense sooner or later, you might not like it as much as you think.

I'll take that risk, says Rust.

OK, says the novel. Don't say I didn't warn you. And by the way, I think you ought to find out something about catastrophe theory.

What for? says Rust.

You'll find out, says the novel. Well, go on then. Get on your Olivetti and pedal into the shit. You don't think I'm going to write myself, do you?

225

7

THE AXEMAN COMETH

Seven thirty in the sick university. All was quiet, apart from the gurgling water in the walkways, and the occasional harsh squawk of a starling. The vast car park was almost empty. Puddles, crisp bags, condoms, a listing Dormobile, a dead Fiat. A small, scruffy looking man was squatting on his heels next to the Fiat, studying it for signs of change. His brow was deeply furrowed, his eyes focussed, if you looked closely, not on the rotting panels, but something invisible in their depths; almost as if the automotive corpse reflected something inside himself. He was so deeply involved in this act of contemplation that he did not hear the battered Mini as it sped in through an EXIT ONLY gate, and with all the yawning acres to choose from, roared straight towards the space next to the Fiat where the scruffy man was squatting.

Ten minutes later, the two nuns, one of them carrying a ghettoblaster turned up to maximum volume, walked across the Piazza and into one of the noxious residential alleys. Without breaking stride, one of the nuns picked up a bottle of milk from a doorstep. The other, also without breaking stride, withdrew a folded *Guardian* from a letter-box. She spread it out as she walked, read the headline and stopped. The other nun stopped next to her. Together they read the front page article. The headline said:

AXE FALLS ON UNIVERSITIES:
25% CUT FOR LOWLANDS, ESSEX, STIRLING,
EAST ANGLIA.

Eight a.m. in the sick university. Ernest Hemmingway, like all good modern executives, and many bad ones, was already in his office and on the blower to Whitehall.

"Bunny? Ernie Hemmingway. It's a nonsense, isn't it? . . . it's not a nonsense. It's a leak. I can't understand this, Bunny. We're squeaky-clean at Lowlands. We're state-of-the-art. We're user-friendly . . . But why? We gave her a doctorate just last year . . . Well, look here, I didn't throw the bloody tomato, did I? . . . Well, what can we do about it? I was hoping to be able to invite you to open our new Science Park, Bunny. And confer a little something . . ."

Dorothy, turning from the personal files, raised an eyebrow. Hemmingway winked at her, then went pale and rigid.

"*What*? No, I'm sorry, Bunny, that's not on. Not in the present climate. Oh, did she. Well, of course we'll be happy to afford them every facility. Delighted. We have nothing to hide at Lowlands. Yes, Minister. Yes. Fine."

He put the phone down. "Twenty-five per cent cut, and it's official," he said. "All for one tomato and that madwoman at Fairlie Hall. *And* they're sending down a factfinding team to investigate waste and inefficiency. The same team that did the Navy."

"Oh, dear," said Dorothy, practising that new smile of hers.

Stephen Daker awoke to the sound of nuns sharpening axes, but he felt no panic or terror. This was because Lyn was sleeping next to him, and because he knew now that the axe-sharpening was in his mind; what was in his room was Chen and a piece of chalk.

"Have you been up all night again?" said Stephen.

"Yeah," said Chen, staring in admiration at his own creation. "Coolie sweats all night while big white doctor snores in his pit. I think what we got here is a whole new dimension of catastrophe theory."

"Please go away, Chen. I don't want any more catastrophes."

"Catastrophe theory doesn't have to be bad," said Chen. "It's just what happens when you push steadily along in one direction, everything nice and logical, then suddenly the whole thing flips inside out. As our national poet puts it, one moment a man is walking through a cool forest hearing the sound of distant flute, the next moment he disappears up his own arsehole. Only I've been thinking about it in four dimensions."

Lyn struggled up to the surface. "Hello, Chen."

"Oh. I didn't see you there," said Chen. "I'm sorry. I intrude. Bugger off now, eh?"

"Not on my account," said Lyn. "I got to get going early, got the headhunters coming after me today. Blimey, is that the time. Bags I first go in the shower, right? Right." She threw the bedclothes back, got up, and walked through to the bathroom.

"That is a wonderful big girl you've got there, Stephen," said Chen.

"Yes, she is," said Stephen pensively.

"This makes you sad?"

"I don't think I've got her for long. The headhunters are after her. She won't stay here."

"She loves you, that big girl," said Chen. "I know all about this stuff."

"Chen," said Stephen. "She's younger than I am. She's cleverer than I am. She's stronger than me, and she can run faster than me, and she's randier than me. And she's . . . you know when I dream about her, she's always running ahead of me, getting further and further away."

"Remember catastrophe theory," said Chen. "Sometimes the whole thing just flips inside out."

"So," said Jock McCannon. "The axeman cometh. Twenty-five per cent overall. Fear stalks the campus, and no one is safe." He surveyed his trusty band of colleagues with a jaundiced eye. Literally jaundiced, in point of fact: the old liver had been taking a bit of a pounding in recent weeks; perhaps one could cut down a little on the morning drinking. No, better stick to what one was used to.

The wee lassie was the first to respond. "I suppose it's only reasonable that Lowlands should make its contribution to the unemployment figures," she said.

"Not volunteering, are you, Rose?" asked Bob Buzzard.

"No, Bob," she said, giving him one of her sweetest smiles. "As a matter of fact, I think the cuts could be a way of rectifying some of the inequalities in the system."

"Inequalities?" said Bob. "Oh, yes, I see, yes, we could get rid of some of those clever chaps, couldn't we, so that the thickies don't feel too inferior. Yes, with a bit more effort we could make this place another Butlins. That the sort of thing?"

"Actually, Bob, I was thinking of inequality as between the sexes."

"Oh, really! Got you now. But, Rose, you mustn't think of it like that. Honestly, Stephen and Jock and I think of you as our equal in almost every way, don't we, chaps?"

"Bob," said Stephen.

"Yes, Stephen?"

"Don't be a prat, Bob. This is a serious situation."

"Oh, is it? Right, yes, thanks for pointing it out."

"It is a tragically serious situation," said Jock heavily. "We can expect loathing and terror on an unprecedented scale. Terrible fallout in terms of psychic damage. A twenty-five per cent cut represents a thousand undergraduates."

"My God, yes," said Stephen. "And more than a hundred academic staff."

"At least two hundred ancillary staff," said Rose Marie.

"Half a nun," said Bob. "Sorry! Sorry!"

"And one doctor from this practice," said Jock McCannon. There was a long silence.

"Er, Jock," said Stephen. "This investigative team they're sending down from London. Do we know anything about them?"

"Well, apparently they played merry hell with the Navy's shore establishments," said Jock. "Apart from that they're just three names." He consulted the crested memo from the VC's office. "Eh, yes, here we are. Soames, Sodd, and Prettiman."

"That wouldn't be P. R. Prettiman, by any chance, Jock?" Bob was sitting bolt upright, keen and alert as a fox-terrier. "P. R. Prettiman? Shrewsbury, Magdalen, and the Treasury?"

"Not an inkling, my dear fellow," said Jock wearily. He had another look at the memo. "The initials *are* P.R. Heard of the man, have you, Bob?"

"Oh, you know," said Bob. "Vaguely."

The chauffeur of the black Ministry Rover had as much difficulty as anyone else in finding his way through the maze of altered priorities and restricted accesses on the Lowlands campus, but it afforded the team a preliminary shufti at the target.

"Fair-sized plant," said Soames, a fine looking man in his fifties with a four-hundred-quid pinstripe suit and an air of having seen most things before and not liked them much. "Have you been here before, Sodd?"

"No, Lord, no," said Sodd, a tough grizzled chap in his forties who had clawed his way up from executive grade. "Reminds one rather of Catterick."

"Catterick. Lord, yes, Catterick," said Soames. "Hope the food's better."

"It won't be," muttered Prettiman. As he was sitting next to the chauffeur his colleagues didn't hear him. He was used to that. He was younger than the other two and a bit on the stout side. He had the right sort of suit, but it didn't look right on him. He had the right sort of haircut too, in principle; but something was wrong with it. Perhaps he had the wrong sort of head.

The Rover glided into the half-empty car park, and slid smoothly into a parking space. Just as it stopped, a battered Mini with two nuns in it shot erratically into the car park, and parked next to the Rover. Right next to it. About two inches away from its nearside doors. The chauffeur got out and helped Soames and Sodd with their briefcases, and they wandered off in the direction of the Reception Lodge,

230

not more than half a mile away. The two nuns had not made any move.

Prettiman was trapped. He tapped on the window. Nothing. The two nuns stared straight ahead. He tapped harder, hurting his knuckles. The nun in the driver's seat turned and smiled, then slammed the Mini into reverse and shot backwards at high speed. Prettiman heard the sound of metal hitting metal. He got out, shut the door, and the wing mirror fell off. As he bent down to pick it up, the Mini shot forward again. Prettiman jumped out of the way, not very nimbly. A hundred yards away, Soames and Sodd turned round.

"Everything all right, Prettiman?" That was Soames.

"Er, yes. Fine." Prettiman thought for a moment, then placed the wing mirror gently on the bonnet, and followed his colleagues towards the lowering concrete cliffs of the Central Complex.

Rose Marie was collating her private files on McCannon, Daker and Buzzard, when Buzzard knocked on her door and came in.

"Panic's started already," said Bob. "Have you seen the waiting room?"

"No, Bob," she said. "But I can imagine."

"Haven't seen such a lot of nervous tics since the VD bug was going round. They're all in there, everything from first year thickies to the Head Porter, shaking like a lot of wet water spaniels."

"You're taking it all very cheerfully," she said thoughtfully.

"Can't help it, Rose. Natural optimist."

"Bob," she said, "what was that business about Prettiman?"

"Oh, that," he said casually. "Bit of a turn up for the book, that. If it's the P. R. Prettiman I think it is, he was at school with me."

"I see," said Rose Marie. "What a bit of luck for you."

"Yes, it was about time old Buzzard's toast came down

231

butter side up. Don't you worry, Rose. I'll put in a good word for you if I get the chance."

"Thank you, Bob," she said.

Robert, Robert, why can't you call me Robert, you'll get a good word from me when hell bloody freezes, thought Bob savagely on his way down the corridor. Some miserable derelict in a leather-patched tweed jacket was mooching about outside his room.

"Hello, young man, looking for Buzzard?"

"Oh, er, yes," said the miserable derelict, who was in fact a middle-aged Education lecturer called Trimble. "I wasn't quite sure where . . ."

"In here," said Bob, speaking slowly and clearly as if to an idiot. "Says Doctor Buzzard on the door, d'you see? That's how you tell you've got the right room. Clever dodge, eh? Right, let's get you fixed up."

Professor Ember was a dark, untrustworthy-looking man in his forties who claimed to be under a strain.

"Well, of course you're under a strain," said Jock McCannon genially. "We're all under a strain. I myself expect to feel the axeblade on my poor old neck at any moment. Yes, of course I'll prescribe you something, Professor Ember. But we're not machines, are we? Even a Professor of Maths is not a machine. How does it feel inside?"

Ember twitched silently for a moment or two. "It feels . . . I haven't published for five years. From *choice*. And now I'm on the verge of a breakthrough. A new development in catastrophe theory. And . . . this is in strict confidence . . . ?"

"Of course, of course."

"One of my research assistants is stealing my ideas."

"Dear, dear, dear," said Jock, perking up. Here was a case of deep sexual anxiety if ever he'd heard one. "A young man, would that be?"

"Yes," said Ember. "An Asiatic."

"Interesting," said Jock. Better and better. This man's libido was clearly in a state of dislocation and turmoil.

232

"You see," said Ember, "if he publishes first . . . they're saying I'm burnt out."

"Burnt out? You're a mere boy?"

"I'm forty-two," said the professor bitterly. "Most pure mathematicians are burnt out by the age of thirty. And with these cuts . . ."

Jock waved the cuts away. It was clear that the cuts were merely triggering an explosion that had been primed for years. "Yes, yes, the cuts. I think I begin to understand. You are not 'burnt out'. The problem is that one of your young men is stealing your fire."

"Exactly," said Ember.

"Yes," said Jock. "I've seldom heard it put more poetically. I'd hazard a guess that John Thomas hasn't been up and about much lately. Hmmmm?"

"What?" The man looked horrified. Deeply armoured against self-knowledge, of course, all these scientists were.

"You're suffering impairment in your sexual drive," explained Jock kindly. "Don't worry. These situations can often . . . how shall I put it? – turn themselves inside out in a matter of moments."

Ember leapt to his feet. "*What*? What do you know about catastrophe theory? Have you been talking to Chen Sung Yau?"

"Not as far as I know, my dear chap. Now sit down, why don't you, and let's have a little talk about libido."

With a wild cry, Professor Ember ran out of the consulting room.

"Poor chap," said Jock. "Poor chap."

"Well, it's quite straightforward as I see it," said Bob. "You've got the screaming abdabs. And I don't blame you."

Trimble, the Education lecturer, stared miserably at Bob's Classic Cars Calendar. "What should I do, Doctor Buzzard? Cate says I've got to go back into school-teaching."

"Well, my wife gets these notions too. Just tell her to belt up and keep taking the tablets."

233

"No, no, you don't understand," said Trimble, almost tearfully. "Cate's an acronym. Council for Accreditation of Teacher Education."

"Ah, yes," said Bob. "With you now. You're on the Mickey Mouse degree. Give lectures on how to control the seething masses, am I right?"

"Er, broadly speaking," said Trimble glumly.

"And now they say you've got to get back in there at the chalk face or out on your ear, right?"

"More or less, yes. Classroom credibility, they call it."

"And you haven't set foot in a school for what?"

"Er . . . fifteen years," mumbled the Education lecturer.

Bob just about managed to smother a cackle of delighted laughter. "Oh dear, oh dear," he said. "Well, some would say you've got it coming to you, but I'm sympathetic. Hairy places these days, state schools. Wouldn't let my own kids near one of them."

"I can't . . . I can't . . ." snivelled the Mickey Mouse man.

"Come on, cheer up," said Bob, relenting. "Give me back that script. I'll write you something stronger." He scribbled briefly. "There you are. Feel no pain with that stuff. And I should get yourself one of those riot shields, second-hand police job. The non-inflammable kind."

"Yes. Thank you," said Trimble. He was blinded with tears of gratitude, or terror. Bob led him to the door.

"That's it. Off you go to Bash Street then. And I shouldn't worry too much, buddy. You'll probably be on strike most of the time."

"Yes, I can see exactly why you're concerned, Alice," said Rose Marie. "It's not an easy time for women." The girl sitting opposite her looked, to be frank, both glum and Neanderthal, but Rose Marie didn't put things in that way, even to herself. An emergent young woman, that was what she was, who needed some help in self-definition in the struggle for authenticity.

"Thing is," said Alice, "I can't concentrate with things like this. Everyone says they're going to kick out a quarter of the second year."

"Well, even if they did, why should it be you?"

"I'm getting steady gamma minuses for everything," said Alice.

"I see," said Rose Marie, making a note. "You're in the German Department, aren't you?"

"Yes."

"I thought so. Who's your tutorial supervisor?"

"Doctor Liebling."

"And he's the one who's sexually harassing you, yes?"

Alice knotted her overhanging brows in a deep frown. "Well, no. Didn't say that, did I?"

Rose Marie took her glasses off and put them on the desk. "Alice, he's giving you steady gamma minuses when you're clearly a highly intelligent young woman. I think that's as clear a case of sexual harassment as any we're likely to see, don't you?"

"Oh, yeah," said Alice. "Never thought of that."

"Alice, I'd like you to go back to the German Department and insist on having a female supervisor for your tutorials. If they ask why, simply say you have your reasons, at this stage."

"But there isn't a female lecturer," said Alice.

"Really? Good," said Rose Marie. "That'll give them something to think about, won't it? And you won't be on your own. The Women's Committee will back you all the way." She smiled at Alice, considering how else her emergence might be hastened. Yes. "And I think you ought to do some assertiveness training at the Well Woman Centre." She handed Alice a small card. "The classes are free. I take them myself."

Alice stared at the card for a while. Clearly a deeply reflective young woman; or perhaps she was just a slow reader. "Right, triffic. Thanks a lot."

"We're going to take care of you, Alice," said Rose Marie warmly. "Oh, and by the way. It might be a good idea to go to some German lectures and read some books. Just in case."

"Oh, yeah," said Alice. "Right, brilliant."

*

Stephen had seen the scruffy little man before, he was sure of it. Yes, that was it. In the bar, and walking by the lake. Always on his own. Always looking guilty, or haunted, or simply confused. And now here he was in the consulting room. Mr Rust.

"So you're the . . ."

"Arts Council Fellow in Creative Writing, right," said Rust.

"And how's it all going?" asked Stephen.

Rust screwed his face up and scratched the back of his head for a bit. "Oh, fine," he said eventually. "Well, not bad. Well, it's horrible really, but you can't complain. Room they've given me, it's like sodding Death Row, but it hasn't got a phone, that's one good thing. My students write about suicide, mostly. Yes, I'm having a whale of a time." While he was talking, Rust was studying the contents of the room with almost obsessive interest, making faces to himself, as it were, rather as if the innocent prints, books and equipment disappointed or offended him in some way. Stephen watched him warily. The University had more than its share of psychotics, and this Rust looked as if he might be one of them.

"Are you able to do much of your own work?" he asked.

"Well, that's the problem, really," said Rust. He stopped glaring at the bookcase and focused his wild stare on Stephen. "I seem to owe the BBC seventeen thousand quid for reasons I can't quite understand, so I thought I'd write off the debt with this little serial set in a place like this." As he talked, he started to fiddle with his shoelace. "You know the sort of thing, sharp satirical black comedy, with a bit of Chekhovian understated pathos. Heaven on wheels, right?"

Now he was doing something else at floor level, but the desk was in the way and Stephen couldn't see. "Well, the thing is," said Rust with great emphasis, "this place is crazy. Every time I think up something really outrageous, sodding reality comes up and tops it. It's as if the University is mocking my powers of creative intelligence. Any damn fool thing I think up really happens, only worse.

I keep getting this feeling that things are seriously out of control."

Stephen's heart went out to the scruffy little man. He might be mad, but he was right on the ball as far as Stephen was concerned. "I do know exactly what you mean," he said. "The thing is, I'm not sure we can help you with it."

"It's all right," said Rust. "Didn't think you could." His head suddenly disappeared below desk level. Stephen hastily revised his opinion. Rust was psychotic after all.

"Er . . . what are you doing?" asked Stephen nervously.

"Just remembered what I really came in for," said Rust, popping up again. "Want you to take a look at this." He plonked his bare foot on Stephen's desk. "Two nuns ran over it in the car park this morning. See what I mean?"

Ernest Hemmingway was abstracting a few delicate documents from the confidential files when Dorothy came in.

"They're here," she said.

"Damn. Already? Couldn't you . . . ?" But it was clearly too late. Using the cool presence of mind that had carried him through many a tricky situation, the Vice-Chancellor slammed the files shut and scuttled behind his desk in time to be able to rise from his chair in a relaxed and hospitable way as the Ministry team came in.

"Come in, gentleman, make yourselves at home," he said, shepherding them towards the conversation area, which featured chairs so easy that they could suck the unsuspecting visitor down like quicksand. "Let's sit over here, shall we, more comfortable. Coffee, I think, Dorothy. We've met before, John, haven't we? Burlington House, wasn't it?"

"Burlington House indeed it was, Ernie." Nice fruity voice. Good firm handshake, been around a bit, fond of his food; John Soames should be all right. "May I introduce Granville Sodd of the Property Services Commission?" Indeed he might. Obviously one of Nature's number twos, was Granville Sodd.

"How d'you do?"

"Delighted."

"And, er, P. R. Prettiman," said Soames, with less enthusiasm. Ernie had been keeping his eye on P. R. Prettiman ever since he had entered the room, and had formed the tentative hypothesis that the chap was not quite all there. Chap's legs didn't seem to go with his body, somehow, and he couldn't seem to keep still. Supposed to be being introduced, and there he was with his back turned, examining one of the sculptures.

"Good to see you, Prettiman," said Ernie heartily. Prettiman turned sharply, cutting his finger on a thorny bit.

"Shit."

"Sorry?"

"Er . . . Treasury."

"Fine!" Probably quite a useful clerk, even if he did have a face like a Mortadella.

"Well, gentlemen." They were all sitting comfortably apart from the clerk fellow, and Ernest Hemmingway didn't propose to kowtow to *him*. "I'll put my cards on the table. This twenty-five per cent cut has come as a bit of a blow, can't pretend it hasn't, and that's why I'm delighted that you're here. I want you to feel free to go anywhere you like, see anything you want to see, talk to anyone you want to talk to. Because I'm confident you'll find you're in the . . ."

The Prettiman fellow had wandered over to the confidential filing cabinet. He opened the top drawer an inch or two, then closed it, leaving a small bloodstain behind him. ". . . in the most cost-effective campus in the British Isles," finished Ernie, rather less powerfully than he had hoped. Why couldn't the fellow sit down?

"Knowing you, Ernest," said Soames, "I think we may well find just that."

"Not as cost-effective as a poly," muttered P. R. Prettiman, who was examining Hemmingway's Jasper Johns in a puzzled sort of way.

"Sorry, Mr Prettiman, didn't quite catch that?"

"Oh, nothing, Vice-Chancellor," said Prettiman apologetically. "Just that, er, polytechnics are in general more

238

cost-effective than universities, that's all." He wound a handkerchief around his finger.

Hemmingway laughed in a panicky kind of way. "Hardly comparable, surely?"

Prettiman put his head on one side to consider this. "Both servicing national needs for first and further degrees . . . both funded for research . . . no, you're probably quite right."

Soames leaned forward soothingly. "We're having to make a lot of noise at the moment about equal funding for the polys, of course, but I shouldn't think that one's a serious runner, Ernest."

"Not when you consider the background of the present Cabinet," said Granville Sodd, bless his heart. Soames, Sodd and Hemmingway had a good companionable chuckle together. Prettiman wandered off and began to examine a large succulent in a pot.

"I've, ah, worked out a possible programme for the rest of the day. Entirely up to you, of course, wander where you will . . ."

A large piece of the succulent fell off.

"Sorry," said Prettiman to the plant.

". . . but I thought you'd want to talk to the chaps in Cybernetics and hear about the plans for the Science Park. That'll be all privately funded, by the way. Then this evening I thought dinner in a rather good little local restaurant. I've made sure a few of the key people from Finance and Development will be along, so that you can make it a working meal, ask any questions you want sort of thing."

"Well, that all sounds like a very satisfactory start," said Soames, and Dorothy came in with the trolley right on cue.

"Over here, Dorothy," said the Vice-Chancellor. "Any initial questions, then, before we kick off?"

"Could you tell me where the lavatory is?" said Prettiman.

"Of course, old man, first on the left outside the door." Prettiman wandered off, managing not to knock himself out on the doorpost. When he was out of sight, Soames leaned forward confidentially.

"No need to be too concerned about Prettiman, Ernest. He's a bit of an oddball. Quite harmless, though. Likes to wander round on his own a bit."

"Bit of a tourist, really," explained Sodd.

"Ah," said Hemmingway, relieved.

"He probably won't be joining us for dinner this evening. Better, really, on the whole."

"Spills soup, all that," explained Sodd.

"Ah. Fair enough," said Ernie. "Well, then, gentlemen. Welcome to the Lowlands!"

Soames and Sodd had a crowded agenda for the next couple of days. They visited all the key departments and they met all the key people and they tried out a great many high-tech breakthroughs and they heard about the creative contacts at the interfaces and they parked in the Science Park and loafed by the lake, and they ate a lot of food and saw a very great deal of Ernest Hemmingway. Prettiman wandered round on his own a bit.

His vaguely amiable face became familiar in the University Pub, which he visited twice a day to drink beer and eat peanuts on his own. He had great difficulty in opening the bags of peanuts, but no difficulty at all in drinking pints of beer. Stephen nodded and smiled to him as he passed his table on his way back to Lyn with the second round of Scotches.

"I think I've got to take it, Stephen" she said.

"Yes," said Stephen. "Suppose you have. No, that's mean. You'd be crazy not to take it. It's an amazing promotion."

"Yeah, couldn't believe the salary. I'll never need to take another bribe."

"They obviously think you're someone special," he said.

"Well, I am something special."

"Yes, you are," he said fondly. "You're unique."

She smiled at him.

Yes, she was certainly unique in this place. Everyone else looked somehow vague and unfocused. Students with

240

their bland faces, years from becoming whatever it was they were going to be. A frightened looking man with a leather-patched jacket reading a book called *Teaching in The Inner City*. The usual job lot of rugby types at the bar. That chap with the odd haircut wrestling patiently with his bag of Murphy's Dry Roasted. Looking back at Lyn, he saw how bright and clear she was, precisely herself in every word and gesture. And he was losing her.

"But will you like it, Lyn?"

"Will I like it? Yeah, I'll love it. Lecturing at Hendon Police College. Fantastic. And it won't be just the ordinary coppers. I'll be sorting out the high fliers, Inspectors and above. Your girl friend will be sensitising the top coppers of tomorrow!" She sounded as if she was gone already.

"Going to miss you," she said.

"Oh, Lyn."

"You could come."

"Not easy to pick up a job these days."

"Come and be my kept man, then," she said. "I can afford you now."

He sighed. "I think I've got to stay here, Lyn," he said. "Till they chuck me out, anyway."

"Yeah," she said. "Thought so." She sounded more subdued now. "It's not that far, you know. You could come and see me. I could come and see you. There'd be parties, one thing about policemen, they throw fantastic parties, and they really like doctors, too."

He couldn't respond; he couldn't play the game. "It won't be the same, though, will it?"

"No, it won't," she said, looking him in the eyes. "Well, how could it be? Everything changes."

"You'll . . . find someone else," he said, and regretted it immediately.

"Well, I might." She sounded almost irritated with him. "I don't know, do I, we'll just have to see how it goes, won't we? . . . Oh, don't let's be sad about it, Stephen."

"Things sometimes have a habit of . . . flipping themselves inside out," he said without much conviction.

"Yeah. Right."

241

Prettiman, with an immense effort, tore his peanut bag in two, showering dry roasted peanuts all over the floor.

When Stephen returned alone to his flat that night he found the door ajar. Not like Chen, he thought. And then: burglars. Oh, really, Stephen. Nothing worth burgling, surely. He must have simply forgotten to close the door properly when he went out. Ah, well. Go to bed and have a good mope. He walked into the bedroom. A thin man in a dark suit was standing by his bed making notes from Chen's calculations on the blackboard.

"Hello," said Stephen, feeling rather foolish.

"Good evening," said the thin man, continuing to take notes.

"You're in my bedroom."

"Are you a mathematician?" The man seemed quite unmoved by Stephen's presence, as if he had just as much right to be there as Stephen had. It was like being in one of those Polish films.

"No, I'm not a mathematician, I'm a doctor," said Stephen. "Look, what are you doing here? How did you get in?"

"Pass key."

"Oh. Ah – are you in this investigative team?"

"In a sense," said the man, still jotting down figures.

"No, you're not," said Stephen with certitude. He had recognised the man now. "You're Chen's professor, aren't you? We met at the VC's party. I'm Stephen Daker."

Professor Ember closed his notebook and peered at Stephen. "Ah, yes. Listen to me, Doctor Daker. The department's rather worried about Mr Sung Yau. He's been playing with fire." He put the notebook in his breast pocket. "It would be better if you didn't mention my visit to him."

"Would it?" said Stephen. "Why?"

"Just take my word for it, Doctor Daker. As his professor. My apologies for any inconvenience. Good evening to you."

*

Early next morning, P. R. Prettiman paid an official visit to the Medical Centre. He looked as if he had slept in his suit, and he had a rather grubby plaster round the fingers of his left hand. Jock McCannon introduced him to the medical team with ghastly bonhomie.

"What's the matter with your finger?" asked Maureen.

"Oh, nothing," said Prettiman, turning from his examination of the photo of Jock McCannon in a dhoti arm in arm with Ronnie Laing and David Mercer. "Little scratch, that's all."

"Will I have a look at it for you?"

"Oh, no, no, no. Please."

"Suit yourself," said Maureen.

"Well, make yourself at home, my dear man," said Jock, waving a vague paw towards the sofa.

"Thank you," said Prettiman, sitting down. A stuffed owl who had been sitting on the arm of the sofa fell into his lap.

"Sorry," said Prettiman to the owl, setting it upright on his knees and smoothing down its feathers.

"Er, yes. Well, the committee's asked me to take a look at the medical practice."

"With a view to recommending one of us for redundancy," said Jock, with gloomy relish.

"Really?" said Prettiman. He looked quite surprised.

"Twenty-five per cent cut, four doctors," said Rose Marie.

"Oh, yes, I see," said P. R. Prettiman. "Yes, that would be logical."

"But . . . you're not necessarily going to do it?" said Stephen.

"Oh, no, not necessarily," said Prettiman to the owl. "No, we have quite a wide range of options." He turned the owl upside down and examined its claws. "Might recommend winding up the practice as a whole."

"*What?*" said Bob.

"There is a notion abroad," said Prettiman apologetically, "that one might do an asset-stripping exercise on the whole University. Move a couple of prestige departments over to

243

Cambridge, say, or into the polytechnic sector, close down the rest, and dispose of the campus as real estate."

All four doctors stared at him in deep shock. Bob gave a little involuntary moan.

"I don't suppose anything will come of it though. Er, don't suppose I should be telling you that. Actually, I'm just the dogsbody. They've told me to spend a day with you, watch you work, get the smell of things. Awfully sorry. Must be a frightful nuisance."

"Not at all," said Jock. He was on automatic pilot, like a man who has just been mugged.

"It's just a question of browsing through some paperwork," said Prettiman to the owl.

"Well," said Bob, rallying, "bit of a snag there, we're living in the twentieth century in this practice, all our records are on floppy disk. So if you're not familiar with the technology . . ."

"I am, thanks," said P. R. Prettiman.

"Ah," said Bob. "Right. Fine. Good."

"And, er, apart from that," said Prettiman, "if you don't mind me mooching about and chatting to you, awful bore, I know . . ."

"I'm not sure that'll be possible, Mr Prettiman," said Rose Marie smoothly. "All of us have a full day of surgery and visits, and even if my job depends on it, I'm not prepared to compromise the doctor-patient relationship by having a lay observer present."

"Oh, dear," said Prettiman contritely. "Yes, of course you're right. Very crass of me. The thing is, you see, I've, er, got to . . ."

Stephen had an inspiration. "Perhaps you could spend some time on the floppy disks and so on today, and chat with us in the evening."

"Right, good idea," said Bob. "We'll work out a programme for you. Still play squash, do you?"

"Still? I don't quite . . ."

"Oops, as you were, nuff said. Do you happen to play squash?"

"Occasionally."

"Fine! Half-past five. On the court. To the death. And we'll take the rest of the evening from there."

Some men in Bob's situation would have contrived to let the investigator win; but Bob was not like that. Show them your throat, and you're asking for it. Much better to let the other chap see who's top dog. Rather to his surprise, he didn't trounce Prettiman, who turned out to have a rather subtle game, though he was clearly out of condition and blowing like a walrus by the time the light went out. Five-two was about right, all things considered. Bob led the way to the changing room, where Prettiman collapsed on to a bench, breathing heavily.

"You don't look too grand, old buddy," said Bob.

"I do feel a bit below par," said Prettiman. "This finger's throbbing a bit."

"Raised circulation," said Bob cheerfully, pulling off his vest. "Nature's way of telling you it's healing. Don't you worry, buddy, you're not going to die, not till you see the old red lines in your armpit. You gave me a damn good game. Takes you back, doesn't it?" He sat down next to Prettiman and started taking off his shoes and socks.

"Yes, it does," said Prettiman thoughtfully.

"Lord, you were a cool one this morning," said Bob. "Could have sworn you didn't remember me. You did though, didn't you?" Prettiman didn't reply. "Look, we can talk in here, perfectly safe, not a beak from here to the horizon."

"Yes, Buzzard. Of course I remember you." Bob stood up and pulled his shorts and jockstrap off, then sat down again, stretching out his strong hairy legs and examining them with satisfaction. "Life's a funny thing, isn't it? All those years ago, and here we are again."

"Yes."

"You can come clean with me, P.R. That was just smokescreen, wasn't it, about all those options? I mean, what you're really looking for is one redundancy in the practice, isn't it? You can tell me. Won't go further than these four walls."

"Well, um . . . yes," said Prettiman. "It does seem the likeliest of the alternatives."

"Thought so. Thought so. Well, present company excepted, you've got quite a choice of candidates, haven't you?" There was a little pause.

"Er . . . what makes you think present company's excepted?" said Prettiman.

Bob was rather taken aback. "What? Well. You know. I mean, we go back a long way, don't we? Happiest days of your life. Two old buddies, P. R. Prettiman and Buzzard Major?"

"I, um . . . I don't think you remember it at all, do you? When you were head of junior dorm, you didn't call me P.R."

"Didn't I?" Bob knitted his brows.

"No, you called me, er, Uglybum, and you slippered me every single bloody night."

"Good God, are you sure?" Bob found himself wishing that he hadn't taken all his clothes off, for some odd reason.

"And it was you," said Prettiman, "who pointed out to the whole lower school that the label on my vests said 'Cherub'."

"So it did!" said Bob rather hysterically. "So it did! Cherub! I remember now."

"And you see," said Prettiman, "I used to lie awake every night, trying not to sob too loudly, and what I used to think was, one day I'd get that thick sadistic bastard Buzzard Major, and I'd f-fucking well crucify him."

"Really?" said Bob. "I see."

"I, er, I will try not to let that influence me too much, Dr Buzzard," said P. R. Prettiman.

The University Pub was full for a Wednesday night. All the regulars were there, but their numbers were swelled by numerous new drinkers, some of whom had never been seen to drink in public before. It was the cuts. Panic and terror were driving people together. They swapped rumours, tried to make useful contacts, shamelessly greased

246

professors, many of whom looked as paranoid as their underlings. The usual subdued roar had taken on a harsh, abrasive tone, a sort of high-pitched snarl, punctuated by the occasional angry outburst or bout of sobbing.

There were still one or two solitary drinkers: a pathetic shivering fellow in a leather-patched jacket who was reading a book on unarmed combat, and a small scruffy-looking man with a walking-stick and a bandaged foot, who was spilling pints of lager and whisky chasers over a thick pile of typescript. Stephen was drinking with Lyn and Chen.

"But he was stealing your work," said Stephen. "I'm sure of it."

Chen was taking it very calmly. "To each according to his need," he said.

"He had this sort of maniacal glint in his eye."

"I'm not surprised," said Chen. "He spent two hours with the investigators this afternoon. I think they sussed out his burnt brain. Desperate man, Stephen."

"But desperate men are dangerous, Chen," said Lyn.

"Maybe. But this is England, not Burma. In England, virtue always triumphs." Chen smiled happily and got up. "I have to go now. I got another great thought coming, I need my blackboards again."

"Be careful, Chen, please," said Stephen.

"Sure." As he was going out he bumped into P. R. Prettiman, who was blinking in the semi-darkness and seemed a trifle unsteady on his feet. Chen pointed him in the right direction.

"Oh, God, here he is," said Stephen. "My turn for the cruel inquisitor."

"He doesn't look too cruel to me," said Lyn.

Prettiman made it to the table without quite managing to knock anyone's table over. "Sorry," he said. "Am I late?"

"Only a bit," said Stephen. "Er, this is Lyn Turtle, Mr Prettiman."

"It's all right," said Lyn, "I'm not stopping. Get you a drink, right? Bitter?"

"Oh, that's very kind of you," said Prettiman. "And I wonder if I might . . ."

"Oh, yeah, you're the peanut man. I'll get you some."

Prettiman sat down, clutching his executive briefcase on his knees. "Oh, dear."

"Squash go well?" said Stephen.

"Not too well."

"I know. Bob took me to play squash my first day here. He's very good, isn't he?"

"As a squash player, yes," said Prettiman. Stephen glanced at him. His puffy face was quite bland and devoid of expression. But he did have this way of saying meaningful things as if they didn't mean anything much at all. Lyn came back with two pints and a bag of nuts.

"Here you are then, one for you and one for you. And the dry roasted for Mr Prettiman."

"Thank you very much," said Prettiman, beginning to struggle with the packet. "Er, congratulations, by the way."

"Thanks," said Lyn, surprised. "What for?"

"The, er, the Hendon job."

"How did you know about that?"

"Oh, sorry, hope it's not confidential. Just a contact. Your name came up in connection with a possible opening in Social Policy. But Hendon got in first. They're very pleased with themselves at Hendon. Er . . . and so they should be."

"Well, thanks."

"I imagine you'll be much missed here," said Prettiman.

"Yes, she will," said Stephen. Prettiman glanced at Lyn and sighed, perhaps because of his lack of success with the peanut bag.

"Come here, Prettiman," she said. She took the packet from his hand, opened it neatly, took his other hand, formed it into a cup, and poured peanuts into it.

"How did you do that?" said Prettiman.

"Just natural talent. I got to go now. See you. Don't drink too much." She went.

"Very gifted young woman, that," said Prettiman.

"Yes, I know," said Stephen.

"Not just with peanuts, you understand."

"Yes, I do understand."

"Four doctors full time in a practice of this kind is a bit of a nonsense isn't it?" said Prettiman, as if they had been talking about this all along.

Stephen took a moment to react. "Well. I wouldn't say that. In fact we have as many patients on our list as the typical four-doctor practice."

"Oh, yes. Quite. But then you have very few young children and over-seventies, and that's where the bulk of the work is, or have I got it wrong?" This man was very quick. He looked extraordinarily dozy, but Stephen was beginning to sense he was in the presence of someone who could run rings round him intellectually. Well, he'd got used to that lately, what with Lyn and Chen and Lilian Hubbard.

"No, you haven't got it wrong," he said.

Prettiman picked up his pint and drained about half of it. "Oh, dear," he said. "I was afraid of that." He did sound genuinely sorry that he had got it right.

"No, you're quite right," said Stephen. "In the context of the medical care most people in this country get, four doctors full time is a bit of a luxury."

"Oh, dear," said Prettiman again. "Look, um, Doctor Daker, I think I ought to say that in these exploratory interviews the usual form is that people tell me lies."

"Oh," said Stephen. "I don't think I'm very good at that."

"No, you don't seem to be." Peanuts were spilling down Prettiman's suit.

"Does it get them very far?" said Stephen. "The people who tell you lies?"

Prettiman considered this carefully. "Um . . . not in general, no. No. Though it's hard to say for certain." He stared into space for a moment, then drained the rest of his pint. "Buzzard took an interesting line, showed me how the practice could be run by one or at the most two doctors, using computerised self-diagnosis and standardised medication strategies. And contract out to private agencies for anything like counselling or night visits. With overseas students paying full private fees, the medical service would become a profit-making sector of the University." He peered owlishly at Stephen.

"I see," said Stephen. It was all he could think of to say.

"I was hoping," said Prettiman humbly, "that you'd, well, persuade me not to adopt that point of view." Stephen did his best to persuade Prettiman not to adopt that point of view, while Prettiman did his best to open another packet of peanuts and had no trouble at all with three more pints of beer. Suddenly Stephen realised that he was very tired. Must be nearly closing time. He looked at his watch and saw that it was only half-past eight. Was it the unusual demands being made on his wits, or the beer? A little of both, probably.

"Yes," said Prettiman. "One does like to know who one's doctor is. Especially in a place like this, I should think."

"It is a crazy place," said Stephen.

"I've seen crazier," said Prettiman. "People we were looking at last month. Big public corporation. The chairman had just had his salary raised to six hundred and seventy-five thousand pounds a year. He did nothing all day. Nothing. I sat there with the watch on him, and he did nothing all day. D'you know why?" Stephen shook his head.

"At that salary, there was nothing important enough for him to do. I filed the report, but nothing came of it, because no one believed it. Ah, well."

"It must be terrible, your job," said Stephen.

"Yes, it is, rather," said Prettiman. "Shamble into a place, no one wants to see you, everybody scared. Try to make sense of it, try to get things right. It's . . . it's an awful responsibility, Stephen."

"But you do share it," said Stephen. "The responsibility. You're part of a team, like us."

Prettiman drank some beer, gave Stephen a brief, odd glance, drank some more beer, and seemed to come to a conclusion. "Well, not really. Shouldn't be telling you this, of course, but Soames and Sodd are just the front men. I make all the judgments. Do most of the work before I visit the place. Read the files, ask around in the right places. . . . Your friend Chen Sung Yau's a gifted man, isn't he?"

"Yes, I think so," said Stephen, surprised.

"Yes, they think so at UCLA too. Still, where was I. . . . Soames and Sodd, yes. Good chaps. They're here to keep the Vice-Chancellor off my back so I can do my work. They're, um . . . they're not actually very bright, you see."

"And you are."

"Yes," said Prettiman gloomily. "Afraid so. Not that it's done me much good. P. R. Prettiman, bit of an oddball, too clever by half. Oh dear, I do feel strange. Is it very warm in here?"

"It is, rather," said Stephen. "Maybe you should go easier on the beer."

"Oh, I shouldn't think it's the beer. I always drink a lot of beer. Your colleague Buzzard is a bit of a fascist, isn't he?"

"Bob's all right when you get to know him," said Stephen.

"Is he really? You should have heard what he said about you. How about the other two?"

"Rose Marie's a brilliant doctor," said Stephen firmly. "Totally dedicated, too. And Jock, well, Jock's about the most distinguished name in the development of student medicine."

"You're not making this very easy, are you? Don't you want to fight for your job, Stephen? Don't you like it here?"

Stephen sighed. "Yes, I do. And I don't want to lose my job. But . . . it's very odd. I feel a curious sense of fatalism about the whole business."

"Yes," said Prettiman. "Know what you mean. Um . . . what'll you do if you're made redundant, Stephen?"

"Oh, that's easy. Go to London, try to get myself locum and night jobs . . . see a lot of Lyn."

251

Prettiman looked sad. "Ah, yes. The sexual life. That's something I've never managed to organise for myself."

"You really should, you know," said Stephen earnestly.

"Well . . . not all that easy." Prettiman gave a funny little shrug that seemed to include everything about him: the odd-shaped head, the suit, the unfocused face, the whole air he had of not quite belonging to the world. "Oh, dear," he said. "Here she comes."

Stephen had never seen Rose Marie in the pub before but she seemed to know her way around it. Looking cool and above it all in a simple black dress, she threaded her way through the tables towards them.

"Look, are you sure you're up to this?" said Stephen.

"No, no, got to be done," said Prettiman. "Woe and duty. And McCannon, before I go to bed."

She was there. "Good evening Mr Prettiman, hello Stephen."

"That's a nice dress," said Stephen. "Can I say that? I've never seen you in a dress before."

"Yes, you can say that, Stephen," she said generously. "Thank you."

"Well, um, shall we have some beer?" said Prettiman.

"I think the idea is that we have dinner, Mr Prettiman. Would that be all right? You haven't eaten already?"

"Um . . . no, I haven't. Actually I don't think I remembered to have anything to eat today."

"Well," she said. "They say the Executive Grill is quite bearable. Shall we?"

An hour later, Prettiman was well into a T-bone steak, and halfway down a bottle of Côtes-du-Rhône. Rose Marie was toying elegantly with her seafood salad, and making wonderful eye contact. It was, as usual, quiet in the Executive Grill. Trimble, the Education lecturer, trying to build himself up with raw fillet, Rust, the Arts Council Fellow in Creative Writing, falling asleep over a paella, a thin man in a dark suit who talked to himself intermittently, and the Reader in Sociology exchanging French kisses with somebody else's research assistant.

"How's the steak?" said Rose Marie. Prettiman was eating it American style, one-handed with a fork. He was making rather a dog's breakfast of it.

"Oh . . . very good, I think," said Prettiman.

"Good," she said, smiling deep into his eyes. "I rarely eat meat myself . . . but I do like to watch a man eat steak. Strange, that, isn't it?"

"Um . . . really quite a good place, this," said Prettiman.

"Yes, it is. Don't usually come here." She poured him some more wine. "It's not a very moral place, I'm afraid." Prettiman glanced, rather wistfully, at the sociological lovers.

"Politically, I mean," she said. "Catering charges the students the full going rate for junk food, so that it's able to subsidise this place quite heavily. Cholesterol and claret for the academic staff at five pounds a head. And, of course, they're waited on by their own students, which makes them feel good."

"Oh, dear," said Prettiman. "Rather like Catterick."

"I didn't realise there was a University of Catterick," said Rose Marie.

"No, no. Army camp. Much the same, though, in essentials."

She put her fork down. "That's amazing," she said. "I'd never have thought of that. Your work must . . . well, you must see very deeply into our society." Her eyes were glowing with girlish admiration.

"S'pose so," said Prettiman, embarrassed. "In a way. Miss most of it, of course. Not very observant. Blunder about, you know." He drank some more wine. His finger had stopped throbbing so badly, but it was curiously difficult to lift his arm.

"You give a very good performance, Mr Prettiman," she said, smiling.

"Performance? Do I?"

"You don't blunder about. You grasp things very quickly, don't you?"

"No, I don't. Not really."

"It must be very interesting, your work. Watching

253

people. The way they try to impress you, the effect you have on them."

Prettiman smiled shyly. "It's awful, sometimes, actually."

"I feel . . . quite out of my depth with you," she said. "I don't usually feel like that with people. But I expect you're always finding that."

"What?" he said. He was feeling a bit out of his depth himself. She had such interesting eyes. And her nose was quite extraordinary. He thought it might perhaps be the most beautiful thing he had ever seen. He decided not to have any more wine.

"Well . . . I suppose you'd have to call it the aphrodisiac properties of power," she said. "It's not something I like to admit to. I'm really cross with myself . . . but there it is. D'you mind?" She filled his glass up again.

"Er . . . no," he said. "Look, really. I'm drinking all this. You have some."

"I don't have a very good head for wine," she confided. And then smiled. "Oh, well." She poured some into her own glass and sipped. Prettiman felt a sudden wave of dizziness and put his good hand to his head. Rose Marie leaned forward. "You're tired, aren't you?"

"Yes, I do feel a bit . . . sorry."

"You must have had a terribly exhausting day," she said. "Look, I've got an idea. Let's skip coffee here. I'll take you back to my flat, it's not far. You can put your feet up and relax for half an hour. Actually . . ." she paused . . . "actually there's something I'd like you to look at, just a few notes on the way we run the practice. Nothing very profound, probably you'd think they were a bit naïve, but I'd love to have your opinion. Or you could just have a nap." She paused again, and smiled. "Whatever you like, really."

Prettiman woke in semi-darkness, finding that he was lying somewhere very comfortable. He looked at his watch. It was half-past eleven. Everything smelt unusually nice. Then he remembered. He was in bed with Rose Marie. He had only the vaguest recollection of how this had come

254

about. They had gone back to her flat, there had been coffee and brandy, he had looked at some very interesting notes, and then somehow . . .

"You're a remarkable person, Mr Prettiman. You're a very unusual man."

"Oh dear," he said. "Am I? It's hard for me to form a judgment about that. In this context. I don't get any practice, you see." There was definitely something wrong with his arm. It felt as if it belonged to somebody else.

"Are you all right?"

"Yes, fine, I think," he said dubiously. "Er, thank you. My arm feels rather strange."

"Only your arm?" she whispered. "I feel strange all over."

"Really?"

"I . . . don't make a habit of this, you know," she said.

"No, you've been awfully kind. I've taken up far too much of your time." He started to struggle up.

"Don't go," she said.

"Dr McCannon's waiting up for me. Woe and duty." He stumbled about in the scented gloom, trying to find his clothes.

"Will we see each other again, Mr Prettiman?" There was a little tremble in her voice.

"Oh, I hope so," he said.

"I'm glad," she breathed.

"Actually," said Prettiman shyly, "there was something else I wanted to ask you."

"Yes?"

"D'you think I could have another glance through those files of yours before I go?" In the semi-darkness he was not able to make out the smile of triumph on her face.

Jock McCannon sat alone in the gloom of his festering cave, one reading lamp casting a harsh light on his ravaged features.

"So poor old Jock is last of all," he said aloud. "Well. It had to come. He poured himself a generous measure of

255

Bell's. "Curious how they delay, the executioners. Always that certain delicacy, that hesitation. As if they're allowing one to reflect . . . to come to terms. I have reflected. I have come to terms. It's all there, all in the book. All, eventually, will be told. Yes." Stumbling footsteps in the corridor. That was wrong. They should come to him in heavy boots and crunching certainty; or silently like knives through water. If they were going to destroy him the least you could expect of them was to get the details right.

"Doctor McCannon!" The executioner's voice was positively feeble.

"Come in, my dear man. The door is open."

"I'm sorry . . . I can't quite . . ."

"Walk towards the chink of light, Mr Prettiman. I'm not going to run away." The door swung open. The bulky shadow wavered in the doorway.

"Er . . . Doctor McCannon. . . ."

"No need to tell me, Prettiman. I know your fell purpose. The old king must be sacrificed so that the lowland may bloom again."

"Er, no, really, it wasn't that . . ." said the executioner.

"Come closer, Prettiman," said Jock. "I want to see my destroyer clearly." Prettiman advanced a couple of steps, then fell down and lay still.

"Good God, he's disappeared. Where are you, Prettiman? No need to crawl on your belly like a snake." There was no answer. Jock got up and began to peer about in the darkness. "Where are you, man? What game is this?" Prettiman groaned. "Oh, there you are. What's the matter with you, my dear chap?"

"I . . . I wonder if you'd mind looking at my left armpit," said Prettiman faintly.

"An odd request. Freemason, I suppose."

"Please," said Prettiman.

"If you insist." Jock laboriously undid Prettiman's waistcoat and started pulling at his shirt.

"Red marks," said Prettiman indistinctly.

"Not for years, no, Freud and Melanie Klein every time for me . . . there. Let's get some light on this." He dragged the reading lamp over as far as the flex would allow. "Ah. I see. *Red marks*. Yes indeed. Prettiman, you've got acute blood poisoning. You're going to die."

"Oh . . . er, morning," said Prettiman. "I'm not dead, then." He was lying in one of the chastely narrow beds in Sick Bay, and Maureen Gahagan was taking his pulse.

"Course you're not dead," she said. "You're full as a gun with penicillin, you are. Up and about tomorrow."

"Oh. Good."

"You've been a bit of a mucky pup, haven't you?" she said.

"How did you know?" he asked, embarrassed.

"You let that little scratch get all infected. Would have been a goner if Dr McCannon hadn't got his act together. Sure you're on the mend now."

"Has . . . has Dr Rose Marie said anything?"

"She's been in to see you. All the doctors have been to see you. You've had four doctors and a nurse on you, you have. You've been treated like royalty."

"You're all very kind." Suddenly he struggled up.

"My case. Where's my case?"

"It's right by the bed here," she said, pushing him back into the pillow. "Don't you worry about it, no one's going to nick that."

"I must see my colleagues. Mr Soames and Mr Sodd."

"You're not ready for visitors yet," she told him.

"It's very important, Maureen."

"Well, I'll see," she said. "If you're a good lad and eat your breakfast."

P. R. Prettiman was a good lad and ate his breakfast; and at ten, Soames and Sodd came to visit him in Sick Bay. He spent the rest of the day writing his report, interrupted by Maureen, who kept snatching his case away from him to give him meals, take his temperature, and shovel more drugs down him. Everybody else waited.

Early next morning, Stephen came into the living room to find Chen packing a couple of canvas bags.

"Chen. What are you doing?"

"Packing my gear. As you see. Things flip round very fast here."

"Christ. What's happened?"

Chen smiled. "University of Lowlands reluctantly finds it has to let Chen go."

"The bastards," said Stephen. "It was Ember, wasn't it? Your own professor."

"Yeah, in a way. But don't worry about Chen. Ember goes to Hemmingway and tells him a load of rubbish about me. Then the bit I don't understand: that guy, what's his name, Pretty Boy, makes this big phone call."

"Prettiman."

"Yeah, that's the guy. Suddenly Berkeley California can't wait to have me. First class air fare, my own blackboard, my own surfboard, my own T-Bird. All I have to do is think there. Well, as our national poet says, I think I could cope with that."

"Yes, I should think you could," said Stephen. "But look . . . what about all this?" Every square inch of all the blackboards in the flat was covered with Chen's calculations. "Your new breakthrough in catastrophe theory."

"Oh, that," said Chen. "I leave it to Professor Ember."

"Chen, you mustn't do that. It's yours. He'll get all the credit for it."

"Well." Chen grinned. "I was looking at it all again last night. I found this big mistake. Right here, in the middle. Everything after that, just a load of rubbish. I think he'll take maybe a year to work it out."

"Ah," said Stephen. He looked at his watch. Eight thirty.

"Look, you're not going right this minute, are you? I've got this group meeting."

"No, no, plenty of time. They send a little car for me about eleven. Plenty of time, Stephen. Relax. Mellow out. Hang loose, baby. See how I practise for California."

*

Prettiman was sitting next to the owl again on Jock's sofa. He had an impressively large dressing on his finger, and he looked rather pale, but was otherwise apparently himself.

"I, ah, thought that as you've all been so kind, you should be the first to know about our, er, recommendations for the practice. And the University as a whole. My colleagues are with the Vice-Chancellor now."

"Glad to see you so much better, P.R.," said Bob Buzzard, who was practically crouching at his feet.

"Thank you, Buzzard." Prettiman began to struggle with his case. The owl fell on him.

"Can I help you with that, P.R.?"

"Oh. Thank you." The case sprang open and Prettiman took out a thin bunch of notes.

"Well, as you worked out for yourselves, four doctors in the present climate constitutes a luxury. The committee's recommendation is that Dr McCannon takes early retirement, with a suitable financial arrangement."

"You miserable ungrateful git," said Maureen Gahagan. The owl fell over.

'Sorry," said Prettiman, perhaps to the owl. "Er . . . however, in view of the tremendous strain the practice will be under, with the coming merger, you'll want to buy Doctor McCannon back again on a freelance basis to give consultation."

"So Jock gets *two incomes*?" Bob Buzzard was practically panting.

Faint smile from Prettiman. "That's how these things usually work. Er, Doctor Daker to take over as head of the practice."

"Congratulations, Stephen," said Rose Marie bravely.

"Yes, absolutely," said Bob, pipped by a point in the sheepdog trials.

"My dear boy," said Jock. "My kingdom will be safe in your hands."

"But . . . I don't think I'm up to it." Another faint smile from Prettiman. "That's, er, that's the usual form too. Sorry. As to the, um, the University as a whole, we're recommending fairly sweeping changes."

"Who's for the chop, then?" said Bob eagerly; nothing like a bit of *schadenfreude* to get a chap going again.

"Well," said Prettiman, "the most important one's the Vice-Chancellor of course." There was a stunned and respectful silence. "Well," said Prettiman almost impatiently, "it was obvious. He's failed to keep his talented people, he's backed all the wrong horses, and he couldn't even flog the campus to the Japanese. I'm afraid his, er, lack of principle is mitigated only by his lack of competence. He'll probably get a Government post and something in the Honours List." Prettiman fiddled in an embarrassed way with the owl's chest feathers while the medical team stared at him in awe.

"Er . . . you said something about a merger," said Stephen eventually.

"Yes. Sorry I can't tell you the details at the moment. It'll necessitate some readjustments, but it should take care of the financial problem."

"But who's it with?" asked Rose Marie. "The Polytechnic?"

"I'm not at liberty to say just yet, Rose," said Prettiman, looking shyly up at her. "But you might be able to guess. What's the fastest growing employment sector in the economy?" They stared at each other.

"Fast food industry?" said Bob.

"DHSS?" said Rose Marie.

Prettiman smiled tenderly at his owl friend. "I . . . really can't say any more than that."

It was Stephen's day off surgery. He went for a walk by the lake with Lyn. Dogs, fishermen, ducks. The peaceful shimmering water. He felt sad.

"Head of the practice, eh?" said Lyn. "Didn't I keep telling you you were wonderful?"

"Yes, you did."

A Border Collie who reminded Stephen faintly of his colleague Bob was racing desperately up and down the bank barking at the ducks, who quacked back cheerfully at him.

"And Prettiman thought you were wonderful too."

"Yes," said Stephen. "He seemed to like us all in a way."

"Well, cheer up then. Here we are. The two big successes."

Stephen stopped and turned to her. "I don't want to be a big success, Lyn. I thought I did, but I don't. I just want to do my job and be happy. I just wish things could go along like this."

The dog was in the water up to his knees now, looking baffled.

"Everything changes, Doc."

"I wish you could stay," he said.

"Yes, so do I. But it wouldn't be me if I did."

"No. I do love you, Lyn."

"I know. Me too. Bleedin' tragic, innit?"

"Yes, it is," he said.

The dog came out of the water, shook himself, and walked into the trees.

"Hey," she said, pulling his ear. "Things work out. Put your trust in catastrophe theory. Still early days."

We started in the Main Car Park. Let's finish there. The rotting Fiat of the Arts Council Fellow in Creative Writing looked definitely finished there. Its tyres were all quite flat; it looked as if it was melting as well as rusting. Stephen, Lyn, and Chen, together with quite a few other people, were watching the team of investigators depart in the black Ministry Rover.

Soames and Sodd were in the back, resting their well-groomed Jermyn Street haircuts against the cushions, two good chaps conscious of a job well done. Prettiman, in the front, was twisted awkwardly in his seat, partly because he had his tie caught in the door, partly because he seemed to be looking for someone or something. He caught Stephen's eye, smiled wanly, then looked past him, and waved his bandaged hand through the open window. Stephen turned to see who he was waving at. It was Rose Marie. It was impossible from her face to tell what she was thinking or feeling. When Stephen turned round again, the Rover was moving away. Someone had operated the electric window, and Prettiman's bandaged hand was caught in the gap.

"Everyone's going," said Stephen. "How am I going to cope?"

"You'll cope," said Chen. "Hang loose. And next summer you can both come out to the Coast to see me. I'll take you for a ride in my little dooce coop."

"Blimey," said Lyn. "Look at this." A dark blue Cadillac limo that looked like the Rover's rich uncle from America was murmuring softly towards them. It stopped, and a man in a peaked cap got out, chewing gum.

"Party here by the name of Sung Yau?"

"Right here, baby," said Chen. "Take my bags." The peaked cap man looked dubiously at Chen's luggage which consisted of one light canvas bag and two kites, then sighed and slung them into the boot.

"Don't forget," said Chen to Stephen. "Sometimes things flip right inside out."

Lyn gave him a kiss and then decided to give him an Irish blow-job as well.

"Come on, man, get in," said the driver. Chen got in the front, and the dark blue Caddy slipped quietly away with a sound like sighing. Chen didn't turn or wave. He had gone into the future.

Stephen and Lyn stood about, as people do. A warm wind had got up, sending the crisp bags and handbills in brisk eddies round their ankles. An empty tube of Fosters rolled in a steady slow diagonal line through the aisles of cars, as if it had a purpose and a destination.

"Don't be sad," said Lyn.

"I'm not sad," he said. "Not really. I'm just waiting for things to flip."

"Doc! Doc!" They turned. A small scruffy man with a walking stick was limping very quickly towards them. It was the Fellow in Creative Writing. His eyes were wild and unfocused, and what hair he had was standing up in tufts all over his head.

"Hello," said Stephen. "How's the foot?"

Rust shook his head violently and dismissed the foot with

a wave of his stick. "Healing fine, healing fine, no problem, but the main things is, I've *cracked the story!* No one could think of this one! Listen." Rust's pale and whisky-sodden eyes were staring into the middle distance with the pure certainty of the clairvoyant, or the dogged Biblical prophet who after years of wrong numbers and crossed lines is at last on the direct person-to-person wire to God.

"Listen," he said again. "The University goes bust, right? So they . . . so they *sack the Vice-Chancellor!*"

"Er . . . Rust," began Stephen gently. But Rust wasn't listening. He raised his stick towards the cold and rook-delighting heaven.

"But *that's not all.* They merge the University with . . . this one you'll never get. . . ." He removed his gaze from the scudding clouds and smiled at Stephen, the gentle beatific smile of a man who has lived on another plane. "Hendon Police College! Heaven on wheels! What do you say, Doc?"

"Stephen," said Lyn. "Look."

A large luxury coach had come into the far end of the car park. The doors opened, and a lot of big men got out. They were all dressed in dark-blue uniforms and peaked caps; and many of them were festooned with medal ribbons. They were looking about them with mild curiosity but also an unmistakable sense of calm proprietorship.

Rust's lower lip began to tremble. His stick shook in his hands and rattled on the concrete. "No," he said. "No, no, no, no, no!"

Lyn turned to Stephen. Her face was startled but there was the beginning of a grin on it. "Hey, you know what this could mean . . . ?"

Behind them, the nuns' Mini coughed suddenly into life and began to reverse towards them, accelerating hard. Lyn saw it first. "Look out!" she yelled, and dragged Stephen clear.

Rust was not so lucky. The back bumper of the Mini knocked his walking stick flying through the air, and as he stumbled, the front offside wheel went over his good foot. He fell on to his back and lay there groaning. The Mini did not stop or slow down. It reversed speedily through a NO EXIT opening, round the corner by the Porter's Lodge, and out of this book.

Stephen knelt by Rust's twitching body, feeling for fractures. "Try to lie still," he said.

"It's my foot, Doc," groaned Rust, twitching and writhing. "They got my other foot."

"Don't move," said Stephen. "You're going to be all right." Lyn knelt down on Rust's other side and held his hand in both of hers. Rust looked wildly from one to the other.

"Help me, Doc. Help me."

"It's OK," said Stephen. "I'm looking after you. You're going to be fine."

"Thank you, Doc," said Rust faintly. "Thank you."

"Don't thank me," said Stephen. "I'm just doing my job." His head was on a level with Lyn's and as he looked up from Rust's mangled foot, his eyes looked into her loving eyes over the writer's twitching body. Some of the big bemedalled policemen were beginning to stroll over to see what had happened.

When Rust visualises the filmed version of this, he hears the music beginning to swell in a heartbreakingly poignant surge at this point, while the camera begins its slow zoom upwards into a fabulously expensive helicopter shot, holding at its centre, frozen, the archetypal group of doctor, patient, dream girl, in a single perfect *gestus*, surrounded by the men of power, the rusted cars, the cracked concrete, the wild-eyed staring students, the whirling paper and the rolling empty cans, the brutal crushing buildings, the still and uncommunicative lake, and all the crazed, corrupt and frightened souls who inhabit and enact the process of the Sick University.

Rust: the Post-Script

Rust is sitting waiting in the large, unbeautiful office of the Head of Series and Serials. He is waiting for Jonathan

Powell and Ken Riddington, and they are late. Rust is getting worried.

He feels even worse when he sees them come through the door. They are both wearing dark suits and black ties. Powell's suit is actually black. Rust forces a cracked smile.

"Terribly sorry, Ron," says Powell. "Funeral."

"Er . . . writer?" says Rust hopefully.

"No. Director," says Powell. He shakes his head sadly. "Heart. Only forty-three." He looks at Rust thoughtfully. Rust feels acutely conscious of being the oldest man in the room.

"Episode Seven, Ron," says Ken Riddington.

"Liked it, did you?" says Rust.

"Oh, heaven on wheels, brilliant," says Jonathan Powell. "But are you sure we've got the right ending here?"

"What's wrong with it?" says Rust.

"I'll tell you what's wrong with it," says Ken. "You've blown it, that's what's wrong with it. For me, you've totally destroyed the reality base of a lovely warm witty . . . *lovable* story."

"We'd like you to consider a rewrite, Ron," says Jonathan gently.

"It's the ending I want," says Rust. "It's the story, and there is no other story. I mean: that's the way it is."

"Well, Ron, I'm sorry to say this, but I don't think I can produce this," says Ken. "Not as it is." A silence develops. Ken's said it. It is crunch time. They are reminding Rust that he is not an author. He is a writer. Writers have only one ace to play.

"Please have a think about this, Ron." Ken's a nice man; he doesn't like confrontations.

Rust has a think about the kind of rewrite he could do. All he can think about is lying on his back on the concrete twitching and writhing. He looks up at Lyn with a desperate plea in his eyes, and with infinite compassion she bends over him, opens her lovely lips, and gives him the longest and tenderest Irish blow-job ever seen on television . . . no. What has to be must be. The doctor gets the girl, but the writer tells the story.

"No good, Ken," he says. "This is the way it has to be. I'm sorry. If you make me rewrite it, or get anyone else to rewrite it . . . I'll take my name off the credits." There. He has said it. The writer's equivalent of the gunslinger's "Let's see how fast you really are." He has often dreamed of this moment, and now he is living it. Rust has realised himself as a writer.

A week or two later, they made him do the rewrites and took his name off the credits. And not long after that, his editor at Hodder and Stoughton expunged all the Rust episodes from the novelisation.

Rust ceased to exist.